In one smooth movement, Mr. Gray caught her by the wrist and held her fast.

"And what if, my dear Mrs. Mornay," he said, "my sister should find herself in this predicament? What advice would you offer then?"

Deborah dimpled up at him. "Assuming the girl has lungs, I would advise her to use them. Scream, Mr. Gray."

"You have an answer for everything," he said in a slow, sleepy voice. He edged closer. "I know how to prevent a scream. What if . . . what if the gentleman in question were to kiss her?" His eyes dropped to Deborah's mouth.

He was close, so very close, and she could feel his warm breath on her cool cheek. It wasn't fear or curiosity that held her captive, nor yet the restraining grasp on her wrist. A strange yearning uncurled inside her, then spread out in ripples, till she was shivering in anticipation. Slowly, inexorably, he tugged on her wrist, bringing her closer. Her lips parted and she forgot to breathe. . . .

❧

DANGEROUS TO KISS

ALSO BY ELIZABETH THORNTON

Dangerous to Love

DANGEROUS TO *Kiss*

ELIZABETH THORNTON

BANTAM BOOKS
NEW YORK TORONTO LONDON SYDNEY AUCKLAND

DANGEROUS TO KISS

A Bantam Book / April 1995

All rights reserved.
Copyright © 1995 by Mary George.
Insert art copyright © 1995 by Franco Accornera.
Cover art copyright © 1995 by Alan Ayers.
No part of this book may be reproduced or transmitted in any form or by any means,
electronic or mechanical, including photocopying, recording, or by any information storage
and retrieval system, without permission in writing from the publisher.
For information address: Bantam Books.

ISBN 0-553-57372-1

Published simultaneously in the United States and Canada

Bantam Books are published by Bantam Books, a division of Bantam Doubleday Dell Publishing Group, Inc. Its trademark, consisting of the words "Bantam Books" and the portrayal of a rooster, is Registered in U.S. Patent and Trademark Office and in other countries. Marca Registrada. Bantam Books, 1540 Broadway, New York, New York 10036.

PRINTED IN THE UNITED STATES OF AMERICA

RAD   0 9 8 7 6 5 4 3 2 1

DANGEROUS TO Kiss

❧ ❧ ❧ ❧ ❧ ❧ ❧ ❧ ❧

PROLOGUE

She came awake on a cry of terror, momentarily disoriented, as if she had been flung back in time to another house, another place. As awareness seeped into her, her heartbeat gradually slowed. She was safe. No one was hunting her. No one knew who or where she was.

The hiss of the rain lashing against the windowpanes had almost soothed her into sleep when lightning flashed and thunder exploded overhead. She raised herself on her elbows in anticipation of Quentin flinging himself into her room. He wouldn't admit that he was afraid of thunderstorms, of course. At eight years old, Quentin was beyond admitting that he was afraid of anything. It would be an amusing charade. Having discovered that his governess was terrified of storms, he would pretend that he had come to comfort *her*. She, none better, understood his bravado.

When the storm increased in ferocity, and still her young charge had not appeared at her door, Deborah felt for the candle on the table by her bed. After several unsuccessful attempts to get it lit, she gave up, and slipping from the bed, reached for her wrapper. It took her only a moment or two to traverse the corridor to Quentin's room, and a moment after that to discover that the boy's bed was empty.

She hesitated, debating whether her employer, Lord Barrington, could have got there before her and carried his son off to his own chamber, or whether Quentin was playing tricks on her again. Deciding on the latter, she groped her way into the corridor, her hand trailing along the handrail, till she came to the banister at the head of the stairs. In that darkly shadowed interior, the light spilling from under the door to his lordship's library on the floor below shone like a beacon. It was then that she remembered her employer had an appointment with Lord Kendal that night. Quentin would not be in the library with them. Then where was he hiding?

She hesitated when she came to the turn in the stairs. "Quentin?" she called softly. "Quentin?" There was no answer.

With a small sound of annoyance, she went to investigate, her mind already jumping ahead to the possible consequences of Quentin's rash prank. His health was not robust. He was just getting over a fever. If he had not donned his robe and slippers, she would give him the rough edge of her tongue.

As she was passing the door to the library, she heard voices, and her steps slowed. She couldn't make out what was being said, but she knew that one of those voices belonged to her employer, and he sounded distraught. The thought that something awful had befallen Quentin leapt into her mind. Her hand reached for the doorknob, then froze in midair as Lord Barrington's voice rended the silence.

"Let the boy go," he pleaded. "For God's sake, have pity. He is only a boy. You of all people. Kendal, Lord Kendal . . . Don't harm him!" The timbre of his voice thickened as his anguish increased. "Quentin, run for it!"

There was a thud, and Deborah was galvanized into motion. A gun went off as she flung the door wide and Quentin came bounding into her arms. The picture of her employer slumped on the floor with a shadowy figure standing over him flashed through her brain, but beyond that she registered nothing. Instinct had already taken over. She slammed the door shut and grabbed for Quentin's hand.

Then they were off and running, running, running, running . . .

❧ ❧ ❧ ❧ ❧ ❧ ❧ ❧ ❧

CHAPTER 1

John Grayson, the Earl of Kendal, had broken one of his own cardinal rules, and now he was paying the toll. In Paris, he'd had a brief affair with a married woman, the wife of one of his colleagues at the Foreign Office no less, and now she was making a royal nuisance of herself.

"Affair" was too grand a word for it. He'd spent the night with her, and that's all it amounted to. He'd felt sorry for her. Her husband's infidelities were common knowledge. He'd been tipsy, and Helena had been lonely, and beautiful, and oh so available. But damn it all, that had been almost three months ago! He'd given her the obligatory trinket, signifying the end of the affair. He'd expected Helena to follow the rules of the game, not corner him in his own house. She was a sophisticated woman of the world. Her string of lovers read like the register of the *House of Lords*. She knew the score.

Unfortunately, he couldn't avoid her altogether. She moved in his circles. And somehow she had worked her way into his mother's coterie of friends. When he'd walked into his mother's drawing room that afternoon and had come face-to-face with Helena, he'd known that the only way to deal with her was to be brutal.

That's why he had offered to escort her home. What he had to say was better said in private.

Being brutal to women, however, did not come easily to him. He should have said something in the carriage. Now he was ensconced in *her* drawing room, in *her* house in Cavendish Square, drinking her husband's prime cognac. It left a bad taste in his mouth.

"I had no idea," he said, "you were so friendly with my mother."

Lady Helena Perrin reclined in languid splendor among the feather cushions on the long white sofa, where she knew her dark beauty was displayed to advantage. "Didn't you, Gray? We met in Paris and took an instant liking to each other." Through half-closed lids, she enjoyed the pleasurable spectacle of her former lover. Sunlight from the window behind his back glinted provocatively in his golden hair. As he stretched, catlike, to adjust his long length to the delicate gilt armchair, she watched the powerful play of muscles in the lean flanks and the long muscular legs.

Now that the earl had parted company with the opera dancer he'd had in his keeping, she was hopeful that she could resurrect their affair. To her knowledge, the little house in Hans Town, which Gray kept for his succession of mistresses, had lain vacant for more than a month. He was between mistresses and that gave her a clear field. She was aware that he was reluctant, and put it down to scruples. Gray and her husband were colleagues. She wasn't going to let that stand in her way.

"Gray," she said confidingly, "Eric is very broadminded. I am free to come and go as I please, as is he."

Gray's lips curved in a cynical smile. Discretion—that was the cardinal rule of their class. Though the whole world might know that he had slept with Helena, as long as they maintained appearances, no one would bat an eyelash, least of all a husband who paraded his conquests as if they were trophies. This was the way of their world. But it wasn't his family's way. His mother, he knew, would be deeply shocked if she suspected he had taken up with a married woman. Hell, it shocked even *him*.

A faint current of irony colored his voice. "Evidently I am not as civilized as he. Helena, that night in Paris was a mistake. It should never have happened. It won't happen again." And he could not be more brutal than that.

He made a movement to rise. "No doubt," he said, "I shall see you at the reception tonight."

"And after the reception?"

"After the reception, I am engaged to attend a private party at Carleton House."

"Then perhaps I shall see you at the Horshams' on Thursday?"

God, did the woman never give up? How brutal could a man get? "That won't be possible," he said. "I shall not be here."

His tone was not encouraging, but Helena was too experienced a player to let that deter her. "Gray," she said, laughing to soften the rebuke, "we have hardly begun to talk, and already you are leaving?"

"What do you wish to talk about?"

"Well . . . your ward, for a start, and Miss Weyman. I have not seen them since we were all in Paris. How are they?"

Gray looked up, his eyes suddenly very wide, very alert on her face. "I was not aware that you knew Miss Weyman."

"I met her once, before the tragedy."

A moment before, he had been pressed for time. Now, his careless posture told her, he had all the time in the world. One booted foot came to rest on a low mahogany table. The other he negligently crossed over one ankle.

"You met her?" said Gray. "Where in Paris did you meet her?"

He couldn't be interested in Deborah Weyman, she told herself. For one thing, the woman was thirty if she were a day. For another, she was a dowd. Now that she remembered it, however, Lord Barrington had seemed to like the woman well enough. He had hovered in the background, smiling a lot, bringing Miss Weyman forward as if she were his protégée, and not his son's governess. Poor Lord Barrington. A week later, he was dead, murdered by a robber whom he had surprised in the act the night before he was due to leave Paris.

It was a horrible business, and all the more shocking because it could have happened to any of them. They were all connected to the diplomatic corps; they had all been in Paris at the time, trying to get out of France before the borders were closed. Lord Barrington had sent his wife on ahead, but had delayed his own departure because his son was not fit to travel, and that delay had cost him his life.

The French had acted with surprising generosity. Though war had been declared between their two countries, they had informed the Foreign Office of the tragedy and had gone so far as to send Lord Barrington's body home for burial. After the funeral, Lady Barrington, Quentin's stepmother, a girl who was hardly out of the schoolroom, had gone back to her family in Devon. As for Quentin and his governess, they were fortunate not to have been detained in France for the duration of the war, as, indeed, had happened to other English visitors who had delayed too long. Once again, the French had acted with surprising generosity, or perhaps not so surprising when one considered that Gray was a personal friend of Talleyrand, the French foreign minister. For whatever reason, Miss Weyman and Quentin had been allowed to leave France and were now residing in one of Gray's estates to allow them a period of tranquility to recover from their ordeal. She had hoped to see them at Lord Barrington's funeral, but the boy's health had prevented them attending. She thought of her own children, and suppressed a shudder.

"Helena," said Gray gently, breaking into her train of thought, "you mentioned Miss Weyman. When and where did you meet her?"

"There was a picnic on the lawns of Lord Barrington's rented house in Paris. All the children and their parents were invited. Miss Weyman arranged the thing for Lord Barrington's boy."

She and Eric had been there with their own children, but Helena said nothing of this. She never mentioned them to Gray unless he particularly asked about them. This was not because she did not love her children. What she wished to avoid was anything that might detract from her image as a desirable woman. A mother who had two growing sons at Eton and a daughter in the nursery was not the impression she wished to create.

"When was this?" asked Gray.

"Now *that* I do remember. It was in May, you know, just before His Majesty declared war on France. Well, you must remember the confusion with everyone trying to get out of Paris before Bonaparte closed French borders?"

"Oh yes, I remember. I should. I was there."

Lady Helena did not know what to make of Gray's odd tone or his interest in Deborah Weyman, but she knew that she did not care for the suspicion that had begun to take hold in her mind.

Gray set down his glass. "I have a particular reason," he said, "for asking about Miss Weyman. Perhaps I mentioned that in Gil's will, Miss Weyman and I are both named as Quentin's guardians?"

"Lord Barrington named a woman as one of his son's guardians? How very odd."

"Yes, isn't it? And since I hardly know her, and we are soon to confer about the boy's future, I wondered what manner of woman I must deal with. Oh, not that it matters. In English law, as Miss Weyman will soon discover, if she does not already know it, a female's title to 'guardian' is a mere courtesy."

"You hardly know Miss Weyman? But I thought . . . well . . . Lord Barrington was your friend, was he not, and a colleague at the Foreign Office? And you were both delegates at the peace talks in Paris. You must have formed some impression of the woman?"

Gray shrugged. "I never went to the house in Saint-Germain, and to my knowledge, Miss Weyman was never invited to any of the receptions at the British Embassy. Well, she wouldn't be, would she, a mere governess?"

"But . . . since then? After she brought Quentin home to England?"

Gray was beginning to regret that he had raised the subject of Deborah Weyman. Helena was no sloth, and if he did not watch his step, she would soon divine that he had never set eyes on the woman. "What I want," he said, smiling, "is a woman's impression of her. She struck me as . . . no, I don't wish to put words in your mouth. How did she strike you?"

Her suspicions collapsing, Lady Helena immediately began on an animated recital of all she remembered about Deborah Weyman. It was soon done, for she had met the girl on the one occasion only.

"Is that how she struck you?" she asked, teasing him.

Before he could reply, a voice from the door said smoothly, "I trust I don't intrude?"

Gray rose as Eric Perrin walked into the room. He was of an age with Gray, dark, darker than his wife, and remarkably handsome. He was smiling, but it was a polite smile, with no warmth in it. *Civilized*, thought Gray cynically as they exchanged the customary pleasantries. He knew from a remark that Perrin had once made to him that he was aware of his affair with Helena. If Helena had been *his* wife, Perrin's smile would have been marred by a few missing teeth.

He did not like Eric Perrin any more than Perrin liked him. This had nothing to do with Helena, but with their work at the Foreign Office. He had been promoted over Perrin's head and Perrin had never forgiven him for it. Gray did not linger, but mentioning the lateness of the hour, soon took his leave.

Nothing was said for some few minutes. Helena sipped her sherry. Perrin went to the sideboard and poured a drink for himself.

"You're back early," she said.

He shrugged and took the chair Gray had vacated. "A man is entitled to take dinner in his own home once in a while."

This was a jarring note and she hardly knew how to answer him. She made light of it. "Have all your flirts deserted you, Eric?"

There was no rancor in his reply. "Something like that. Is Kendal your new flirt?"

There was no rancor in her reply either. "Something like that. Why do you ask?"

"No particular reason. No reason at all." He bolted his drink and rose. "I shall be with Gwen in the nursery if you want me," he said, and sauntered from the room.

❧

When Gray arrived at Kendal House in Berkeley Square, he made straight for his library. For some reason, Helena's perfume clung to his clothes and he had no wish to explain himself to his mother, the dowager countess, whose nose was infallible, or to his young sister, Lady Margaret, who had a penchant for ferreting out scandal. His brother, Nick, was even more obnoxious. The young pup would immediately wager a large sum of money that he could tell the lady's identity from one whiff. And what was even more obnoxious was that he could do it too. The thought made Gray smile, but the smile faded when it occurred to him that Nick was in Bath, waiting for him to arrive so that they could finally settle accounts with Miss Deborah Weyman.

On entering the library, he strode to a side table between two long windows meaning to pour himself a glass of sherry. Before he could do so, a cough alerted him to the presence of his secretary, Mr. Philip Standish. He glanced round, and seeing the look on Philip's face, he said with distaste, "You are right, Philip. I smell awful. Women should learn to be more discriminating in their choice of fragrance. That reminds me. See that Lady Helena Perrin receives a . . . oh, whatever . . . as a token of my esteem."

"Very great esteem?" inquired the secretary, forcing a blush to recede.

"Moderate esteem," corrected Gray. He had already parted with a diamond pin in Paris, and was annoyed that ridding himself of a woman could prove so costly.

Mr. Standish dipped his pen in his inkpot and duly noted that the lady was to receive a bracelet with a ruby attached to it. One could tell a lot from the gifts Lord Kendal dispensed to his women.

"Do you have those letters for me to sign?" asked Gray.

"They are on your desk."

"How's the vicar?" asked Gray, as he perused the letters.

Philip was gratified by the question. His lordship's interest in his employees was quite genuine. He removed his spectacles and began to polish them with his handkerchief. "He is very well, thank you, sir, and sends his compliments."

Gray noticed the smile and his brows lifted.

Philip laughed and shook his head. "I received a letter from him today in which he took me to task for burning my hand with sealing wax. I felt like a small boy again."

"Parents will do that to you every time," said Gray. "How is the hand, by the way?"

"It's as good as new." The injury was three months old, and long healed, but Philip refrained from pointing this out to his employer.

As Gray went back to reading his letters, Philip's thoughts wandered, as they often did, to their Oxford days, when he and Gray had first met. Even then, Gray had cut a glamorous figure, tall, athletic, and into every sport that was going. He, on the other hand, had a weak chest. He kept his nose in his books. He did not have Gray's advantages to fall back on if he did not do well in his studies. He had never run with Gray's set. They had too much money and were too wild for him. But the two young men had formed a friendship of sorts when Philip had undertaken to tutor Gray in Homeric Greek for his final examinations. Gray never forgot a good turn, and when, a year ago, he discovered that Philip was eking out a living as a junior clerk in the Admiralty, he had immediately offered him the far more lucrative and prestigious position as his private secretary at the Foreign Office.

Philip's father, the sainted vicar, had tried to persuade his son to stay on at the Admiralty. Even as far afield as Chester, rumors of Gray's sexual exploits circulated among the gentry, and the vicar feared the influence of such a man on Philip's morals.

There was another side to Gray, Philip had written to inform the vicar. Gray was one of that elite group of young men who had been singled out by the then prime minster, Mr. Pitt, and groomed to take their places in government service. Gray's natural bent was foreign affairs, and so he had ended up at the Foreign Office, where he had made quite an impression on the Secretary. He worked long, hard hours, especially now that the war with France had been resumed. And lest the vicar think that his only son was wasting his talents, he had pointed out that his duties involved far more than domestic trivia. By and large, he worked with Gray at the Foreign Office. His work was highly confidential. He rubbed shoulders with men who were becoming legends in their own time. Under Lord Kendal's sponsorship, there was no saying how far he might go. The vicar was persuaded and the matter was dropped.

"What else needs my attention before I leave?" asked Gray.

Philip picked up a document and cleared his throat. "The lease on the house in Hans Town has fallen due. Do you wish me to renew it or allow it to lapse?"

He couldn't be bothered with these trifles, not when other more weighty matters were pressing on his mind. "Renew it," he said. "Is that all?"

"One other thing. Where might I reach you in the next week or two if it becomes necessary?"

"Gloucestershire," said Gray.

"How is Quentin?"

Gray was already rising to his feet. "As well as can be expected. I shall see you at the reception tonight, Philip?"

Philip knew better than to argue when Gray employed that particular tone of voice. "I look forward to it," he said simply.

"Good."

There was a thoughtful look on Philip's face as he stared at the door Gray closed on his way out.

❦

On entering his own room, Gray threw off his coat and flung himself down in a stuffed armchair. His thoughts were grim, and at the same time, he was possessed of a restless energy. For three months, he had been playing a part, living a lie, promoting the fiction that all was well with his ward and his governess. The playacting would soon be over, and everyone would know that Deborah Weyman had abducted Quentin and gone into hiding. It had taken his agent more than a month to track her down, and almost a month after that to verify information and observe her movements. *But by God, they had found her!* And this time, she would not escape him; this time, he would be there in person to see that nothing went wrong.

Rising, he strode to the bell rope beside the fireplace and yanked impatiently. When a footman arrived, Gray bade him go to the cellars and bring him a bottle of his finest cognac. This was soon done. He drank the first glass in one long swallow. Shaking his head at his intemperance, he poured himself another and, seating himself, sipped it slowly. Then, closing his eyes, he focused all his thoughts on the sequence of events that had led to the present moment.

Paris. It had all started in Paris during those last frenetic days when war was declared. They had known it was coming, and those attached to the diplomatic corps had taken the precaution of sending their wives and children home before the French decided to close French borders. He had been one of the last to leave, as had his good friend, Gil Barrington. Gil had delayed because Quentin was not fit to travel. All the same, he had been onto something before he met his death, close to unmasking someone who was betraying sensitive information to the French during the peace talks.

Gray had known that information was being leaked to the French, but he had failed to discover its source. He'd had an appointment with Gil on the night he was murdered so that they could compare notes, an appointment that Gil had subsequently canceled. At the time, Gray had thought nothing of it. He hadn't been thinking clearly, of course. Everything was in chaos. Everyone was trying to get out of Paris. He'd expected to meet up with Gil in London. Instead, a week after he returned, Talleyrand sent word that Lord Barrington had been tragically murdered by a thief whom he had surprised in the library of his house in Saint-Germain.

When the shock of the news had dulled, on thinking it over, he could not accept Talleyrand's account of Gil's murder. It was too pat, too much a coincidence. Before his death, Gil had stumbled across something significant. He'd had no proof, but he had a name for him. If he had only kept that appointment with Gil, the traitor in their midst might well have been unmasked by now, and Gil might still be alive. It was then that he began to question the note Gil had sent him canceling their appointment. Was it forged or was it genuine?

He'd made up his mind to reserve judgment until Miss Weyman arrived in England. He didn't suspect her of anything, not then. He simply wanted to question her since she had been one of the last people to see Gil alive. He knew approximately when she would be arriving in England. This was something else Talleyrand had arranged. She and the boy had been given a safe-conduct as far as Calais. They had arrived in Dover all right, but his suspicions had taken a new twist when both Deborah Weyman and Quentin had slipped away from the escort he had provided to convey them to London. It was quite deliberate on her part, and on the boy's too. There could be no mistake in that. His coachmen had pursued them both, but had lost them in one of Dover's busy thoroughfares.

From that day to this, the chase was on. He might have raised the alarm and set militia from one end of the country to the other to flush her out. He had rejected that idea for only one reason. Nothing must be done that would put the boy's life in jeopardy. A panicked woman was a dangerous woman. Quentin's welfare and only Quentin's welfare counted for anything now. He had one consolation. Quentin knew nothing of the danger he was in. His willingness to go with Miss Weyman convinced Gray of that. He didn't know what story she had told the boy, but he was glad, for Quentin's sake, that he was not going in fear of his life.

Before charting his course, he had weighed everything in the balance. At first, he'd taken no one into his confidence except the coachmen she'd run from in Dover, and they had been well paid to keep their mouths shut. Anticipating that she would demand ransom for the boy, and fearing that if word of the abduction got out she would be scared away, he had let it be known that Miss Weyman and his ward had arrived safely in England and were now secluded in one of his distant estates. When a week had passed, and no ransom was demanded, he had not known what to think. If she didn't want money, what did she want?

He'd gone over it in his mind a thousand times. The only other thing of value he could supply was information that she could sell to the enemy. Then why hadn't she communicated with him? When another week went by with no word from her, he had quietly approached Lord Lawford, head of Intelligence at the War Office, and he'd put the whole matter before him. Lawford's view, which Gray soon came to accept, was that she was holding the boy hostage for some nefarious scheme that had yet to unfold. They had to find Quentin, and soon. With this in mind, Lawford had loaned Gray his best agent, a man he trusted implicitly.

Campbell, the agent, had asked him questions he could not answer. What was Miss Weyman's background? Who were her parents, her friends? Where was she likely to go? Who had employed her before Lord Barrington? It soon became clear that Miss Weyman was a woman of mystery. For four years she had been Quentin's governess, yet none of Gil's friends seemed to know anything about her. Few of them had even met her. She never ventured out in society, but kept to herself.

The next few weeks were the longest of his life. He had almost given up hope, and was on the point of making everything public, when Campbell's report reached him. He'd gone down to Devon to question Gil's widow, Sophie Barrington, not openly, but posing as Miss Weyman's long-lost cousin who had lost her direction. In the course of the conversation, he learned that Deborah Weyman had come to Quentin from a girls' school in Bath. It wasn't much to go on, but it was the only lead they had. What Campbell finally came up with was a certain Mrs. Deborah Mornay, a widow, newly come into Bath to take up a teaching position at Miss Hare's School of Deportment for Young Ladies. One of the coachmen who had been at Dover to meet the girl was dispatched to help Campbell identify her. He was almost sure that Deborah Mornay and Deborah Weyman were one and the same person.

It wasn't all good news. In fact, some of it was harrowing. The boy was no longer with her.

Becoming aware that his fingers were wrapped around his glass in a death grip, he forced himself to relax. Quentin was safe. He would stake his life on it. She would not have dragged him across the length of France only to kill him in England. It was far more reasonable to suppose that she had hidden him away somewhere close by. She couldn't keep him with her, not now that she had taken up a position as a teacher in a girls' school. At any rate, he had to proceed on the assumption that Quentin was safe and well. Anything else was unthinkable.

Suddenly straightening, he reached for the drawer in the small table that flanked the fireplace. Inside, he found letters written in a round, childish hand, letters from Quentin thanking him for various gifts he had sent him on his birthdays and at Christmas. For a long, long time, Gray stared at those letters. There was no need to read them. He knew them by heart. He'd read them more than a dozen times since Quentin had been abducted.

He saw now what he had not seen when he had first received them. Quentin was a lonely little boy. There were no uncles and aunts, no cousins to play with, no relatives to care for him. That's why he and Miss Weyman had been named as Quentin's guardians in Gil's will. Quentin's only living relative was Gil's brother, a young man who had settled in the West Indies and had hardly troubled to write to Gil in years.

The boy's stepmother was not much better. When he'd told Sophie he thought it best for Quentin's peace of mind if he remained quietly at his estate in Gloucestershire, she had not protested or demanded to see the boy. She would write to Quentin, she'd told him in an offhand way as she had entered the carriage that was to take her to her parents' home in Devon. But no letters had been forwarded to him in London.

He shouldn't judge her too harshly. Sophie was very young, and she had been married to Gil for less than a year. She and Quentin had hardly had time to get to know each other. But, damn it all, there should have been *someone* to demand access to the boy! There wasn't a single soul, and though it suited Gray's purposes, it also saddened him. A boy deserved better than that!

A clock chimed the hour, breaking into his reveries. Setting down his glass, he stretched, rose, and began to prowl the room. He felt like a caged tiger. What he wanted was to be off and doing. All along, he'd wanted to be in the thick of things, helping Campbell with the investigation. Lord Lawford had cautioned patience. No one knew what the woman would do if she were panicked, or whether the traitor at the Foreign Office was working hand in glove with her. He must do nothing to alert them to their danger. The time to act would come, but not yet. And because Lawford knew his business and Gray respected his opinion, he had played a waiting game.

This last month, it had been almost impossible to carry on as though nothing were happening, for by this time, they had found her. He'd forced himself to do nothing until he was sure of his ground. Now, Campbell's part was over, and he had returned to his duties with Lord Lawford. The rest was up to him, and for what he had in mind, there were only two people he was willing to confide in. One was his brother, Nick, and the other was his brother-in-law, Lord Hartley. Nick and

Hart were already in Bath, waiting for him to arrive so that he could set things in motion.

In his mind's eye, he reviewed the information he had received on Mrs. Mornay that had helped him devise his plan of action. She was nervous, very nervous. The position at the school was only temporary. She was seeking a position in the country with a congenial family. On every second Wednesday, without fail, Mrs. Mornay took a party of girls to Wells, to visit the famous cathedral or to do a little shopping. No other teacher from the school visited Wells. Only Mrs. Mornay.

He hoped to hell he wasn't miscalculating. He thought about it for a moment, and his nerve steadied. The plan he had come up with posed the least threat to Quentin. At any rate, it was too late to draw back. Still, he wasn't underestimating his adversary. Deborah Weyman had proved that she was a clever, resourceful woman. She might well be implicated in Gil's murder.

A cold, wintry rage settled over him. Soon, very soon, Deborah Weyman would be in his power, and she would know how foolish she had been to cross swords with him.

❧ ❧ ❧ ❧ ❧ ❧ ❧ ❧ ❧

CHAPTER 2

Deborah studied her reflection in the small looking glass above her washstand, and she nodded her approval. The lady who nodded back at her appeared to be on the wrong side of thirty. Her skin, though unlined and fine-pored, had lost its first bloom of youth. The wire-rimmed spectacles added a little dignity. Her hair, what little could be seen of it for the muslin cap that was pulled low on her brow, was dull and mousy. Her high-necked, dark kerseymere gown was as drab as the rest of her. Well satisfied with what her mirror told her, Deborah quit her chamber.

In the corridor, she paused for a moment. She had learned from experience that hunching her shoulders gave her a backache. She could do nothing with her erect carriage, but there were other measures a young woman could take to add a few years. Her movements must be slow and sedate. Slow and sedate, she repeated to herself, and glided toward the stairs.

"Good morning, Sarah."

" 'Morning, Mrs. Mornay."

"Good morning, Millicent."

" 'Morning, Mrs. Mornay."

As she greeted the girls she met on the stairs, Deborah set her lips in a careful half-smile. As much as possible, she tried not to smile. She had been cursed with dimples, and dimples ruined the effect she had labored so hard to achieve.

Arriving at the headmistress's office, she knocked once before entering. She was expected. At the sight of her, Miss Hare reached for the teapot on her desk and poured Deborah a fresh cup of tea.

With Miss Hare, there was no need for pretense. "Morning, Bunny," said Deborah, and dropped a kiss on the top of Miss Hare's capped head before accepting the proffered cup and saucer.

The relationship between these two ladies was much more than that of employer and employee. There was real affection here, and it showed. Deborah's childhood had not been a happy one. Miss Hare, or "Bunny" as Deborah had nicknamed her, had been the source of what little security she had known. Miss Hare had once been Deborah's governess. Over time, she had become Deborah's bastion, the one sure refuge in a treacherous world.

"Good morning, Deborah." Miss Hare's voice was as no-nonsense as the rest of her. She was tall and well built, verging on the stout side. Her mode of dress was not unlike Deborah's, though not quite so old-fashioned. She'd had her dressmaker lift the waistlines and hems on all her gowns to suit the current mode. In her clothes press, swathed in tissue paper, was one of those new, square-necked, puff-sleeved muslins that was becoming all the rage. When the right moment arrived, that is, when the fashion became universally accepted, she intended to wear it. Though Miss Hare had no real interest in fashion, she believed it her duty to set an example in taste to all her pupils. She wished her teachers would adopt her rule. In her opinion, they were too conservative by half. Deborah was no exception. But then, Deborah had good reason to disguise her appearance.

"I think," said Miss Hare, "that I may have found a position for you."

This was good news to Deborah and it showed in her flashing dimples. "Bunny, you are an angel."

Miss Hare did not share in Deborah's enthusiasm. Leaning forward in her chair, she said seriously, "Deborah, are you sure this is what you want? Why not stay on at the school? This is as safe a haven as any you are likely to find."

"You know I'm not cut out to be a teacher. I do much better with only one or two children in my charge. Besides, I dare not stay in one place for long, not until I am quite certain I have thrown Lord Kendal off the scent."

A level look was exchanged, then Miss Hare sighed.

"Bunny, you know I am not exaggerating. The man is dangerous. I swear it."

"Are you sure? Forgive me, my dear, I know you hate to speak about that night, but isn't it possible that in the confusion you somehow misheard the name Lord Barrington cried out? I can hardly credit that a man of Lord Kendal's eminence would stoop to murder. Besides, Lord Barrington was his friend."

Deborah gave the answer she had repeatedly given Miss Hare since she had arrived at the school seeking asylum. "I heard it, I tell you, and there is nothing wrong with my hearing. Lord Barrington addressed his assailant as 'Lord Kendal,' not once, but twice. Besides, they had an appointment that night. Who else could it have been?"

"But you didn't see his face?"

"It was too dark. The candle was behind him."

Miss Hare sat back in her chair and considered Deborah thoughtfully. "Deborah," she said finally, "even if everything is as you say, you must surrender the boy. Surely you see that?"

"I do intend to surrender Quentin." Deborah spoke eagerly. "You know I do, just as soon as I receive a response to the letters I have sent to his uncle."

"The uncle who owns property in the West Indies and whose correspondence with Lord Barrington has been irregular, to say the least, in the last several years?"

Deborah looked away. "Yes."

"And if there is no response to your letters?"

"Then I shall take Quentin to him in person and lay

the whole business before him. What would you have me do? If I give Quentin up to his stepmother or anyone else, you know he would be handed over to his guardian, Lord Kendal, the man who murdered his father. And what do you think would happen to Quentin then?"

Seeing Deborah's agitation, Miss Hare tactfully busied herself setting out a plate of sugar biscuits and macaroons. It was Deborah who eventually took up the conversation where it had left off.

"It would be different if Quentin could corroborate my story. But I told you what happened. It was all too much for him. The horror of seeing his father murdered before his eyes is not to be borne. 'Trauma,' the physician called it. One day the memory of it may come back to him, then again, it may not. Meanwhile we go in fear of our lives, helpless to bring Lord Kendal to justice."

She swallowed hard. "Don't you think I have been tempted to go to the authorities with what I know? What good would it do? They would start probing into my past, and when they discovered the truth about me, they would discount every word I said." She gave a short laugh that held no humor. "They might even charge *me* with Lord Barrington's murder. After all, a woman who is accused of murdering her own betrothed would not cavil at murdering her employer."

"Don't speak like that!" said Miss Hare sternly. "You did not murder Albert. You were defending yourself from his attack."

Frowning, she reached for the teapot and replenished their cups. Inwardly, she was calling the Deity to account for the whole sorry mess. It was more than time He began to take a hand in Deborah's affairs.

She glanced at Deborah and her expression softened. Deborah had always had this effect on her. From the moment she had assumed her position as her governess, she had adored the child. Deborah had been starved for affection, and all Miss Hare's mothering instincts had come to the fore. Deborah could not be more like her daughter if she had been born of her own body.

Often, in that bleak, unhappy house, she had wondered how someone as innocent and as lovely as Deborah could have survived. Where had she come by that warmhearted nature, that quick intelligence, that sensitive spirit? Certainly not from her father. He was a coldhearted monster, a dangerous man with a will of iron.

She pressed a hand to her eyes. "You haven't had much of a life in the last number of years." Her eyes wandered over Deborah's drab outfit. "Dressing to look older, trying to disguise your appearance, always wondering if someone will recognize you. That is no life for a young woman, Deborah."

"You mustn't think I have been unhappy. These last four years as Quentin's governess have been the happiest of my life. Everything was going so well until . . . until." She gulped and fished in her pocket for her handkerchief. When she had blown her nose, she sat up straighter, then took up a different thread. "I am so thankful that you have always believed in my innocence, first with my betrothed, and now with Lord Barrington."

"I know you, my dear. It is not in your nature to deliberately hurt anyone or anything."

A tremor ran over Deborah, but she managed a smile. "Thank you, Bunny. I shall never forget those words, nor all you have done for me."

Miss Hare made a small sound of impatience. "Stuff and nonsense!" she exclaimed, but she was smiling one of her rare smiles.

"And now," said Deborah, "tell me about the position you mentioned."

For a moment, Miss Hare debated inwardly whether she should return to the subject of Quentin and what was to become of him. One quick glance at the angle of Deborah's stubborn little chin convinced her that further argument would be pointless. Sighing, she took a moment or two to set her thoughts in order. "I had an interview with a certain Mr. Gray," she began. "Initially, he had it in his mind to place his sister in the school in order to give the girl a little polish. Well, that's what we do for all our girls, isn't it? The more we conversed, however, the more it came to me that the girl and her brother would be better served by employing their own private tutor. Naturally, as soon as that thought occurred to me, I thought of you."

"Tutor? Not governess?"

"Perhaps I should have said 'mentor.' You see, Mr. Gray has come up in the world. I think he said his people made their fortune in breweries. But the point is, he got himself elected to Parliament. You see what this means?"

"No," said Deborah.

Miss Hare eyed Deborah askance. "It means that he and his sister will be taking up residence in London and moving in more exalted circles. Miss Gray must act as her brother's hostess, but the poor girl is hardly out of the schoolroom. She doesn't know the first thing about court protocol, or how to go on in society, leastways the kind of society she will meet with in London."

"You can't be suggesting that I go to London, Bunny? Why, I could run into my father or my stepmother. Then what would become of me?"

Miss Hare allowed herself a small smile. "But that's the beauty of it. Mr. Gray has no wish to remove his sister to London until she is well versed in the social graces." She sat back in her chair and paused deliberately for effect. "He has a place where the girl resides, quite off the beaten track."

"Where is this place?" asked Deborah.

Miss Hare watched Deborah's face intently. "Wells, Deborah. Mr. Gray's country villa is on the outskirts of Wells."

Deborah's startled expression gradually gave way to one of acute interest. "Wells," she said, and breathed deeply.

"Yes, Wells. And there is more. He is willing to pay handsomely for the privilege of employing someone of your unquestionable talents. And it's only for a few months."

It seemed too good to be true, and that worried Deborah. "What exactly did you tell him about me?"

"No more, no less than we agreed I should tell anyone who asked about you, and, of course, my personal recommendation of your character and abilities."

It had been a glowing testimonial, but Miss Hare would not allow that one word of it was exaggeration. Deborah really was an accomplished young woman. She should be when she, Miss Hare, had had the training of her for most of her young life. As was natural, Mr. Gray had asked a good many questions about those early years which she had answered diplomatically but without betraying anything of the least significance. The one question that had taken her aback was the one to do with Deborah's failings.

"Come now," Mr. Gray had said. "No one is perfect, not even Mrs. Mornay. Everyone has some flaw or failing that could stand to be improved."

He must have seen something in her expression for his nice eyes had narrowed on her in a most disconcerting way, and she had found herself saying something to the effect that Deborah's failing was that she allowed people to take advantage of her, which was no failing at all from a prospective employer's point of view.

Deborah watched the play of emotions that were reflected on Miss Hare's face, and she quickly set down her cup and saucer. "Bunny, you do understand that Lord Kendal is clever, more clever than you or I? He could send constables after me, or even the militia. He has that power. Or," she added significantly, "he could send his agents."

Miss Hare emitted a long, drawn-out sigh. "Frankly, Deborah," she said, "I think you are letting your imagination run riot. No, no, I refuse to enter into a debate. When you meet Mr. Gray, you will laugh at your own words. Why, a more harmless, unassuming gentleman I have yet to meet. I liked him on sight."

The stiffness in Deborah's spine gradually relaxed. Miss Hare was a shrewd judge of character. If she liked Mr. Gray on sight, he must be a very presentable gentleman. "I take it," she said, "he will wish to interview me?"

Miss Hare's eyes twinkled. "He wants to take you

unawares, you know, see for himself how you manage the girls."

"Oh no," groaned Deborah.

"Tomorrow," said Miss Hare. "You may expect him tomorrow."

❧

By the end of the day, Deborah's head was pounding. Her conversation with Miss Hare had made it impossible for her to concentrate on what she was supposed to be doing, and the girls had made the most of it.

Sighing, her shoulders drooping, she stared at herself long and hard in the looking glass above the washstand in her chamber. Suddenly, with a little cry of anguish, she threw off her spectacles, tore off her muslin cap, then flung herself facedown on the bed. When and where would it all end? Her youth was passing, and she was doing her best to hurry it along! She must be out of her mind! It wasn't fair, oh it wasn't fair! When she had been offered the position with Lord Barrington, she could hardly believe her luck. After five years of working with Miss Hare, she had known that teaching large groups of adolescent girls was not for her. And the position with Lord Barrington had seemed ideal. His country estate was isolated and he never entertained there. And later, after his marriage, when she had been invited to accompany Quentin to Paris, she had thought herself the luckiest girl in the world. If only Quentin had not come down with a fever! If only they had left for Calais with Lady Barrington! But Quentin had come down with a fever, and she had stayed on to look after him. And they had both witnessed a murder.

Murder. How was it possible for one girl to become involved in two murders in her short life? With her balled fists, she dashed her tears away. This was no time to be indulging in a bout of self-pity. She must think.

She rolled on her back and looked up at the ceiling. It was reported in the newspapers that her employer had been murdered by a thief who broke into his house in

Paris. But this was only a theory. She could well imagine the outcome if it were known that his son's governess was accused by her own father of another murder which had taken place eight years before. She would be suspected of Lord Barrington's murder also. Then she would surely hang. At least she would have the satisfaction of knowing her father's machinations had come to nothing!

She checked the hysterical laugh that bubbled to her lips. In her present circumstances, her father was the least of her worries. She should be thinking of Lord Kendal. She had never met the man nor ever wished to, but she had taken his measure from what Lord and Lady Barrington had told her. He was reputed to be the most respected man in England. But that was the public figure. His private life did not bear too close a scrutiny. It went without saying that he would be tall, dark, and handsome. His sort always were, the sort women swooned over. She could well imagine the supercilious slant to his brows, the cynical smile. Ugh!

Hauling herself into a sitting position, with her back against the headboard, she focused her thoughts, trying to recall what she knew of him. Though he was Quentin's godfather, to her knowledge, he had seen very little of the boy in the last four years. Lord Barrington had excused his friend's neglect by pointing out that London was Lord Kendal's milieu, while Quentin remained in the country. True, he had sent Quentin gifts, and they had kept up a correspondence, but even in Paris, Lord Kendal had made no effort to become reacquainted with his godson. He had not even appeared at the picnic she had arranged. He had sent his secretary in his stead. It was all very well for Lord Barrington to say that the peace talks completely absorbed his friend's time and energies, but a godfather . . .

She broke off at this point in her reflections and shuddered in horror. What was she thinking? It would have been better for them all if Lord Kendal had *never* come near Quentin. And to think that Lord Barrington's voice had always been shaded with admiration whenever he spoke of Lord Kendal! Until that last night.

She couldn't begin to understand what had gone wrong in that friendship. One thing she knew. They had been arguing about something before the gun went off. It was no accident. She was sure of that too. Lord Kendal had come after her and Quentin and might have had them if the servants had not scared him off. Oh God, it was so reminiscent of that other time. Who would believe her if she told the truth? How could she persuade anyone that the most respected man in England had murdered his best friend? People were too easily taken in by outward appearances. They did not know of the hatreds and passions that could smolder beneath a charming façade. But she knew. Her father had taught her that.

Her thoughts strayed, remembering Lord Barrington in happier days, easy-going, charming, with an attractive twinkle in his dark eyes. It was impossible not to like him. When he was in residence, the whole house seemed to come alive. It was as if the prodigal had returned from the far country.

Quentin had adored his father. When they were together, it was like watching two children at play. She had wished, though, that Lord Barrington would spend more time with him. Quentin was a very lonely little boy. She'd sympathized with her employer's position. He had important work to do at the Foreign Office. For his part, he understood that Quentin missed a mother's touch. That's why he had employed a governess to care for his son and not a tutor. When he'd married, she'd thought things would change. Though it tore at her heart, she was prepared to give Quentin up to his new mother. As it turned out, the girl Lord Barrington married didn't care for country life, though she had been born and bred in the country. She rarely came down to see Quentin. Sophie liked parties, and shopping, and taking in all the entertainments the city had to offer. Even in Paris, they had hardly ever seen her. Lord Barrington had tried to remonstrate, but it made no difference. That was one failing in her employer that occasionally irked her. He was too nice for his own good. Sometimes, just sometimes, she wished he would put his foot down, not only with his wife, but with Quentin also. Oh God, how could this have happened? It wasn't fair! Oh, it wasn't fair! He was such a good man.

She wasn't going to cry, she told herself, and blinked the tears away. Lord Barrington was gone, but she was here. Somehow, someday, she would make Lord Kendal pay for what he had done. For the present, her first duty was to Quentin. She had to get him away. She had to.

Her chin trembled and she closed her eyes, thinking of Quentin. She'd come to him shortly after his mother's death, and she remembered the first time she had met him. She had no conception then that the solemn-faced, four-year-old boy who viewed her with open suspicion would, very soon, become the most important thing in her life. She remembered his first pony, and how her credit had soared in the boy's eyes when he saw that his governess was an accomplished rider. She remembered sitting by his bed, bathing his face and his body with cool washcloths when he was burning with fever. She remembered rocking him in her arms when he wakened from a dream, crying for his mother. And she remembered her own fear when she realized how much he had come to mean to her. She could not keep him forever. She wasn't his mother. She was only his governess.

Abruptly rising, she moved to a dresser on which sat a small carved coffer made of oak. She felt in her pocket, extracted a key, and unlocked the coffer. Inside was a black velvet pouch. She emptied the contents of the pouch into the palm of one hand. Tiny diamonds set in an oval silver locket winked up at her. She pried the locket open and stared at the miniature inside. A young, dark-haired girl with a trace of a smile on her lips stared back at her. This was all that was left to her of her mother. Looking at that sweet face, she was filled with a flood of memories, not unlike the ones she'd had of Quentin a moment ago, only this time she was the child.

Swallowing, she turned the locket over. Her name was engraved on the back, her real name. This was her most prized possession, given to her by her mother on the last Christmas they'd spent together. Because her name was on it, she could never wear it. Since she'd become a fugitive from the law, she'd been reduced to keeping it hidden away, and brought it out only on odd, reflective moments when there was no one there to see it. If Lord Kendal was after her, it was even more dangerous to have it in her possession. The thought made her shiver. It would be far wiser to give it to Miss Hare to keep for her. She thought about this for a moment, and came to a decision. When she left here, she would give it to Miss Hare to keep for her until . . . until what? She couldn't envisage the day when she would be free to wear the locket without fear of discovery. A more prudent woman would get rid of it, but she couldn't bring herself to do that. She would give it to Miss Hare, and one day, God willing, she would reclaim it.

She slipped the locket inside the pouch and replaced them in the coffer. With the tips of her fingers, she massaged her forehead. Her mind was churning with doubt and anxiety. Had she done the right thing in coming to the school? None of the other teachers had known her from before, and she had taken such pains to change her appearance that even her own father would not recognize her. And she did not think there was any way Lord Kendal could trace her. She was always so careful not to betray anything that would connect her to anyone in her past. Even Lord Barrington had been told a pack of lies to persuade him that she was the right person to be his son's governess. Lies, lies, lies. It had become a way of life for her, only this was a worse catastrophe than before. Before she had only herself to think about. Now there was Quentin. What confounded her was that there had been no outcry when Quentin had disappeared, nothing in the papers, not one word. Lord Kendal must be responsible. He would want to silence Quentin and her before they could do him any real harm. She hoped that he was trembling in his boots as much as she trembled in hers. What he could not know was that, for the present at least, he was safe from detection.

If Quentin had been able to corroborate her story, she would have taken her chances and gone directly to the authorities with what she knew. But Quentin had no memory of that night. The storm had awakened him and that was all he remembered until they had boarded the packet in Calais. He had not even known that his father was dead.

Another shudder passed over her, and she hugged herself tightly. Lord Kendal would never find Quentin, she assured herself, not unless he found her first, and even then, she would never lead him to the boy. Just thinking about it made her sick with fright. If anything happened to her, what would become of Quentin?

With a stifled moan, she began to pace the floor. Nothing was going to happen to her. She had made her plans, and she would abide by them. She dared not stay in one place for long. Mr. Gray had come upon the scene at just the right moment. And if Lord Kendal sent his minions to nose around asking questions about her, Miss Hare would know what to do.

It was imperative that she make a good impression on Mr. Gray. It shouldn't be too difficult. He was a provincial, and she had the knowledge and skills to smooth his sister's way in society. She must convince him of it.

CHAPTER 3

In the pink and white drawing room of Miss Hare's School of Deportment for Young Ladies, the ritual of taking tea was in progress. This was no empty ritual as was to be found in legions of drawing rooms throughout England on almost any day of the week. This was an exercise in deportment, a way of putting the girls through their paces, testing their competence in the social graces. That was the theory.

In practice, thought Deborah dismally, it was sheer torture, not least because the guest of honor on this particular afternoon happened to be a handsome, personable gentleman whom Miss Hare had vaguely introduced before abandoning him to his fate. It was he, of course, Mr. Gray, the gentleman who was seeking a mentor for his young sister, and Deborah could have wept in frustration. Of all the times to be caught unawares, this was unquestionably the worst. She could do nothing with the girls. They did not give a straw about learning the rudiments of drawing-room conversation. They were all man-mad, and were flirting outrageously. Miss Hare frequently arranged for gentlemen guests to be present when the girls took tea, but no one of Mr. Gray's attributes had ever visited them. It was inevitable that these brazen hussies would be thrown into a twitter.

He was certainly handsome. In her experience, most men with his looks had the conceit to go with them. They fed on feminine adulation and knew how to charm a female into doing whatever they wanted. Mr. Gray wasn't like that. It had taken her only a few minutes to sum him up. She could see at a glance that he wasn't used to being the center of attention. He was ill at ease and seemed more than happy to allow her to do most of the talking. His modesty, his ineptness around females, was quite touching.

As her gaze lingered, his head turned, and eyes as blue and clear as a mountain stream caught and held her stare before the gentleman looked away. She had a flash of unease, a quick impression of a cat among the pigeons, then sanity returned. She was overwrought. She was imagining things. If Lord Kendal's minions ever caught up with her, they wouldn't waste time by taking tea. They would swoop down like vultures and carry her off in pieces. This quiet, unassuming gentleman was exactly what he appeared to be. She had nothing to fear here. Then why was he smiling? What was he thinking?

Gray was congratulating himself on the approach he had decided to take with the girl. His first inclination had been to swoop down and carry her off by force. His interview with Miss Hare had persuaded him to a more subtle course of action. There was no doubt in his mind that Miss Hare would raise Cain if her protégée were to be mishandled. Not only would she call in the constables, but she would pursue the matter with the tenacity of a British bulldog. The last thing he wanted was to involve others in how he meant to proceed with Miss Weyman.

The more he observed her, the more the conviction grew that he was not dealing with an enemy agent but a guileless innocent who had somehow got in over her head. It would be no great feat to terrify her into submission. He had every confidence that in a matter of days, if not sooner, she would be willing to tell him all that he wished to know. Yet, a small part of him regretted that he must be so hard on her. It was not his way to make war on defenseless women. He dismissed this thought almost as soon as it occurred to him. He could not be sure that she was as innocent as she appeared, and even if she were, she had abducted Quentin, and Quentin's safety took precedence over everything.

Deborah touched a finger to the furrow on her brow, willing an incipient headache to retreat, and she did her best to ignore the fluttering eyelashes and simpers that emanated from her charges. When, however, Millicent Dench rose to offer Mr. Gray another cucumber sandwich, Deborah sat bolt upright in her chair. One never knew quite what to expect from Millicent. It wasn't that the girl was wicked. It was simply that she could not refuse a dare. One quick look around at the girls' faces convinced Deborah that mischief, in bold letters, was brewing.

She was on the point of rising to head the girl off when Mr. Gray's voice arrested her. "Thank you, Miss Dench," he said, "but I prefer something sweeter. Miss Moir, I'll have a slice of that cake, if you would be so kind."

The hush that descended eddied with hidden currents. Deborah knew that she had missed something, but could not begin to guess what it was. She was aware that Millicent had received a snub—the girl's blushes attested to that fact—but there was more to it than that. Something had happened and she was the only person present who had missed it. She was aware of something else. The balance of power had shifted to Mr. Gray, and his innocuous words were responsible for it.

She looked at him curiously, and saw things about him that she had missed before—the breadth of his shoulders, the powerful masculine physique, and now that she came to think of it, that pleasantly modulated voice had carried an edge of steel. Had she mistaken his character? If so, it hardly mattered. The gentleman could be as masterful as Jupiter, just so long as he did not try to master her. There was no fear of that. His business would take him to London almost at once, and she and Miss Gray would be left to their own devices in the seclusion of his country estate. It was perfect, if only she could manage it.

When he turned to look at her, she saw that his eyes were smiling, and an unspoken message flashed between them. There was a joke in this somewhere, and later he would share it with her. When she nodded imperceptibly, Mr. Gray gave his attention to the cup and saucer in his hand. The smile on Deborah's face lingered.

She hadn't been mistaken in him. He really was a nice man, the sort of man a woman could make a friend of, up to a point. The only other men she had befriended had all been elderly, with the exception of Lord Barrington. Her thoughts drifted and a wistful expression came over her face, an expression that was not lost on the gentleman who was assiduously drinking his tea.

She came to herself with a start to discover that the girls had taken advantage of her preoccupation and were firing off questions like English archers releasing their arrows at the Battle of Agincourt. Was Mr. Gray married? Betrothed? How old was he? What was his profession? Where did he live? Why had he come to Bath? As the only mistress present, it was Deborah's duty to give the girls a push in the right direction when conversation flagged, or restrain them when they got the bit between their teeth. Though she was curious to know more of Mr. Gray, experience had taught her that if she gave the girls an inch they would take a mile, and there was no saying what they would come up with next.

"Girls," she said, and got no further. A gong sounded, loud and clear, and Deborah tried not to let her relief show. A lady who earned her bread by caring for other people's children must always appear in command of every situation.

"Study hall," said Deborah brightly, addressing Mr. Gray, and all the girls groaned.

With a few muttered protests and a great deal of snickering, the girls began to file out of the room. Deborah assisted their progress by holding the door for them, reminding them cheerfully that on the morrow they would be reviewing irregular French verbs and she expected them to have mastered their conjugations. As the last girl slipped by her, Deborah shut the door with a snap, then rested her back against it, taking a moment or two to collect herself.

Suddenly aware that Mr. Gray had risen at their exit and was standing awkwardly by the window, she politely invited him to be seated. "You'll have a glass of sherry?" she inquired. At Miss Hare's, the guests were invariably treated to a glass of sherry when the ordeal of taking tea was over. At his nod, Deborah moved to the sideboard against the wall. The glasses and decanter were concealed behind a locked door, and she had to stoop to retrieve them from their hiding place.

As he seated himself, Gray's gaze wandered over the lush curves of her bottom. There was an appreciative glint in his eye. The thought that was going through his head was that Deborah Weyman bore no resemblance to the descriptions he had been given of her. Spinsterish? Straitlaced? Dull and uninteresting? That's what she wanted people to think. She had certainly dressed for the part with her high-necked, long-sleeved blue kerseymere and the ubiquitous white mob cap pulled down to cover her hair. An untrained eye would look no further. Unhappily for the lady, not only was he a trained observer, but he was also an acknowledged connoisseur of women. Advantage to him.

Since her attention was riveted on the two glasses of sherry on the tray she was carrying, he took the liberty of studying her at leisure. Her complexion was tinged with gray—powder, he presumed—in an attempt to add years and dignity to sculpted bones that accredited beauties of the *ton* would kill for. The shapeless gown served her no better than the gray face powder. She had the kind of figure that would look good in the current high-waisted diaphanous gauzes or in sackcloth and ashes. Soft, curvaceous, womanly. When she handed him his sherry, he kept his expression blank. Behind the wire-rimmed spectacles, her lustrous green eyes were framed by—he blinked and looked again. Damned if she had not snipped at her eyelashes to shorten them! Had the woman no vanity?

"I missed something, didn't I?" said Deborah. "That's why you are smiling that secret smile to yourself."

"Beg pardon?" Gray's thick veil of lashes lowered to diffuse the intentness of her look.

Deborah seated herself. "I missed something when Millicent offered you a cucumber sandwich. What was it?"

If he had the dressing of her, the first thing he would do was banish the mob cap. There wasn't a curl or stray tendril of hair to be seen. "A note."

"A note?"

"Mmm." Red hair or blond. It had to be one or the other. Unless she had dyed it, of course. He wouldn't put it past her. If this were a tavern and she were not a lady, he would offer her fifty, no, a hundred gold guineas if only she would remove that blasted cap.

"Are you saying that Millicent passed you a note?"

Her voice had returned to its prim and proper mode. He was beginning to understand why she had kept out of the public eye. She couldn't sustain a part.

"The note," Deborah reminded him gently.

"The note? Ah yes, the note. It was in the cucumber sandwich." She was trying to suppress a smile, and her dimples fascinated him. No one had mentioned that she had dimples.

"Oh dear, I suppose I should show it to Miss Hare. That girl is incorrigible."

"I'm afraid that won't be possible."

"Why won't it?"

"On her way out, she snatched it back. I believe she ate it."

When she laughed, he relaxed against the back of his chair, well pleased with himself. That wary, watchful look that had hovered at the back of her eyes had completely dissipated. He was beginning to take her measure. The more he erased his masculinity, the more trustful she became. Unhappily for him, there was something about Deborah Weyman that stirred the softer side of his nature. Advantage to her.

Deborah sipped at her sherry, trying to contain her

impatience. As her prospective employer, it was up to him to begin the interview. He lacked the social graces. She wasn't finding fault with him. On the contrary, his inexperience appealed to her. It made him seem awkward, boyish, harmless. Besides, she had enough social graces for the two of them.

"Miss Hare mentioned that you were seeking a governess for your young sister?" she said.

He was reluctant to get down to business. All too soon, things would change. That trustful look would be gone from her eyes, and Miss Weyman would never trust him again. Pity, but that was almost inevitable. Still, he wasn't going to make things difficult for her at this stage of the game. That would come later.

Deborah shifted restlessly. "You will wish to know about references from former employers," she said, trying to lead him gently.

"References?" He relaxed a little more comfortably against the back of his chair. Smiling crookedly, he said, "Oh, Miss Hare explained your circumstances to me. Having resided in Ireland with your late husband for a goodly number of years, you allowed your acquaintance with former employers to lapse."

"That is correct."

"I quite understand. Besides, Miss Hare's recommendation carries more weight with me."

"Thank you." She'd got over the first hurdle. Really, it was as easy as taking sweetmeats from a babe. Mr. Gray was more gullible than she could have hoped. The thought shamed her, and her eyes slid away from his.

"Forgive me for asking," he said, "Miss Hare did not make this clear to me. She mentioned that in addition to teaching my sister the correct forms and addresses, you would also impart a little gloss. How do you propose to do that?"

There was an awkward pause, then Mr. Gray brought his glass to his lips, and Deborah shrank involuntarily. She knew that she looked like the last person on earth who could impart gloss to anyone.

For a long, introspective moment, she stared at her clasped hands. Seeing that look, Gray asked quietly,

"What is it? What have I said?" and leaning over, he drew one finger lightly across her wrist.

The touch of his finger on her bare skin sent a shock of awareness to all the pulse points in her body. She trembled, stammered, then fell silent. When she raised her eyes to his, she had herself well in hand. "I know what you are thinking," she said.

"Do you? I doubt it." He, too, had felt the shock of awareness as bare skin slid over bare skin. The pull on his senses astonished him.

His eyes were as soft as his smile. Disregarding both, she said earnestly, "You must understand, Mr. Gray, that governesses and schoolteachers are not paid to be fashionable. Indeed, employers have a decided preference for governesses who know their place. Servants wear livery. We governesses wear a livery of sorts too. Well, you must have noticed that the schoolteachers at Miss Hare's are almost indistinguishable, one from the other."

"You are mistaken. I would know you anywhere."

The compliment was unexpected and thrilled her until she remembered that he saw her as an aging dowd. She'd seen his kind in action before. She'd wager her last groat that he was quite the gallant in the presence of elderly ladies. In another moment, he would be pinching her cheek and swearing that, in her salad days, she must have been a breaker of hearts. It was too mortifying to be borne.

"The thing is . . ." she began.

"Were you happy as a governess?"

"Beg pardon?"

"It could not have been easy, submerging your own personality to fit someone else's preconceived notions of what you should be."

She didn't mind being a governess. It was the necessity for her elaborate disguise that was hard to bear. In some ways it was like a prison sentence, but she couldn't tell him that. Behind the spectacles, her lashes flickered. She didn't want his sympathy, she wanted his respect. She had to convince him that she was the right candidate for the position.

"Mr. Gray, the point I am trying to make is this." Conscious that her tone verged on the tart side, she tried to sweeten it with a smile. "You may not think it to look at me, but I have knowledge of court life; I know what it is to prepare a girl for her first season; I am well versed in the modes and manners that prevail in the upper echelons of court circles. I don't have the credentials to prove it, but I am quite willing to be put to the test. Ask me something, anything you like, and I shall endeavor to answer you."

He could almost taste the desperation behind her words. He had her in the palm of his hand. The thing to do now was to bring the interview to a speedy conclusion and arrange a time convenient to them both to convey her to the "villa" Nick had rented outside Wells. He did not wish to bring the interview to a close, not yet. There was something about Miss Deborah Weyman, a sadness, a wistfulness, and yes, a heart-tugging bravado that drew him like a magnet. If only for a few moments, he wanted to prolong the pleasure of her company. It might well be the only time she would look upon him with favor. Once again, he felt the sting of regret, and was taken by surprise.

"I don't know what to ask," he said, throwing her a helpless look.

"Think of your sister. What is it you wish for her?"

That was easy to answer. The real Margaret was quite a handful, and likely to give him a crop of silver hair before he had safely married her off. "Well . . ." he began, warming to his part.

"Nothing you can say will embarrass me, I promise you."

His lashes lowered to half mast. If the lady was eager to play games, he was willing to indulge her. "As Miss Hare may have told you," he said, "my sister, Margaret, is quite an . . . um . . . heiress. Oh, don't mistake me. Margaret is no fool. She knows about fortune hunters and men of that ilk. It is experience in turning them off that she lacks. What advice would you give her?"

"Nothing could be simpler," said Deborah, bringing to the question the same directness she would bring to a problem that one of the girls had raised in class. "Avoid such men as if they were poison."

And that's exactly what he had told Meg, not that she'd listened to him. For all her paucity of years, she thought she knew how to handle men. He'd wager that Meg knew more than Miss Weyman did.

Her bright eyes were watching him. Making a steeple with his fingers, he said, "With some gentlemen, that only makes them more persistent. They see it as a challenge. What if . . . what if she were caught unawares, like . . . like you, for instance, alone, with me, behind closed doors?"

Deborah's eyes flicked nervously to the closed door, then back to Gray. Cautiously inching forward in her chair, she looked with alarm at his left shoulder.

"What is it?" asked Gray, frowning.

"Don't move," she whispered. "There's a wasp crawling inside your collar."

"What!"

While Gray lurched to his feet and batted ineffectually with his hands, Deborah darted to the door. With her hand on the knob, she turned back to laugh at him. "It's all right, Mr. Gray," she said. "There was no wasp."

By degrees, his glare gave way to a sheepish grin. Shaking his head, he said, "That was diabolical!" and he strolled toward her. When he came to the door, he negligently propped one shoulder against it. "You have convinced me that Margaret could do no better," he said. "In the interests of harmony, though, I think we should avoid the word 'governess' and substitute 'companion.' What do you say, Mrs. Mornay?"

Deborah's eyes were brilliant. Her voice wavered. "You won't regret it, Mr. Gray. I promise you."

"No, I daresay I won't. Then it only remains to arrange the day and the hour when I may convey you to my sister."

"I must speak with Miss Hare first."

"Naturally."

Deborah pulled on the doorknob to no avail. "Would you mind, Mr. Gray?" she said, indicating that the door would not budge because he was still propped against it.

In one smooth, unthreatening movement, he caught her by the wrist and held her fast. There was no fear in Deborah's eyes, only a question.

"And what if, my dear Mrs. Mornay," he said, "my sister should find herself in this predicament?" He raised her wrist and resisted her feeble struggles when she tried to free herself. "What advice would you offer then?"

Deborah dimpled up at him. "Assuming the girl has lungs, I would advise her to use them. Scream, Mr. Gray. She should scream, and when she is rescued, as she is sure to be, she should give out that a wasp crawled inside *her* collar."

"You have an answer for everything," he said in a slow, sleepy voice, and he edged closer. "I know how to prevent a scream. What if . . . what if the gentleman in question were to kiss her?" His eyes dropped to Deborah's mouth.

He was close, so very close, and she could feel his warm breath on her cool cheek. It wasn't fear or curiosity that held her captive, nor yet the restraining grasp on her wrist. A strange yearning uncurled inside her, then spread out in ripples, till she was shivering in anticipation. Slowly, inexorably, he tugged on her wrist, bringing her closer. Her lips parted and she forgot to breathe. His head descended. Hers lifted.

A gong sounded, just outside the door. Gray's eyes flared. Deborah blinked rapidly, then she looked about her as though she had no recollection of how she had got there.

When she gasped, he released her and took a quick step back. She was still gazing up at him, horror-struck, when he opened the door with a flourish and motioned her to precede him.

"If I'm not mistaken," he said, "study hall is over."

Her cheeks flooded with color and her eyes anxiously searched his. "Mr. Gray, I don't know what—"

He spoke at the same moment. "You were going to stamp on my foot. That's it, isn't it?"

"What?"

"You were playing up to me. Then, when I was distracted, you were going to stamp on my foot?"

She fastened on his words as if he had thrown her a lifeline. "Y-yes." Then more emphatically, "Yes. That's exactly what was in my mind."

When they came into the corridor, they were caught up in the rush of girls who were coming and going to their various classes. Deborah was glad of the confusion, and embarked on a disjointed flow of small talk that lasted till Mr. Gray had taken his leave of her. As soon as the door closed upon him, she spun on her heel and made for the long pier glass in the teachers' common room.

Her reflection was vastly reassuring, she told herself. Mr. Gray could not possibly have been flirting with her. It was all in her head. Her steps were slow and heavy as she made her way to Miss Hare's office.

❧

In the library of the house that Gray had rented while he was staying in Bath, two gentlemen were playing a game of cards. One of those gentlemen was Nicholas Grayson, Gray's younger brother. Like Gray, Nick was tall and blond and possessed his fair share of good looks. He was, however, a younger son, which made all the difference between them. Gray had responsibilities that Nick neither coveted nor thought much about. He was financially independent, and pursued a life of pleasure and ease, and if sometimes he found that life a bit of a bore, it was infinitely preferable to the one his mother, the dowager countess, had mapped out for him. Marriage and babies did not figure prominently in Nick's scheme of things. That sad duty, he was frequently heard to airily protest, fell to the unhappy lot of his brother, the earl.

The other occupant of the room was Lord Hartley, their brother-in-law, who had married their older sister, Gussie, nine years before. Hart, a sober-looking gentleman, was in his late thirties, dark haired and dark complexioned. Though he was fond of his brothers-in-law, he was a little in awe of them. He considered himself a slow, plodding sort of fellow, while they were as changeable as quicksilver. Sometimes, in conversation with them, he found it hard to grasp their train of thought. A lesser man, not wishing to appear stupid, wouldn't have troubled himself, but Hart was nothing if not persistent. For some time now, he had been mulling over Gray's plan of action and he was not satisfied that he understood all the implications of it.

"I suppose," he said, "this is the best way to handle things?"

"Meaning?" Nick gathered the cards that were on the table. "My trick, I believe?"

"What? Oh yes. What I mean is this. Wouldn't it be simpler to hand Miss Weyman over to the authorities?"

"You heard Gray. Magistrates and constables are sworn to uphold the law and must follow a set procedure. That takes time. Besides, Gray won't make a move that might tip the hand of the traitor at the Foreign Office. That's why we are doing this in stealth." There was a twinkle in Nick's eye as he waited for the next question.

Hart looked at the cards in his hand and rearranged them. At length, he said, "And Gray is no nearer to discovering who this traitor is?"

"You heard him. He has set dozens of traps without result. Not one bite. Not even a nibble."

"What do you make of it?"

"That our spy is either very cautious, or he has given up the game. Perhaps he's waiting for something big, something connected with Miss Weyman and the boy."

"Is it possible that Miss Weyman is the traitor?"

"Oh no," said Nick. "Quite impossible."

Though Hart was relieved to hear it, he said carefully, "Why is it impossible?"

"Because Miss Weyman did not have access to the information that was passed to the French. The only way she could have known anything was if Gil told her, and he was hardly likely to do that."

Hart frowned down at his cards. "None of it makes

sense to me. No one suspected her. Why would she suddenly run with the boy when she arrived in England?"

Nick sighed. "Hart, you will just have to accept that some questions cannot be answered until Gray has questioned Miss Weyman."

For the next few minutes, they played out their cards in silence. Nick was not surprised when he won the next hand. Hart had that expression on his face that told him his thoughts were elsewhere.

When Nick began to shuffle the pack, Hart said, "I don't believe she murdered Gil."

"Oh? Why not?"

"Because," said Hart, "Miss Hare could not recommend her highly enough, and Gil named her as Quentin's guardian. That does not sound to me as if she were capable of committing murder."

"No, but she might know who did. And there's no getting round the fact that she abducted Quentin. She must be guilty of something, Hart, or why did she take the boy and run?"

But Hart had no answer to this and stared glumly at his cards. When a door suddenly slammed, both gentlemen looked up. They heard Gray's quick stride in the hall, then a moment later the door opened to admit him. He hardly spared them a glance as he strode to the table with the decanters and glasses. Having poured himself a small measure of brandy, he took a long swallow, then swung to face them.

"You are to leave at once for Wells," he said. "You will be happy to know that everything went off without a hitch. Miss Hare trusts me. The girl trusts me. So you see, we are well on the way to success."

Nick's brows had risen. "Gray, what the deuce has happened? You act as if Miss Weyman had flown the coop."

Gray's smile was arctic. Hart could feel the chill of it on the back of his neck. Raising one hand, he absent-mindedly smoothed the fine hairs into place.

"What has happened," said Gray in a voice that matched his smile, "is that I am perfectly sure I shall be able to break Miss Weyman in a matter of days, if not hours."

His words were met by silence. Nick and Hart exchanged a quick look, then Nick said carefully, "But that's capital, Gray, and if that's the case, perhaps there's no need to, um, go on with the charade."

Gray bolted the dregs of his brandy and set down the glass with a snap. "Use your head, Nick. Miss Weyman has proved that she is a clever, resourceful woman. I have every confidence that I can break her, but only when pressure is brought to bear."

Hart, who had a vision of thumb screws and boiling oil, swallowed convulsively. "I say, Gray, old fellow, don't you think—"

Gray's voice lashed out like the crack of a cat-o'-nine-tails. "Don't be a fool, Hart. I won't harm her, not in any real sense."

Though the words were hardly comforting, Hart lapsed into silence.

Gray looked from one gentleman to the other. "Then I shall see you in Wells before the week is out. And Hart, remember what I told you. I don't want you getting into conversation with the girl. You are to look grim and say as little as possible. You are too nice for your own good, that's your trouble. Just think of Jason," he went on, referring to Hart's eight-year-old son. "Think how you would feel if he were abducted."

Hart looked very grim indeed, and Gray nodded. He turned to Nick. "Nick?"

"I know my part. I'm to be her friend and savior."

"Just see that you remember it."

His hand was on the doorknob when Nick called out, "I say, Gray, aren't you going to tell us something of your interview with Miss Weyman?"

"What do you wish to know?"

"Well . . . what is she like, for a start?"

"Frightened. Vulnerable. Unsuspecting. Does that answer your question?"

"I suppose, but . . . do you still think she may have murdered Gil?"

"Why shouldn't I?"

"Well . . . do you?"

Gray turned away with an impatient oath. "I'd be a fool to let myself be deceived by a pair of huge, innocent eyes and those taking ways of hers. And I am no fool."

"I see," said Nick, mystified.

"Fine. Now, if you will excuse me?" and Gray left his companions staring at a closed door.

Hart cleared his throat. "I've never seen him in this mood." He spoke in an undertone, as though eavesdroppers might be lurking on the other side of the door.

"Neither have I," said Nick.

"What do you suppose has got into him?"

"If I didn't know better . . ." mused Nick, then trailed to a halt.

"What?"

"It can't be." Nick was still staring at the closed door, his brow knit in a perplexed frown. "No, I must be mistaken." A moment later, he was smothering a laugh behind his hand.

"I wish you would share the joke," said Hart, not bothering to hide his annoyance.

A wicked light kindled in Nick's eyes. "Poor Gray!" With an expression of arrested surprise, he turned to face his brother-in-law. "Do you know, Hart, I've never said those words before."

"What words?"

" 'Poor Gray.' "

Hart was wishing that he was in the bosom of his family in Kent. His wife might be a Grayson, but at least she was comprehensible. Throwing down his cards, he got to his feet. "We'd best do what Gray says."

Nick rose also. "What we'd best do," he said, flinging an affectionate arm around the older man's shoulders, "is tread very carefully around Gray until this is over." He was still laughing when they left the house.

CHAPTER 4

The journey to Mr. Gray's villa was made in the most dismal weather. There was a steady drizzle, and a fine mist had blown in from the Bristol Channel. As a consequence, the coachman held his team at a snail's pace. These small aggravations were offset to some degree, in Deborah's opinion, when, just out of Radstock, Mr. Gray chose to relinquish his mount and travel in the coach with her.

"Filthy weather," said Gray, and settling himself on the opposite banquette, he vigorously brushed raindrops from the collar of his cape. Angling her a smile, he said apologetically, "Pray forgive the intrusion, ma'am, but my horse has no more taste for a drowning than I do. That's the trouble with these Thoroughbreds—they are too fastidious in their notions. Jupiter balks without fail whenever he steps in a puddle. Lord, one would think I was asking him to swim the English Channel."

Gray eased into the corner of the coach, one arm resting negligently along the back of the banquette. He was careful to keep the smile of apology in place. His thoughts were not nearly so pleasant as his expression.

The last place he wanted to be was in the intimacy of the coach with Deborah Weyman. He cared nothing for the elements, and neither did Jupiter. What he wished to avoid was any softening in his attitude toward the girl. So long as he kept his distance, he felt relatively safe from all her unconscious appeals.

Circumstances beyond his control had frustrated him. What Miss Weyman did not know, thankfully, was that on their way through Radstock, as they were passing the White Hart, he had been recognized and hailed by Lady Pamela Becket, one of Helena's particular friends. Until that moment, it had slipped his mind that the Beckets' country place was on the road to Wells. It was entirely possible that her husband, the marquess, was there now for the hunting season with a party of guests. He therefore judged it prudent to travel in the obscurity of the coach.

Deborah hastened to put him at his ease. "Come now, Mr. Gray, you are not responsible for the rain. You could not have foreseen . . ." Her voice faded as it occurred to her that there had been no change in the weather for the last two days. He must have known that it was folly to ride a horse that would balk every time he came to a puddle.

Correctly reading her mind, Gray said: "But you see, I did know. It was Farley, my old valet, who convinced me that the weather would break almost before we left Bath. His lumbago is something of a barometer, you see. I've never known it to fail before now. And . . . well, I knew I should not ride in the coach with you. You see how it is?"

She liked him. She really liked him, and she most particularly liked his gentlemanly conduct toward herself. There were hot bricks for her feet, and a traveling rug draped across her knees. In addition, his very evident reluctance to travel in the coach with her, as though this small disregard for decorum would blacken her name, both amused and warmed her. Mr. Gray had that happy knack of making a female feel safe and cherished. She thought his sister must be the most fortunate of girls.

Leaning across the distance that separated them, she said earnestly, "No one could fault you for coming in out of the rain. My advice to you is to put it out of your mind."

His look was long and inscrutable, and Deborah eased back, increasing the space between them. As that look lengthened, her heart skipped a beat, but when he smiled, it gradually steadied itself.

Gray made a note of the distance she had set between them and he was seized with the temptation to pounce on her. In all ignorance, the woman was rousing the primitive in him. He did not know how much longer he could go on playing the part of a gelding. He did not know why she wanted him to, but it was one of the things about Deborah Weyman he was resolved he would find out. But all in good time.

"Had I been thinking properly," he said, "I would have asked one of Miss Hare's maids to accompany us, to act as chaperon."

Teacherlike, she clicked her tongue. "You may believe, Mr. Gray, that I am beyond the age of requiring a chaperon. I am no green girl."

She gave her trust too readily. That was her fatal weakness, and without scruple, he had used it against her. He should be pleased that matters were progressing just as he had hoped they would. Instead, he felt, not guilt, but a faint distaste. And regret. Losing patience with himself, he brushed his misgivings aside. Quentin, and only Quentin, must be his first consideration.

Seeing that some response was expected of him, he said carelessly, "I take leave to doubt that," and turning his head, he stared out the window.

Deborah accepted his response for what it was, an unthinking commonplace, and her spirits sank. It was so depressing. To him, she must appear as well on the way to her dotage. As for herself, she had never met a man she liked half as well.

Once again, she found herself longing to confide in him. He had such a kind face, such an unselfconscious grin, and his marked attention for her comfort went well beyond common courtesy. She dared not say a word. She was Mrs. Deborah Mornay, and for Quentin's sake,

Mrs. Mornay she must remain until she had got the boy safely away.

When her train of thought made her suddenly shiver, he put out a hand, then quickly withdrew it. "What is it?" he asked softly.

She lifted her shoulders and tried for a laugh. "Nerves, I suppose. I'm always like this when I take up a new position."

He held her eyes in a searching stare, then he smiled. "I've seen you in action, Mrs. Mornay. I'm counting on you to hold your own."

It was an odd thing to say, but it soothed her just the same. "Thank you," she said, and lapsed into silence.

❧

When they entered the small, medieval town of Wells, Deborah gave a cursory look out the window. "The mist is lifting," she said, "and it's stopped raining."

"Most people," observed Gray easily, "show a little more interest when they see Wells for the first time."

"This isn't my first time. I've been here with some of the girls from school. We've even been as far afield as Glastonbury. The area is so rich in history, and legends and so on, that Miss Hare considers such outings essential to the girls' education."

Interesting, thought Gray. Though her words flowed easily, her hands were knotted together in a stranglehold. "Are these regular outings?" he asked in an offhand way.

"Oh no, nothing like that, just whenever the fancy strikes us." Uncomfortable with this subject, she remarked on the façade of the King's Arms as the carriage made an abrupt turn and entered the inn's stable yard.

Like many of the houses in the area, the inn was a low, half-timbered building with small windows and an uneven roofline. Deborah had been here before and knew that in spite of alterations, the small, low-ceilinged rooms and narrow twisting passageways had hardly changed in the last several centuries. They were dark and dank and put her in mind of the coal cellars she had once played in as a child. Shivering, resigning herself to an uncomfortable half hour, she allowed Gray to assist her from the carriage.

As ostlers came running to unharness the horses, Gray led Deborah through the back door of the inn. The noise emanating from the taproom indicated that the King's Arms was a popular watering hole. Deborah kept very close to Gray as he found the landlord, who soon ushered them up a dark, steep staircase to a private parlor at the back of the house. Having seen to Deborah's comfort, Gray withdrew on the understanding that he wished to instruct the stable boys respecting Jupiter, upon which he would ask their landlord to serve them a glass of wine.

"Oh, and for your own peace of mind, I advise you to lock the door while I am gone," he said.

This was soon done, and having thrown off her cloak, she went to stand by the blaze in the grate, lifting her skirts to toast her frozen limbs. Mr. Gray, she reflected, was the most considerate of employers. Not many of her acquaintance would have gone to so much trouble for a mere governess. Somehow, without embarrassing him, she must find a way to thank him. He really was a dear.

Now that there was no one to see her, she removed her spectacles and did a little pirouette around the furniture. She would have liked to have removed her lace cap and shaken out her hair, but it could not be put back together without a great deal of bother. She stilled, imagining for a moment how Mr. Gray would respond if he could see her as she truly was. Would he think she was pretty? Would he be completely bowled over? Would he want to . . . kiss her? She touched her fingers to her lips, remembering. But he hadn't wanted to kiss her. They had been playing a game, nothing more.

Resolutely turning from such vain speculations, she veered off to stand by the small window. There was nothing to be seen but the inn's courtyard and stable block and off in the distance, the Mendip Hills. But Quentin was here. Here! And Mr. Gray's villa was only a stone's throw from Wells. Soon, very soon, she would be in a position to see the boy more regularly. No one would think it odd if Miss Gray's companion chose to spend her leisure hours in Wells.

She was gazing out at the Mendip Hills, her mind dwelling on Quentin, when she heard the knock on the door. Reaching automatically for her glasses, she shoved them on her nose before going to answer what she supposed was the landlord with their wine.

The lady who stood on the threshold was a study in elegance. Her high-waisted tan carriage coat was of the finest velvet and trimmed with black braid. Her matching hat was adorned with long black feathers. Color was high on her cheeks and her hazel eyes held a friendly glint. Deborah could easily picture her riding to hounds or presiding at some county assembly. The word "picnic" slipped into her mind and she felt a flash of unease.

"Miss Weyman," said Lady Pamela Becket, "so it is you. I saw you at the window as I alighted from my carriage. May I come in for a moment?"

Deborah fell back as though felled by a blow. The last time she had heard that cultured voice was on the lawns of Lord Barrington's house in Paris, when they had entertained Quentin's friends to a picnic.

Lady Becket advanced, her brows knitting in a worried frown. "What is it, my dear? You look as though you had seen a ghost."

Deborah's thoughts were racing off in several directions at once. One thought took precedence. She had to get rid of Lady Becket before Mr. Gray returned.

Summoning all her powers of control, she bobbed a curtsy and said, in a voice that gave no indication of her agitation, "Lady Becket, this is a pleasure. Unhappily, I am not at liberty to receive guests. You see, my employer—"

Lady Becket laughed and waved her to silence. "Oh, you need not fear that your employer will object to my presence. Lord Kendal and I are well known to each other, on account of Helena, you know." She made a small sound of exasperation. "What am I saying? Of course you wouldn't know. Forgive my unruly tongue, Miss Weyman."

After Lord Kendal's name was mentioned, Deborah had heard almost nothing of Lady Becket's conversation except in a vague way. She felt as if her tongue were glued to the roof of her mouth and her feet weighted with lead. Her brain seethed with a confusion of thoughts.

"Lord Kendal?" she said faintly.

As she spoke, Lady Becket moved to the fire and stationed herself so that the blaze warmed her back. "I recognized his horse, you see. Jupiter, is it not? Had I known he was coming into the area—Lord Kendal, I mean—I would have invited him to our little house party at the Hall. That's why I am here. Nothing ventured, nothing gained, so to speak, and Lord Kendal's presence would be in the nature of a coup for me, if I can persuade him."

Her ladyship eyed her frozen companion with no little curiosity. Deciding that she had thrown Miss Weyman into confusion with her muddled explanation, she started over. "I was alighting from my carriage at the White Hart, when Gray, that is, Lord Kendal, passed me on horseback. That is, he was on horseback. Oh, you know what I mean. So I gave my coachman the order to follow your carriage. I know Gray is here somewhere because Jupiter is in the stable. However, the landlord knew nothing of Lord Kendal, but when I described him, he directed me to this parlor. I say, Miss Weyman, are you sure you are all right? Sit down, why don't you, and I shall fetch you a glass of wine."

"What description?" demanded Deborah. She was debating inwardly, telling herself it couldn't be true. Lord Kendal was tall, dark, and handsome. She didn't know how she knew this, but she knew that she did. He looked nothing like Mr. Gray.

Lady Becket sighed. "Oh dear, I really am making a muddle of this, aren't I? Well, you know—tall, blond, and with the face of an angel. Lord Kendal, I mean. Are you sure you wouldn't like me to fetch you a glass of wine?"

Deborah was already reaching for her cloak. Though her brain was reeling from the shock of discovery, she forced herself to act naturally. "I'm a little shaken after the ride in the carriage," she said. "It's of no consequence, really. Pray be seated, Lady Becket, and I shall undertake to find Lord Kendal for you."

Lady Becket's eyes were fixed on the cloak which Deborah was clutching to her bosom. "Oh, is he not on the premises, then?"

"I believe he is in the stable block," answered Deborah, and without more ado, she whipped herself out of the room.

As her momentum carried her to the top of the stairs, she flung her cloak around her shoulders. Her brain was churning as it made connections of trifles that had puzzled her. But they weren't trifles. They were indications that all was not as it appeared to be. She could have wept for her gullibility.

She had just begun to descend the stairs when she heard the tread of footsteps ascending and the word "Gray." Doing a quick about-face, she hared off in another direction, praying that she would come upon the back staircase. She was in luck. Without looking to left or right, she clattered down the wooden stairs and did not stop till she was outside the building. Here she hesitated, taking her bearings.

Gray, meantime, had ascended the stairs and was striding along the corridor to the parlor where he had left Deborah. Having conferred with Nick and Hart in the taproom, he had made up his mind to forgo the small repast and remove Miss Weyman forthwith. He was right about the Beckets. They were hosting a house party, and when their guests were at a loose end, they sometimes made forays into Wells. He wasn't going to chance meeting up with any of them.

He knocked on the parlor door and waited for Deborah to unlock it. The moment it swung open and he came face-to-face with Pamela Becket, he knew the game was up.

"Gray! Well, I must say that was quick."

"Where is she?" His tone was imperious and not at all friendly.

Lady Becket peered up at him in some uncertainty. This was not the reception she had anticipated. "Oh dear, I knew Miss Weyman was upset. Was it something I said? You see—"

"Dammit, woman, just tell me where she went."

"She went to look for you, to—"

With a violent expletive, Gray spun on his heel and took off at a run. He found Nick and Hart in the taproom, in the act of settling with the landlord. "Hart," he said, "pay for my shot and meet me out front. Nick, fetch the horses and follow us. The bird has flown the coop."

Nick and Hart exchanged a startled look, then quickly complied with Gray's instructions.

Having taken her bearings, Deborah was striking out along High Street in the direction of the market. Though everything in her was tempted to make for where she knew she would find sanctuary, where Quentin was, instinct went deeper. She must protect Quentin at all costs. She must lead Lord Kendal away from the boy. If she managed to evade him, she would decide later what was best to be done.

Two things stood in her favor. This was market day, and in spite of the inclement weather, the town was bustling with farmers and merchants as well as their customers. In addition, she knew Wells like the back of her hand, had made it her business to know it in the event that she and Quentin might be forced to flee for their lives.

"Halt, thief!"

At Lord Kendal's cry, Deborah looked back over her shoulder. He had just flung out of the King's Arms. Passersby were stopping to look and stare. The din of the street sellers as they called out their wares worked to her advantage. No one paid any heed to the man who was chasing her. Picking up her skirts, she slipped between two stalls and pushed her way to the edge of the throng, toward Penniless Porch on the far side of the square, the towered gatehouse that gave access to the cathedral precincts. By the time she reached it, she was gasping for breath.

It took every ounce of her nerve to remain immobile under that great arched gatehouse where once the poor had begged for alms. Her prayers were no less fervent than theirs and were answered when stragglers moved off, leaving her alone. Her movements were jerky as she searched for the hatpin that secured her lace cap. Panicked now, she tore it from her head, hardly aware of the sting to her scalp as cap and hatpin came away together. Her spectacles were similarly dealt with. Stuffing everything into her pockets, she shook out her hair. A torrent of auburn tresses liberally laced with gray powder fell about her shoulders. Brushing out the powder as best she could, she moved swiftly through the little close and entered the cathedral.

No sound of the bustling marketplace penetrated the thick walls of that vast sanctuary. The great vaulted ceiling soared above her head, and beneath her feet the tombs of ancient bishops and knights kept silent vigil. There were a few visitors, but not as many as there would have been in the summer months. Nevertheless, one of the cathedral divines was leading a party of people down the length of the nave, pointing out some of the features of the architecture. Though he spoke in hushed tones, there was a slight echo, as though the buttressed walls that had stood for six centuries were weighing every word.

The click of Deborah's first few steps on the flagstoned floors brought the cleric's head in her direction. Mumbling an apology that no one could hear, she rose on her toes. She knew exactly where she was going. Moving smartly and silently, she traversed the length of the nave. She had almost reached the party of visitors when the door creaked open and a gust of damp autumn air, smelling faintly of wood smoke and rotting leaves, swept in. Without breaking her step, Deborah turned aside to join the spectators, edging her way round so that she had a clear view of the west wall. Her heart raced. Lord Kendal stood with hands on hips, surveying the interior. He would be looking for a bespectacled dowd with a lace cap on her head. From this distance, surely he would not recognize her?

"You will note the scissor arch," said the divine, pointing upward.

All eyes obediently lifted. Not so Deborah's. She took advantage of the moment to elbow her way to the very center of the group. When Gray advanced a few steps, spurs jangling, and carefully scrutinized faces, her knees began to knock together. It never once occurred to her to appeal for help to her neighbors. Magistrates and constables would not accept her word against Lord Kendal's. Then Quentin would be handed over to his guardian to do with as he pleased. She would never let that happen.

Her nerves steadied as Gray crossed the nave to the north porch, but when a dark-haired gentleman entered it and joined him, Deborah went sick with fright. Now there were two of them.

"This way, ladies and gentlemen," said the cleric, and eyeing the two spurred gentlemen with hostility, he led the way toward the famous clock in the north transept, bringing his little flock to within a few yards of Gray and his companion.

"Watch for the knight."

"What?" Deborah glanced abstractedly at the lady who had addressed her. She was plump, with rosy cheeks, and her garments were not unlike her own, that is, well made though far from fashionable. A prosperous farmer's wife, by the look of her, thought Deborah.

"Watch for the knight," repeated Mrs. Farmer's Wife. "On the clock, you know."

"Now, Mavis, don't spoil things for the little lady."

The not unkindly voice belonged to a gentleman with the look of a prosperous farmer. They appeared to be ordinary, decent folk who were happy with their lot. She envied them. Her fate had cast her in a more exalted role, but it had not brought her happiness.

Mavis either did not hear her husband or she affected to be deaf. "The knight is struck down. Watch the clock, dearie."

Deborah's eyes fixed on the clock, but she was excruciatingly aware that Lord Kendal and his companion were systematically combing the north and south aisles under the Gothic arches. She could trace their progress by the sound of their spurs. They jangled lewdly in that hallowed silence. Gentlemen did not wear spurs in church. These men evidently thought themselves above the common decencies.

A bell tinkled.

"Ah, here he comes," said Mavis.

No sooner were the words out of her mouth than a miniature knight exited a little door above the face of the clock. Deborah had stopped breathing. Lord Kendal had suddenly appeared at the entrance of the transept and his eagle eyes were scanning every face. By judiciously bending her knees, she managed to knock several inches off her height, giving the appearance, she hoped, that she was little more than a child.

"I told you he would be struck down," said Mavis with all the satisfaction of a seer whose prophecy has come to pass.

There was a round of applause. The cleric was not amused. Pinning Mavis with an intimidating stare, he embarked on his rehearsed discourse. "The clock dates back to the fourteenth century. Be pleased to note the little doors above the clock face."

As his voice droned on, Deborah bobbed her head, as though listening to every word, but all the while she was aware of Lord Kendal signaling to his friend, upon which he passed beneath the scissor arch and into one of the chancel aisles, becoming lost to view. The dark-haired man, meantime, strode to the west wall where he took up a position as sentry at the exits. Two things were becoming clear to her. They must be very sure that she was still in the cathedral, and Lord Kendal seemed to know his way around.

But all was not yet lost. One step into the chancel aisle and a quick left turn and she would reach her object. Beneath the Chapter House and the Vicars' Hall were a warren of small rooms. Moreover, this part of the cathedral was not open to the public and would make an excellent hiding place.

Deborah bided her time in quaking silence. When the cleric's discourse was at an end, and he led the way to the stone pulpit, she made her move. Taking a deep breath, she stepped boldly into the chancel aisle. There was nary a sign of that hateful man. She was beginning her turn when, to her horror, from the corner of her eye, she spied him coming out of the chancel. She ruthlessly checked the almost overwhelming impulse to take to her heels. Trusting that the dim light and the changes she had made in her appearance would deceive him, she completed her turn.

"Excuse me, ma'am," said Gray, advancing toward her.

Taking a leaf out of Mavis's book, Deborah gave no indication that she had heard him. Her eyes were fixed firmly on the door ahead.

"Sir, you cannot go in there." That was the cleric's voice.

"The devil I can't!" That was Gray's. "Deborah? I know it's you."

Her nerve broke and she made a dash for it.

"Deborah!" roared Gray.

There could be no chance now of finding a hiding place, no time to think out a plan of action. It was do or die. As she flung herself at the stairs to the Chapter House, a body of divines descended. Papers and books went flying in her frantic haste to get by them. It slowed her progress but not half as much as it slowed Gray's. More clerics were descending, choking the staircase and small corridor. She could hear Gray cursing at them, and the obsequious apologies of the bishops and priests as they "lordshiped" him all over the place. It made her sick.

Heart pounding, chest burning, she pushed on, through the Chain Gate and into the open air. There was no mist now to conceal her from her pursuers, no shops, no taverns where she could slip in the front door and out through the back. She was in one of the cathedral closes, a row of medieval cottages with thatched roofs and little walled gardens that seemed to go on forever. There wasn't a soul in sight. Either the priests were at their prayers or they were the ones she had encountered at the Chapter House. Though it registered in some part of her brain that she had lost, the will to go on was stronger. She bolted up that narrow close as if she were running the race of her life.

There was no sound of pursuit. Chancing a quick look back, she saw that Lord Kendal and his dark-haired companion had somehow got hold of two horses. They were tightening girths and making ready to mount up. There was no haste to their movements, indicating that they were very sure now that they could run her down. Fear gave her a strength she had not known she possessed. Her feet flew over the cobblestones, and she dashed into the main thoroughfare as if she were crossing a finishing line.

Then she saw him. He was on his great roan, and he was coming toward her. As he advanced, she fell back, shaking her head, unable to believe her eyes. *He was following her.* She knew that he was following her. She turned her head and focused on the two riders who were walking their horses toward her. Not Lord Kendal, then, but someone who looked very like him, a brother or twin. Now there were three of them. She whipped back to face him as the sound of horseshoes on cobblestones struck an ominous note. Edging away, she retreated, falling farther back into the close. He was herding her toward his companions. In another moment, they would be upon her. He had her in a vise.

She looked at him, really looked at him, and she hardly recognized him. There was no sign now of her nice Mr. Gray. His eyes were cold and hard. His features were set like granite. He rode his horse with all the grace and arrogance of the lord of the manor. He was a man who knew his own worth. But he did not know where Quentin was, or there would have been no need for all this playacting.

He leaned down, offering her his hand. "You have run your race," he said. "Don't make this hard on yourself. Come, Deborah, give me your hand. We shall ride together."

She could playact as well as he. Lowering her eyes, she began to weep copiously.

"Deborah," he said, and she detected a softening in him.

She groped in her pocket as if searching for a hand-kerchief. "Please," she warbled, "please."

Her fingers curled around the lace cap with the hatpin in it. The men at her back were closing in. She could hear their horses' hooves striking the cobble-stones. Lord Kendal had relaxed his grip on the reins, assuming she was beaten.

Suddenly lunging, she drove her hatpin into the roan's flank. There was a great commotion as the rear-ing animal bellowed in terror and Gray fought to con-trol it. Deborah did not wait to see the outcome. She ducked beneath flying hooves and hared up the close.

When she came onto the thoroughfare, she turned right. There were vehicles on the road, but these were mostly farmers' carts coming and going to the market. Her brain had ceased to function. It was blind instinct that kept her going, blind instinct that made her dash into the middle of the road when she heard the thunder of galloping hooves at her back. She heard a shout and twisted her neck. A curricle traveling at breakneck speed was bearing down upon her. Rooted to the spot, she stared in disbelief. Without warning, she was swept off her feet as Gray swooped down from the saddle and carried her safely to the other side.

The ensuing uproar brought Deborah to her senses, and she struggled to free herself.

"I think the lady has fainted," said Gray.

When she felt his fingers tighten on a sensitive spot at the base of her neck, she opened her mouth to scream. No sound came. Her lungs tightened horribly, as if they would burst, then everything faded, and she slipped into a pit of darkness.

CHAPTER 5

Deborah awoke as if from a drugged sleep. Awareness stole over her gradually. She registered the steady rhythm of the horse beneath her, the soft twilight, the rain, her head pillowed on a man's shoulder, the solid support of his arms and thighs. Her lashes fluttered and slowly lifted. Mr. Gray, she thought, nestling closer. Suddenly, her mind cleared and she was fighting like a deranged woman. Only then did she discover that her wrists were bound behind her back.

There was a furious curse and the arms supporting her tightened violently. Undaunted, Deborah increased her struggles. She had only one thought in her mind. She was in the arms of a murderer. She had to get away from him. Panting, sobbing with fear, she kicked out with her legs.

Her wild blows missed their target and struck the horse's neck. Jupiter danced and whinnied, and pranced sideways, but Gray's sure hand on the reins kept him from bolting. Deborah felt her lungs squeeze tight with the pressure of those unrelenting arms, and her panic increased tenfold. Thrashing, tossing her head, she caught Gray a glancing blow on the chin. The arms around her slackened, the horse reared, and she went tumbling to the ground.

She knew how to take a fall. Twisting so that one shoulder and thigh bore the brunt of the impact, she used her momentum to roll clear of the flailing hooves. Lying in a heap, with all the breath knocked out of her, she could do no more than gasp for air. When she heard the jangle of spurs she found her wind and, scrambling to her knees, twisted to face her abductor. Chest heaving, eyes spitting fire, she rose unsteadily to her feet.

In her panic, she had forgotten that there were three of them. The dark-haired man held the horses' reins while the other two came at her on foot, circling her with outstretched arms.

"Your wench," said the younger man, laughing, "is a rare handful, Gray. Somehow, I had the impression she would come quietly. Why does she continue to fight you, when she knows she can't win?"

Gray was unsmiling. "I don't know, unless it's because she is as guilty as hell."

Deborah glanced around, trying to assess her chances of escape. Against the horizon, she could see the outline of hills. On either side of her were hedgerows, and beyond that, farmers' fields with neatly stacked hayricks which were drooping under the weight of the rain. The road they were traveling was no more than a farm track and wound its way up between two dense copses. Soon, the darkness would be impenetrable.

Her eyes darted back to the men on foot. When the younger one lunged for her, she turned and ran. Gray was on her before she could clear the hedge. She went sprawling, and as she tried to rise, his knee pressed into the small of her back while his hand caught in her hair and dragged back her head. His other hand was raised threateningly, ready to strike her.

Every nerve in her body tensed for that blow. Her eyes went wide and her lips parted. When the seconds ticked by, she made an involuntary movement to relieve the pressure of his knee on her back, and the hand in her hair tightened, eliciting a sharp cry of pain.

"Yes," he said, his narrowed gaze wandering over her face, "you would do well to fear me."

The warning was superfluous. She had never feared

or loathed a man more. Now that she was seeing him in his true colors, everything about him repelled her. He was the antithesis of the man he had pretended to be. He was merciless, brutal, a murdering devil. When her usefulness to him was over, she knew that he would kill her too. Her only hope was to delay the evil hour for as long as possible, and when the right moment presented itself, she must be ready to act.

With a little cry of surrender, she went as limp as a rag doll.

"That's more like it," said Gray and yanked her to her feet. "Try anything like that again and I'll thrash you to within an inch of your life."

"I say, Gray—"

"That's enough, Nick!"

Deborah kept her eyes blank, but she was conscious of the tension between the two men. She flicked her gaze to the one who was called Nick. He might yet prove to be an ally. It was too soon to say. As she watched, he gave an indifferent shrug and turned aside. The dark-haired man looked as grim as her abductor. She would get no help from that quarter.

She cried out when she was given a shove in the direction of the horses. Concealing the blaze of hatred in her eyes, she stumbled over ruts and mud holes till she stood shivering in front of the huge roan. When Gray was mounted, Nick lifted her onto the saddle. Once again, she could feel the strength of the arms and thighs that cradled her. She could feel more than that. With her hands bound behind her, she was more intimate with him than she wanted to be. Gasping, she jerked forward. He chuckled and pulled her back. "Don't wriggle or move," he whispered for her ears only, "or I shall not be able to vouch for my good behavior."

She half turned to look up at him, her brow drawn in puzzlement. His own brows shot up. Shaking his head, laughing, he clicked his tongue and touched his spurs to his mount's flanks.

❧

To Deborah, it seemed like an aeon before they turned into a rundown farmyard and reined in the horses. The events of the day had taken a toll on her. Her arms ached; she was dropping from fatigue; and the pain in her shoulder and hip made her wince with each jarring step. She knew she looked a fright.

Her abductor, who had dismounted first, seemed as fresh and vigorous as when they had started out. His movements were easy, and his garments, she did not doubt, would be immaculate beneath the sodden cape. It galled her that their confrontation, which had brought her to her knees, had made so little impression on him.

When he helped her down from the saddle, sheer willpower kept her legs from buckling under her. She listened with an inward sneer as he issued orders to his companions in that soft, cultured intonation of his. Issuing orders seemed to be this man's forte.

She learned something from their exchange. The dark-haired, sinister-looking man was called Hart. As Nick went off to stable the horses in what appeared to be a barn, Hart entered the farmhouse to get a light going. Her abductor, meanwhile, pulled on the bonds that held her wrists together, and the rope came undone.

It was a point of pride to feign indifference to the burns that the bonds had made on her tender flesh. She would get no sympathy from him. Turning from him, she allowed her gaze to drift over the farmhouse, and she gave a start. It was an abandoned hovel, and not fit for human habitation. Every window on the ground floor was boarded up. The thatch on the roof was so bare in places that the joists were showing.

"Is this your *villa*, Lord Kendal?" Outrage made her voice shake.

Propelling her with one hand on her elbow, he answered mildly, "For my purposes, it will do very well, Miss Weyman."

She wrenched her arm from his grasp. "I am Mrs. Mornay, as you know very well."

"Lady Becket does not think so."

"Lady Becket does not know me."

"It won't wash, Deborah. One of my coachmen identified you."

"Coachmen?" Her expression was puzzled.

He answered patiently. "The coachmen I sent to meet you in Dover."

"I am Deborah Mornay, I tell you, a widow. Miss Hare will vouch for me. You have made a ghastly mistake." Her eyes shimmered with resentment.

His held a trace of humor. "Have I, Deborah?" he said in a languid drawl. He had removed his gloves, and one finger touched her cheek, tracing the path of a tear that had long since dried. She jerked her head back. Her flashing eyes seemed to amuse him. "Be careful," he said softly, "that you do not tempt me to put you to the test."

"And what might you mean by that?"

He rubbed the bridge of his nose with one finger. "One presumes that Miss Weyman is a maid, and Mrs. Mornay . . . is not."

She stared at his smiling face for one uncomprehending moment, then she flushed scarlet from throat to hairline. As she stumbled away from him and entered the house, his laughter followed her.

The room she entered was as crude as she had feared it would be. The furniture, for want of a better word, consisted of a broken-down table and three horsehair chairs that had seen better days. A long, cluttered sideboard filled one wall. At the boarded window, there was a stone sink, but there was no sign of a pump. On the floor in front of the cast-iron fireplace was a litter of blackened pots and pans. Tinkers would scorn to live in such filth.

At least Hart had got a couple of lamps going and was trying, not very successfully, to light some kindling in the grate. When he turned to her with that fierce look of his, her courage faltered, and she made haste to shore it up. Though she did not consider herself a particularly brave person, she had learned how to overcome her terrors. Anger and outrage were her best weapons. When one dwelled on one's grievances, one forgot to be afraid, and her grievances against the man who had engineered her abduction were grave, indeed.

"Sit!" The peremptory command came from Lord Kendal.

For a moment she hesitated. Deciding that the point was not worth arguing, she accepted the chair he indicated. "I demand that you explain your outrageous conduct," she said.

He seated himself on one of the chairs. His outer-things had been discarded, and she took no pleasure in having her conjectures confirmed. The man was immaculately turned out, except for his boots. Shirt, dark coat, buckskins—there wasn't a mark on him. Her own clothes were mired to the knees and she smelled of wet horse. She hoped he stank as much as she did. Without asking his permission, she undid the clasp on her cloak and eased out of it. It was as she feared. Her gown was no improvement on her cloak, but looked as though she might have slept in it.

Her temper was simmering, and she counted that a blessing. "The transformation in you, Mr. Gray," she said acidly, "—or should I say Lord Kendal?—is mind-boggling. You started the day as a mere commoner, and now you are a peer of the realm. I think I deserve an explanation."

He answered her without heat. "I might say the same of you. You began the day as an elderly governess, and now look at you. If there is any explaining to be done, since I hold the upper hand, I leave it to you."

She took a moment to moisten her lips, putting her thoughts in order. "Parents and guardians have a decided prejudice against youthful-looking governesses. I tried to make myself appear older. There is nothing more sinister to it than that."

At this point, Nick entered. He glanced in her direction, then moved to the fireplace to help the other man get the fire going. It wasn't much of a look, but she sensed his concern. She hoped she wasn't imagining things.

When her eyes returned to Lord Kendal's, she had the uncanny feeling that he had read her mind. Hoping to distract him, she went on with her explanation. "You are right in this. When Lady—Becket, is it?—came to my door, she did mistake me for someone else. You may imagine how I felt, however, when she revealed that the man I understood to be Mr. Gray was no less a personage than the Earl of Kendal."

"Oh yes, I can well imagine your feelings," said Gray dryly.

"How could I know what you meant to do with me? Gentlemen belong to such strange clubs and societies. For all I knew, you might be a libertine or . . . or worse."

"Strange societies?" said Gray.

"The Hell-Fire Club . . . Oh, I know it's no longer in existence, but I've heard that there are others that have taken its place."

This was no lie. Such clubs proliferated, and decent women went in dread of them. It was rumored that the aristocratic lechers who made up the membership abducted young virgins and had their way with them, and afterward sold them to Eastern potentates for their harems. Deborah was skeptical of all such reports, but it suited her now to pretend she believed them.

"And that was the reason you bolted like a terrified rabbit? You suspected that I, a libertine, might have designs upon the virtue of an aging schoolmarm?"

Put like that, it did sound a bit ridiculous, but in lieu of a better story, she had to stick to it. "I wasn't sure what you meant to do with me," she said stiffly, "but I feared for my very life."

"Indeed. Then why didn't you appeal to someone to help you? There was ample opportunity. Good God, at one point, we were in the thick of a bevy of saintly clerics. Why didn't you appeal to them?"

Her look was scornful, withering, and conversely, anxious. "And would they have taken my word over yours? I think not. I am a mere female. You are a nobleman. Nothing I could say would have persuaded them of my innocence. On the other hand, whatever story you cared to offer, however farfetched, would have been accepted as the gospel truth."

"It sounds to me," said Gray, "as if you are speaking from experience. Who are you, Deborah Weyman? I know that you came to Gil from Miss Hare's. But where were you before that?"

She swallowed the lump of fear in her throat. "I told you, until recently, I lived in Ireland with my husband. And who is Gil?"

The blue eyes, with their startling intensity, seemed to probe into her very soul. She wanted to look away but she was caught and held by a force she couldn't resist.

"One way or another," he said, "I mean to get the truth from you."

It took her a moment or two to realize that she had been given a reprieve. He motioned to Nick, and when he approached the table, she turned to him eagerly.

"Mr.—"

"Oh, do call me Nick," he said easily. "No need to stand on ceremony. Here, I've brought you a glass of wine. You look as though you could do with it. Old Hart is warming up the stew. I daresay you haven't eaten a thing since breakfast."

His kind words, his obvious concern in the face of Lord Kendal's cruelty, was almost her undoing. She had to swallow several times before she found her voice. "Thank you, Nick. But I was wondering . . . that is . . . could you direct me to the . . . um . . . ah . . . convenience?"

"The . . . ? Oh, the . . . ah, of course. How remiss of us not to think of it before. If you would step this way." He gestured with one hand.

"Hart will take her to the latrine," said Gray.

The crude word as much as the tone of voice brought a sudden pall. Once again, Deborah was aware of the faint animosity between the two men. She would have sworn that they were brothers and that their animosity, which was largely resentment on Nick's part, had got its start when they were boys. She didn't care how it had got its start, she knew only that so long as Nick was present, she felt relatively safe.

The dark-haired man, Hart, had taken one of the

lanterns and was holding the door for her. No word was spoken as he led her to the side of the house, along a well-worn path to the ubiquitous privy. There was no need for a lantern. From the stench of the place, she could have found her way in the dark.

Though this was no ruse on Deborah's part—she really had to go—she had hoped to use these few minutes to get a sense of where the farmhouse was situated in relation to Wells. She knew it could not be more than a mile or two away. They had left Wells as the sun was setting and had arrived at their destination before dark. If Nick had taken her to the privy, she would have questioned him about it. She couldn't bring herself to speak to the man called Hart. There was something about him that made her tremble—the way he looked at her, glared at her, glowered. Lord Kendal might kill her once he was done with her, but it would be clean and quick. This man would make her suffer first.

The return journey was made in equal silence. On entering the kitchen, Deborah halted. Her eyes swept the small interior, but there was no sign of Nick. Her abductor made a motion with one hand, and with that signal, Hart withdrew, closing the door behind him.

Steeling herself to act naturally, she returned to the upright chair she had previously occupied and took several fortifying sips of wine. When the silence lengthened, and she could no longer sustain his stare, she turned her attention to the hearth. The fire in the grate blazed merrily, and the aroma from the blackened pot which was suspended above it reminded her that she had not eaten since breakfast. The thought that he meant to feed her was vastly comforting.

More minutes dragged by. Finally, subduing her terrors, she said conversationally, "Where are the others?"

"I sent them away so that we could be private."

The fear she had experienced before was only a pale shade of what she experienced now. Without Nick's presence, she felt defenseless, and those words had an ominous ring to them.

When he rose she started to her feet. Shaking his head, mocking her, he moved to the hearth and returned almost directly with a tray of food which he set on the table.

"Eat!" he said, and indicated the bowl of stew he had set out for her.

Eat! Sit! Mount up! Do this! Do that! She was heartily sick of taking this man's orders. It did not sit well with her, either, that she had betrayed her fear to him. Though her stomach was rumbling, she said indifferently, just to defy him, "I have lost my appetite, thank you."

He smiled grimly. "But not your hearing, one hopes. Let's try again, shall we? Sit and eat."

Her hands fisted helplessly at her sides. Fuming, she sank into her chair and picked up a spoon. There were no knives or forks to be seen.

He grinned devilishly. "I don't underestimate you, you'll observe."

It was a compliment of sorts, she supposed. If she had a knife, she really would be tempted to use it on him. He was watching and waiting, his eyes glinting with humor. Head down, she lifted the spoon to her lips. After the first bite, she needed no urging. She really was famished, and the stew was edible. There was a hunk of coarse bread beside her plate, and she ate that too. There were no napkins, and when she had finished, she groped in her pocket and found a handkerchief which she used to dab her lips. Only then did she chance a look at her companion.

He had finished before her, and was reclining at his ease, sipping his wine. She hated that gloating look. Reaching for her wine, she took a small swallow.

"Where is Quentin?" he asked.

Her hand jerked, and droplets of wine spilled over the front of her gown. Mopping at it with her balled handkerchief, she said uncertainly, "Quentin?"

"Yes, Quentin. Don't bandy words with me, Deborah, or it will be very much the worse for you."

"I don't know anyone by that name," she said miserably.

He leaned closer, one hand on the table, eyes boring

into hers. She could hardly credit that she'd once thought he had a kind face. He was the devil incarnate.

"What happened, Deborah? Did you get in over your head?"

Her voice was painfully hoarse. "You're not making sense. I don't understand you."

"No? Then let me tell you what I think happened. You were recruited in Paris. I don't believe you murdered Gil, but when your accomplice murdered him, you became frightened. That's why you ran from my coachmen in Dover. Is that what happened? Listen to me, Deborah. If you take me to Quentin, I shall let you go. I swear it."

If he was trying to confuse her, he was succeeding remarkably well. The horrible, perverse truth was that she wanted to believe him. But she knew there was no one else involved. He had an appointment with Lord Barrington that night. His was the name Lord Barrington had spoken only moments before he was murdered. If this man had his way, he would have murdered Quentin too. That's why he was trying to confuse her. It was only a trick so that she would lead him to Quentin.

Think. She had to think how Mrs. Mornay would act if this had suddenly been sprung on her. Her legs would hardly hold her when she rose to her feet. "I think you have taken leave of your senses," she cried, trying to sound outraged. "How many times must I tell you that I am not Deborah Weyman? Don't think you will get away with this. If anything happens to me, Miss Hare will see you hang for it."

He leaned back in his chair and eyed her dispassionately. When he spoke, his voice was slow and reasonable, as though he were talking to a witless child. "It could be weeks before Miss Hare comes to suspect anything and by that time, there will be no trace of Mr. Gray or Mrs. Mornay. As far as she knows—as anyone knows for that matter—you left Bath to take up another appointment. Months could pass before you are missed. Oh, I'm not saying that Miss Hare won't suffer a few pangs of uneasiness when there is no word from you, but when she remembers that you are under the protec-

tion of that 'nice Mr. Gray' "—he smiled diabolically—
"she won't act with undue haste. It wouldn't surprise
me if six months, no, a year were to go by before any
real push was made to find you, and by that time the
trail will be stone cold."

Mentally, Deborah was dredging up every vile name
in her limited vocabulary that could describe this black-
hearted scoundrel. *That nice Mr. Gray*—that's what got
her goat, and didn't his snide smile show that he knew
it? He'd seen through her disguise from the very beginning. He'd deliberately worked his charm on her, and
like an idiot she had succumbed to it. He knew that too.
He wasn't "that nice Mr. Gray." He was a thoroughgoing bastard. The word wasn't fit for a lady's lips, so she
knew she had hit on the right word to describe him.
Bastard, she repeated inside her head, wishing she had
the courage to fling it in his face. Better still, she wished
she had the courage to pick up her glass of wine and
dump it on his head. It would almost be worth it just to
ruin his insufferably flawless appearance. Wiser counsel
prevailed. He would make her suffer for it. His kind
always did.

When he rose, she squared her drooping shoulders.
"At last," he said in that lazy drawl which she was coming to detest, "you appear to understand the seriousness
of your position. Think about it, Deborah. I have you in
my power. There is no one here to save you. No, we
won't discuss this further tonight. In another minute or
two, you will be willing to confess you are the queen of
England just to please me. Now there's a thought—you,
wishing to please me."

His little joke fell on deaf ears. "Where are you taking me?" She sensed a new peril, and every muscle
tensed.

"To bed," he answered succinctly, and reached for
the lantern.

Fear and rage unfurled inside her. That's why he had
sent Nick and Hart away. He was going to put her to
the test, just as he said he would, to prove that she could
not possibly be a married woman. Then, when he had
his answer, he would question her in earnest. Every

nerve straining, she reached for her half-empty glass of
wine.

"What the—" Gray straightened.

"Monster!" she shrieked, and flung the glass at him.
She had a gratifying glimpse of red droplets of wine
spilling over his immaculate shirtfront, then she bolted
for the door.

He caught her in the hallway. She was lifted off her
feet and hoisted over his shoulder like a sack of coal.
Bucking, beating at him with her fists, she tried desperately to free herself. Her struggles were rewarded by several ferocious swats to her backside. A couple of those
swats landed on her sore hip, and pain exploded
through her in waves. She hadn't the strength to fight
him. Blackness hovered at the edge of her consciousness.
When he returned to the kitchen and picked up the lantern, she was hardly aware of it.

The chamber was at the top of a steep flight of stairs.
There was one window, boarded up like those on the
ground floor, and a couple of straw pallets on the bare
floorboards. In one corner, nestled under the eaves, was
a washstand with a pitcher and basin and an assortment
of towels. The fire was unlit.

Setting the lantern on the floor, he dumped her none
too gently on one of the straw pallets, then stood over
her, feet splayed, hands on hips.

"You little fool," he bit out. "Don't you know when
you are beaten? Are you determined to make me hurt
you?"

She stared at him with huge, frightened eyes.

His brows slashed together, then, as comprehension
dawned, he threw back his head and laughed. Shaking
his head, he said, "You can't believe I meant to ravish
you?"

Pride dictated only one answer. "It never even entered my head."

His look was skeptical. "In the first place, you look
like a scarecrow."

"Thank you," she snapped.

"And you smell . . . rank. My dear Miss Weyman,
I assure you my tastes run to something quite different."

She was relieved to hear it, naturally, but no woman liked to hear herself described in such unflattering terms. With a little sniff, she cast a disdainful eye around the room. "Am I to understand," she said scathingly, "that you expect me to sleep in this vermin-infested hovel?"

He grinned. "Fear not. I shall be close by to protect you from . . . um . . . spiders and mice or what-have-you," and he indicated the other straw pallet.

The eyes that met his were fiery with temper. "You mean . . . we are to share this room?"

"That's exactly what I mean. In short, Deborah, I fear you are not to be trusted. Either I or one of the others will keep you in sight at all times. Now, are we going to have another fight about it, or are you going to give in gracefully?"

She folded her lips together.

He waved a hand airily in the direction of the wash-stand. "Ladies first," he said.

For a moment, she hesitated. Deciding that argument was useless, she hauled herself to her knees, then to her feet. Her hip was so painful that she was sure each halting step would be her last. Pride kept her back straight and her feet moving. To betray weakness to this man could prove fatal.

The water in the pitcher was ice-cold. What she really wanted was a hot bath; what she allowed herself, under his prying eyes, was a quick splash with cold water on her face and hands. There was a piece of broken comb by the basin, but it was so filthy she wasn't even tempted to use it. Having completed her ablutions, she returned to her pallet.

"Remove your clothes," he said. "Please, no more fuss, Deborah, just do as I say. Oh, you may leave on your shift."

She could tell by his voice that he was enjoying himself enormously. She turned her back on him so that he could not witness her shame. Tears pricked her eyes. This was the man who had pretended to be so nice in his notions that he was reluctant to travel in the coach with her. One day, God willing, she would see him dangle at the end of a rope.

"Be quick about it," he said, "or I shall strip you myself."

She dragged her gown over her head and then began on the tapes that held her petticoats in place. When she was down to her chemise and drawers, she halted. This had gone far enough.

"The drawers, Deborah," he said, "or I swear I shall take them off you."

He would do it too. The remnants of her resistance ebbed away. She was so weary that every movement felt weighted. Again, the blackness hovered and she blinked it away. Wordlessly, she undid the tapes of her drawers and removed them. She felt like a whipped cur when she stretched out on the pallet. Even the sight of his far from immaculate shirt had not the power to cheer her. She made to lie on her side, away from him, but her hip was so painful, she gave up the attempt. Stretched out on her back, she gazed unseeingly at the blackened ceiling.

A quilt was thrown over her. She heard his movements as he padded around the room, but they hardly penetrated. Every cell in her body demanded a respite. Before long, her lashes fluttered, and she succumbed to the blackness.

Using a taper to get a flame from the lantern, Gray lit the kindling that had been set in the grate. When he heard snuffling noises coming from Deborah's pallet, he left the fireplace and moved quietly to her side. Sinking on one knee, he let his eyes roam over her. Her abundant auburn hair curled around her pale face in a mass of tangles. Small freckles dusted her nose and cheekbones; violet smudges made hollows of her eyes. With one finger, he caught a tear that hovered on the tip of one butchered eyelash. Her brows were drawn together in a frown. He had known that when he unmasked her, she would turn out to be a pretty girl, but this transformation was more than he had bargained for.

Without thinking, he touched his tear-dewed finger to his lips, and the taste of her spread over his tongue, tantalizing him, filling him with a hunger to take more. Ruthlessly quelling his errant thoughts, he waited a moment till the impulse had passed, then he deliberately pulled back the feather quilt which covered her.

He did not expect her to waken, nor did she. The few drops of laudanum with which he had dosed her bowl of stew had finally taken effect. With an expert eye, he examined first one wrist, then the other. The marks from the bonds were raw, but not so severe that he felt they required doctoring. He was not so sure about the knocks she had taken in her fall from Jupiter. It had seemed to him that in the last little while she had been favoring her right foot, and when he had swatted her, he was sure he had felt her wince. She wouldn't confide in him, of course. He was the monster who had abducted her. His hands were not quite steady when he raised her shift.

Her body was perfectly made, lush and lean in all the right places. Scowling now, he concentrated on her injuries. When he gently touched the bruise on her left hip, she whimpered and flinched away. He got the same reaction when he touched her left shoulder. She made no sound when he examined her ribs. Satisfied that she was not hurt in any real sense, he covered her with the quilt, returned to the fire, and added a log to the blaze.

Staring at the flames as they licked around the log, he went over in his mind the merits of the strategy he had decided to employ. He had to make her fear and hate him. He glanced at the sleeping girl. He had not expected such a hard core of resistance in her. Most women of her station would have been reduced to a quivering mass of jelly by this time. He admired her pluck, but at the same time, he regretted that she was making things so hard for herself. She wouldn't admit when she was beaten. More than ever it made him wonder about her. Nothing was known of her before she had taken up a position as Quentin's governess, except that she had come to him from Miss Hare's school. Campbell, Lord Lawford's agent, had tried to dig deeper, but no one knew anything about her. Miss Hare was the key, of course, but Miss Hare kept a close guard on her tongue. Who was Deborah Weyman, and what was she hiding? Miss Hare, whom he liked and respected, had nothing but good to say of her. As for Gil, she must have made quite an impression on him before he named her as one of his son's guardians.

The thought turned in his mind as he added another log to the blaze in the grate. Gil had mentioned Quentin's governess in passing, but he had paid scant attention at the time. The thing he remembered was Gil's very evident relief that his son was happy and gradually getting over the loss of his mother. Quentin was happy, Miss Weyman was a treasure, and Gil felt free to devote himself to his work at the Foreign Office.

He was wishing now that he *had* visited Gil's house in Saint-Germain, if only to meet Deborah. He'd made a point of avoiding it. Sophie Barrington was the reason. She was a born coquette, and it had made things awkward between him and Gil. He'd had the impression that Gil was not happy in his marriage. Not that Gil had said anything to him. He was still the same old charming Gil, but though he could talk and laugh with gaiety, sometimes his cheerfulness seemed forced and not as natural as it used to be.

He shook his head, smiling, remembering that it was Gil's charm that had got them out of many a scrape when they were schoolboys at Eton. The masters always believed that it was he, Gray, who was leading Gil astray, and because they were loath to punish the one they believed was innocent, Gray got off scot-free too. The truth was Gil could talk his way out of anything. He'd been well suited to a career in diplomacy.

For a long time, he stood at the fireplace, one hand resting on the mantelpiece, his thoughts roaming far and wide. The smile on his face gradually faded, and his expression became hard and inflexible. He was reminding himself that Gil had been murdered, and Deborah Weyman might well turn out to be the one who had committed the crime. If she were not the murderer, she could be an accessory. At the very least, she had abducted Quentin, and that in itself was a capital crime. He shouldn't be softening toward her. He should be trying to break her. He must do whatever was necessary to find Quentin.

He had to make her fear and hate him, and her obvious distrust of his "unbridled passions" had put the germ of an idea in his head. With that sober thought, he began to undress himself.

CHAPTER 6

It was a shocking, lurid dream, such as she had never experienced before. In some dark corner of her mind, it registered that when she chose to, she could awaken, and the dream would recede. But not yet. She was too drowsy, too languid, and far too curious about the unfamiliar though pleasurable sensations that held her in thrall. It had never occurred to her that she would like the feel of a man's hairy leg rubbing against her bare skin, that she would like the feel of his hands as they gently kneaded the soft cheeks of her bottom. She knew that she should put a stop to it, but it was, after all, only a dream, and she couldn't be held responsible for her dreams.

Even in sleep, it troubled her that she could be susceptible to a man she both loathed and feared. If she was going to have romantic fantasies about anyone, she would have expected them to be about a man she liked, someone like Nick, or even Mr. Gray. That was the thing about dreams—they turned harmless people into ogres and ogres into lovers, and there was no accounting for it.

The hands on her bottom clenched and unclenched and she moaned as tiny shivers swept over her. All her senses were focused on what he was doing to her. Her breathing was uneven, her body throbbed, and her loins ached in anticipation of she knew not what.

"So," said the husky voice of her dreams, "now I know how to provoke those delectable dimples. You wouldn't believe how much I have missed them."

Her smile vanished, and she squeezed her eyes tight before slowly, slowly opening them. From a few inches away, his wicked blue eyes twinkled back at her. She swiftly closed her eyes and tried again. He was still there when she opened them a second time.

"And," said Gray, "I have wanted to do this almost from the moment we met," and he caressed her bottom with both hands, sinking his fingers into her tender flesh, tracing the furrow between her voluptuous curves.

She became painfully aware of several things at once. Their two straw mattresses were pushed together on the hearth, and the only thing separating bare skin from bare skin was her inadequate shift and the thin lawn of his drawers. Most humiliating of all, however, was the knowledge that he wasn't restraining her in any way whatsoever. She was a full participant in this amorous encounter. In point of fact, she was restraining him! Her hands were clutching his bare shoulders as if she were afraid he would try to get away. It went without saying that he wasn't putting up any resistance. What man would?

There was a moment of pent-up silence, then she exploded in a flurry of flailing limbs and flying fists.

"Whoa!" Gray grabbed for her wrists and rolled on top of her, effectively subduing her struggles. He was helpless with laughter.

She lay there shivering, staring up at him with murder in her eyes. The pain in her hip and shoulder from the press of his weight was the least of his transgressions. He had made her look ridiculous and that was unforgivable.

"You told me," she said, grinding her teeth together, "that your tastes ran to something quite different. I should have expected something like this."

He shook his head. "You are far off there. For my part, which I readily confess, I did drag your pallet closer to the fire, but that was to stop your caterwauling when the roof started to leak. One would have deduced from your shrieks that I was trying to drown you. The whole house was in an uproar." She had, of course, been almost insensate from the laudanum she had ingested before going to bed, but Gray, prudently, said nothing of that.

Brows drawn, she glanced around the room. It was barely dawn, but there was enough light filtering through the slats of the boarded window to illuminate her cramped quarters. She had a vague recollection of water dripping on her face. Sure enough, there was a pool of water where her pallet had been laid out the night before.

If he was waiting for her to thank him, he would wait till doomsday. She hadn't asked to be brought to this pigsty. Had it not been for him, at this moment she would be tucked up in her warm bed in her pristine room at the school, waiting for the maid, Betty, to arrive with a cup of steaming hot chocolate. If he had wanted to, he could have held her in a more comfortable prison. She understood his reasoning. He didn't want her to be comfortable. By heaping humiliation upon humiliation on her, he thought he could break her.

Those shrewd blue eyes were glinting down at her from beneath raised brows. It galled her that he was so handsome, and so unconscious of it. It galled her more that she was fool enough to be affected by it—at least in her dreams. She would wager her last farthing that he had this effect on most women. How could he help it? Women were so gullible. They wouldn't look beneath those arrogantly molded features, those broad shoulders, that powerful torso that hadn't an ounce of spare fat on it. It was to be expected that many females had given in to the itch to brush back those strands of silky blond hair that fell across his brow, or caress that golden skin that put her in mind of—

"Deborah, are you flirting with me?"

Her eyes jerked up to meet his. The mockery that so often incensed her was in full bloom. She gasped, she squawked and gasped again before she could get the words out. "Your conceit is matched only by your stupidity. Does a prisoner flirt with her jailer?"

He relieved her of some of his weight, and breathing became a little easier until he began to slide the backs of his fingers along her bare arms. "She might," he said quietly, "if she thought it would persuade him to go easy with her. Is that why you were trying to seduce me earlier, Deborah? Because if it was, I should warn you that it won't work with me. I want that understood between us at the outset."

Squawking was so undignified. Keeping her voice low and steady, she replied, with just a hint of haughtiness, "I was not trying to seduce you." As if she would, as if she could. She didn't know the first thing about relations between the sexes. She almost told him so until she remembered that she was trying to maintain the fiction that she was a widow.

"No?" he asked whimsically. "It felt very much like a seduction to me. When I wakened this morning you were plastered against me. I, of course, just did what comes naturally to any red-blooded male who wakes to find a woman in his bed."

"Oh, of course," she snapped. He would. And she could well imagine the succession of women he had wakened with over the years. Her voice was very prim, very proper. "If you must know, I was dreaming of my, um, late husband."

There was a silence, and she couldn't prevent a quick peek up at him. His eyes had turned opaque, shielding his thoughts from her.

He shifted to his side, and pillowed his head on the mattress close to hers, one arm flung loosely around her waist. She was steeling herself for another laugh at her expense. One thing was certain, she wasn't going to fly at him like a terrified virgin when he had made it patently, insultingly obvious that she wasn't his type. On the other hand, no decent woman would remain in this position with a man who was not her husband. Inch by imperceptible inch, she began to edge away from him.

"Do you miss being married?" he asked.

Sensing a trap, she said carefully, "It's too painful. I . . . I don't wish to talk about it."

His lashes lowered to half-mast. "Do you miss having a man's arms around you?"

Never in a million years. "There is that," she agreed, trying to sound as though she knew what she was talking about.

"And his kisses?"

She couldn't help looking at his lips. They were made for kissing, and by her reckoning, there would be scores of women who could vouch for it from personal experience.

It gave her great pleasure to say, with just the proper degree of shyness, "Tom's kisses were incomparable. I shall remember them to my dying day." This was no exaggeration. Tom had been a stable boy at Belvidere. She could well remember the day he had pounced on her and slobbered all over her. It was disgusting. Poor Tom. The other stableboys had made game of the black eye she had given him for his pains. She wished she could do as much to the man who was tormenting her.

"I presume," said Gray, "that you enjoyed the conjugal bed, otherwise you would not have been so eager to seduce me when you awoke this morning?"

It was all so confusing, so subtle. She had the distinct impression that whatever answer she gave, he would use it to his own advantage. Yes. No. She couldn't begin to see where it was all leading. Sensing that she was out of her depth, she made a stab at changing direction.

"Lord Kendal," she said, trying to sound coherent, then caught back a great breath when the brush of his hand accidentally touched the fullness of one breast.

"Yes?"

Her voice lost force, and she whispered hoarsely, "What are you going to do with me?"

He raised slightly on one elbow to lean over her. There wasn't a trace of laughter or mockery in his eyes, and that surprised her. "Tell me where Quentin is," he said, "and I shall let you go. Persist in this fiction that you are a widow, and I shall take great delight in proving you a liar."

She was a liar, a practiced liar, and she used all the skill that she possessed to say indignantly, "There is no use talking to you. You are determined to believe what you wish to believe. If I knew anything of the boy, don't you think I would tell you?"

His eyes narrowed to slits, and the hand that was brushing along her arm stilled. "What boy?" he asked softly.

She understood that she had made a blunder, but she failed to see what it was. Swallowing, she whispered, "Quentin."

"I never said that Quentin was a boy."

She stuttered and stammered and finally got out, "You must have done, or I would not have known it."

"That lie won't save you. You see, Miss Weyman, I made it a point to tell you nothing of Quentin in hopes of entrapping you. And by damn, it worked."

Desperate now, she cried out, "Then Nick must have told me."

"By my orders, Nick was forbidden to speak of Quentin. Besides, when could he have told you? You have not spoken two words together that I was not there to hear. You are Deborah Weyman. I want to hear you admit it."

"Even if it is not true?"

His gaze held her silent as he brought his hand to her throat in a gently caressing threat. Deborah's heart stopped beating as she waited for the pressure of those long fingers to clamp down and choke the life out of her.

His beguiling voice belied the malice in his words. "Tell me what I wish to know, Deborah, or I shall prove that you are no widow woman. No, really, you would be doing us both a favor. I have no taste for virgins."

Staring straight into his eyes, she made no attempt to shade her opinion of him. He was a monster and she could expect no mercy at his hands. How could she have forgotten it? And she had forgotten, there was no doubt in her mind about that. He was like a chameleon, changing before her eyes, confusing her with his many masks.

"Resigned, Deborah?" he asked, taunting her.

Only one thing kept her from blurting out the truth

like a panicked child. Quentin. She must protect Quentin whatever the cost to herself. As his massive shoulders loomed over her, she tried one final, delaying tactic. Eyes glistening, she said fiercely, "Nick will kill you for this."

She could see that her words had an effect. Those brilliant, all-seeing eyes went as dark as the muddied waters of the Thames, but it wasn't enough to make him change his mind. His answer came softly, deriding her. "But my sweet, Nick is not here. And the door is locked."

When he lowered his head, she went for him with her balled fists. Then he was upon her, his hands snagging her wrists and forcing them behind her back. There was a rending sound as he tore her shift from throat to waist. Bucking, twisting, she tried to throw him off. He subdued her with his weight, crushing her into the depths of the mattress, forcing her legs apart with his powerful thighs. His kiss was bruising, punitive, and she snapped at him with her sharp teeth, surprised and afraid when she bit into the soft swell of his bottom lip. Numb with fear, she waited for what he would do next. He retaliated in kind, and she cried out as her own blood filled her mouth.

He drew back, staring down at her, all emotion concealed behind half-hooded eyes. Her fear and anger ebbed away. He had hurt her, and deep down, she really had believed he would go so far and no further.

"Deborah?" he whispered.

She lowered her lashes, shutting out the sight of him.

She heard him sigh, then his lips were on hers, washing away the pain and blood. This newfound gentleness was her undoing. She wanted to be held and comforted, but she didn't want *him*. She wanted her mother, or Miss Hare, or some other, kindly lady who had her best interests at heart.

She wasn't given a choice. Rocking her now, he held her to him, lavishing her bruised lips with soft kisses, lifting her tears with the tip of his tongue, returning to her lips, opening them with gentle pressure to tenderly assuage the hurt he had inflicted. Her head was nestled in the crook of his arm. Her protests were feeble and lacked conviction. He ignored them and angled her head back, taking his fill of her with lips and tongue.

His touch was so different, his softly murmured words so soothing, that she found it hard to believe he was the same man who had terrorized her only moments before. She couldn't face a return of the man she feared. Just thinking about it made her dissolve in a fresh bout of hiccups. She was so tired of trying to outwit him, so tired of being brave.

There was solace to be had in the hands that were moving over her, drawing her close to the warmth of his body, and if anyone needed solace, it was she. She'd been through hell in the last several months. There was only so much one person could withstand.

"Yes," he whispered, when she turned into him. His fingers were lost in her hair, separating each silky strand, savoring the texture. "I knew it would be this color. Kiss me, Deborah."

She couldn't fight him and win. The thought kept her passive as he took her lips again, but at the first touch of his hand on her breast, she tried to pull away. The flat of his other hand curved around her bottom, holding her steady, and her dream came rushing back to her in a flood. Her body was throbbing, her breathing was labored, and the ache in her loins was as palpable as any pain. She moaned and when he heard that small pleasure sound, his breath became suspended, then accelerated as he sensed her arousal.

In the blink of an eye, the pattern of his sweetly comforting caresses changed. His kisses seemed to suck the very lifeblood out of her; his hands slipped over skin and bone, caressing, touching her intimately. There wasn't a part of her that did not receive the homage of his lips and tongue; her breasts, her waist, her calves, her knees. She was burning; she was drowning; the pressure in her body tightened in a delirium of pleasure.

It was some time since Gray had given thought to anything but his driving need to possess the woman who, he readily admitted, had tantalized him from the first. He was positioning himself to take her, lifting her knees, when, from the rooms below, he heard faint movements as Nick and Hart roused themselves for another day. He didn't want to think about Nick and Hart. He was only a moment away from burying himself in her delectable body, a moment away from completion.

The outside door slammed, and the focus of his thoughts shifted. There was a purpose to this, and he would do well to remember it. He was supposed to be terrorizing her, not lusting after her like a callow youth with his first woman. What the hell had come over him?

He shook his head as if to clear his brain of the mist that had gathered there. This could not be him, taking advantage of a woman's inexperience! He knew better! One of the few times his father had ever lifted his hand to him was when, as a boy of fifteen, he had tried to seduce the vicar's daughter in the barn behind the church. A man did not seduce an innocent young girl, not even if she was willing, and Sally Wentworth had been more than willing. A man treated all women with courtesy and respect, whether they deserved it or not. That lesson had been drilled into him by both parents since he was in the schoolroom, and he, in turn, had drilled it into his younger brother. Deborah Weyman was a special case. He had to break her, but she did not deserve this from him.

Deborah, sensing the subtle change in him, lifted her head and gazed up at him with uncertain eyes. There was a moment when she read the same uncertainty in his expression, then his eyes clouded over and his features hardened into a cold mask.

"Last chance, Deborah," he said. "Tell me where Quentin is, or I shall well and truly fuck you."

The crude word acted on her as he hoped it would. Her knee came up like lightning and struck him full on the stomach, sending him sprawling. Even if he had wanted to deflect the blow, which he didn't, he doubted if he could have acted quickly enough. Wonderful! While he was doubled over in agony, she had scrambled to her feet, and was reviling his lecherous designs with all the facility of a fishwife from Billingsgate. That ought to bring Nick rushing to the rescue and not a moment too soon. He ducked as first one shoe then the other came flying at him. With no other missiles in sight, she backed away from him. At the first sound of feet thundering on the stairs, Gray reached for his breeches and stepped into them.

A fist hammered against the door and the handle rattled. "Unlock the door." Nick's voice. "Deborah, are you all right? Unlock the door, I say, or I shall break it down."

Deborah was crouched in a corner, the back of her hand pressed to her mouth, staring at Gray as though he had suddenly sprouted another head. Ignoring that shocked look, he said tersely, "Cover yourself, woman, unless you want Nick to finish what I started." She continued to stare at him until he made a sudden move toward her, then, diving for one of the quilts, she quickly wrapped it around herself. Only then did Gray produce a key from his pocket and answer Nick's frenzied blows on the door.

As soon as Gray unlocked the door, Nick pushed past him and strode into the room. One look at Deborah's bloodied lip and he turned furiously upon Gray. "What the devil is going on? What have you done to her? I warn you, Gray, I won't have her harmed."

Gray's handsome features betrayed not a flicker of unease. "Why don't you ask the lady what happened?"

Deborah answered before the question could be put to her. She could not bear to look Nick in the eye. She felt shamed to the depths of her soul, knowing she had participated in her own seduction. Voice breaking, she said, "He said a word to which I took exception."

Bewildered, Nick looked from one to the other. "What word?"

Gray shrugged. Deborah turned away and began to pick up her clothes.

"And that's all there was to it?" Nick's voice was still rife with suspicion.

Gray folded his arms across his chest. His tone was conversational, his words were lethal. "If I want to take her, Nick, I shall, and I won't ask your permission."

The silence these words produced was long and profoundly frightening. Deborah was afraid to breathe.

Nick stared at Gray for long moments. By degrees, his hostility seemed to ebb away. "This one is different, Gray, you know she is."

Gray laughed, neither agreeing nor disagreeing. "Come along, Nick, and leave Miss Weyman to get dressed." He flung an arm around Nick's shoulders and led him from the room, carefully locking the door behind him.

"What really happened, Gray?"

They were on the stairs, and Gray put a finger to his lips, silencing Nick. Once in the kitchen, he said easily, "I put the fear of God into her, or more precisely, the fear of her ruthless captor. She is halfway persuaded that I mean to have my wicked way with her. 'Morning, Hart."

Hart looked up from the bacon he was frying and grunted a greeting.

Nick sprawled on a chair. "She's halfway persuaded?" he asked incredulously. "Gray, you can't gull me. If you could only see yourself! Your lip looks as though it has been caught in a mangle, and Miss Weyman's lip looks no better. Is this how you make love to a woman? Is this an example of the famous charm which has divested women of their wits if not their clothing since you graduated from the schoolroom? If so, I think you should be looking to your laurels, old sport. Even I can do better than that."

A pot clattered, but neither brother paid any heed to it. "I don't wish to make love to her," said Gray. "Our purpose is to break her, remember?" He snagged a thick slice of bread that was toasting at the open fire and bit into it.

"I might believe you," said Nick, snickering, "had I not walked into a room where the ripe smell of passion almost choked me. Talk about being knocked over with a feather!"

There was a commotion at the fireplace as Hart dropped the frying pan he was holding, then an oath as he picked it up without benefit of a pot holder and subsequently slammed it on a trivet. When he turned upon Gray and Nick, his expression was wrathful. Theirs was startled.

"If you have dishonored that lady, you shall answer to me," he declared. "This was no part of our understanding."

The brothers exchanged a quick look. "Hart! Hart!" said Gray, pulling a long face. "Have you so little faith in me? Nick is exaggerating, as usual. He doesn't mean anything by it."

"Oh, don't I?" taunted Nick.

"Nick, tell him!"

"Oh, very well. Hart, you know me. I was merely enjoying a bit of fun at Gray's expense. The trouble with you, Hart, is that you don't have any brothers. If you had, you would know that there is nothing we like better than to torment each other. Isn't that so, Gray?"

At these reassuring words, Hart unbent a little. It had never seriously entered his head that Gray would dishonor Miss Weyman, whatever the ultimate goal. The Graysons weren't like that. He well remembered the intimidating interview with Gray, when he had finally screwed up his courage to ask for Gussie's hand in marriage. Gray wasn't interested in his wealth or his title. He wanted his sister to be settled with a man who would make her happy. The Graysons had been raised to cherish their womenfolk, and if Hart failed in his duty, Gray would take a very dim view of it. Hart was left in no doubt that in that event he would be facing Gray at some distant dawn with a dueling pistol in his hand.

Miss Weyman would not be designated as a member of Gray's "womenfolk," but she was still a member of the weaker sex. He had never known Gray, in spite of his cynicism, to treat females with anything but respect and gentleness, yes, even the bold hussies. Miss Weyman was different, of course. It was quite possible she was implicated in the murder of Gray's friend. Gray could be ruthless, but Hart did not think he could throw off the tenets by which he had been raised. At least, he hoped he could not.

Aware of two pairs of eyes on him, Hart ventured, "I

won't be a party to anything . . . well . . . dishonorable."

"Nor would Nick. Nor would I." Gray's voice became brutally soft as he continued. "But you will allow that these are exceptional circumstances? She knows where Quentin is. I mean to find him. If there was another way, don't you think I would take it?"

Though the belligerence had faded from Hart's expression, he was persistent. "I can't believe that she was involved in Gil's murder, or that she would do anything to harm Quentin."

"I find it hard to believe too."

"Well, then?"

"I have been known to be wrong before now."

Eyes glinting, Nick said, "Hart, didn't I tell you he fancies the girl? She won't come to any harm with Gray. He took one look into those big baby-blue eyes of hers, and—"

"Her eyes are green," corrected Gray.

Nick's shoulders shook with laughter. "What did I tell you, Hart? As I was saying, he looked into those big, baby-*green* eyes of hers and read his fate in bold letters. She's his wench. He doesn't believe she is a murderess any more than you or I do. And when this is all over, he's got to face the music. You should feel sorry for him, Hart. I know I do."

Amusement stirred in Gray's eyes. "When this is all over," he said, "I shall be happy if I never set eyes on the wench again. By the way, Nick, do try for a little less melodrama when you charge to the rescue. I thought it was a little overdone."

"Anything to oblige," answered Nick cheerfully.

"And Hart, just keep on as you are doing. I think she fears you almost as much as she fears me."

Hart made no comment other than to slam a kettle of boiling water on the rickety table. "You need a shave," he told Gray, indicating the kettle.

"One does so miss one's valet on these missions," said Gray. "I take it my portmanteau is in the other room?"

"As is Miss Weyman's," replied Nick. "Shall I take it up to her?"

"Hardly, when the point of the exercise is to make her feel as miserable and uncomfortable as possible. Please, Hart, I don't think my nerves can stand any more rattling of pots and pans." He reached for a tin mug and filled it from the kettle. "Now," he said, "this is how we shall bring matters to a speedy conclusion."

CHAPTER 7

When Gray locked the door, Deborah lost no time in seeing to her toilette. The water in the pitcher, the little that remained after her ablutions of the night before, was ice-cold. Finding no washcloth, she dampened one of the threadbare towels and rubbed it briskly over her body. Her hands and face received no more than a quick splash. It took her only a few minutes to don her clothes. Her hair was a mess of tangles. For long moments, she gazed with loathing at that filthy, broken comb before finally snatching it up and dragging it through her hair.

Having tidied herself, she threw down the comb and waited expectantly till someone should come to the door to escort her to the outside privy. After pacing impatiently for several minutes, convinced that no one gave a thought for her comfort, she looked around the room for the indispensable commode with its equally indispensable chamber pot. There was no commode, but she found the chamber pot. It was in the washstand, behind the slop pail, and it was crawling with maggots.

Smothering a scream, she dropped the chamber pot and took a quick step back. He had done this on purpose, in an effort to wear her down so that she would tell him what he wanted to know. Furious at such base tactics—another example of the man's crudity—she used the water from the slop pail to drown her uninvited guests, and wished she could do as much to her ruthless abductor. It was horrible. She would burst before she would use that filthy, broken-down thing.

Indignation bolstered her courage. She moved purposefully to the door and used one of her shoes to hammer upon it. Within minutes, the key turned in the lock and she was confronted with the fierce-looking, dark-haired man, the one they called Hart.

The hot words of reproach died unsaid. She didn't know how to read this man and decided not to provoke him. "May I be permitted to visit the outhouse?" she asked, managing a faint smile.

He gave her an unreadable look before leading the way down the steep staircase and into the kitchen. There was no sign of Lord Kendal or Nick but she could hear their voices in the next room. The kitchen looked as though an army had been through it. The sink was piled high with dirty dishes, and pots and pans were strewn over the table and floor. The smoke from burned bacon hung on the air. She smirked, thinking it would take them a month of Sundays to clean up the place. She just wished she were there to see it.

She wasn't smirking a few minutes later when she was marched back to her room and the key was turned in the lock. She didn't care to eat a cooked breakfast, but she would have given anything for a piece of dry toast and a cup of something hot to drink. She had been offered nothing. Lord Kendal was lower than the lowest rodent.

She looked around her small prison and examined every nook and cranny to see if there was a way of escape. Deciding that the window would be her best bet, she grasped one of the boards across it and yanked with all her strength. It would not budge, and there was nothing in that room that she could use as a lever, no candlestick, no fire tongs or poker. Lord Kendal was a very cautious man. If she were to escape, she would have to go out through the door. It wasn't impossible, but she would do well to choose her moment with care.

There was no chair, but by arranging the mattresses and quilts, she managed to make a sofa of sorts. It was hardly comfortable, but it would do. Gingerly seating herself, she leaned back against the wall for support and began to take stock of her position.

Kendal was a formidable enemy, but he was not infallible. He thought she could easily be cowed into doing whatever he wanted, and that's where he had made a colossal error. He needed her. Alive, she was worth something. If anything happened to her, his plans would come to nothing.

She made a sound that was not quite a sob, not quite a laugh. Who was she trying to fool? She *was* easily cowed. She wasn't a heroine. And if sometimes it seemed that she was brave, as Miss Hare seemed to think, that was only because she had been backed into a corner and could do no other. Even a cornered rabbit would put up a fight. If Albert had only realized it, he might still be alive to this day.

It was her way, when memories of that appalling time came back to her, to ruthlessly suppress them. This time, she found them hard to suppress. She was all at sea. Fear had done this to her. Her ability to think clearly was fast disintegrating.

Restless now, she rose and began to pace. Realizing that she was chilled, she retrieved her cloak from the floor and threw it over her shoulders, then went to stand by the window. Through one of the slats, she could make out a field of barley, and beyond that, the hills silhouetted against the pink haze of a new dawn.

At Belvidere, where she had been born and raised, the landscape owed nothing to nature though it gave the appearance of great natural beauty. It was all created by man—the lake, the streams, the gentle rises and dips, the copses, the plantations of oaks and elms. The house itself was far more a private palace than a home. She remembered mile upon mile of cold white marble, and Greek columns, and state rooms adorned with priceless paintings and antiquities, and other valuable collectors' items.

It had taken a great deal of money to maintain that

magnificent house and estate. *Money*. That was all she had ever meant to her father. Shivering, she rested her head against the boarded window, and closed her eyes, willing the memories to recede, but it was hopeless. Resigned, she let them flow into her.

As a child, she had not known that her father had married her mother only for her fortune, had not known of his hatred for a wife he regarded as so far beneath him. Her mother's people had been of the merchant class, and her father regarded his wife as the daughter of a "tradesman." There was no lower word in the earl's vocabulary.

Deborah and her brother, Stephen, had known of his vicious temper, and went in fear of him, but they never suspected that it was their mother who bore the brunt of it. They saw very little of him, and were glad of his indifference, and though they spent a good part of each day in the schoolroom, the rest of the time was spent with their mother, and it was glorious. Together, the three of them roamed the woods and pastures on horseback; they collected wildflowers and pressed them between the pages of books; they made friends with gypsies and the local people. Their mother was the center of their small world and they adored her.

All this changed the day she bundled them into a coach and told them they were going on a long holiday. They knew that something was very wrong because she was tearful and anxious for the coachman to drive faster. They did not get far before their father caught up with them. They were ordered out of the carriage, and their mother was sent on her way alone. It was the last they ever saw of her.

Years were to pass, long painful years, before she and Stephen were able to make sense of what had happened to them. From servants' gossip and other sources, they pieced the story together. Their mother had been terrified of her husband's ungovernable rages, and after one harrowing experience, when she feared he would kill her, she had taken her children and fled. There was to be no rescue for her. After the aborted escape attempt, the earl banished his wife to an isolated cottage on the estate while the children were kept at Belvidere. The law gave him that right.

The law gave him other rights. Not one penny of her mother's fortune was ever returned to her. She was destitute, and even if she were free, she could not have supported herself let alone two young children. But she hadn't given up hope. She'd written secretly to her lawyer in an attempt to prove that her husband was unfit to have custody of her children. Magistrates had come to the house and they'd questioned the children, and they, in turn, had ingenuously supported their mother's claims. There was never any doubt, however, whose word the magistrates would accept. Their father was charming, reasonable, and so obviously a man of breeding. By the time the earl had finished with the magistrates, it was his wife's sanity that was called into question, a wife who very evidently had poisoned her children's minds against their father.

Then the earl took his revenge. It was not long before he had committed his wife to an asylum. Within the year, she was dead. And for the children who, in his warped mind, had aided and abetted her by telling the magistrates tales out of school, he reserved his most virulent hatred.

Deborah's eyes pooled with grief as other memories rushed through her mind in quick succession. Stephen being sent away to school only days after her father had presented them to his new wife. Their stepmother, whose bloodlines, their father never let them forget, were as pure and exalted as his own. The birth of her half sister, Elizabeth, and her joy turning to horror as her stepmother screamed not to touch the child in case she would harm her. London, and her first season that turned out to be a nightmare. Her father's house in the Strand, and her sixteenth birthday, when she was introduced to her betrothed, Albert Hollander. Albert, who tried to rape her, and the look on his face when the rail at the top of the circular staircase gave way and he fell to his death three floors below.

She rested her head against the hard board at the window, and fought to control her breathing. Albert hadn't deserved to die. She hadn't meant to kill him. But hers *were* the hands that had pushed him in her desperation to be free. She'd been cornered, and she'd fought like a wildcat.

The memories that followed were almost as bad. Her father telling her what would happen to her if she proved as rebellious as her mother; Windsor, and Stephen who had betrayed her to the authorities when she arranged to meet him there.

Stephen's betrayal was the greatest hurt of all, for they had been united in the loss of their mother and in their contempt for their father. Had he suffered the pangs of a guilty conscience for what he had tried to do to her? She thought he must have, for she'd heard that afterward he had run away from school and enlisted. Last she had heard, he was still in India with the British army.

If it had not been for Miss Hare, she did not know what would have become of her. When her father had announced her betrothal, Miss Hare had been dismissed. But Deborah had known where her governess was to be found, and after her narrow escape at Windsor, she had taken refuge with her.

Her father would be at Belvidere now for the hunting season. Her half sister, Elizabeth, must be old enough for her first season. That would take money, a lot of money. She, Deborah, might not be able to touch her fortune, but neither could her father, not now that she had reached her majority. That could only happen if she fell into his clutches again. She had no doubt of the outcome if that happened. He would force her to marry someone like Albert, or he would commit her to an insane asylum.

A sudden intuition warned her that she was not alone, and she spun to face the door. Gray's smile faded the moment he saw Deborah's expression.

He spoke to her curtly. "There's no need for so much anguish. Tell me what I wish to know and I shall let you go."

She pressed a hand to her temples. "What? Oh, it's you."

"Who did you think it was?" He advanced toward her.

Her smile was bitter. "Someone very like you."

"Who?"

She shook her head. "Even a prisoner is entitled to her own thoughts."

It surprised him how much he wanted her to confide in him, how much he wanted to comfort her. He sensed that whatever had upset her went beyond their present differences. Her past was shrouded in mystery. It gnawed at him, or perhaps it was just the woman, herself, who gnawed at him. He was baffled by the contradictions in her character. She feared him, yet she was reckless in her defiance. She was fragile, yet she was as hard as nails. Looking at her now, he could see nothing of the timid, vulnerable creature who had been wary of the bloodless Mr. Gray. With her head thrown back and her eyes fearlessly trained on his, she had the look of some mythical warrior queen. It was bravado, of course. Every instinct told him she was close to collapse.

Gentling his tone, he said, "Deborah, I want to help you. If there is someone or something you fear, I can protect you, but first you have to tell me where Quentin is."

For a moment, he saw her resolve waver, then her eyes flashed her scorn. "I've had a taste of your protection, thank you, and quite candidly, it does not impress me. In plainer terms, I'd sooner trust myself to a den of vipers than trust a man like you." Conscious that her control was fast slipping away, she turned aside to fold the towels on the washstand, taking these few moments to compose herself.

His disappointment was as keen as his anger. She was forcing him to go on with the game. He didn't want to go on playing the part of a tyrant, didn't want to frighten her or hurt her. He wanted her to give in before he was forced to utterly crush her.

He pulled himself up short, recognizing that he was falling into the same trap again. He didn't know the first thing about her, he reminded himself. She must be guilty of something. An innocent woman did not abduct a helpless boy and flee as if the hounds of hell were after her.

He didn't know what was the matter with him. No woman had ever moved him the way this woman moved him, and of all women, she was the one he should trust least. He would do well to remember it.

"Your breakfast is ready," he said, and held the door for her.

In the kitchen, Nick and Hart were seated at the table. They both rose at Deborah's entrance.

"No need to stand on ceremony with Miss Weyman," said Gray, motioning them to take their seats.

Nick sank back in his place, but Hart moved to the fireplace. Because the windows were boarded up, the lamps were lit, and Deborah's gaze flitted to each gentleman in turn.

"Sit down, Deborah," said Gray.

She looked at him carefully. He was immaculately turned out in a fresh set of clothes. There wasn't a stain on his white shirt, not a drop of the wine she had flung at him the night before. Nick and Hart were also as fresh as new-minted pennies.

Righteous anger began to simmer. While she was beginning to look and smell like a tinker, they were decked out as though they were about to begin on a day's round of pleasure. "Where is my portmanteau?" she demanded. Her attention was distracted as Hart put a plate of congealed fried eggs and bacon in front of her, then a mug of steaming hot liquid. "Thank you," she said, noting absently that this time around she was to be trusted with a fork.

"Oh," said Nick, "it's in the—" He halted when Gray silenced him with an abrupt motion of one hand.

"Where did you leave it?" asked Gray.

"In your carriage, as you know very well." Just looking at those congealed eggs turned her stomach. She picked up the mug and took a small sip. Coffee? Tea? It might have been either, or a combination of both. She couldn't tell by looking at it. It was as dark and thick as molasses. She set down the mug.

"I left my carriage in Wells," said Gray.

"With my portmanteau in it?"

He inclined his head.

"And your own portmanteau and Hart's and Nick's?"

His amusement made her straighten her shoulders.

"Oh, we had the foresight to bring those with us."

And his grin made her want to rake his handsome face with her nails. Stabbing a piece of bacon with her fork, she brought it to her lips. Crisp was scarcely the word for it. It was so hard, she felt as though she were chewing on a mouthful of nails. To prevent herself choking, she was forced to swallow some of the vile-tasting brew Hart had set down for her.

Conscious that she was the only one eating, she said, addressing Nick, "Aren't you going to eat breakfast?"

He looked abashed. "Well . . ." he began.

Gray answered for him. "Nick and I are going into Wells this morning. We shall break our fast at the King's Arms. They do a very good breakfast, I understand."

There was only so much a girl could stand. In one abrupt movement, she scraped back her chair and rose to her feet.

"Where do you think you are going?"

"This is no better than a pigsty," she cried out. "If you mean to poison me, why don't you simply hand me a cup of hemlock? It would be preferable to this pig's swill you call breakfast."

Gray turned with a chuckle to Hart. "I don't think Deborah appreciates your culinary talents any more than Nick and I do." Then turning to Deborah, "Tell me what I wish to know, and I'll buy you breakfast at the King's Arms. What's your fancy? Ham? Kippers? Or some tender braised kidney? Nick and I—"

Those twinkling eyes were the last straw. With one swipe of her hand, she sent plate and contents to the floor then took a quick step toward the door.

"Take one more step, Deborah, and I'll make you regret it."

The atmosphere in that small room was charged. Deep inside, Deborah began to tremble. Very slowly, she turned to face her captor.

Nick, too, had risen from the table. His eyes took in the pallor of Deborah's complexion and the stark fear in her eyes. "I say, Gray, is this really necessary?"

"Saddle the horses, Nick."

"But—"

"Do as I say." Gray's voice was deathly soft.

With a troubled look at Deborah, Nick went to do Gray's bidding.

"Hart, go with him."

When the door closed upon Hart, Gray said, "Come here, Deborah." When she hesitated, he bit out, "At once."

She had to will her feet to take the steps toward him. He was a killer. What was wrong with her that she kept forgetting it? How could she have been so stupid as to goad him to violence? She flinched when he grasped her chin and turned her face toward the light.

His eyes scanned her face. "Yes," he said, "you are wise to fear me. Now listen carefully to what I have to say. You should think yourself fortunate, Deborah. You are to be given a short reprieve. Nick and I are going to pay a call on Lady Becket, just to make sure she doesn't suspect anything. We should return by nightfall. That should give you time to reflect on what is in store for you if you refuse to tell me what I wish to know." He nodded, satisfied with the look that came into her eyes. "Yes, Deborah, we shall begin where we left off this morning.

"As for this place—" His gaze traveled the disordered room and finally came to rest on the debris of her breakfast. "You are right. It is a pigsty. I shall expect you to make it habitable. In other words, I want it so spotless by the time I return that we could eat off the floor. Do you understand?"

Wordlessly, she nodded, but her thoughts were racing in every direction. She shouldn't be defying him. She should be thanking her lucky stars that he and Nick were leaving. Then, there would be only one person to guard her. Wells could not be far away. She was in no condition to walk the distance, but if she could get to Hart's horse, there was a chance she could escape.

He laughed softly, and shook his head. "Don't even think it, Deborah. Hart is not as civilized as I. If you try to escape him, I can't vouch for what he might do."

His words on Hart were well taken, but it shook her that he could read her thoughts so easily. "I don't know what you are talking about," she said.

He smiled that devilish smile of his and released her. "Oh, I think you do," he said, and left the room.

She heard a muted conversation, just outside the door, then Hart entered. He wasn't as tall as Kendal, but he was a good three stone heavier by Deborah's reckoning. He was one of those men whose jawline would always be shadowed by the growth of his new beard, giving him a sinister appearance.

"Gray wants the place cleaned up," he said.

She eyed him nervously. Those were the first intelligible words he had spoken to her. Perhaps, if they got a conversation going, she wouldn't be so afraid of him. "I shall need hot water and lots of it," she ventured.

He pointed to a wooden bucket by the sink, then indicated the barred window. "The pump is in the yard, right outside that door."

Moistening her lips, she tried again. "There is hardly enough light to see what I am doing."

Without a word, he moved to the window and grasped one of the boards across it. With one yank, it came away in his hands, as did the next, and the next. The man was as strong as an ox.

Swallowing, Deborah began to roll up her sleeves.

※

By nightfall, every muscle in Deborah's body ached with fatigue. She paused in her labors at the sink, straightened, and rubbed the small of her back with one hand to ease the tension that knotted her spine. Her eyes strayed to the silent man who had been sitting at the fire for the last hour or two, staring at her as if he were a starving cat and she were a mouse in a cage. She had been a fool to think she could escape him. With his master gone, his vigilance had increased tenfold. She could not even go to the privy but he stood on guard right outside the door, and when *he* went to the privy, he took the precaution of locking her in her room first.

She had cleaned the kitchen from top to bottom, and it had been all for nothing. Lord Kendal had had the foresight to take Hart's horse with him when he rode out that morning. Just thinking about that scoundrel made her want to spit. While he was out gallivanting, she had worked her fingers to the bone, cleaning his house for him. Her eyes traveled the interior of the small room, noting the results of her labors.

Her cast-iron grate gleamed brightly, and an array of spanking-clean pots and skillets hung on their proper hooks from the oak mantel. The table was still scratched and rickety, but every speck of filth had been removed from it. The flagstoned floor had been swept and scoured. The slop pail was empty, and a tub of fresh water sat on the bench next to the sink. Even her own room had received its fair share of attention. There was a pitcher of fresh water on the washstand and, most gratifying of all, the iniquitous chamber pot had been immersed in a tub of scalding hot water.

She shouldn't be so angry. Had she not agreed to clean up the kitchen, God only knew what he would have done to her. He had already murdered one man. He wouldn't hesitate to punish her if she defied him. Yet, she was alive and unharmed, and though Lord Kendal had made many threats against her, he had not carried out a single one. The more she thought about it, the more convinced she became that she had Nick to thank for that. She had no way of knowing what had passed between them in private, but she was sure Nick would have taken her part. He liked her, was sorry for her, and looked askance at his brother's rough and ready methods of subduing her. If it really came down to it, she was sure Nick would champion her cause.

The last thing she wanted, however, was a face-to-face confrontation between Nick and Kendal. Nick would lose, nothing was surer, then she would be worse off than before. Somehow, she must persuade Nick to help her escape, and it must be done quickly. She had to find a way to speak privately with Nick. She had to escape Kendal's power. She *had* to.

As she absently dried her hands on a coarse towel, she turned the thought over in her mind. She didn't know what was the matter with her. She knew what Kendal was, yet she could not seem to hold on to that thought for more than a few minutes at a time. When he had asked her, so quietly and earnestly, to confide in him, she had been shaken to the depths of her soul. For a second, a fraction of a second, she had actually teetered on the brink of indecision. In that moment, there was nothing she wanted more than to lay her burdens on his broad shoulders. When it came to her that *he* was the burden she wanted to lay on his broad shoulders, her wavering had turned to outrage. All the same, she had come perilously close to betraying herself. She had to escape before she completely lost the use of her wits.

It wasn't only that moment of indecision that set her teeth on edge. She'd had time to reflect on the episode that morning, when she had awakened to find herself plastered against him. Just thinking about it made her go hot all over. It wasn't as if she were attracted to the man or anything of that sort. He was the antithesis of everything she admired in a male. It pained her to admit it, but she had behaved with all the modesty of a wanton hussy. She was inexperienced, that was her undoing, and he was a man of the world. The intelligence on which she prided herself had not entered into it. It was one more reason why she had to leave this place as quickly as possible.

He was a murderer, she reminded herself. She hated him, feared him, wished with all her heart that he would meet with his just deserts. And if she ever again felt herself softening toward him, she would cut her own throat and save him the bother.

She was spreading out the dishcloths to dry on the sink, when she heard the sound of a horn blowing. There followed several more blasts on the horn and Lord Kendal's voice raised in a rousing sea chantey. Deborah recognized the tune, but not the words.

"What shall we do with the wanton maiden?" roared his lordship at the top of his lungs.

Another voice answered him, Nick's voice, and Deborah did not appreciate the tone or content of his lewd reply. By the sound of them, they were as drunk as lords.

Hart flashed her one of his forbidding looks, then rose and went quickly through the door that led to the front of the house. Deborah's brows came down. She was almost tempted to reach for her rolling pin. Both voices now were loud enough to raise the rafters. Hart was trying to shush them, to no avail.

Crude, thought Deborah. She had expected better of Nick. Drunk wasn't the word for it. Hard on that thought came an electrifying flash of perception. She might never be handed a better chance to escape.

CHAPTER 8

She gave a start as the door crashed open and Gray, one
arm looped around Nick's shoulders, came ambling into
the room. In his free hand, he held a coachman's tin
horn which he proceeded to blow with great gusto. In
that small kitchen, the blast of noise was ear-shattering.

Deborah crossed her arms beneath her breasts.
Though both gentlemen were in a similar state of disar-
ray, it was Gray she eyed with mounting ire. He was
dressed in the same garments he had worn that morning,
but he was anything but immaculately turned out. Her
eyes moved over him slowly, missing nothing. His hair
was windblown and damp from the rain. His neckcloth
was askew, and both shirt and waistcoat were unbuttoned, displaying his sleekly muscled chest and the
strong column of his throat. The breeches that sheathed
his slim flanks and taut thighs were wrinkled beyond
redemption. Her gaze dropped to his boots. Adorning
each tasseled Hessian was a frilly lace garter garlanded
with red rosebuds. Her eyes jerked back to his hair. Not
windblown, she decided then, but disarranged by a
woman's fingers.

She prided herself on having hit on just the right
combination of amusement and contempt in the snort

she emitted. "Is this how Lady Becket entertains her guests?"

Nick cleared his throat. "Actually, Deborah, we, um, left Lady Becket's place some hours ago."

Her gaze narrowed on Gray, and swept over him, making a more thorough inventory than before, then she sniffed and turned her nose up.

Gray's face broke into a slow grin. "By damn, Nick, I can't resist her when she flirts with me," and shaking off Nick's restraining arm, he crossed the room and enfolded her in a bear hug.

Deborah buckled under his weight, but before she could protest, his lips took hers in an openmouthed kiss that sent flashes of heat all the way to her loins. She felt the burst of something sweet inside her, and then she smelled him. The brandy she could tolerate, but the reek of cheap perfume on his bare skin set up a different kind of heat on the palm of her hand. She itched to slap him.

Dragging her head back, she glared up at him. "You smell like a, like a—" Her bosom was heaving.

"Bawdy house?" he supplied. "Oh, that was Nick's doing. The Jewel Box, do you know it? It's right behind the King's Arms." His face fell. "It didn't work. I told Nick it wouldn't."

Over Gray's shoulder, Deborah saw Nick shrug eloquently as he pulled out a chair at the table and seated himself. "I don't know, Gray," he said. "It seemed to me that you were tolerably well amused."

Gray leered down at Deborah. "Amber and Garnet do very well in their way. I'll even go so far as to say I found them quite inventive. But their tricks are tainted. You can't blame a man for wanting the fresh meat that's keeping in his own larder."

Nick gave Deborah a very direct look and shook his head.

Deborah knew well enough that Nick was trying to reassure her. The crude drunken sot who was a deadweight around her neck was so worn out with his amorous exploits that he posed no immediate threat to any woman. She was glad to hear it, and exceedingly grateful to Nick for his timely intervention. All the same, it was galling to discover that while she had been working her fingers to the bone, cleaning his house for him, he had been amusing himself with ladies of easy virtue. *Inventive* ladies of easy virtue, whatever that meant. She knew she was badly out of her depth with this man, and it irked her. It damn well infuriated her.

Her move was so ferocious, so sudden, that even she was surprised by the result. Gray staggered back on his heels, did a little half-turn, and went spinning toward the open fire. Nick sprang to his feet. Deborah got there before him. With a squeal of fright, she made a dive for Gray and caught him by the coattails not a moment before he went sprawling on the hot coals. One yank brought him teetering back on his heels to fall with a thump on his rear end.

"I say, Deborah," began Nick.

Gray waved a hand airily above his head. "No, don't meddle, Nick. That's her love play. She's quite the Amazon once she gets started. No, really, I'm coming to appreciate the strong, masterful type of woman. It makes a man wonder who is going to come out on top."

This was evidently a huge joke, for both gentlemen chortled into their hands.

Glaring furiously from one to the other, Deborah took a few quick paces around the room. "You are a disgrace to your rank and class," she stormed at them.

"Yes, so you have already told me," said Gray, looking more like a mischievous schoolboy than a thoroughgoing degenerate. "Look, I've brought you a present."

She took the garters from him without thinking, then gasped.

He flashed her a cozening grin. "I was sure you would like them, you know, because your own things are so plain and serviceable."

Her voice rose alarmingly. "And you thought to please me by giving me another woman's cast-offs?"

"They're not cast-offs. I won them in a game of dice."

He stopped speaking when she stomped to the fire and threw the garters with great deliberation on top of the glowing coals.

There was a silence, then Gray said sulkily, "If they don't suit, perhaps something else will. That's not all I won, by any means."

When he began to fish in his coat pockets, and Nick made a warning sound, Deborah stamped her foot. "Have you no sense of—" She stopped in mid-sentence, suddenly struck by her own stupidity. This conversation was ludicrous. She was berating him as though he were an errant husband and she were a jealous wife. He was her *abductor*. She was his *captive*. Moments before he had entered the room, only one thought had possessed her mind. Escape. Yet here she was again, going off like a rocket over something that could not possibly be of any interest to herself. Worse than that was the fact that she had saved him from toppling onto the hot coals. If she had been in her right mind, she would have given him a push. She must be mad. Oh God, she had to escape before she completely lost her senses.

Ignoring the frilly piece of underclothing Gray held out to her, she said to Nick, "Where is Hart?"

"He's taking care of the horses, and, um, lighting the way for the company we are expecting."

"Company?" she repeated carefully.

"Mostly for Hart's benefit," said Gray, "though not entirely." He pulled to his knees, then to his feet, and with a helping hand from Nick, managed to seat himself at the table. As he stuffed the article of female clothing back into his pocket, he watched her from beneath the concealment of his lashes. "Like myself, Hart is a connoisseur of fine jewels. He will appreciate the gesture."

"Jewels?"

He smiled. "Even you could not be that innocent, Deborah. Amber? Garnet? Pearl? Ruby? Oh, no need to look disgruntled. You are still the diamond, still the prize."

She could not believe what her mind was telling her. Not even *he* could be that steeped in vice. A glance at Nick's painfully apologetic expression destroyed that faint hope. A warm tide of color crept under her skin. He was going to turn the cottage into his own private den of iniquity, and she was to be a part of it. Numb with fear, she watched as Nick went to the sideboard and fetched glasses and a bottle of brandy. Sloshing liquid into two glasses, he handed one to Gray.

"I want to go to my room," she said, looking beseechingly at Nick.

Gray gulped down a fortifying swallow of liquor. "Oh no, Deborah," he said. "That does not suit me. You, my pet, are going to take part in the orgy."

Orgy. The very word brought to mind every wild rumor she had ever heard about the depravity of men of his class. She would be forced to take opium and be passed from man to man, and when they were finished with her, they would sell her into sexual slavery in some brothel or other.

"I'm going to be sick," she whispered, and made a dash for the door.

Gray half rose to his feet, but Nick was faster. "I'll see to her," he said, and grabbing for her cloak, he followed her outside.

Deborah stumbled down the steps and leaned against the outside wall where she retched several times in dry spasms. She was leaning weakly against the wall when Nick caught up to her.

"If you were any kind of man, you would put a stop to this," she said, trying to sound angry instead of terrified out of her wits.

"I intend to."

"You are as bad as . . . what did you say?"

He wrapped her cloak around her shoulders. "Trust me, Deborah. I've taken care of everything."

She wasn't quite ready to believe him. "What have you taken care of? Why should I trust you?"

"I persuaded Gray to while away an hour or two in the Jewel Box, did I not? Oh, I know. That ploy was not as successful as I had hoped it would be. You've become an obsession with him, you see. Women have always come easily to Gray. He doesn't take rejection well."

Her mind fastened on the one thing that really mattered to her. "How can I get away from here? The others will prevent it."

"Gray is in no condition to prevent anything. And you may leave Hart to me."

Her pulse was pounding with excitement. "Oh Nick, if you would only saddle one of the horses for me."

He shook his head. "Then Gray would know I had a part in your escape. It's more than my skin is worth."

"But I can't walk all the way to Wells in this kind of weather and in the dark," she cried out.

"I'm not asking you to. Listen to me carefully. The consignment from the Jewel Box will be here at any moment. The coachmen have orders to return for the girls some time tomorrow. You, my dear Deborah, are going to be in that empty coach tonight when it makes the journey to the King's Arms. After that, you will have to fend for yourself."

"Why the King's Arms?"

"That's where Gray is stabling his horses, and where the coachmen are putting up. You must see that we can't have them here."

"But what about Lord Kendal and Hart? Won't they come after me?"

"As I said, you may leave them to me."

A confusion of questions raced through her mind, but before she could put any of them to Nick, the sounds of a coach and horses approaching came from the other side of the house.

Nick's hand closed around her arm. "It's now or never," he said, and began to propel her along the path that led to the front entrance. They paused in the shadows at the corner of the house and watched as the coach came to a shuddering halt. Hart, with a lantern in his hand, stepped forward and opened the coach door. Gray stood, none too steadily, on the front step, with light streaming out from behind him.

"Stay here until I give the signal," said Nick softly, and he went to join the others.

Deborah shrank back against the wall of the house, concealing herself behind a screen of climbing ivy. Everything was happening so fast that there wasn't time to sift through all that Nick had told her. But she trusted him. She clung to that thought, ruthlessly suppressing her vague uncertainties.

Her eyes went wide when the coach's passengers began to alight. For all that it was September and raining, these ladies looked as though they were dressed in nothing more substantial than diaphanous veils. The wind gusted and the veils flew up, revealing a wide expanse of pink flesh. The girls giggled. The men laughed appreciatively. Deborah shut her mouth with a snap.

She counted five girls. Two of them looped their arms around Gray's neck. She almost snorted. By the look on his face, it would be hours before he would remember the existence of Deborah Weyman. He led the way into the house, and Hart and the other girls followed. There remained only the coachmen and Nick.

"We shall see you tomorrow, then," said Nick, "toward noon."

"Aye, sir. That you will," answered the driver.

"Hang on a moment. This door is not shut properly."

Nick strode to the nearside door and jerked it open with one hand, signaling to Deborah with the other to come out of her hiding place. She crept forward, flattened herself against the back of the carriage and quickly moved to the door Nick held for her. When she had climbed in, he slammed the door closed.

"That's better," he said. "One of the girls must have left it open. Goodbye, Jenkins. Goodbye, Rankin. Oh, and good luck," and with that cryptic remark, which Deborah knew was meant for herself, he entered the house.

The stench of cheap perfume inside the coach put Deborah in mind of the perfume she had smelled on Gray's skin. It was just the right note to steady her nerves. Teeth chattering, she shrank into the folds of her cloak, not daring to draw breath as the coach lurched into motion.

It was the longest drive of her life, not because Wells was far distant from the cottage, but because the driver went at a snail's pace, fearful, she supposed, of coming to grief with his lordship's horses in that filthy weather.

At every moment, she expected to hear the thunder of hooves in hot pursuit. There was nothing but the moan of the wind and the driver's incessant chatter to the other coachman, cataloguing his master's amorous adventures, which were legion by the sound of it. From their laughter, she deduced that the coachmen did not take as dim a view as she of Lord Kendal's depravity.

By the time they reached Wells, her nerves were stretched taut. She could not believe how easily everything had worked out. She gave Nick the credit for it. Without his intervention, she would never have made it so far. He had deliberately engineered her escape, from the moment he had persuaded Lord Kendal to while away an hour or two in that disreputable bawdy house to the carriage that had been made available to convey her to Wells. Even now, he had provided the means to keep Kendal and Hart occupied while she made good her escape. One day, God willing, she hoped she would be in a position to thank Nick for all he had done for her. As for his brother, the earl . . .

She would never see Lord Kendal again. The knowledge did not act on her as she thought it would. She should be ecstatic. Instead, she felt an odd tightening in her chest, and she was appalled. She wasn't sorry to see the last of him, she told herself devoutly. She couldn't be. He had wormed his way into her confidence, tricked her, abducted and abused her. A sane woman would hate him with a passion. A sane woman would be thinking of boiling oil and the rack in her lust to be revenged on that cur. If there was any lingering regret, it was for Mr. Gray, and since that gentleman did not exist except in her own imagination, there was nothing to lament.

She came to herself with a start when the carriage made a turn and rolled into the stable yard of the King's Arms. Ears straining, heart thudding, she sank down and carefully closed her fingers around the door handle. As soon as the carriage came to a stop, she opened the door and jumped down.

Ostlers came running, but they paid her scant attention as they ran to unharness the horses. She slipped by them, then chanced a quick glance over her shoulder.

Lord Kendal's coachmen were only now descending from the box, and even if they had caught sight of her, she did not think it would occur to them that she had been a passenger in the coach. Anyone seeing her now would take her for a woman of the lower orders whose business had taken her to the inn. She wore no gloves or hat. Her shoes were scuffed; the dress that peeked from beneath her cloak was mired and stained from her labors that morning. She looked like a scullery maid or a washer woman, and it suited her to play that role. An unescorted lady would attract attention. A working woman could come and go as she pleased.

It surprised her that the inn's common rooms were filled with patrons. Wells was a small place, and country people went early to bed. From the cultured accents and snatches of conversation, it seemed that most of the inn's patrons were visitors. Head well down, she traversed the corridor, passed the common rooms, and came to the front doors.

Here, she hesitated, and made as though she were glancing around casually. Having assured herself that no one was watching her, she pushed through the doors and into the High Street. It was dark, much darker than it should have been given the hour. She looked up, but an overcast sky veiled the moon and the constellations of stars. The only light to guide her steps came from lanterns hanging outside every other house and building.

Turning up her collar against the light drizzle, she struck out in the direction of the marketplace. Before long, she turned left onto a street of two- and three-storied buildings, many of them commercial properties, which overlooked the wide expanse of the cathedral green. There were still pedestrians about, and the odd carriage and rider, but they seemed as eager as she to make for home and get in out of the rain. No one gave her a second glance. As she approached a draper's shop, her steps slowed, and she looked up at the private dwellings above the shop front. From one of the windows, a lone candle cast a feeble glow. Deborah tried not to stare, tried not to give in to the flood of emotion that threatened to overwhelm her. She shouldn't be here, she shouldn't be putting Quentin in danger like this, but without money or friends, she didn't know where else to turn.

Moving with less caution now, she made a turn, then another, and came out onto the walled lane at the back of the houses. There were no lights here, and she exclaimed softly as she stumbled unsuspectingly through puddles and muddy potholes. At the fourth gate along, she stopped and crouched down, tracing the pattern of the bricks in the wall till she came to the one she wanted. Beneath a loose brick, she found the key to the back gate. Her breathing was audible and her fingers trembled as she let herself into the garden and locked the gate behind her. At the back of the draper's shop, there was an outside stone staircase leading to the floor above. On mounting that steep staircase, she paused to even her breathing. From this vantage point, she could see over the walled lane to the backs of the houses in the next street. There were a few lights at windows, but all was quiet, all was as it should be. Not even a cat was stirring in that dreary night.

She used the edge of her cloak to blot the moisture from her face. Exhaling a long, shivery breath, she rapped softly on the stout wooden door that barred her entrance. Some moments passed, and Deborah rapped on the door again, this time with more force. When the door creaked open, Deborah swiftly pushed into the house and shut the door behind her.

"Deborah! What brings you here at this time of night?" Mrs. Nan Moffat was close to sixty, and her light brown eyes, which were usually as bright as buttons, were shaded with alarm.

Deborah knew she must look like a wild woman with her dripping wet hair plastered to her head, and her mud-spattered garments, but she was in no mood for explanations. There would be time for that later. She had to see Quentin, had to assure herself that he was safe and well.

"Quentin," she said, swallowing the lump in her throat. "Give me a few minutes alone with him, all right? Then I shall come down and speak with you both.

No, there's no need to look like that. Everything is fine, really. I just want to see him."

Mrs. Moffat looked as though she might argue the point, then her plump face softened. "I'll put the kettle on," she said, "and tell John you are here."

"Nan? Who is it? Who are you speaking to?"

As John Moffat came out of the back parlor, Deborah turned and quickly mounted the stairs that led to the attics. Quentin's door was the first she came to. Turning the handle, she pushed open the door and quietly slipped into the room.

Though the boy was sleeping, the candle on the wooden mantel was lit. Ever since the night of his father's murder, Quentin had been afraid to go to sleep in the dark. Crossing the room on tiptoe, Deborah halted by the bed and stared down at the sleeping child.

In looks, he took after his father, dark hair and eyes, but whereas Lord Barrington had enjoyed robust health, his son was delicate. It had been a great cause of concern to them all, and still was. Added to that was a new anxiety. Quentin never talked about his father and Deborah never forced him to.

Had she done right by him? There was no sure answer to that question. She had done the best she could. She had left him with people he knew and trusted. Before her marriage, Nan Moffat had been nurse to Quentin, and to his father before him. John Moffat had once been Lord Barrington's steward. When the time came for them to retire, they had surprised everyone by marrying and setting down new roots in Wells where they had opened a draper's shop.

They'd been shocked when Deborah had shown up at their door with Quentin, and even more shocked at the story she had told of events in Paris. She had told them almost everything. What she had kept from them was Lord Kendal's name. The Moffats had known him since he was a boy. They liked him, trusted him, and Deborah was afraid they would not believe a word she said if she accused him of murdering Lord Barrington. And so she had told them she didn't know who was pursuing them, but that Quentin's life was in mortal danger. She'd done more than that. She'd told them a bare-faced lie. She'd said that Quentin's uncle in the West Indies was now his guardian, and they must wait until he came to fetch the boy.

If Quentin's health had been more robust, she would not have hesitated to take him to his uncle in person. As it was, she did not wish to chance that long sea voyage, not yet. But she would, if it became necessary.

Sinking onto the bed, she touched her fingers to his hair, brushing it away from his forehead. His lips turned up in a smile.

"Deb?" he said, and his eyes opened.

"I thought you were asleep."

"And I thought you were Aunt Nan until I smelled you. Where have you been? You didn't come on Wednesday."

There was no reproach in his tone, only a matter-of-fact curiosity, and Deborah felt a rush of gratitude to the Moffats for the care they had so obviously lavished upon him.

"I told you how it would be," she said lightly. "I can't get away from school as often as I would like. What happened to your tooth?"

He touched a finger to the gap in his front teeth, then diving under his pillow, he came up with a small porcelain tooth. "Look," he said.

Deborah examined it closely. "There's blood on it," she said.

Quentin beamed up at her. "Uncle John tied a string from my tooth to the doorknob, and when Aunt Nan opened the door, she pulled the tooth out. It was *agony*. Uncle John said I was as brave as a lion."

"Did he, indeed? And why is the tooth under your pillow?"

"Oh, you know. It's supposed to change into a penny when I'm asleep. But I know there's no such thing as magic. That's why I stayed awake. I was sure Aunt Nan was going to take away my tooth and leave a penny in its place."

His grin was magic. It wrenched at her heart. "You don't believe in magic?"

"Of course not! I'm not a baby."

She smiled at this, then her whole body went rigid as a terrible thundering came from below. Paralyzed with shock, she stared at the open door. When she heard voices raised in anger, she rose quickly, crossed to the door, and crept to the head of the stairs. What she saw made her fling herself flat against the wall. Lord Kendal, as sober and fierce as a judge, was tapping his riding crop against his thigh. Behind him stood Nick. The Moffats were wringing their hands, obviously trying to placate him. Deborah did not wait to see more. Though she felt the shock of discovery all through her body, she did not give in to it. Her thoughts were already leaping ahead to Quentin and how she could get him away.

"Deb, what is it?" Quentin was already out of bed and pulling on his breeches.

There was no key in the lock. "We are going on a journey," she said. "You remember, I told you it might come to this? No, leave your nightshirt on, and tuck it under your breeches. You'll need your coat and your shoes. *Hurry, Quentin.*" As she spoke she dragged a small upright chair to the door and set it at an angle against the doorknob. That should delay their pursuers for a moment or two.

"It's him, isn't it?" Quentin's voice held a betraying wobble. "The man who is after us? The man who murdered my father?"

Her blood was humming, and every sense was razor sharp. Her voice was low and controlled. "Yes, it's him. Go stand by the window while I blow out the candle."

No sooner had she blown out the candle than she heard feet taking the stairs. Forcing down her panic, she quickly crossed to the dormer window which gave direct access to the roof. "I'll go first. Don't worry, darling. Nothing will happen to us. Uncle John will send for the magistrates. All we need do is stay on the roof until they get here."

She didn't know where the soothing words were coming from. She didn't believe a word of what she said. If it had been only herself, she would have been screaming her head off. "As brave as a lion," she whispered to him softly, and clambered over the sill.

He took her hand with all the confidence of a child who believes that those watching over him possess the powers of demigods. Deborah was well aware that she was far more frightened than he. She pointed to the row of chimneys standing high on the roofline, and he nodded. If they could make it to the other side of the stacks before Lord Kendal thought to look on the roof for them, they might yet stand a chance of evading capture.

When they were both on the roof, she slid the window shut, then, crablike, they crawled toward the smoking stacks. It was much worse than Deborah had anticipated. The rain had made the slates slippery and the wind gusted about them like a mad dervish, tugging at their clothes, stealing their words before they were half out of their mouths. If she'd had time to prepare, she would have roped Quentin to her. As it was, she held on to his hand for dear life.

They heard the noise of a door shattering and Lord Kendal's voice raised thunderously, demanding that they show themselves.

"Don't look back!" shouted Deborah, and she tugged on his hand, urging him on. They had almost reached their goal when Quentin was overcome by a fit of coughing. They dared not delay. Murmuring words of encouragement, she slipped an arm around the boy's waist, and with the remnants of her strength, dragged him the last yard or two, till they were sheltering on the other side of the stacks. The bricks were warm to their touch, and they huddled against them, catching their breath.

"Deborah? Quentin?" Lord Kendal's voice reached them from the other side of their hiding place. "I know you are out here. You barred the door. There is nowhere else for you to go. Answer me, damn you!"

Cursing herself for that foolish mistake, Deborah looked around wildly. So he knew they were on the roof, but he didn't know which way they had gone. With luck, Kendal would go in the opposite direction.

She must find a way to get them off the roof, perhaps through one of the other dormer windows or . . .

Her glance was caught and held by a depression in the roof only three or four yards farther on. She rose to her feet to get a closer picture. It wasn't a depression. It was a skylight into the attics of one of the other houses. Excitement shivered through her. All was not yet lost. Motioning Quentin to remain where he was, she slowly edged her way toward it. The wind whipped at her, almost overbalancing her.

Quentin's cry of alarm had her spinning on her heel. The boy had risen to his feet to face the man who stalked them.

Gray held out one hand. His voice was soft and as soothing as he could make it in that near gale. "Come to me, Quentin. It's Uncle Gray. Don't you remember me?"

"You are not my uncle," warbled the boy. "You can't be. Deb!" he cried out, and lunged for the safety of her arms.

She was already edging back toward him, reaching for him. Their fingers touched, but rain-slicked skin slid over skin and she could not hold him. She shrilled his name as he slipped away from her. Aghast, she sank to her knees and went after him, desperately grabbing at empty air.

"Get down on your knees, boy!"

Quentin obeyed Gray's terse command, but it could not save him. Whimpering, he slipped closer to the edge of the roof. Deborah was paralyzed with terror. Her mouth opened, but the scream in her head came out as a moan.

As in a dream, she saw Kendal dive for the boy. They rolled, and came to a stop on the one place on that long ledge where there was a decorative pediment.

She was sobbing quietly as other shadows moved into her line of vision.

"I'll take the boy, Gray." Nick's voice. "Come along, Quentin. Don't you remember your uncle Nick? That's the way, son. Put your arms around my neck. You're safe now."

"Is it really you, Uncle Nick?"

The voices faded as man and boy passed behind the chimney stacks. Then *he* was there before her, and she slowly lifted her head to look into his face.

He held out his hand and she grasped it, blinking away tears and raindrops, trying to clear her vision. She couldn't see his face, but his voice left her in no doubt of his sentiments.

"I have never been more tempted in my life to thrash a woman," he said.

CHAPTER 9

"You thought *what?*" roared Gray.

Deborah reached for her cup and took another sip of tea with the reviving measure of brandy Gray had insisted on adding to it. She coughed to clear her throat. "I thought you had murdered Lord Barrington," she said.

Her voice shook almost as badly as her fingers, and it wasn't only in reaction to the catastrophe that had almost overtaken them on the roof. The intimidating man who towered over her visibly quivered in masculine outrage. She was afraid to look him in the eye.

Gray glowered down at her. Her eyes darted up to meet his, then quickly dropped away. Her mouth trembled, and she shrank into the folds of her warm dressing gown in an unconscious attempt to make herself look smaller.

"Drink your tea," said Gray, and reaching for the fire tongs, he turned aside to add several lumps of coal to the embers in the grate.

Deborah was relieved by his altered tone and, at the same time, anxious about the coal he was adding to the fire. It looked to her as though the interview with Lord Kendal were far from over. It would be another hour before the fire died down and they could all troop off to their beds. Having bathed and changed into her night clothes, she longed for the oblivion of sleep in a soft, comfortable bed.

Her eyes strayed to the closed door, willing someone to enter the little parlor and distract Lord Kendal's attention from her. There was little hope of that happening. Quentin was sleeping in his bed, and Mr. and Mrs. Moffat were ensconced in the kitchen with orders to wait there until his lordship could question them also. She wasn't sure where Nick and Hart were. They had fetched her portmanteau, and after spending some time with Quentin, they had gone off on some errand or other for his lordship.

Gray seated himself on the chair facing Deborah's. "Now," he said, "shall we go through this again? You ran off with Quentin in Dover because you were convinced I had murdered his father and would do the same to the boy?"

"Yes," she whispered, and sniffed.

"You thought that I was the murderer?"

She nodded once and edged into the corner of her chair. Her enormous eyes were brimming.

"The murderer," said Gray, forcing his voice to remain neutral when what he really wanted to do was yell at her. His legendary control was slipping away from him, and he knew why. Those few minutes on the roof had shaken him badly. For one heart-stopping moment, he had thought he was going to lose both of them. He hadn't understood her panic, hadn't guessed at the lengths she would go to evade him. Now that she had given him the reason, it didn't put him in a better frame of mind. *Murderer.* His whole life had been devoted to serving his country. No one had ever questioned his integrity. True, in the last few days he had deliberately tried to intimidate her. But murderer? That was going too far.

He surveyed her intently. She was very pale and she couldn't seem to stop shaking. "I told you to drink your tea," he said.

She hastened to obey him, and took several long swallows, eyeing him warily over the rim of her cup.

"You didn't act as though you thought I was a murderer," he said moodily, recalling those moments when she had melted in his arms, and other occasions when she had given him the sharp edge of her tongue.

"No," she said in a constricted tone, then tilted her cup to drink the dregs of her tea.

He drummed his fingers on the wooden armrest. "Do you still think I am a murderer?"

She shook her head vigorously. "Oh no. When you saved Quentin out there on the roof, when I couldn't hold him," she gulped, "I knew I had made a ghastly mistake."

Just remembering what she had put him through when she had slid toward the edge of the roof as she reached for Quentin revived his fury. His voice rose alarmingly. "Do you realize you might both be dead by now? Can you imagine how I would feel? I would hold myself responsible for the rest of my life, and I would never know why—" He broke off as her mouth began to work and fresh tears flooded her eyes.

Sighing, he reached in his coat pocket and produced a handkerchief. She accepted it gingerly and dabbed at her eyes.

When she began to twist his handkerchief into hopeless knots, he plucked it from her. "Let's start again, shall we?" he said gently, and managed a forced smile. "Tell me what happened that night."

She nodded her compliance. "There was a thunderstorm, and Quentin's bed was empty. I saw a light under the library door and went to investigate, thinking, you see, that Quentin was playing a trick on me."

When she paused, he said quietly, "As I understand it, Lady Barrington left a few days before, to return to England, but you stayed on because Quentin was not fit to travel?"

"Lord Barrington had arranged for the three of us, that is, Lady Barrington, Quentin, and myself, to travel with the Capets. But when Quentin came down with a fever, I stayed behind to look after him."

"I see. So whoever came that night to meet Gil had no way of knowing that you and Quentin were still there?"

She thought about this for a moment. "I shouldn't think so. With Quentin feeling so poorly, Lord Barrington rarely left the house, so I don't think he had the opportunity to mention it to anyone. But I can't be sure."

"Go on. You saw a light coming from under the library door? Then what?"

"Then I heard voices."

"What did you hear?"

She swallowed as the memory came back to her. "Lord Barrington, pleading with you"—she sucked in a breath when his eyes flashed—"pleading with someone to spare the boy's life."

"I don't understand. Where was Quentin?"

"He was there, in the library."

"So Quentin witnessed the murder? Is that what you are saying?"

She gave a little hiccup and nodded.

His tone rose sharply. "And the boy said he saw *me?*"

"No, no. You don't understand. Quentin has no recollection of what happened between the time he entered the library and the moment he found himself on the packet that brought us home to England. The physician says he may never remember. The shock of seeing his father murdered before his eyes was too much for him. He doesn't want to remember."

He stared at her for a long interval. "We shall return to this later," he said. "Go on. Tell me exactly what Gil said."

"I can't remember his exact words, but he said your name, not once but twice . . ."

"What did he say?"

She looked down at her clasped hands. "He said, 'Kendal, Lord Kendal, don't harm the boy.' Then he said, 'Quentin, run for it.' That's all I remember."

"You are sure he said 'Lord Kendal'?"

"Yes," she said, carefully avoiding his eyes.

"Gil would never call me by my title." Her eyes flew to his and he went on deliberately. "We had known each other since we were schoolboys, long before either of us came into our titles. If we were conversing face-to-face, he would call me Gray, just as I would call him Gil. If I were to speak of him to someone else, someone who did not know him well, I would refer to him as Lord Barrington. Do you understand what I am saying? It seems to me that I was the subject of conversation between Gil and whoever it was he met that night."

She looked at him fixedly. "It wasn't only that. I knew you had an appointment with him. As soon as I saw the light under the library door, I remembered it."

"I received a note canceling that appointment."

"I knew nothing of that."

After a moment, he said, "Did Gil have an appointment with anyone else?"

"Not to my knowledge."

Observing that her cup was empty, he reached for a bottle on the floor by his chair and poured some brandy into it. He did the same with his own cup.

"You are beginning to shake again," he said. "This will steady your nerves. Drink it." He waited until she had brought the cup to her lips before he took a long, fortifying swallow of his own drink.

After a moment or two, he said, "Let's leave that for the moment, shall we, and tell me what happened next."

She looked longingly at the closed door and he said gently, "Yes, I know. You are exhausted. These last two days have been far from pleasant for either of us."

"And whose fault is that?" she demanded, managing a faint edge of defiance in spite of her quivering lips and brimming eyes.

His brows went up, but he was not displeased to see that she was rallying. He had debated about questioning her in the morning, after she was rested, but had decided against it. At the moment, she was receptive because he had saved Quentin's life. There was no telling how she would feel in the morning, but he suspected that she might put the blame for everything onto his shoulders. For the moment, the advantage was with him and he intended to press it.

"Tell me what happened next," he prompted.

She took a minuscule swallow from her cup before

answering him. "I must have acted instinctively. I flung the door open just after the gun went off, and Quentin came bounding into my arms."

"You saw the murderer?" he asked sharply.

"I saw someone in the shadows, standing over Lord Barrington's body." She gave a strained laugh. "I didn't think about what I was doing, didn't think about going to Lord Barrington's assistance. I grabbed Quentin, and we ran."

"And Gil's assailant saw you?"

"No. I had no candle, and the hall was in darkness. It's highly unlikely that he saw more than a shadow. On the other hand, it would be easy for him to work out that if Quentin was still in the house, his governess would be there also."

Gray nodded at this. "Then what happened?"

Her lips quivered. "It was horrible. I slammed the door shut, but still he came after us. The servants were in their beds and though I suppose I knew the shot would waken them, I did not think they would reach us in time. We hid behind the curtains in the blue saloon." She shuddered. "I knew he was there. I could hear his harsh breathing in the darkness, and was terrified that he would hear us too. Then . . . then . . . I don't know. The servants must have frightened him off."

"And afterward? What did you tell the French authorities?"

"Nothing, at least, nothing of any significance." When he gave her a blank look, she said quickly, "We were at war with the French. And anyway, what could they do? I didn't want to delay in case they kept us in France for the duration of the war. There was no one there to help me. I had to get Quentin home. I had to. So, I told them nothing."

"I see. And afterward, when you reached Dover, you took Quentin and ran?"

She dropped her eyes and nodded. "I got the scare of my life when your coachmen approached me and told me that you had sent them to fetch us."

There was a long, uncomfortable silence, then Gray said, "You could not hope to hide Quentin here indefinitely. What were you going to do with him in the years to come?"

Her lower lip trembled. "I've written to his uncle in the West Indies. I was hoping he would take him."

"George?" said Gray. "You wrote to George?" One part of his mind admired her ingenuity, another part was appalled by it. This girl stopped at nothing.

"Yes," she said miserably. "I didn't know what else to do."

"Why didn't you go to the authorities? When you reached England, why didn't you go to the authorities? It's what a sane person would have done."

She stuck her nose in the air. "What was I to tell them? That I suspected *you*, a peer of the realm? If you denied it, as I had no doubt you would, what then? I knew you were named as Quentin's guardian. He would go to you. I wasn't going to let that happen." A thought occurring to her, she burst out, "I might ask you the same question. Why didn't you go to the authorities if you thought I had abducted Quentin? I read the papers and there was nothing."

He spent the next few minutes describing his own actions and the reasons behind them once it became clear to him that she had abducted Quentin. He held nothing back, going so far as to tell her of the traitor at the Foreign Office and how he had been sure she was working hand in glove with him. It pleased him enormously that by the end of his recitation, she was glaring at him like a scalded cat. It was evident that she was no more pleased to have been suspected of murder than he had been.

Ignoring that look, he said, "You were named as Quentin's guardian also. Were you aware of that, Deborah?"

"Hmm," she snorted. "Much good that would have done me. I am a woman, and therefore of no consequence. My opinions would carry no weight. How could I oppose you?"

Abruptly leaning forward, he grasped her chin and held her face up to the light. She emitted a startled cry, but made no move to evade him. "You sound," he said, "as though some man has treated you badly. Who are you, Deborah Weyman? What are you hiding from me?"

There was a flash of fear in the eyes that stared doggedly into his, then her lashes swept down and when she lifted them the fear was gone. "I am hiding nothing," she said, "and if I were, you are the last person in whom I would confide. After tomorrow, I pray that our paths may never cross again."

"That's an odd thing to say if you hope to see Quentin again."

"You mean . . ."—she took a slow breath—"you would still allow me to see him, from time to time, after everything that's happened?"

His tone was thoughtful. "I haven't made up my mind what I am going to do with you yet."

She jerked out of his grasp. "I see. You are going to hand me over to the magistrates for abducting Quentin, is that it?"

"Don't be ridiculous. All things considered, you behaved with remarkable intelligence in the boy's interests. I can't fault you there."

Slightly appeased, she said, "Then I don't understand why you are threatening me."

"Do I threaten you, Deborah?" he asked whimsically.

His cool blue eyes met hers in a curiously speculative look. She felt the power of that look all through her body. It made her exceedingly self-conscious. What did he see with those shrewd blue eyes of his? Having bathed and donned her high-necked linen night shift, and her warm woolen dressing gown, she was perfectly respectable. When that look lingered, she fought the temptation to touch a hand to the tendrils of damp hair which curled around her face, or clutch at the edges of her robe as though to shield herself from his gaze. Suddenly conscious that her bare toes were peeking from under her voluminous garments, she quickly hid them. His lips quirked. When he moved his hand, she jumped.

"Deborah," he said, "I was merely reaching for my snuffbox."

They both looked up at the ceiling as something fell to the floor in the room above. A moment later, when Quentin's voice was heard calling for Deborah, she sprang to her feet and raced to the door. Gray followed at a more leisurely pace.

Quentin's room was in darkness. Deborah lost no time in striking a flint and getting a candle lit.

"It was so dark, I could hear him breathing," sobbed Quentin. His arms were around Mrs. Moffat and he was sobbing into her motherly bosom. "And when I tried to run from him, I tripped and fell."

Deborah sat on the other side of the bed and placed one hand on his shoulder, patting him comfortingly. "There, there, darling. Don't think about it. It was only a bad dream."

Quentin turned into her arms and burrowed close to the warmth of her body.

"Whose breathing did you hear?" Gray had come to stand at the end of the bed. Deborah flashed him a warning look which he ignored. "Whose breathing was it, Quentin?"

Quentin blinked rapidly, coming to himself. "It must have been Uncle Nick's. He read me a story, but I fell asleep. When I awakened, the room was in darkness."

Mrs. Moffat clicked her tongue. "I never thought to tell your uncle to leave the candle lit. There, there now, dearie. The candle is lit and Miss Weyman is going to sleep in this room with you, so you see there is nothing to fear."

Quentin's face visibly brightened. "Are you going to sleep in my bed with me, Deb?"

"If you want me to," she said fondly.

"Certainly not." Gray's tone was just short of being impatient. His eyes were fixed on Deborah's. "I won't have the boy babied."

Her hackles rose, but before she could say anything annihilating, Quentin forestalled her. "I'm *not* a baby. It was only a joke, Uncle Gray. Truly."

Gray smiled. "You and I both know that, old sport, but women can't help being women. They like nothing better than to fuss over us poor males as though we were puppies. My advice to you is to head them off before they get started."

"I do not fuss!" declared Deborah wrathfully. "Furthermore, I think I know what is best for Quentin."

"Perhaps," said Gray, folding his arms across his chest, "but that is by no means established yet."

Mrs. Moffat looked uncertainly from one to the other. "I made up the trundle bed for you, Miss Weyman," she said nervously, indicating the bed by the wall. "And you are to sleep in the spare bedchamber, Lord Kendal."

"No," he said. "I prefer to sleep in this room, with Quentin. Miss Weyman may take the spare bedchamber."

Once again, Deborah's retort was stayed by Quentin's excited intervention. "Do you really mean it, Uncle Gray? You don't mind sharing a room with me?"

"I should be honored. Besides, we men must stick together."

"And . . . and . . ." Quentin swallowed before going on resolutely. "I don't mind if you put the candle out. I'm not afraid of the dark. I'm not afraid of *anything*."

Deborah could hardly believe her ears. Quentin was terrified of the dark. She had tried, repeatedly, to cure him of this fear, to no avail. Now, after an hour or two in Kendal's company, the boy would do anything to please him. It was as though she had ceased to exist.

She looked away and her glance was caught by Gray's before she dragged her eyes from his.

Though Gray addressed his remarks to Quentin, his eyes were on Deborah. "Douse the candle? Why should I do that? I always sleep with a candle lit, and no one has ever accused me of being afraid of the dark. Let them dare, and I should call them out." He bent over the boy and pulled the covers up to his chin. His voice was very soft, very soothing, and Deborah felt a burning sensation at the back of her eyes. "Now off to sleep with you, there's a good fellow. I wish to speak with Aunt Nan and Uncle John, then I shall come to bed. This will only take a few minutes. Say your good-nights to the ladies."

In the corridor, when Deborah made to descend the stairs, Gray stopped her with a look.

"Good night, Deborah," he said deliberately.

Mrs. Moffat continued on down the stairs without a backward glance. Evidently, this was to be a private conversation.

"Good night," retorted Deborah, and turning on her heel, she marched into her chamber and shut the door with a snap.

Sleep did not come as quickly as she thought it would. Though every bone in her body ached with fatigue, her brain felt as if an electric storm were trapped inside it. She couldn't hold one thought for more than a few minutes at a time. She shuddered convulsively as the memory of the chase on the roof came back to her. She bristled when she recalled the indignities she had been made to suffer at *his* hands. But the thought that finally lingered was that Quentin was no longer hers. She was glad, exceedingly glad, that things had turned out the way they had, but now that her terrors had been relieved, she couldn't help thinking of the future, and the future looked bleak and empty.

There was no place for her in Quentin's life now. A boy of eight would have a tutor. She'd known that from the day she had become his governess. He would write to her, of course, when she found a new position, but gradually his letters would dwindle and dry up altogether. Miss Hare had warned her what to expect.

But she was his guardian! Surely that counted for something? She would be entitled to see him occasionally, and receive reports on his progress. Oh God, she didn't know if she could bear it.

Sniffing, she turned on her side and tried to think of something pleasant. The voices from below, faint though they were, distracted her. Though she could not hear what was being said, she was convinced that she was the subject of conversation. Lord Kendal was a tenacious man. He would be questioning the Moffats in minute detail, trying to find discrepancies in her story.

Who are you, Deborah Weyman? What are you hiding from me? She drifted into sleep wondering if the time would ever come when she could be truly herself.

An hour later, when Gray entered the bedchamber he was to share with Quentin, he was reflecting on what the Moffats had told him. They had corroborated Deborah's story except in one particular. She had told them she didn't know who the murderer was. He understood her reticence. She must have known that if she had accused him of the murder, the Moffats would not, could not have accepted it. They had known him from the time he and Gil got up to deviltry as schoolboys at Eton, to their scrapes in the petticoat line, years later, as young bucks on the town. Even if a judge and jury convicted him of the crime, they would still believe him innocent.

He was, however, no nearer to plumbing the mystery surrounding Deborah's past. Deborah was a darling, according to Mrs. Moffat, and that was about the sum of it. They knew nothing of her origins, or her life before she had become Quentin's governess.

Gray could picture, without much difficulty, the solitary existence Deborah must have led. A governess's position was awkward at the best of times. In Deborah's case, it must have been painfully lonely. Before his marriage, Gil rarely entertained. For the most part, he lived in London, while Quentin spent his days in the country, under Deborah's supervision. It would have been better for her if she had found a place in some respectable family of less distinction, where there were opportunities for her to meet people of her own age. Instead, she had accepted a position with Gil, knowing that she would be stranded in the country. Later, after Gil's marriage, she had accompanied Quentin to Paris. But to Gray's knowledge, she had not mixed with the diplomatic corps. This was not Gil's doing, he was sure, but Deborah's preference.

That the Moffats were her most trusted confidants next to Miss Hare he found truly disturbing. A girl like Deborah would have no difficulty in making friends of her own age or in finding herself a husband. In spite of his suspicions, he had taken to her at once, as had Nick and Hart. Then what reason did she have for shunning society?

It did not take much imagination to deduce that Deborah was running from something in her past, something that made her change her appearance whenever she came into the public eye. He couldn't begin to guess what it was, but at the same time, he didn't think it was anything he couldn't fix. How much trouble could a girl of eighteen or nineteen, as she must have been then, get into? Whatever it was, it no longer mattered. He owed her something for her care of Quentin, and he would do whatever was necessary to protect her.

He sank onto the small trundle bed and began to ease off his boots. He was on the second boot when he paused, his mind taken with the image of Deborah, not as she was but transformed into a beautiful young woman dressed in the height of fashion. He could easily picture her pouring tea in a lady's drawing room, or surrounded by beaux at some grand ball. His imagination took him further—Deborah married to some eligible young gentleman, in her own establishment, with a brood of infants hanging on her skirts. Auburn-haired infants with big green eyes and irresistible dimples, he thought, and chuckled. Deborah and marriage to some eligible young gentleman? The thought had merit. It could be done, under his mother's sponsorship. He thought about it for some time, and the more he thought about it, the more the idea appealed to him. It was the perfect solution to Deborah's problems, but whether she would accept it was another matter.

It went without saying that he must learn to keep his hands off her. He wasn't going to chastise himself for what had almost happened in the cottage. Though she was inexperienced and unaware, she was also a caldron of suppressed passion. Any red-blooded male would have fared no better than he. The man who finally won her was going to be a very lucky man, indeed. But it would not be he. She looked upon him as she might look upon a worm she'd found in an apple she was eating. No. That was not precisely right. She looked upon him as a ravening beast of prey, her ruthless captor, and that impression had stuck in her mind. He wondered if it would ever be possible to dislodge it. He wondered why he should even want to try.

He was gazing into space, lost in reverie, when the candle sputtered and went out. Cursing under his breath, he rose to his feet, and with one boot on and one boot off, hobbled to the candles on the mantel. Halfway there, he fell headlong over some obstacle that had been left lying carelessly on the floor. His roar of rage not only wakened Quentin, it also disturbed Deborah in the room next door.

She awoke to the sound of Quentin's laughter and a string of expletives that made her eyes widen with wonder. There was the sound of a flint repeatedly striking, and Quentin giving advice between gasps of hilarity. Then Lord Kendal's voice raised alarmingly, damning Miss Deborah Weyman for leaving her valise in the center of the floor for some poor unsuspecting male to break his leg on.

She shrank down in her bed and pulled the covers up to her cold nose. Lord Kendal had lost his temper and she was responsible. She fell asleep with a smile on her face.

CHAPTER 10

There is nothing like the aftermath of needless terror to rouse a person to a paroxysm of fury. This was Deborah's thought as she banged about her bedchamber, readying herself for the new day, which was already halfway over if the porcelain clock on the dresser was anything to go by. Last night, as was to be expected, she had been ravaged with remorse for having misjudged the situation and endangered Quentin's life. This morning she was cataloging all the needless terrors she had been made to suffer at *that man*'s hands, and now that she no longer feared him, her rage knew no bounds.

The sound of laughter led her to the kitchen. She knew that Hart and Nick were putting up at the King's Arms. When, however, she entered the room and found that the only occupants were Quentin and Lord Kendal, she was taken aback. What had they found to talk about? What were they laughing at? She dismissed Gray with a flick of her lashes before her gaze fixed on Quentin. There was a sparkle in his eyes and his cheeks were flushed with excitement.

Gray was reclining on a wooden chair, his booted feet resting comfortably on the flat of another chair. One look at Deborah's face told him all he needed to know. It was just as he had imagined. Now that she had recovered from her terrifying ordeal of last night, she no longer saw him as her savior. Once again, he was the ruthless abductor who had terrified the life out of her, and he would be made to pay for his sins.

At sight of Deborah, Quentin burst into a spate of excited chatter which the earl silenced by raising one hand.

"Mustn't forget the observances to the ladies," he said, and suiting action to words, he gracefully unwound himself from his chair and rose to his feet.

Quentin eyed him carefully, then followed suit.

When Deborah simply stared at them, Gray said gently, "I believe it's customary for a lady to curtsy when a gentleman pays her the compliment of recognizing her presence."

Conscious that Quentin was watching the exchange with avid interest, she bobbed a grudging curtsy and seated herself. When Gray resumed his place, so did Quentin.

Keeping her tone light, she said, "Where is everyone? What happened to my breakfast? And why wasn't I wakened before the day was half over?"

At these words, Quentin clapped a hand over his mouth and gazed dumbfounded at the clock on the mantel. "Gadzooks!" he said. "We forgot about you, Deb."

"You forgot about me?" she asked, trying not to sound offended.

"Uncle Gray was telling me stories about Papa, you know, when they were both at Eton."

"You know how it is," said Gray, unconcerned. "We got carried away. Besides, I thought you could do with an extra hour or two's rest."

"And Uncle Gray says I am going to Eton, too, just like Papa. Isn't that famous, Deb?"

"When are you going to Eton?" she asked sharply.

A look passed between man and boy. "That has yet to be decided," said Gray.

She opened her mouth to argue the point, but a speaking look from Gray quelled the impulse. One did not argue in front of servants or children.

"We have already eaten," said Gray, "but we are under orders to wait on you. The Moffats are in the shop, looking after their customers, and Hart and Nick are running a few errands for me. No, don't move from that chair. Quentin and I are quite capable of fixing breakfast."

As she watched, they moved around the kitchen, conversing amiably, opening drawers and cupboards, removing dishes and cutlery and the makings of a cold meal. They seemed to be enjoying themselves enormously, as though finding their way around a lady's kitchen was a grand adventure. Before long, there was a kettle of water set on the hob to boil and the table was laden with a selection of savory pies and cold cuts of meat.

She was so lost in thought that she was only half aware when Quentin excused himself to work on his lessons, or that she had given Gray permission to fill a plate for her. Picking up her knife and fork, she absently began to toy with the food on her plate.

There was no doubt in her mind that for the first time in months, Quentin looked happy and healthy. And that the earl had managed to get the boy to speak about his father without bursting into tears was no small victory. Lord Kendal, she acknowledged, had a way with children. Or it could be that Quentin was in sore need of a man's companionship. Mr. Moffat was fine in his way, but he could never be a model for the boy. Quentin was a viscount. On his father's death, he had succeeded to the title. It was right and proper that he turn to some suitable gentleman, someone he could admire, whose guidance he would accept. Then why was she angry?

She wasn't angry so much as hurt. Lord Kendal had made a grand entrance, and suddenly, she was invisible. They were even making plans for Quentin's future, and no one had consulted her. Oh no, she was only the governess.

"Deborah," said Gray, breaking the long silence, "it's only natural for Quentin to turn to me at this time. I was his father's best friend. I have a fund of stories I can tell the boy. Don't you see, it makes his loss easier to bear? You haven't been displaced in his affections, as you seem to think. Give him time."

She glanced at him, then looked away. His kindness made her want to pour out all the terrors she had endured these last few months, and all the fears she had for the future. At the same time, she wanted to throw his sympathy back in his face. He had abducted her, terrorized her, made her fear for her very life. She could never make a friend of this man, not in a hundred years.

"I want you to know," he said, as humble as she had ever heard him, and just as though he could read her mind, "that I deeply regret what you were made to suffer these last few days. Don't you see, I had to break you as quickly as possible?" When she bit ferociously into a crust of bread, Gray's eyes glinted wickedly. "I didn't like what I was doing. It was a job that had to be done and quickly. You must see that I am not the man I pretended to be. When you get to know me better, Deborah—"

"Get to know you better?" she said, mimicking his reasonable tone. She leaned across the table until they were nose to nose. "I'd as soon get to know a rabid dog."

"Dammit, woman, will you listen to me?" he suddenly thundered, making her cower. "We have more to discuss than your petty grievances. There is a murderer on the loose, and it's quite possible that you and Quentin are his quarry." He nodded at the shocked expression on her face. "Yes, Deborah. The murderer. Try to put yourself in his shoes. What must he be thinking? He knows Quentin saw him that night. He must be wondering why the authorities have not arrested him by this time." He gave her a moment to absorb his words, then went on, "I told everyone that you and Quentin were secluded in my estate in Gloucestershire, yet, to my knowledge, no one has come sniffing around asking questions about you, and the murderer would, Deborah, unless he thought he had nothing to fear."

Her mind was working like lightning. "Perhaps he's in France? Perhaps he was afraid to return to England?"

"Not if he is who I think he is. No, I don't know his

identity, except that I am convinced he is the traitor Gil was close to unmasking, and since none of my colleagues at the Foreign Office has bolted in the last little while, it means that our murderer is carrying on as usual. Now, what does that suggest to you?"

She shook her head. "I don't know."

"Think about it," he said tersely.

She did, then said, "He must be shaking in his boots. I don't know what else to think."

"Or he must know that Quentin has lost his memory, and be quite sure in his mind that you did not get a clear look at him that night."

She stared at him blindly as her mind sifted through his words. "But nobody knows about Quentin's memory lapse except Miss Hare and the Moffats, and no one has been asking them questions."

"Yes, I know. Think carefully, Deborah. Did you say anything to the French authorities when they questioned you?"

"No," she said uncertainly. "I told them that Quentin and I had come running when we heard the shot. I didn't tell them he had witnessed the murder. They could see Quentin was in shock, but they didn't know he had lost his memory. I didn't know myself until the night before we left Paris. I was so worried about him, I sent for the physician."

"Quentin was examined by a doctor the night before you left Paris?"

She nodded.

"Ah," he said, and relaxed against the back of his chair. "Now I begin to understand."

"What do you understand?"

"That the report of Quentin's memory loss has been relayed to the murderer in England. That's why he has made no attempt to find you." He turned his sparkling eyes upon her. "Don't you know how lucky you were, Deborah? How lucky we all were? You got clean away before the French realized that you and Quentin posed a threat to their agent. Now everything is beginning to make sense."

She said glumly, "It seems to me that their agent is

the lucky one. If what you say is true, he knows he is safe, while Quentin and I must always be on our guard. That's why I don't want Quentin to go away to school."

"Hmm? Oh, you need not think I would send him to Eton until I am quite satisfied that no harm will come to him."

She gestured helplessly. "Then what's to be done? I want Quentin to live a normal life, but I'm so afraid that if he shows himself, he may become a target."

He was watching her closely. "Are you never afraid for yourself, Deborah Weyman?"

She was so startled by his tone that she jerked her head up and stared at him with wide, questioning eyes. Caught by the softness in his expression, she answered unthinkingly, "Mortally afraid, but there is nothing new in that." When his look sharpened, she quickly retreated. "So, where do we go from here? I presume you have given the matter some thought?"

"A great deal of thought." He allowed her to turn the conversation, but he made a mental note of her unthinking remark. *Mortally afraid, but there is nothing new in that.* He opened his snuffbox, took a pinch of snuff, then shut the box with a snap.

Finally, he said, "We must demonstrate to the murderer, without a shadow of a doubt, that neither you nor Quentin can identify him."

"And how do you propose to do that?"

"Quite simply, by taking you both to London and showing you off. There's no point in concealing Quentin's loss of memory, but we won't make a great fuss about it. We will simply say that the death of his father affected his mind. If someone makes a bolt for it, I shall have my man, but it's unlikely. He would have done it before now. No. Our murderer will breathe a little more easily when he sees with his own eyes that he is free and clear."

He had hardly finished speaking when she burst out, "That's not it! You are hoping that the shock of seeing his father's murderer will jog Quentin's memory. That's it, isn't it? There's a spy at the Foreign Office, and you are counting on Quentin to catch him for you."

A muscle in his jaw jerked. "That's a damn lie! You told me the doctor didn't hold out much hope of Quentin ever recovering his memory. However, if it did happen, and he could identify the person who murdered his father, so much the better. What's wrong with that? Don't you understand anything? Until that person is apprehended, you and Quentin must always go in fear of your lives."

She was on her feet, her weight braced with both hands on the flat of the table. "Oh, I understand, all right. Who better to understand than one of your victims? Quentin and I are just pawns to you. Bait, in fact."

His eyes leapt with fury. "Don't be ridiculous! The risks entailed in exposing you and Quentin to his father's murderer are slight. Haven't I explained it all to you? The murderer thinks he is safe. Besides, you and the boy will be well guarded. Afterward, in a week or two, you can go down to my estate in Kent. If you have a better plan, I should like to hear it."

"I don't have a plan, but what you suggest is too dangerous. I won't allow it, do you hear? I won't allow it."

"*You* won't allow it? You have no say in the matter, Miss Weyman. You can do as you wish, but whether you like it or not, Quentin goes to London with me."

Their eyes battled as Gray's implacable stare met her stormy, resentful glare head-on. In a low, angry voice, she declared, "I would not dream of leaving Quentin until I know he is no longer in danger."

"Does this mean you accept my invitation?"

"Invitation?" Her bosom quivered. "That was no invitation! You were commanding me in your usual high-handed fashion."

He studied her for a long, contemplative moment, then a gleam of amusement lit his eyes. "I beg your pardon," he said. "You seem to have this strange effect on me. I assure you, I am not so autocratic with other ladies. In fact—you will hardly credit this—I am renowned for my charm."

Unaffected by her dark scowl, he went on. "It won't be so bad. You'll like my mother, and I've no doubt she will like you. You are Quentin's guardian now, and that makes a difference. You'll be a guest in my home, my mother's guest, and you will be treated as a member of my family. Of course, I shall expect you to be guided by me in all things. I want that clearly understood between us before we set out. I must know that you trust me implicitly, or our charade won't work.

"It's only for a few weeks, then you and Quentin can go to my house in Kent. I promise you, I'm *not* setting Quentin up as bait. There are other ways of apprehending this scoundrel. When I unmask my traitor, I shall have him. All I am trying to do is make him feel so safe that he will become careless. Sooner or later, he will make a mistake."

In the end, of course, she had relented, as he must have known she would. As long as he had Quentin, he had the upper hand, but she did not like what he had proposed. It was all very well to say that the murderer felt safe knowing that Quentin had lost his memory, but nothing was certain. And she was not convinced that the traitor at the Foreign Office and Lord Barrington's murderer were one and the same person. But Lord Kendal was convinced, and nobody else's opinion held any weight with him. There were just too many "ifs" in his reasoning for her comfort.

What she really wanted was to take Quentin to his uncle in the West Indies, but she knew Lord Kendal would never agree to that. He would look upon it as the act of a coward. She sniffed. So, she was a coward. She would rather run away than stay and fight. She could not change what she was, any more than Lord Kendal could change what he was. The man was tenacious, ruthless, implacable, and though those qualities repelled her, she was very glad, for Quentin's sake, that his guardian was no weakling but a man who would know how to protect his own.

For some time after he had left her, she did nothing but stare at the untouched food on her plate, debating inwardly the advisability of taking up residence in London in Lord Kendal's household. She could never think of London without remembering Albert and her father's house in the Strand. She would only be in London for a few weeks, she chided herself. Her father and stepmother rarely showed their faces in town until the season was under way, and she and Quentin would be in Kent by then. And come what may, she was not going to let Quentin out of her sight until Lord Kendal had caught his traitor.

Gray, meantime, was congratulating himself on his easy victory. He had known that Quentin would be the irresistible bait to lure her to London. Her loyalty and devotion to the boy were unquestionable. As was natural, she mistrusted him, her ruthless abductor.

He had told her no lies when he had revealed his motives for taking them to London. True, he had toyed with the idea of using Quentin as bait and, as a last resort, it might come down to that, but only as a last resort. In that event, he was going to have the battle of his life with Deborah. He shook his head when he realized he was smiling.

All the same, he had not been transparently honest with her. He'd set dozens of traps for the spy at the Foreign Office, and had failed to tempt him. The trouble was, nothing much was happening in the war right now. Both France and England were arming themselves to the teeth. It could be months before the fighting began in earnest, months before their spy was tempted to pass information to his masters. And he had covered his tracks well. That's why he had silenced Gil.

He had one of those flashes, when Gil's face came sharply into focus—a roguish smile and merry brown eyes with a laugh always lurking in their depths. No one had understood their friendship, least of all themselves. They were complete opposites. He was a born cynic. Gil, on the other hand, was inclined to accept everything at face value. That's why neither of his marriages had added one iota to his comfort. Both times, he had married pretty girls with nice manners and no substance.

This thought led him quite naturally to Deborah. He couldn't fault Gil there. He must have seen her sterling worth before he named her as Quentin's guardian. And how well she had repaid his trust! It was more than time that someone did something for Deborah Weyman.

In London, there would be time to gain her confidence, time to dig a little deeper into her background. Then, when he had fixed whatever it was that brought that hunted look to her eyes when the past was mentioned, he would see her settled with some—he grinned wickedly—eligible young gentleman, who would cherish her as she deserved.

As he mounted the stairs to Quentin's room, he was mentally ticking off the eligible young gentlemen of his acquaintance whom he considered worthy of a young woman of Deborah's mettle. To his astonishment, he could not come up with a single name.

CHAPTER 11

On the morning of their departure for London, Deborah opened her eyes to see Mrs. Moffat packing her valise. Quentin stood at the side of the bed, his eyes sparkling.

"I've brought your chocolate, Deb," he said.

She accepted the glass of chocolate, but her eyes were trained on the gown Mrs. Moffat had laid out for her. She had never seen it before in her life.

Quentin couldn't contain his excitement, and burst out, "Uncle Gray did it, Deb. He arranged everything."

"What," asked Deborah ominously, "did Uncle Gray arrange?"

"New gowns! And . . . and everything!" exclaimed Quentin.

"He's done *what*?" She hauled herself up and set down the glass of chocolate.

Mrs. Moffat looked up, and seeing the look on Deborah's face, made a small sound of impatience. "I know what is going through your mind, my girl, and you can just take that stubborn look off your face. There is nothing improper in accepting clothing from a gentleman when he is acting on his mother's behalf. Lord Kendal explained the circumstances to me. Deb, you should be grateful that he went to so much trouble. His mother knew you would not wish to arrive in London looking like a charity case."

A charity case. The words hurt. "Is . . . is that what he called me?" asked Deborah, her spirits plummeting for some unknown reason.

"Of course he didn't. He is a real gentleman. And I am only telling you for your own good. He likes you, Deb. I can tell. If you would only smile at him, talk nicely, you know what I mean, I think you might be surprised at the results." And smiling, she left Deborah to mull over her words.

Marriage, that's what was on Mrs. Moffat's mind. Deborah felt the rise of hysterical laughter and swallowed it. Swiftly rising, she went to inspect the clothes that were laid out for her. Beneath the folds of a green twill carriage dress, cunningly concealed, was a set of fine lawn underwear adorned with rows of Mechlin lace, as well as white silk stockings and frilly lace garters embroidered with blue forget-me-nots.

"Where are my own clothes?" she asked Quentin.

"Uncle Gray told Mrs. Moffat to take them away."

"Oh, he did, did he?" Her whole body quivered in outrage.

Quentin's eyes anxiously searched hers. "Deb, don't you *like* Uncle Gray?"

"Your uncle Gray, let me tell you—" The look on Quentin's face brought her up short. One word from her, that's all it would require, and she could begin to drive a wedge between Quentin and his guardian. She took a deep breath and started over. "Your uncle Gray certainly knows how to please a lady."

He studied her face, then satisfied with what he saw, plumped himself down on an upholstered stool. "Did you know," he said, "that Uncle Hart has a boy the same age as me?"

So it was "Uncle Hart" now, thought Deborah uncharitably. "No, I didn't know." She managed a smile.

"He says Jason and I will become the best of friends, you know, like Papa and Uncle Gray."

She heard the note of uncertainty in his voice, and gave him her full attention. "And?"

"Best friends are supposed to tell each other secrets."

She knew the secret he was thinking of, and answered carefully, "You may tell him that you can't remember things, and that's all you may tell him. Do you understand, Quentin?"

This was one point she and Gray had agreed on. It was one thing to let the world know that Quentin had suffered a loss of memory, but nothing would be gained by revealing that he had actually witnessed the murder. In fact, it would only invite a great deal of unnecessary speculation and make things unpleasant for Quentin. The murderer would know what to make of everything, and that's what counted.

Quentin nodded. "Uncle Gray explained it to me. If I tell people that I was in the library that night, they'll badger me with questions."

"Then, what is it? What's wrong?"

"Why can't I remember, Deb? I've tried and tried and nothing happens. Papa . . . Papa . . ."

His face crumpled and he reached for her. She drew him into her arms, rocking him as he sobbed brokenly. "Papa must hate me. Why can't I remember who shot him?"

His words shocked her. She had known that he chafed because he could not remember that night, but it had never occurred to her that he would feel guilty about it. She smoothed back his hair and held him till his tears had run their course. After a while, he sniffed, gulped, and dashed his tears away, then looked up at her. "You're crying," he said.

She didn't try to hold him when he pulled out of her arms. Kneeling beside him, praying earnestly for the right words, she said, "Your uncle Gray loves you, doesn't he, and he knows you can't remember. Your papa loved you best in the world. Why should he be different from Uncle Gray? They were best friends, and friends think alike, don't they? Your papa could never hate you, Quentin. I told you what happened. He saved you. He told you to run, and I was there to help you."

He sniffed, thinking over her words. "I still wish I could remember," he said.

"Your papa knows that too. And one day, it will all come back to you, you'll see."

"Truly, Deb?"

"Truly."

His little face suddenly turned fierce. "Good," he said. "Then we'll catch the man who killed Papa and hang him."

Deborah watched him go with an uneasy feeling in the pit of her stomach. She didn't care if Lord Barrington's murderer was ever caught, just as long as Quentin was safe.

She dressed swiftly in her new clothes, but it wasn't until she entered the parlor where she found Gray that she remembered she had a bone to pick with him.

"I should like to know what you mean by this," she said, indicating the green twill carriage dress she had donned.

Gray set aside the newspaper he had been reading and glanced at her coolly. "Sit down, Deborah," he said. "There are some matters I wish to discuss with you before we are joined by the others."

She threw him a fulminating look, but recognizing that particular tone, she accepted the chair he had indicated. Back straight, hands folded in her lap, she tapped her foot on the wooden floor, just to let him know that she wasn't completely cowed by his imperious manner.

When he leaned forward slightly, pinning her with his stare, her foot stilled. "I told you yesterday," he said, "that you were to be a guest in my home. That being the case, you will dress for the part. To continue as you were would be to invite unnecessary speculation, if not suspicion. If you are worried about being in my debt, you may consider it as part payment for your services for looking after Quentin these last few months. Damnation, girl," he broke out as she opened her mouth to respond, "I do as much for any of my servants by providing their livery, and that's a costly business, let me tell you. You are Quentin's guardian, and my mother's guest. I won't have you mistaken for a poor relation. It would reflect badly on my family."

"Poor relation" was almost as bad as "charity case."

Did he think she enjoyed dressing like a frump? As much as any girl, she liked fine clothes and pretty things. There had never been the opportunity or the money to indulge herself. She didn't want to indulge herself, not if it meant drawing attention to herself.

Her eyes burned with resentment, but she wasn't in the mood to do battle with him. Compared to her anxieties for Quentin, her grievances seemed trivial. "What matters do you wish to discuss?" she asked.

He seemed surprised at her capitulation, and gave her a searching look before saying, "I have taken the liberty of engaging a maid for you, at least to accompany us as far as London. Once there, I'm sure my mother has maids in plenty to attend you. Then the girl can return to Wells."

She knew she was just being contrary, but she couldn't seem to stop herself.

"I see no need for a maid. I am well beyond the years of requiring a chaperon."

"How old are you, Deborah?"

"Four and twenty."

"And I am almost ten years older than you, so you see, the maid is obligatory. Oh, I'm not thinking of your reputation, but my own. Should I be so foolish as to compromise you, the results would be dire, indeed. Marriage, Deborah, and to a rake, nothing could be more disastrous."

When she smiled, his eyes narrowed. "Let me set your mind at rest, my lord," she said. "Neither you nor all the king's combined armies and navies could ever force me into that lethal trap."

"I've used the same words myself, on occasion."

She gave an exaggerated sigh. "At last we agree on something."

Leaning back comfortably, Gray crossed his hands behind his neck. "You'll change your mind when you meet the right man."

His typical masculine response almost tempted her to put him straight about a few things. Almost, but not quite. She didn't want him probing, didn't want him to use that shrewd intelligence of his to start putting two and two together.

"You said," she reminded him gently, "that there were some matters you wished to discuss with me. If that is all, my lord, I should like to say my farewells to the Moffats before we leave."

"That's not all," he said, straightening in his chair. "In a few minutes, Nick and Hart are going to come through that door, and I expect you to treat them with cordiality and respect. You will wipe from your mind the events of these last several days as though they had never happened. Do you understand what I am saying, Deborah?"

"I shall never be able to wipe the events of the last several days from my mind!"

Gray appeared unmoved by her indignant outburst. "Then you will become the consummate actress. You will act as though nothing happened. I'll not have you subjecting Nick and Hart to your temper tantrums for merely following my orders. If you would only think about it, you would see that they were as reluctant as I to use you as we did, more so in fact, for I am not so easily taken in by the tears and protestations of a beautiful young woman."

She stared at him blankly. The last time she had seen Nick or Hart had been right after Gray had carried her from the roof. Since then, there had not been the opportunity to see them. With the Moffats' quarters being so cramped, they had been staying at the King's Arms, and they rarely came to the house, and never before she was in her bed or had yet to rise. For the first time it occurred to her that they had been avoiding her, or they had been ordered to avoid her, and she wondered why.

The answer that came to her was self-evident. They were afraid to face her until her anger had time to cool. This seemed reasonable for Hart, but Nick was her friend. He had taken her part against his own brother, going so far as to help her escape. It was not Nick's fault that Lord Kendal had been too clever for them. Nick could not be afraid to face her unless—

As comprehension dawned, she leapt to her feet, and

her chair went tumbling to the floor. "You devil!" she cried out. "Nick and Hart were merely following your orders! I was never meant to escape. From beginning to end, it was a trick. Nick was never my friend!"

"I thought you knew. I thought you would have worked it out by now."

"My god, you brood of vipers! Is this what I may expect from your mother and sisters when I arrive in London? Are all you Graysons tarred with the same brush?"

He surged to his feet, a sudden fury blazing in his eyes. "You may call me any vile names you choose, but when you speak of my mother and sisters, you will speak with respect."

She whirled away from him, intent only on escaping his hateful presence. Gray was too quick for her. Seizing her by the arm, he jerked her back to face him.

"You gave me your word that you would obey me in all things. If you wish to renege on that promise, tell me now. I'll not have my family set on its ears by an ill-bred termagant. But think on this, Deborah, before you give me your answer. If you desert Quentin now, you forfeit all chance of seeing him again."

So intent were they on each other that they barely heard the voices in the hallway.

"Even you could not be so cruel!" she cried out.

"Try me!" he retorted.

"I say, aren't you two ready to leave yet?" Nick stood on the threshold, a sheepish grin on his face. Hart stood behind him, his wary eyes trained on the overturned chair.

She jerked her arm free from Gray's clasp and turned to face them. What a fool she had been, what a blind, gullible fool! The words to flay them trembled on the tip of her tongue.

"Deborah!" Gray's eyes were flinty. His tone promised swift retribution if she disobeyed him.

She executed a deep, respectful curtsy which she held for an inordinate length of time. "Gentlemen," she said, rising, "I have not had the opportunity to thank you for your hospitality, and your many kindnesses to me."

The cordial tone encouraged Nick to advance into the room. The significance of her remarks had yet to register. Hart, who had more experience of a woman's humors, retreated strategically to the far side of a long sofa. At her side, Gray stiffened.

She smiled sweetly upon each gentleman in turn. "Words are inadequate to express my feelings. May I say merely that one day I hope to repay you all in full measure?"

Nick watched her with a bemused smile on his face as she made a graceful exit. Hart let out the breath he had been holding. Gray combed his fingers through his hair.

"Well," said Nick, turning to face his companions. "I think that went off rather well. That girl has the sweetest, most forgiving disposition of anyone I know. Gray, you are a lucky fellow."

Gray let out a furious expletive and he, too, left the room. Hart rolled his eyes and told Nick not to be more of a simpleton than he could help.

"What did I say?" demanded Nick querulously, following on Hart's heels as he descended the stairs to the waiting carriage. "What did I say?"

※

The carriage halted and Deborah's head jerked, awakening her from the light sleep she had fallen into. Using her glove, she cleared the mist from one pane of glass and looked out. A light drizzle was falling, obscuring her view, but she knew that Gray was out there somewhere, mounted on his roan. It had been like this from the moment they had begun their journey two days before. Though the carriage could hold six comfortably, the three gentlemen rarely entered, but preferred to ride on horseback, resting every hour or two as they came to various hostelries. They were giving her a wide berth because they thought that was what she wanted. She would not see any of them again until they came to their next stop.

She sank back against the cushions of the banquette

and allowed her lashes to fall. This time, sleep eluded her, but she had plenty of thoughts to keep her company. The strain of keeping her companions at arm's length was beginning to tell on her. They deserved a lot worse than her long silences for what they had done to her. All the same, it seemed to her that by ostracizing *them*, she was also punishing herself. The maid who had been hired to act as her chaperon was a pleasant enough companion, but Treana was little more than an adolescent. She was no conversationalist, and Deborah was starved for adult conversation. More than once, as they dined, she had been tempted to join in one of the conversations that was going on around the table. From Gray's expression, she suspected that he was deliberately trying to draw her out of herself. She had devoted herself to Quentin, but the trouble with Quentin was that he hung on every word that fell from his idol's lips. He didn't notice her silences, or if he did, he thought that she, too, was hanging on every word Lord Kendal said.

Sometimes, she could hardly believe that the fine gentlemen who solicitously saw to her comfort on the long, tedious journey were the same men who had terrorized her when she was their captive. Hart, in particular, had undergone the greatest transformation. He addressed her in the most respectful tones, but it was his kindness to Quentin that made the greater impression. His son, Jason, he promised, was eagerly awaiting Quentin's visit to their home so that the boys could have glorious times together. Hart spoke of his wife and son in such fond terms that Deborah had a hard time remembering that when she was his prisoner, one look from him had made her knees knock together. That was the thing about men. Until a woman was completely in their power, she had no way of knowing whether they would use their superior strength to protect her or crush her. Hart's wife was fortunate, but it could just as easily have gone the other way.

She opened her eyes a fraction to find that her maid was covertly studying her. There was nothing new in this. Treana was under the illusion, which Nick had maliciously fostered for reasons known only to himself, that Lord Kendal had a romantic interest in *her*, Deborah. From that moment on, Treana had minutely scrutinized her mistress, her clothes, her manners, her conversation, as if she were Deborah's understudy in a play they were rehearsing.

The girl fancied Lord Kendal. Treana didn't exactly make a spectacle of herself like some of the females they had encountered at posting houses along the way. She merely trailed his lordship with her big, soulful brown eyes, and let out little telling sighs whenever her hero addressed a few careless words to her. The looks she bestowed on Deborah, when she wasn't studying her, were closer to a reproach. She could not understand why Deborah held herself aloof from Lord Kendal and Deborah did not enlighten her.

It was all beginning to grate on Deborah's nerves and she was not sorry that once they reached London, the little lovestruck maid would, almost immediately, make the return journey to Wells. His lordship had promised that his mother had plenty of maids to see to her needs. She hoped they weren't all as gullible as Treana.

It galled her that he was attractive to women, and not just the young, pretty ones either. That he possessed a surfeit of good looks, she had never denied. But that was not the only reason for his effect on the opposite sex. To alleviate the boredom of their journey, she had made a study of *him*, in much the same way as her maid studied her. The man unconsciously evoked an impression of power and authority, a man who was not to be trifled with. Well, she could vouch for that. It was, however, the charm which got her goat, if "charm" was the right word for it. He wasn't like Nick. He didn't have a repertoire of roguish smiles and grins that invited a woman to respond in kind. He simply gave a woman his complete and undivided attention, as though she were the last woman in the world, and it worked. He never wasted those looks on her. She was a lost cause, and she hoped he knew it.

When they pulled in to the Castle Inn in Marlbor-

ough, the last stop of the day, and Gray helped her
alight, she spoke to him in a friendly way as she did
whenever Quentin was watching them. As far as Quentin knew, they were the best of friends. The laughter in
Lord Kendal's eyes told her that he knew what she was
up to.

❧

Gray knew something was wrong the moment he answered the knock on his bedchamber door. "What is it,
Treana?" he asked.

The maid gaped in astonishment, as though she had
never seen a man with his shirt unbuttoned before. Gray
did not wait for the maid to recover. His coat was
thrown over the bed. Reaching for it, he said impatiently, "Is it Miss Weyman? For God's sake, girl, tell me
what's happened."

Lowering her eyes as though to shield herself from
the potent effect of that muscular chest, she stammered
out the message she had been told to deliver. "If it please
your lordship, Miss Weyman says you are to come at
once. The boy is not well."

Gray did not attempt to elicit further information
from the flustered maid. The door to Quentin's room
was only a few steps away. Shrugging into his coat, he
quickly traversed the corridor, gave a perfunctory knock
on the door and entered the room. Deborah was sitting
on the edge of the bed, brushing back the hair from
Quentin's forehead. The boy's face was flushed. At sight
of Gray, his breathing became labored and he groaned.

Deborah rose and came to meet him. She was already attired in her nightclothes. Above the dark green
collar of her robe, Gray absently noted the white lace of
her night shift. Her wide, luminous eyes betrayed her
fear. His hands reached for her and she grasped at them
convulsively.

"Easy," he said. "Don't be afraid. I'm here now. Just
tell me what happened."

"I've never seen him like this. I don't know if it's

something he has eaten, or if it's more serious. I think we should send for the physician."

Gray crossed to the bed and leaned down over the prostrate boy. Quentin stared back at him with eyes that were just a shade too innocent. Gray breathed deeply and caught the whiff of something he instantly recognized. Shaking his head, he straightened and turned to Deborah. "Where is the sherry I sent to your room earlier this evening?"

"Sherry? I don't remember any sherry."

In answer to Deborah's questioning look, the maid shook her head.

"I think," said Gray, "that Quentin can answer that question."

Quentin licked his lips. "I drank it," he said hoarsely.

"How much did you drink?"

Quentin's eyes strayed to the walnut wardrobe. "I don't know."

Inside the wardrobe, Gray found the bottle of sherry and a used glass. "About two glasses, I should say," he said, holding the bottle up to the light.

Deborah gasped. "Is . . . is that bad?"

Gray forced his lips to remain straight. "Bad enough, but they are small glasses. You had better leave us alone, Deborah. This is men's business, so don't interfere. Treana, I want a carafe of cold water. At once, girl," and so saying, Gray shut the door in their faces.

Deborah's eyes never wavered from that door. A time or two, when she heard prolonged retching followed by animallike moans, she started from her chair, then sank back as the moans faded away. In due course, the carafe of water arrived. Taking it from the maid, she tapped lightly on the door and entered at Gray's bidding.

He was sitting on the edge of the bed, washing Quentin's face and hands with a washcloth. Quentin smiled weakly as she approached the bed.

"I'm sorry, Deb," he said. "It was a stupid thing to do." He glanced at Gray's face then went on manfully, "I should be horsewhipped for giving you such a fright."

Gray laughed. "Did I say that? Well, I did not mean it literally, so don't go adding any more to your Deb's worries than you already have. There will be no whipping. What you are suffering now and what you will suffer tomorrow is punishment enough." He held out his hand and took the carafe from Deborah. "He'll feel better when he gets this down him, and even if he doesn't, it's the price he must pay for trying to ape the modes of his uncle." He nodded an affirmative to her raised brows. "Oh yes. Young Lord Barrington, here, has been studying my habits and thinks that by emulating my example, it will make him a man. He knows better now."

Deborah stood a little off to one side, observing Gray as he forced Quentin to drink back the whole carafe of water. He had taken command of the situation and she could have wept in gratitude.

When Quentin was comfortably settled, she walked Gray to the door and into the corridor, leaving the maid to watch over Quentin. She looked at him with wide, tear-bright eyes. "I suppose you think this is my fault for not watching him more carefully?"

"I think nothing of the sort. Quentin only did what any boy would do given the opportunity. Deborah, haven't you heard the old saw 'Boys will be boys'?"

She swallowed hard. "Then you think I fuss over trifles?"

He slowed his steps and stared at her intently. "Don't be so hard on yourself. I would never reproach you for your care of Quentin."

"It's very good of you to let me off so lightly."

"Deb," he murmured, "don't cry. Please don't cry."

At these soothing words, the tears that had been held in check welled up and spilled over. When he reached for her, she went into his arms without protest.

"I . . . I don't know what's the matter with me," she choked out. "It's just that I've been so alone. And now . . ." She swallowed back her words, not even sure what she had meant to say.

"Shhh. You've been through a lot in the last little while, more than most grown men could handle. You are human, Deb. You just need someone to take care of you for a change."

When he kissed her chastely on the brow, she sighed and nestled her head against the crook of his shoulder. The arm around her waist tightened, bringing her closer to the warmth of his body. She pulled back slightly and looked up at him.

"I'm glad you are Quentin's guardian," she whispered. "He'll do very well with you. I'm sorry I was rude to you. From now on, I promise, I won't fight you."

He smiled. "Don't go all submissive on me, Deb, or I won't know you."

At this, her dimples flashed, and he brought one hand up to trace them with his fingers. When they winked out, he frowned, and lifted his eyes to search her face. He could feel her soft breasts quivering against the hard wall of his chest. She felt so soft and womanly, so right in his arms.

"Don't start that," she warned him, and tried to wriggle out of his clasp, one hand braced defensively against his broad chest. When she gasped, he looked down. Her hand had slipped inside the edges of his opened shirt.

Horrified, she cried out, "You are practically unclothed."

He grinned down at her red face. "Deb, you've seen me in a lot less. Don't you like the feel of your hand on my bare flesh? You did once, don't you remember? I know I like it."

She gave a little squeal of indignation, stomped on his toes, and twisted out of his arms. "You told me to forget all about the time I was your prisoner." Her eyes darted over his shoulder to the door to Quentin's room. She couldn't reach it without going past him. "I'm trying to forget, I'm really trying, but I won't succeed if you keep throwing it in my face." She squared her shoulders and lifted her chin. "Now, if you would be so good as to step aside, Lord Kendal, I should like to retire to my room."

"Don't you think 'Lord Kendal' is a bit formal considering all that we have been to each other? You don't call Hart 'Lord Hartley,' do you, or 'my lord' in that annoying way of yours? Call me Gray. It sounds more friendly."

She glared into his laughing face. When she retreated a step, he advanced. He wasn't seriously pursuing her, he told himself. This was, after all, a public hallway. At any moment, someone might appear. He hoped that someone would. He just couldn't seem to resist baiting her. No sooner had that thought occurred to him, than he discarded it. He wasn't baiting her, he was playing with her, and damn if she wasn't the one who always provoked it.

When he pounced, she let out a shriek. Arms like vises dragged her against him. "Gray," he said, laughing down at her. "I want to hear you say it."

Her eyes flashed. "Then you will wait till doomsday, my lord."

He wasn't going to let that challenge pass. He kissed her quick and hard. "Gray! Say it, Deborah!"

She pressed her lips together. He kissed her again, then again. When her lips softened, he increased the pressure until her mouth was open and pliable beneath his. He shifted her till her body was flush against him. The game was forgotten as he felt her yielding to his demands. His hands dipped to the rounded swell of her bottom, kneading, lifting her into him, pressing her against his hard groin.

Deborah tried to fight his power. He was a rake. This was all a game to him. Her body didn't seem to care. Hot and cold chills shivered through her, making her cling to him for support. The ache in her breasts spread out and sank into the lower half of her body, settling between her thighs. Without volition, she spread her legs. He groaned and flattened her against the wall.

"Gray!" she cried out. "Gray!"

When he pulled back, his eyes were wildly dilated, as were hers. Neither said a word. Both remained frozen, staring at each other as their labored breathing punctuated the silence. Gray came to himself first. His hands fell away and he took a step back. Feeling herself slipping without his support, Deborah made a determined effort to straighten her knees. Her cheeks were flaming.

"Now that wasn't so bad, was it?" Even to his own ears, his voice sounded shaken. "*Gray,* Deborah. From now on you will call me Gray."

She picked up her skirts and quickly slipped by him. At the door to Quentin's room, she made a half-turn. Even in the candlelight, he could see that the glint of challenge had returned to her eyes. "Good night, Uncle Gray," she said with false sweetness, and she whisked herself into the room.

He was laughing softly when he turned toward his own chamber, but the laughter died when he caught sight of Nick in the shadows, arms folded across his chest, one shoulder propped against the wall.

"How much did you see?" asked Gray, coming abreast of him.

"Enough."

"There's no need to look like that. It didn't mean anything."

"Oh, didn't it?" Nick followed Gray into his room and shut the door. "I presume you *will* offer the girl marriage?"

"Good grief! Why should I do that? Deb is not the first pretty girl I have kissed. Did I marry the others?"

Without waiting to be invited, Nick uncorked a bottle of sherry and poured out two glasses. "You call that a kiss?" he asked, taunting him. "You were practically devouring the poor girl."

Gray accepted the glass Nick held out to him. "Deb and I are worlds apart," he said.

"What does that mean?"

"You know." Gray shrugged indifferently. "I'm too old for her."

"Too old? I'd hardly say you were in your dotage. There can't be more than—what?—eight or nine years' difference in your ages?"

"In experience is what I meant."

Nick folded himself into an upholstered armchair. His eyes were dancing. "I see," he said. "She deserves something better. Is that it?"

Gray's lashes drooped, concealing his expression. "Well, doesn't she?"

Nick threw back his head and laughed. "Oh, Gray," he said, "I should have known you would fight this every inch of the way."

Gray's hands. Deborah's attention was caught.

"Well, there's that."

Nick threw back his head and laughed. "Oh, Gray," he said, "I would have given my world's worth to see the look of the man."

CHAPTER 12

Kendal House in Berkeley Square was a three-storied, brick-terraced house with stone pediments decorating the upstairs windows. It was inevitable that Deborah's mind would stray to her father's houses, Belvidere, his country estate near Windsor, and Strand House, just around the corner from Charing Cross. Those were palaces, and could quite easily have swallowed up Kendal House ten times over.

None of this occurred to her consciously as Gray ushered her into a white marble hallway hung with a delicate blue paper. She was clinging very tightly to Quentin's hand, trying to bolster his confidence by her own cheerful example. Quentin wasn't to know that her knees were knocking together. At least Gray was not springing them on his mother without warning. He had sent Nick ahead to inform her ladyship of what she might expect.

A door banged on the floor above, and several voices cried out at once. Quentin edged a little closer to Deborah, and she, in turn, edged a little closer to Gray.

"Uncle Gray, where is Papa?"

A boy with tousled dark hair appeared at the top of the stairs and began a perilous descent. In his wake came three ladies, and in the rear, trailing them, came Nick.

Hart, entering the vestibule at that moment, exclaimed, "Jason! What are you doing here? And where is Mama?"

"We came to visit Grandmama." The boy's eyes alighted with interest on Quentin, but it was evident that he was bursting with some important communication. "Papa, we are going to have a baby. I heard Mama tell Grandmama."

"I know," said Hart, "but that is not for general knowledge." He stared pointedly at the two grinning footmen who were carrying valises and portmanteaux into the hall.

"You know?" Jason could not hide his disappointment. "But how can you know?"

Hart grinned sheepishly and shrugged.

There was a moment of stunned silence, then everyone was laughing and talking at once. Gray and Nick pounded Hart on the back, exclaiming at his good fortune. When one of the ladies detached herself from the others, Gray sprang on her and enfolded her in a bear hug.

"Gussie, I could not be happier for you."

"I had almost given up hope." She sniffed into his collar.

"Not you," said Hart, extricating his wife from her brother's embrace and taking her into his own arms, "else I would still be a bachelor."

This brought more laughter. As several conversations started at once, Deborah stood there arrested. In her whole life, she had never witnessed such informal manners. Babies as yet to be born were never mentioned in mixed company. She wasn't being judgmental. She was simply marveling at the exuberance of this strange family.

With everyone laughing and talking, she took a moment to study Gray's mother and sisters. She had an impression of tawny good looks and wealth and breeding, then a silence descended as all eyes turned to her and Quentin. For a moment, she experienced a shaft of pure panic. Her arm went around Quentin's shoulders; his arm crept around her waist. Then Gray was beside them, making the introductions, and the moment passed.

The countess considered Deborah gravely for a long moment before she smiled. "So this is Deborah," she said. "And you are Quentin. My dears, welcome to our home. Those words seem so inadequate, but I mean them sincerely." She reached for Deborah's hands and took them in a firm clasp. "You've both had a bad time, but that's over now. We are going to do our best to make you forget it."

For a moment, Deborah thought that the countess was referring to her abduction, but a quick look into Gray's calm, untroubled eyes corrected that impression. He had intimated that he would tell his family only what he intended to tell the world, that the shock of his father's death had caused Quentin to lose his memory, and they had spent a few months in the country to get over the tragedy. No one was to know that they had witnessed the murder, or that they had gone into hiding when they reached England. It would rouse too much curiosity, too much speculation, and add nothing to her peace of mind. She was here because she was Quentin's guardian, and because she and Gray had to decide on the boy's future.

The warmth of her reception was more than she had expected. A lump formed in her throat. She liked the countess on sight, and intuition told her that the feeling was mutual. She was clearing her throat, trying to find her voice to reply to these kind words, when Gray drew one of his sisters forward to meet her.

"My sister Gussie," he said, slipping an affectionate arm around his sister's shoulders. "You wouldn't know it to look at her, but Gussie was once the bane of my existence. Older sisters tend to be tyrants, you know, but now that she has Hart and Jason to manage, we rub along tolerably well."

Gussie ignored the ensuing laughter. She, too, reached for Deborah's hands and held them in a firm clasp. "Deborah," she said, and smiled warmly. "I hope you do not believe everything this rogue tells you. As though he would allow a mere female to lord it over him! He is the tyrant, though you would not know it to look at him."

"Yes," said Deborah, "I believe you."

"Oh ho!" Gussie threw Gray a challenging look. "There is a story here, if only I could discover it."

"Gussie!" Hart laughed, not very convincingly, and pulled his wife to his side again, where he anchored her with one arm fast around her waist. He spoke to Deborah. "These Graysons take a bit of getting used to. This kind of teasing is second nature to them."

"Yes, I believe that too," said Deborah demurely.

Jason and Quentin were becoming restive. There was a short consultation with Hart, then making their excuses, they went charging up the stairs to the old nursery where a set of tin soldiers was set out for battle.

Deborah watched Quentin go with a start of alarm. Without him, she felt lost. She felt the touch of Gray's hand on her shoulder and glanced up, and the look he gave her helped steady her nerves.

Gray, aware that his mother was avidly watching the interesting byplay between himself and Deborah, drew Deborah's attention to the last member of his family to be introduced. "And this is my sister Meg."

The girl was lovely—heart-shaped face dominated by the Grayson eyes. Her hair was fair, though not so blond as her brothers' and sister's, and her expression was frankly curious. Deborah had a fleeting recollection of Millicent Dench, the girl at Miss Hare's who would try anything for a dare. Precocious, she thought, and was very glad she was not Lady Margaret Grayson's governess.

"Lady Margaret," murmured Deborah, acknowledging the introduction.

"Oh, please call me Meg." Her eyes scanned Deborah in a slow perusal. "I have never had a governess who looked anything like you. I wish I had green eyes and hair the color of vintage sherry. Blond hair and blue eyes are so common."

"Only," said Gray dryly, "in this family. Meg, where are your manners?"

"Oh." Crestfallen, Meg looked from Deborah to

Gray. "Did I say something out of turn? It seems to be a failing of mine."

"Not to my ears," interposed Deborah. "I have never yet heard of any female objecting to a compliment. Thank you, Meg. That was very nicely said."

The countess linked her arm through Deborah's. "Come along, my dear, and I shall show you to your room. You will want to get settled before we dine. Quentin has the room next to yours. I hope that is convenient?"

Deborah was swept away on the countess's arm, with Gray's sisters following them. As soon as they had taken the first turn in the stairs, Gray rounded on Nick.

"Oh no," said Nick, answering that look, "I told Mother exactly what you told me to tell her. I never even hinted that your interest in Miss Weyman was anything but brotherly. Well, I wouldn't, would I? You might decide to repay me in kind, and I wouldn't appreciate it any more than you would."

"Nick, let's get one thing straight. I have no interest in Deborah Weyman, brotherly or otherwise. I feel a responsibility for the girl, and that is all. Do you understand?"

"Oh yes," said Nick, clapping Gray on the shoulder. "I understand perfectly. I say, let's open a bottle of champagne. It's not every day that a fellow hears he is going to be an uncle."

Hart threw one arm over Gray's shoulders and the other over Nick's and began to propel them toward the library. He was grinning from ear to ear. "An uncle is all right in its way, but just you wait. One day, you will hear that you are going to be a father, then you'll really have something to celebrate."

Nick cocked one eyebrow. "How do you know we haven't already heard it?"

Speechless, Hart stopped in his tracks, and stared first at Nick, then at Gray. "You don't . . . I can't . . . surely . . ."

Nick decided to put his brother-in-law out of his misery. "Don't worry, Hart. To my knowledge, there are no little . . . um . . . unhallowed Graysons running around the country, though I can't vouch for Gray. What do you say, Gray?"

Gray was no more amused than Hart. "It's that kind of loose talk that starts up vicious rumors. What if it got back to Mother, or one of our sisters?"

Nick winked at Hart and sailed into the library. "Or to Miss Weyman? Poor Gray! She is going to hear plenty and there is nothing you can do about it." Unperturbed, grinning, he pulled on the bell rope to summon a footman.

❧

The rumors reached Deborah sooner than Nick had foreseen and came from a most unexpected quarter. After dinner, while the gentlemen lingered in the dining room, enjoying their port and brandy, the ladies retired to the drawing room for tea and conversation. Before long, Gussie and Meg were practicing a duet at the piano, and the countess had picked up her embroidery.

For the first little while, the countess, very subtly, delved into Deborah's background. Deborah was prepared for the questions, and told, very candidly, a tissue of lies that would take a month of Sundays to disprove, but which satisfied the countess's curiosity. After this, they talked of Quentin and how his father's death had affected him. Finally, there was a silence.

After a quick glance at the piano assured the countess that Gussie and Meg were absorbed in their music, she smiled confidingly at Deborah. "Gray is very grateful for all you have done for Quentin."

"Yes?" said Deborah carefully.

"He feels that these last few months have been very hard on you, and he wishes to make it up to you." Deborah made no response to this, and the countess went on brightly, "You are to look upon your time with us as a holiday from all your cares. Gray has asked me to sponsor you in society, arrange parties and so on."

This was news to Deborah and she opened her mouth to argue, then thought better of it. It was all part and parcel of Gray's plan to protect Quentin, and she had given her word to be guided by him. All the same, she felt a little uneasy about the idea of being sponsored in society, and more uneasy still at the interpretation the countess might put on all this unwarranted attention for a mere governess. She smiled and uttered the first inanity that came to mind. "His lordship is too kind."

The countess nodded, reflecting that it really was mere kindness on Gray's part, and that's what was so disappointing. When he had come to her room before dinner for a quiet tête-à-tête, and had given her explicit instructions respecting Miss Deborah Weyman, she had leapt to the conclusion that at long last her son had met a woman who could hold his interest. She should have known better.

Her hopes had been dashed almost at once. Miss Weyman was a guest in their home, he told her, because she was indispensable to Quentin's peace of mind. She had been with the boy for four years, and had devoted herself to Quentin, especially in these last months following the tragedy. They owed her a debt of gratitude that could never be repaid. Now that Quentin was soon to go off to Eton, some provision must be made for the girl. He did not see why she could not make a suitable match with one of the many eligible young gentlemen who flocked around Meg.

The countess could think of many reasons, not least the disposition of his own sister. Meg was no shrinking violet. She would not take kindly to another woman poaching on her preserves. Not wishing to provoke an argument, the countess had said nothing of this. Instead, she had mentioned the lack of a dowry. Gray had waved away this objection. Gil had left Miss Weyman a handsome legacy, and so the matter was settled with one caveat. Deborah was proud to a fault. She must not suspect that they aimed to marry her off.

Now, facing Deborah, the countess got down to business. "It would be a grave mistake, Deborah, to put too much weight on my son's interest in you."

"What!" exclaimed Deborah, startled.

The duet at the piano died a sudden, discordant death.

The countess groped for the right words to convey her message tactfully. "You are a guest in my home, Deborah. I feel responsible for you. I like you and don't wish to see you get hurt."

"Hurt?" Alarm coursed through her. Were they going to abduct her again?

"What Mama is trying to say," said Gussie, coming over and making a place for herself on the sofa beside Deborah, "is that she hopes you are too sensible to lose your heart to Gray."

Meg flounced over and plumped herself down on a stuffed armchair. "It's so pathetic the way women moon over him, like dogs salivating over a juicy bone. Haven't you noticed? There are no maids in Mama's employ under the age of fifty. They never last a week. It's too comical for words, don't you agree?"

"Meg," remonstrated the countess, "you make it sound as though Gray encourages them. You know he never would."

"Oh, wouldn't he? That's not how my last governess told it. Miss Peachum, you remember her, Mama?"

"Well, of course I remember her. I had to give the woman notice, didn't I? And what do you mean, 'that's not how Miss Peachum told it'?"

Meg's eyes sparkled. "She said that though Gray had spoken no words to her, none were necessary. His speaking eyes said it all. I had to put her wise about a few things." She plucked a sugar plum from the dish on the tea table and popped it in her mouth. "It did the trick."

"What did the trick?" demanded the countess, torn between terminating a conversation that was not fit for Meg's innocent ears and her desire to know more.

"I told her about the little house in Hans Town. It was cruel, I suppose, but in the end it was better for her to know that there was no hope for her."

"You know about the house in Hans Town?" asked the countess, thunderstruck.

"Of course I know," replied Meg, and she reached for another sugar plum. "Doesn't everybody?"

Deborah, who had been trying with diminishing patience to get a word in edgewise, suddenly pressed her lips together. She looked with interest at each lady in turn. When the silence lengthened, and no one made a move to satisfy her burning curiosity, she gently prompted, "The little house in Hans Town? That's in Knightsbridge, isn't it?"

Gussie said, "It's best if she knows, Mama."

The countess mopped her brow with a scrap of white lace. Finally, coming to a decision, she said, "You must remember, Deborah, Gray is a single man."

"A rake, in fact," said Meg merrily.

The dowager pinned her younger daughter with a flinty eye. "Meg, one more word out of you, and you may retire to your room."

Deborah reinforced that message with her own flinty eye. At this rate, she would never hear the salacious details of Lord Kendal's private life. Soon, the gentlemen would be joining them and the opportunity would be lost. Convinced that Meg had got the message, she turned back to the countess.

"A single man," she repeated encouragingly.

"Yes," said the countess. "But you must not think that, when the time comes, Gray will not make a worthy husband. He hasn't met the right woman yet, 'tis all. When he does, the house in Hans Town will become ancient history. You may take my word for it."

Meg made a sound that suspiciously resembled a smothered snort.

Gussie shook her head. "Mama, you are not explaining this very well. May I?"

"Please do."

"What Mama means to say is that Gray does not lack for female companionship. That is why he has a house in Hans Town. Oh, you need not fear Gray has designs on you. His mistresses are all experienced women of the world. He would never dream of taking up with a virtuous girl. Governesses and so on are not his style."

"What exactly," said Deborah, unashamedly fishing, "do you mean by 'women of the world'?"

When Gussie hesitated, Meg said, "Mrs. Brewster

for one. Mama, you need not look so shocked. I am practically eighteen years old. These morsels of gossip are bound to get back to a man's sister."

"*That* is not what shocks me," said the countess. "But Mrs. Brewster! Oh dear! She is so *vulgar*, though she is an actress. What on earth does Gray see in her?"

"She is probably *inventive*," said Deborah acidly.

This contribution to the conversation meant nothing to the others, and after a moment Gussie went on. "That's old history, Meg. Last I heard, Mrs. Brewster was sporting a bracelet with a ruby clasp, and the new tenant of the house in Hans Town was Caterina Cesari. She's an opera dancer at Covent Garden, and there is nothing vulgar about Miss Cesari. No, really, Mama, she speaks with a cultured accent, and since Gray has the dressing of her, she is quite elegant. Even Hart says so."

"That's something, I suppose," said the countess faintly.

"A ruby clasp?" said Meg. "I would have thought Mrs. Brewster would have rated a diamond. Still, it's better than a plain gold bracelet." To Deborah's questioning look, she responded, "You can tell a lot about what Gray thinks of his mistresses by the bracelets he gives them when the affair is over. Some few are rewarded with a diamond necklace."

The countess moaned. "You ought not to know about such things, Meg. Nor should we be talking like this. What would Gray say if he knew?"

"Nonsense, Mama," said Gussie. "All young girls are curious about such things. I was no better at Meg's age." She turned a very direct gaze upon Deborah. "The point is, Gray has a way with women. He can be charming, he can be kind, but he doesn't mean anything by it. It would be a mistake to read too much into it."

Deborah relaxed against the back of the sofa. Her face was flushed. "You are telling me all this because you think I stand in danger of losing my heart to him?" Their solemn expressions answered for them, and she gave a start of laughter. "I promise you, I won't fall in love with him." She knew that for a certainty. "Lord

Kendal and I are not exactly the best of friends. To be perfectly honest, I find him a mite autocratic for my taste."

The countess's blue eyes widened in surprise. "I believe you mean that."

For two pins, Deborah would have put these ladies wise to the true colors of the charming degenerate who had a way with woman and whom they seemed to revere. She couldn't tell them, of course, because she was here for a purpose, and that took precedence over everything.

She forced a smile. "You forget, Lord Kendal and I are Quentin's guardians. We have a business relationship. In plain terms, we do not always see eye to eye, and when Lord Kendal is thwarted, his 'charm' flies out the window. He has a temper, ma'am, which he has never tried to conceal from me."

"Now this is truly interesting," said Gussie. "I never yet met a woman who was unaffected by Gray's considerable appeal."

"You have met her now," said Deborah. "Might I have more tea?"

When the gentlemen entered the drawing room, Deborah was at her most gracious. She knew that Gray's mother and sisters were watching her closely, and she schooled herself to appear quite unaffected by the worldly earl. She didn't ignore Gray, but she never allowed her gaze to wander to him when she was in conversation with someone else.

And she was unaffected, she told herself. Nevertheless, as soon as she could manage it, she excused herself to go to Quentin.

CHAPTER 13

"A toast, gentlemen. Here's to a glorious British victory with the French on our own shores!"

The group of noisy celebrants, who were seated at a corner table in the dining room of White's Club, the most exclusive gentlemen's club in St. James's, loudly seconded the speaker's sentiments before draining their glasses. Gray and his companion watched for a moment in silence before turning their backs on them.

"I'd say," said Lord Lawford, "that the war fever is beginning to sound hysterical. A toast to a French invasion! Young Leathe should know better. He, at least, is a real soldier."

"Do you think so?" said Gray. "I hear that when he sold out, he saved his commanding officer the trouble of a court-martial."

Lawford was surprised by Gray's lack of charity. He glanced again at the table of young men, some of them in officers' uniforms of the militia, Britain's reserve army of volunteers and amateurs. "Those coxcombs don't know one end of a musket from another. I suppose they expect to repel a French invasion with a pair of dueling pistols. If they get their wish, they'll learn that it will take more than fancy uniforms and empty boasts to frighten Bonaparte away."

Leaning back in his chair, Gray studied his companion. Oliver Lawford was in his early fifties, with stooped shoulders and a face with the features of a monkey. His clothes were shabby. Lawford's looks, however, were deceptive. His relatives included two dukes, a marquess, and an earl. His mind was razor sharp and his memory phenomenal. His field of operations was intelligence, but whereas Gray was affiliated with the Foreign Office, Lawford was affiliated with the War Office. They were not exactly friends, but they trusted each other. And as Gray had discovered when he was looking for Deborah and Quentin, Lawford was a useful man to know.

Lawford was making his own appraisal. He liked Kendal, though he wasn't sure why. The earl was not really his type. He was too glamorous, too wealthy, too much a man of the world. Lawford was none of those things. His tastes ran to fine port and quiet evenings spent at home in the company of his dogs. Yet, he enjoyed these dinners with Kendal and supposed that it had something to do with the fact that the earl did not take himself too seriously. Some called him cynical. Lawford suspected that Kendal was bored, and that only his work at the Foreign Office meant anything to him.

Gray raised his glass of burgundy and took a small sip. "Now tell me what you've discovered about this traitor of ours."

"Damn little, if you want the unvarnished truth. There are too many people to investigate, too many people who were in the know, and all of them above reproach, pillars of the diplomatic corps. These people have influence." Lawford paused to marshal his thoughts. "I agree with you about trying to work from the other direction. You suspect the informer is the person who murdered Barrington, and I think you are right."

"Why?"

"What?"

"Why do you think I'm right?"

For a moment, Lawford appeared to be nonplussed. "Because . . . well, because everything points to that conclusion. Lord Barrington knew something and made

an appointment to see you. You received a note canceling the appointment, a note that, in my opinion, is
highly suspect. I don't believe Barrington canceled that
appointment. My instincts tell me that the murderer got
to hear of it and decided to keep it himself. And so he
sent you that note canceling the appointment."

"That's what my instincts tell me too," said Gray.
"That means he must have been someone close to me, or
close to Gil." He glanced over his shoulder as a burst of
laughter came from Leathe's table. Turning back to his
companion, he picked up a new thread. "Let's talk
about alibis. Where was everyone on the night Gil was
murdered?"

"Who knows? Everyone was trying to get out of
Paris. Take yourself, for example. Where were you, Kendal, when Lord Barrington was murdered?"

Gray almost laughed. "I was halfway to Calais."

"Can someone verify that? Your secretary, for instance?"

Slightly taken aback, Gray said, "I was alone. My
secretary and I became separated in the confusion. I was
in London when the report of Gil's death reached me."

Lawford smiled. "That's what they all say, more or
less. You see the problem? We've got hardly anything to
go on. Most of those who could tell us anything are
behind French lines where we can't get at them right
now. All we've got are Lady Barrington, your ward,
Quentin, and his governess."

Gray did not respond to Lawford's speculative look.
He had confided the essential facts of Gil's murder and
Deborah's flight to Wells with Quentin. The only thing
he had left out was her abduction and the time she had
spent as his captive, not because it showed him in a bad
light, but because he wanted nothing to tarnish Deborah's spotless reputation.

"Are you sure Miss Weyman has told you everything
she knows?" asked Lawford.

"Perfectly sure."

"And there's no evidence that the boy's memory is
coming back to him?"

"None whatsoever."

"Then you know as well as I do that there's only one thing to be done."

Gray took a moment to refill their empty glasses before replying. "I won't have my ward used as bait. The boy has been through enough already. Besides, the whole point of displaying him is to let the murderer see that he poses no threat to him."

"If I were the murderer," mused Lawford, "I would always fear that the boy's memory would come back to him."

"He is well guarded. And that's exactly why we have to find our traitor, so we'll have the murderer, and Quentin will be safe."

"And how is Quentin?"

There was a pause as Gray thought about his reply. "He's doing remarkably well. He's at Channings right now—you know, Hart's place."

"Yes, I know it. It's right next to your estate, isn't it?"

Gray nodded. "Hart took Quentin along with his son to get in some riding and fishing. Gussie stayed on in town. Ladies weren't invited."

"It's good to get away from females sometimes," said Lawford with a laugh.

"Yes, isn't it?" said Gray.

But it had caused the most almighty row between Deborah and him. She'd wanted to go with Quentin, in spite of the fact that it was supposed to be a male-only event and the rest of the family would be going down there in a week or so. He'd said some harsh things, accusing her of wanting to keep the boy in leading-strings. In the end, he'd told her to discuss it with Quentin. Whatever they decided together would be fine by him. The look on Quentin's face when he realized Deborah meant to tag along had settled the argument. Deborah made light of it, saying it was only a suggestion, but he could see she was hurt to the quick. He'd gone after her, but she wasn't in the mood to be comforted, at least not by him. So he'd sent Quentin to her. They'd spent an hour together, and though he had no idea what they had talked about, it had made all the difference to Deb. But he knew she was counting the days till they would all go down to Channings.

"And Miss Weyman?" said Lawford. "How is she?"

"Very well," said Gray, and smiled to himself.

Lawford lounged back in his chair and surveyed Gray curiously. Just that morning, his nephew had casually mentioned that Lord Kendal was turning respectable now that he was the guardian of Lord Barrington's boy. The house in Hans Town had stood empty for quite some time, and no lady's name had been linked with the earl's since someone had seen him leaving Helena Perrin's house on the afternoon of Lady Melbourne's reception. That had been more than a month ago, right before the earl had gone off secretly to Bath to find the boy and his governess. In the weeks since they had taken up residence in Kendal House, the earl had given up his old haunts. When he wasn't at the Foreign Office or at his club, he was at home, in the bosom of his family, or he was seen squiring one or another of his female relatives and Miss Weyman about town. Lawford had assumed that Kendal was keeping a close eye on Miss Weyman and his ward as a precautionary measure, but he wondered now if there was more to it.

"My nephew," he said, "tells me that Miss Weyman is making discreet inquiries about the possibility of finding another position once your ward goes off to school." This was a blatant lie, but like any intelligence officer worth his salt, Lawford knew how to fish for information.

Gray's head snapped back. "Your nephew is mistaken."

Behind his sleepy-eyed gaze, Lawford studied Gray's hard, blue-eyed stare, the bunched muscles that were tensed for action. "Really?" he asked mildly, smiling to himself. "I expect you are right. I am only repeating what Roger told me."

Gray signaled to a waiter to bring the bill. "I'd be obliged," he said, "if you would keep your eyes and ears open. Something may cross your desk that will give us a clue to the traitor's identity."

"I've already alerted some of my key operators,"

said Lawford, "but I don't hold out much hope unless your spy becomes active again. Thank you for the dinner. Next time, it's on me."

No more mention was made of Miss Weyman, nor did Lawford expect it. He had touched a raw nerve, and now he could hardly wait to make the lady's acquaintance. Though he wasn't one who enjoyed the social scene, he had made up his mind that for Deborah Weyman, he was willing to endure the tedium of sprucing himself up and braving the perils of drawing-room conversation. In his desk drawer were several invitations to parties and receptions. One of those invitations bore the earl's seal.

Having finished the burgundy and settled the bill, they scraped back their chairs. They were almost at the door when a young man with a thin, handsome face fringed with dark hair came barging into the room and stumbled against them. This was the Viscount Leathe who had made the toast which had soured Lawford's mood. He righted himself almost at once, and had begun on an apology when he suddenly recognized Gray and drew back violently.

"Leathe," acknowledged Gray, icily polite. The last time he had seen Lord Leathe was in the Bois de Boulogne in Paris when he had helped him onto his horse after knocking him senseless for daring to kiss and fondle his sister, Meg. Had it not been for the threat of scandal, he would have called him out. "I had heard," said Gray, "that you were fixed in Yorkshire for the hunting season."

Leathe spoke with deliberate insolence. "The hunting in London suits me better."

A muscle tensed in Gray's cheek. "Then no doubt we shall meet again before long."

"I look forward to it," drawled Leathe.

During the short walk home to Berkeley Square, Gray was seething. He had promised Leathe that the next time he came near his sister, he would put a bullet in his brain. During that terse exchange in White's, Leathe had practically taunted Gray with the promise that Meg was still his quarry, and if that meant a duel with her brother, so be it. Leathe was an insolent pup who was begging to be taught a lesson. He was wild and had an ungovernable temper which his years with the army had done nothing to improve. Scandal had followed on his heels from one posting to another, from the plains of India to the garrison at Dublin.

About six months ago, he had appeared in Paris like an ill-omened comet. Gaming, dueling, wenching—that was the sum of Leathe's ambitions. This did not surprise Gray. It was common knowledge that bad blood ran in his veins. His mother had died in an insane asylum. His sister had disappeared off the face of the earth after her betrothed had died in suspicious circumstances. And Leathe himself had escaped some scandal at school by running away and enlisting in the British army. It was the father who had Gray's sympathies. The Earl of Belvidere put a brave face on things. Though estranged from his son and heir, it was rumored that he had left no stone unturned to effect a reconciliation, but his efforts had been futile. Leathe was intent on burning himself out before he reached his next birthday. And the boy was no older than Nick!

If it were up to him, every door in London would be barred against the viscount. There was little hope of that happening. Leathe had one asset hard to resist. He had more money than sat in the vaults of the Bank of England. In fact, even Gray's considerable fortune paled into insignificance when compared to Leathe's. And for this reason, ambitious parents would willingly overlook the viscount's unsavory character in hopes of establishing their daughters in style. Gray snorted. If Leathe had marriage on his mind, his name wasn't John Grayson. No. What Leathe wanted was to set the world on its heels, just for the hell of it.

On arriving at Kendal House, he removed his greatcoat and made straight for the drawing room where he knew his mother would be hosting one of her informal assemblies for a few invited guests. This was something new at Kendal House, and the idea had come from Gray. He wanted to ease Deborah's way in society, to enlarge her group of friends and acquaintances so that she would feel comfortable when she attended larger receptions. It also gave him a chance to look over the young men who might be suitable candidates for her hand in marriage. To his chagrin, the first person his eyes alighted on when he entered the room was Lady Helena Perrin. She was seated on a long sofa, talking animatedly to Deborah. He didn't want Helena Perrin anywhere near Deborah.

Standing unseen, just inside the door, he took a moment or two to contemplate Deborah. Her profile was to him, giving him a glimpse of her beautiful long throat and the soft swell of her breasts. In the pale peach silk that he himself had chosen for her, she looked as pretty as a picture. She looked so right in his house, with his mother and sisters, wearing garments he had chosen to enhance her femininity.

It wasn't enough for him. He wanted to lift the burdens from her shoulders. He wanted her to be safe and happy. She shouldn't have to worry about money, or earn a living by looking after other people's children. He wanted the best for her, and, by God, he was going to see that she got it.

Lady Helena looked up and caught sight of him. "Gray!" She smiled and patted the empty space beside her on the sofa.

He ignored the invitation and took a straight-backed chair from where he could face both ladies. Deborah's expression was unclouded, and he experienced a rush of relief. As his look lingered, Deborah's brows winged up, coolly questioning him. He smiled into her eyes, conveying his pleasure at the pains she had taken with her appearance that evening. She had not given in gracefully to this transformation. He was still in her black book, and he sensed that someone had warned her against him, probably his own mother. He didn't mind Deborah's cool stares or her flashes of temper for himself, in fact, he relished crossing swords with her, but he would not permit anyone else to embarrass her, especially not a discarded mistress.

Lady Helena was taking in this silent exchange. She had already noticed that Deborah Weyman was hardly the drab little governess she had been in Paris. This vision of elegance could hold her own in any setting. It struck her forcibly, now, that she had never seen that softened expression on Gray's face, had never seen that warm, intimate smile. She could hardly believe what her eyes were telling her.

Deborah broke the silence. "Lady Helena did not recognize me when we met this evening."

"No, indeed," said Helena, managing to pull herself together. "Miss Weyman's appearance has undergone a remarkable change."

Gray looked at Helena, and there was a warning to be read in the hardness in his eyes. "Deborah," he said, "was convinced that she would be taken more seriously as a governess if she made herself look older."

Helena smiled sweetly. "So she told me. But you saw through her ruse?" Gray inclined his head, and Helena laughed before continuing lightly, "Watch him, Miss Weyman. He is a born predator." She rose gracefully. "It was a pleasure to meet you again, Miss Weyman." She looked over at her husband, signaling that it was time to go. "Gray, would you mind waiting for me while I take my leave of your mother?"

When she and Gray were in the corridor, Helena slipped a gold bracelet from her wrist. "You bastard," she hissed, slapping the bracelet into the hand that came up automatically to receive it. Then, ignoring the presence of two silent, startled footmen, she walked off.

Gray had just slipped the bracelet into his pocket, when Eric Perrin came out of the drawing room. "What happened to Helena?" he asked.

"She went to get her wrap." Gray did not elaborate, and after a slight hesitation, Perrin bade him a civil good-night and began to descend the stairs. When Perrin had taken the turn in the stairs, Gray went back to his guests.

❧

"You're very quiet tonight, Eric."

Eric Perrin gripped the safety strap as the coach

turned the corner into Bond Street. When the coach straightened, he looked over at his wife. "I was thinking of Miss Weyman. I saw you speaking to her earlier, and wondered what you had found to talk about."

"Eton," said Helena. "Quentin will be going there soon, and she wanted to know my opinion of it."

"Why didn't she ask Kendal? He is the boy's guardian."

"Yes, but Kendal doesn't have two sons who are pupils there. I think she was anxious, but I did my best to put her mind at rest. Besides, she is the boy's guardian too."

"Where was Quentin, by the by? I thought, since this was an informal party, he might be allowed to join us for a few minutes."

Helena looked curiously at him, then shrugged. "I believe he has gone into the country to be with the Hartleys' boy. Jason and he have become almost inseparable."

"That's an odd business about his memory, isn't it?"

"Miss Weyman explained it to me. Quentin and she found his father's body. The shock did something to the boy's mind." She felt suddenly cold, and shrank into her wrap.

"That's not all that's odd!"

"What do you mean?"

"Miss Weyman is the boy's governess, but while he goes off to the country, she stays in town. What do you make of it?"

Helena did not care for what she made of it, and she spoke sharply. "She is not a paid employee. She is Lady Kendal's guest. It's my opinion that Gray means to marry her."

There was a silence, then Perrin said, "I'm sorry I spoke."

She closed her eyes and let out a breathy sigh. "It doesn't matter."

"I don't like to see you hurt."

The coach made another turn, and she opened her eyes, staring at her husband as though he were a stranger. In some respects, he was a stranger. She had never really understood him though they had been married for ten years. She had been sold to him, quite literally, to pay off her father's debts. She considered herself fortunate that it was he who had offered the highest price for her and not one of her father's friends, all of them elderly, revolting roués who had a taste for young flesh. Eric was not much older than she; he was handsome, he was rich, and could have had his pick of any number of girls. Whether he regretted the bargain, she had no way of knowing. They were not in the habit of confiding in each other. On balance, she thought the bargain suited him very well. For what it was worth, his children had blue blood in their veins. She was highly connected and used those connections to advance her husband's career. She presided over boring dinner parties with charm and grace. She never complained about his infidelities, never reproached him for neglecting her. There was nothing to reproach. He was openhanded, never begrudging her a new gown or whatever took her fancy. And he turned a blind eye to her own string of lovers. She wondered if he was happy with his new mistress in their lovers' nest in Kensington.

"What is it?" he asked softly.

She breathed out slowly. "I don't want to be alone. Don't leave me tonight, Eric."

His eyes seemed to burn brightly in that dimly lit coach. "Do you want me, Helena, or will any man do?"

She sensed his arousal and laughed tauntingly. "Any man will do, as long as he is as handsome and as virile as you."

He made a small sound that she could not interpret, then he was reaching for her.

❧

After the Perrins' departure, Gray felt more comfortable in his role as host. He exchanged a few words with Lord Denning, who had arrived late, and was sulking over finding Deborah monopolized by Philip Standish. Having exhausted the subject of Denning's new bay, Gray appraised the other gentlemen in the room. He approved of Hay and Banks, the young men who formed part of Meg's court. Their credentials were impeccable; they came from good stock; they conducted themselves like gentlemen; and though he was aware that each dabbled in the petticoat line, he did not hold that against them. They were men. Besides, no plaster saint would ever hold Meg. That reminded him of Viscount Leathe, and he went to join his mother at the tea table.

She smiled when he sat down beside her. "I think," she said, "that Deborah and Mr. Standish are quite taken with each other. They met in Paris, did you know? At some picnic or other."

Gray followed her look. Deborah and Philip were cozily ensconced on the sofa, and Philip was laughing at something she had said. Gray frowned. "Philip and Deborah? I hardly think so."

"Mmm," said his mother with a complacent twinkle in her eye. "Why won't they suit?"

He gave her the obvious explanation. "Philip is as poor as a church mouse. It would be a foolish match for them both."

She sighed dramatically. "I fear you are right, yet again."

"Yet again?" asked Gray absently. Deborah had turned one of Philip's hands over and she appeared to be reading his palm, much to that gentlemen's embarrassment.

The countess began to tick off names on the fingers of one hand. "Mr. Daniels, you said, was too old for her; Mr. Markham was too young; Lord Tweedsdale, and I can hardly credit this, would never offer marriage but only the position of mistress. Now who else was there? Oh yes, Crossley's heir was too spoiled, and Denning only wants a nurse for his motherless children. But Gray, these are all gentlemen that you particularly told me to cultivate because they are so suitable. I wish you would tell me what has made you change your mind. At this rate, we shall never get Deborah married off."

Gray heard not one word of his mother's deliberately provocative prattle. He was absorbed in watching Deborah as gradually others drifted over to her and laughingly demanded to have their palms read.

"Gray?" said the countess, bringing his attention back to herself.

"Mmm? Oh yes, Deborah. Don't worry about it, Mother. There's plenty of time to get her married off. What I wanted to talk to you about is Leathe. He's back."

"Leathe." The countess's gaze strayed to her daughter. She had a shrewd idea that Meg was more taken with young Leathe than she let on. In fact, it wouldn't surprise her if Meg encouraged the young man. She understood his appeal only too well. Good girls were always attracted to bad boys, thinking they would be the one to reform them. That was mere wishful thinking. Poor Meg.

She heard herself agreeing to Gray's suggestion that they go down to Hart's place before the week was out.

"Meg will be safe from Leathe there," said Gray, "and Channings is close enough to town to make it easily accessible for visitors. Besides, I know that Deborah will be more than happy to be with Quentin again." This reminded him of something else. "By the way, has Deborah said anything to you about finding another position as a governess?"

The countess smiled to herself. "I believe," she said, "Lord Denning could tell you more about that."

"Denning?" Gray's eyes fixed on the gentleman in question. Denning was all right in his way, thought Gray dispassionately. He was a bit of a dandy, but not vulgar with it. His looks were passable. However, he was a widower with two young daughters still in the nursery. Now that he'd had time to think about it, he had decided that he did not want Deborah saddled with a brood of infants before she had time to enjoy herself. He watched her for a moment as she responded to something Denning had said. He could detect no interest on Deborah's part, and that made him feel marginally happier about the riding expedition to Richmond Park he had arranged where Denning was to be one of the party.

"What," he asked at length, "has Denning to say

about Deborah finding another position as a governess?"

The countess choked back a laugh. "I gather the poor man was trying to hint Deborah into marriage, but she jumped to the conclusion that he was offering her the position of governess."

Gray smiled. "And did she accept it?"

"No. She told Denning that she already had a position, but she would be quite happy to write to her old governess to see if she could suggest someone for him. The poor man was utterly confused." Her expression turned serious. "Do you know, Gray, I don't think Deborah wishes to marry? Oh, she's very agreeable to all the young men who come to the house, but she never encourages any of them."

"Nonsense. Every young woman wishes to marry. Would you excuse me, Mother?"

The countess watched curiously as Gray joined the group beside Deborah and deftly plucked her out of it. He then led her to the piano and stood over her like a watchdog while she selected a piece of music to play to the assembled guests. Gray and Deborah? The thought made the countess smile.

Nick, also, watched Gray with Deborah, and when his chance came, he droned in Gray's ear, "This has all the makings of a farce."

"What has?" asked Gray absently.

"You, watching Miss Weyman, watching Philip, and Mother, weighing every word and change in expression."

"You are imagining things, Nick."

Nick allowed that to pass. "I suppose," he said, managing to sound serious, "Philip would do very well for our Deborah?" Gray's brows came down. Taking that for encouragement, Nick went on in the same vein. "He is of good family, and with your patronage, he should go far in the diplomatic corps. Moreover, he is youngish for someone who is over thirty, handsome and virile. And Deborah seems taken with him. What more can I say?"

Gray's eyes met Nick's in a steady stare. "Actually,"

drawled Gray, "I was thinking of someone closer to home, someone like you, Nick."

Nick's jaw dropped. "Oh no you don't! You're not going to palm her off on me, Gray. She's too old for me."

"Nonsense," said Gray. "You are about the same age."

"I'm only a stripling! You have said so yourself on many occasions. I have years ahead of me yet in which to enjoy my freedom before I tie myself down to one woman. Besides, you are joking. You want her for yourself. You know you do."

Gray merely smiled, and eventually Nick went off huffing to join Denning in a game of chess.

Gray settled back in his chair and went through the motions of taking snuff. Philip and Deborah? He just couldn't see it. Philip was too prim and proper and Deb had enough of those traits for the two of them.

As for Nick, he could not see that either. Nick was too young, too inexperienced. Deb would have the bit between his teeth before the ink had dried on their marriage lines, if not sooner. There was another reason, a more compelling reason to keep them apart. If Deborah married Nick, she would become his sister, live in the same house with him, be closer to him than was good for him. That must never be allowed to happen. There was no hurry, he told himself. It was months before Quentin would be going off to school. In that waiting period, some suitable candidate was bound to turn up.

CHAPTER 14

"Sophie! This is a pleasant surprise!"

Deborah was descending the stairs when she heard Gray's cordial greeting. She looked over the banister and saw a young woman, dressed from head to toe in unrelenting black, holding out both gloved hands. Gray quickly crossed to the girl, clasped her hands briefly, then dragged her into a bear hug. Deborah wasn't surprised. Bear hugs, back poundings, exuberant kisses, and so on were a particular idiosyncrasy of all the Graysons. They never stood on ceremony with their friends.

When Gray released the girl, Deborah had a clear view of glossy dark ringlets peeking from beneath the brim of an elaborate bonnet, and a beauty that was almost childlike in its purity. This face was well-known to Deborah. It belonged to Sophie Barrington, the young widow of Gil Barrington. The last time Deborah had seen her ladyship was when the Capets had called for her in their carriage to convey her from Paris to England. Just as she had then, she was weeping delicately into a lacy white handkerchief. Tears and swoons were not uncommon with Sophie Barrington. Her nerves were so fragile that it didn't take much to reduce her to a quivering jelly, and most people avoided that at all costs.

"Gray," said Lady Barrington, one hand clutching a lapel of his blue coat. She gulped back a teary sob. "I had to come when you wrote me that Quentin had lost his memory. I had no idea that the poor boy had suffered so much. I had to see with my own eyes that he is as well as you say he is. We were always so close."

"What a pity you've missed him. He's at Channings right now, but the family will be there before the week is out. Why don't you join them when they go down?"

"Unfortunately, I have appointments this week."

"Then the week after? I know my sister won't take no for an answer. She'll be delighted to see you, Sophie."

"Will you be there, Gray?"

"Unfortunately, no. There is a war going on, and my presence is required at the Foreign Office. But I should manage to get down there on odd days."

Sophie laughed. "How can I refuse? Oh Gray, it's so good to see you again."

Deborah was on the point of continuing her descent, when Sophie's next words froze her to the spot.

"And what is this I hear about Miss Weyman, Gray?"

"What have you heard?"

"That there has been an extraordinary change in her appearance?"

Gray answered easily, "Oh, that. Yes, Deb tried to make herself look older to impress her employers. She thought if Gil knew how young she was, he might have reservations about her abilities as a governess."

Deborah peeked over the banister just as Sophie let out a trill of musical laughter. She was looking up at Gray with a teasing smile on her face. Gray's arms were still around her.

"What a bore for Miss Weyman," said Sophie. "And really, it was not necessary. She's a plain-looking girl, as I remember."

"Is she? I couldn't say. My mother thinks she's quite pretty."

Deborah did a quick about-turn and headed for the servants' staircase. Inwardly, she excused herself for avoiding Sophie Barrington on the grounds that Nick and Meg were with a party of friends in the mews behind the house, waiting for her to join them for an outing to Richmond Park. It would be inconsiderate to keep them waiting. Besides, she had no wish to intrude on *that* tender reunion.

We were always so close. Deborah almost snorted. She could count on one hand the number of times her ladyship had entered the schoolroom, or included Quentin in any of her plans. It had all been a great disappointment to Lord Barrington. *She is very young,* Deborah told herself, trying to be fair, *young and flighty, and man-mad, just like the girls at Miss Hare's.* And her ire had nothing to do with the soft, stupid smile on Gray's face when her ladyship had batted her long, curly eyelashes, blatantly flirting with him.

Only a few more days and she would be reunited with Quentin. She had felt lost without him. She was bored with sewing and shopping and playing the piano and being on display like some porcelain figurine in a china shop. She couldn't rest easy not knowing where Quentin was, and what he was doing, not as things stood. It wasn't fair to say that she wanted to keep him on leading-strings, as Gray had flung at her. It was fear that put her on edge.

Her throat burned when she remembered her quarrel with Gray. She would just be in the way if she went down to Channings with Quentin, he had told her. And the look on Quentin's face, anxious and guilty at the same time, when she had suggested it, only confirmed Gray's opinion.

Later, when she was in her room, lying fully clothed on top of her bed, Quentin had come to her. Without saying a word, he had taken her hand. He understood even if Gray did not. She didn't want to spoil Quentin. She wanted to keep him safe.

Finally, Quentin had broken the silence. "The grooms at Channings are all armed and crack shots, Deb. Uncle Gray told me. It's quite safe."

That's when she had burst into tears.

She smiled now at the groom who raced to catch up

with her as she left the house. He, also, was a crack shot, and it was more than his life was worth to lose sight of her. Where oh where would it all end? Her smile became more fixed when she entered the mews.

"What kept you?" asked Meg. She was already mounted and looked very striking in her new plum riding habit with its matching feathered bonnet.

"Nothing in particular," Deborah said, then smiled an acknowledgment to the other riders who had assembled.

There were six in the party, not counting two grooms. Mr. David Banks had brought his sister, Rosamund, and Lord Denning had brought his carriage with a feast fit for kings, or so he said.

It was a fine day; the company was pleasant, and the prospect of Richmond should have been inviting. Deborah squared her shoulders, stepped lightly onto the mounting block and swung into the saddle.

❧

Though it was good weather for riding, it was quite cold, and when they came to the park, Lord Denning suggested that they repair to the nearest inn for hot toddy or tea to take the chill out of them. This Meg refused to do. They had come to Richmond Park for the riding, and she was not ready to give up yet. There was a good-natured debate, and finally they decided to stay with the original plan. While the ladies waited in the comfort of the coach with hot bricks and fur wraps to keep them warm, the gentlemen would put their mounts through their paces, after which they would all ride together. Then they would have their picnic.

Nick was first away. He touched spurs to flanks and his horse shot forward. There was a shout, and Banks and Lord Denning went bounding after him. The ladies watched them until they disappeared over a rise of ground, then they sat back, exchanging smiles.

"A regular cavalry charge," said Rosamund Banks. She had a pleasant face fringed with fairish red hair. She also had dimples, and Deborah always felt sorry for anyone who had been cursed with dimples.

It was Rosamund and Deborah who kept the conversation going, while Meg stared out the window at passing riders and carriages. Deborah was happy to have found someone who shared her love of Paris, and did not notice Meg's preoccupation.

The two girls were exchanging reminiscences when Meg rudely interrupted. "I shall die of boredom sitting here doing nothing. Don't worry about me, Deb. I shall take one of the grooms with me."

"What?"

Deborah and Rosamund were caught off guard. Before they could prevent it, Meg was out of the carriage and untethering her horse. She summoned one of the grooms, and the next thing they knew, she was sprinting to the far side of the turf with the groom galloping at her heels. They watched dumbfounded as a rider on a huge black stallion came forward to meet her.

"Oh dear," said Rosamund. "David will be so disappointed." She shook her head. "If Nick were here, he would put a stop to it. It really is too bad of Meg."

Deborah's stint as a teacher at Miss Hare's school had taught her a thing or two about adolescent girls. She knew exactly what was going on. Meg, quite deliberately, had arranged to meet with one of her beaux when she knew the gentlemen in her own party would not be there to prevent it.

She peered out the window but could not make out the gentleman's identity. "Who is he, do you know?"

Rosamund shook her head. "All I know is he isn't someone her brothers would want her to meet, otherwise he would have approached her quite openly."

"Millicent Dench," said Deborah, remembering the bane of her existence at Miss Hare's, and she ground her teeth together. "I should have expected something like this. At least Meg had the good sense to take a groom with her." Which was more than Millicent had done.

The words were hardly out of her mouth, when the groom wheeled his horse and came cantering back in their direction. Under Deborah's horrified gaze, Meg and her beau disappeared behind a stand of evergreens.

"Oh dear," said Rosamund. "She has sent the groom back. Now there is no one to chaperon them."

"I'm going after them," Deborah said. Ignoring Rosamund's plea to wait until the gentlemen returned, she flung open the carriage door and was soon mounted. When the remaining groom made to go with her, she ordered him to stay with Miss Banks, then she took off in a flash of thundering hooves.

She could ride. Rosamund, who considered herself no mean equestrienne, admiringly watched girl and mount streak across the sward.

The horse was spirited, but Deborah controlled it effortlessly. As she passed the groom, he called out something which Deborah could not make out. Then he, too, dug in his heels and went racing after her.

She plunged off the turf and into an area of woodland. Leaves were thick upon the ground but the bridle path was still clear. She checked her mount's pace and took a moment to get her bearings. There was no sign of Meg or her companion. To her left, there was what appeared to be an old ruined lodge. Ahead of her was the path, and all around, the silence of dense evergreens. She pulled on the reins and her mount left the path and made for the ruined lodge. The groom, coming upon the bridle path a moment later, went galloping by without looking to left or right.

❧

"No one ever kissed me like that before." Meg touched her trembling fingers to her lips.

Stephen Montague, Viscount Leathe, smiled slowly. "And you've had plenty of kisses, I suppose?"

"Not as many as you, if rumor is anything to go by." Unsmiling, she pulled out of his arms and wandered aimlessly around the stone ruins, all that remained of this ancient hunting lodge that had once belonged to kings.

"Rumor is right," he said, watching her closely. "I never pretended I was a monk."

She turned her head in his direction. "Do I detect a sneer behind those words?" When he didn't answer, she laughed without humor. "I must be mad, meeting you here like this. There's going to be the devil to pay when I go back to the others. If only you would try to get along with my brothers! If only you would make an effort to establish yourself as a respectable gentleman!"

The sneer was more pronounced. "I thought I had when I asked you to marry me. What could be more respectable than that?"

She looked at him helplessly. She knew it wasn't wise to love him. He was everything her brothers said and more. They didn't know the half of it, but she knew because Stephen had told her, not confiding in her, but laughing it off as a huge joke. He wasn't like her. He hadn't been raised in a family where love and discipline were inextricably bound up together. He had known discipline, a ferocious discipline, and he had rebelled against it. He wasn't as bad as Gray said. But he wasn't good either.

"You told me," he said, "that you would give me your answer today. What is it to be, Meg? Do we elope, or do we part forever?"

He sounded flippant, as though her answer hardly mattered to him, and that angered her. Her lips compressed, but she managed to keep a firm grip on her temper. "I can't elope with you, Stephen. You must see that. And really, there's no need for it. If you would only do as I ask, in time, my family will come round."

"Your family?" His lip curled derisively. "What the hell have they got that makes them so proud? If they can't accept me as I am, then to hell with them, to hell with you."

She was Lady Margaret Grayson, the daughter of an earl, and no one, not even Leathe, who was the son of an earl, was permitted to speak to her like this. She spoke passionately. "I'm proud of my family, Stephen, proud of my brothers. I could not marry a man who would make me ashamed to be his wife."

There was a long, tense pause and she could see his shoulders stiffen. He said softly, "Then it appears we have both had a lucky escape."

"Lady Margaret! You will mount up at once and return to the carriage."

Deborah's command brought both heads whipping round. She had slowed her horse to a walk, and as they watched, she reined in where one of the walls of the lodge had crumbled into rubble. Though she was still some distance from them, and the sun was in her eyes, she had a quick impression of a lovers' quarrel. Meg seemed to be on the point of weeping.

Deborah softened her tone. "Come along, Meg. If we ride out of here together, no questions will be asked, or at least, none that we can't brazen through. To delay is foolish. There is a groom following me and he is bound to carry tales to your brother."

When Meg gave a little sob and stumbled toward her horse, Deborah allowed her eyes to stray to the stranger. He made no move to help Meg as she struggled to mount up.

"You must be the inestimable governess," he taunted. "Miss Weyman, is it not?" He looked at her intently, and he said more naturally, "I know you from somewhere, don't I?"

"Not to my knowledge." The words were automatic. There was something familiar about him, something that worried at her. Shading her eyes with one hand, she began to edge her horse over the rubble, trying to get a clear view of him. "You have the advantage of me, sir," she said. "I am sure Lady Margaret's brothers will wish to know the name of the gentleman to whom they may apply for satisfaction." This was an empty threat. Deborah did not believe in dueling, nor would she carry tales out of school. She was simply trying to bring home to the young man and to Meg the seriousness of their situation.

"Leathe," he flung at her. "You may tell them Leathe."

It was the last name she had expected to hear. The color in her cheeks receded, leaving her complexion bone-white, and she dragged convulsively on the reins, making her mount rear up at the sudden pressure on its mouth. She controlled it with difficulty.

"Deborah, what is it?" cried Meg.

Leathe took a step forward, then another. When Deborah swayed in the saddle, he swiftly crossed to her and reached for the reins. This was the first clear view he had of the face beneath the plumed bonnet. "Deborah?" he said, frowning, and he turned her horse to face the sun. "My God, it is you!"

Green eyes gazed intently into green eyes and the silence stretched out endlessly.

"No!" cried Deborah suddenly, and she wrenched the reins from his grasp. Meg was forgotten in this greater peril to herself. She dug in her heels and her mare sprang forward.

"Deborah, wait!" Leathe was already springing into the saddle as he called out to her.

Instinct made her head for the carriage. She came out of the trees like an arrow shot from a bow. She could hear the thundering of hooves at her back, knew that her mare did not stand a chance against his powerful black stallion, but still she pressed on. He streaked by her and cut her off. Her mount reared and plunged to avoid him, and he deftly turned aside and plucked the reins from Deborah's hands, bringing her horse to a standstill. He was an excellent horseman as she well knew. It was an accomplishment all the Montagues shared.

She put up a fight as he wrestled her from her mount, but her struggles hardly made an impression on him.

"Damn you, Deborah!" He had her by the shoulders and gave her a hard shake. "What's got into you? Is this any way to greet me after all these years? Why didn't you send word to me? I have gone through hell imagining what might have happened to you. I thought you were dead."

"You betrayed me," she cried out. "I trusted you and you betrayed me!"

"I never betrayed you! I swear it."

"Liar! They were waiting for me! Father and the militia were waiting for me."

"I know they were. I saw the whole thing. I don't know how Father knew we were to meet there, but I swear it wasn't my doing. And how could you believe such a thing of me? I hated our father. I still do."

They were intent only on each other, oblivious of their surroundings. A shot from a pistol brought them to their senses. They looked around startled to see riders converging upon them. Nick was in the lead, waving a smoking pistol above his head, and his expression was murderous.

Deborah looked pleadingly into her brother's eyes. "Tell them nothing, do you understand? *Nothing!* I am Deborah Weyman, and you came to my rescue when my horse bolted."

He nodded slowly. "I understand. But this isn't the end of it. We must meet again and soon."

There was no time to say more. Nick had flung himself from his horse and was within earshot, and in the next moment, they were surrounded by a group of bristling, furious gentlemen who all seemed intent on calling Leathe out. The viscount, to everyone's surprise, refused to be provoked, and though he remained aloof, he supported Deborah's story of her horse bolting. Short of calling her a liar, everyone had to accept what she said, but they did so reluctantly.

Meg said nothing, but her eyes were rife with suspicion, and she stared hard at Leathe when he kissed Deborah's fingers. He did not acknowledge her when he rode off.

❧

The story had to be gone through again for Gray's benefit when he came home later that evening. He questioned Deborah in his library, and by this time he had several versions of what happened. The contradictions hardly bothered him. He had a fair idea of the truth. It seemed to him that Meg and Leathe had made an assignation which Deborah had foiled. The part about the bolting horse was an obvious pretext to prevent a duel, for if she or Meg had accused Leathe of insulting them, a duel would have been unavoidable. Women would lie through their teeth to prevent men dueling.

There were, however, two points which nagged at him. The first was Meg's pettishness. Though she had substantiated Deborah's story, she had hinted that Leathe and Deborah knew each other and seemed to be on the best of terms. Gray did not see how this was possible. Deborah was closely guarded, and if she had met Leathe, he would have been told about it, unless, like Meg, she had met the viscount in secret. This Gray would not believe of Deborah. The second point that made him wonder was Leathe's conduct when Nick ordered him to take his hands off Deborah. The viscount was all sweetness and light, according to Nick, and could not be needled into offering the challenge which Nick would have accepted on the spot.

"Your horse bolted," said Gray, idly watching the play of candlelight on Deborah's face. "Now that surprises me. I know you to be an exceptional horsewoman."

"Thank you," said Deborah and pressed her lips together. She had already made up her mind that the less said the better.

Gray smiled, recognizing the ploy. "What really happened, Deborah? Did you say something to Leathe that made him come after you when you caught him with Meg? I believe the fellow has a vile temper."

He must know that her story was a tissue of lies from beginning to end, but she had to stick to it for all their sakes. She moistened her lips. "As I already told you, Meg and I went riding and met the viscount quite by chance. His black stallion nipped my mare and she bolted. That's all there is to it. I knew nothing of his vile temper. He was perfectly charming. Ask Nick. Ask anyone."

There was an interval of silence as he digested this. Finally, he said, "It has been suggested to me that this was not your first encounter with Leathe, that you and he are on terms of intimacy."

This came from Meg, of course. The girl was jealous. Deborah tried to brush it off as a triviality. "Yes, I know him. Well, one meets so many young gentlemen when one is out riding. Stephen is very knowledgeable about horses."

"Stephen?"

She saw her blunder and tried to correct it. "That's what I heard Meg call him." Her eyes were as clear as crystal.

He pondered that look that was just a shade too innocent for his liking, and in an instant the tiny seed of doubt Meg had planted in his mind began to grow. He spoke harshly. "I'll not see you take up with someone like Leathe. You had better make up your mind to it. He is a wastrel. If you knew his family's history, you would not encourage him."

She'd already heard about Leathe and his notorious family from Nick and the others before they had started for home. She had listened in silence as they poured contempt not only on her brother but on the whole tribe of Montagues. It had hurt her, but not half as much as this.

The heedless words spilled over as though a dam had burst. It was more than his contempt for her family. The jealousy she had diligently suppressed since his mother's scandalous revelations found an opening and erupted in full spate. "You're a fine one to talk! What makes you think you are better than he is? Has he abducted innocent young women and tried your filthy tricks on them? And who gave you the right to judge what is best for me? You are not my guardian. If I wish to take up with Viscount Leathe, or . . . or take a lover, or whatever, it has nothing to do with you, just as your lovers have nothing to do with me."

She knew he could move fast when the occasion demanded it, but she was taken by surprise when he reached out, seized her by the shoulders, and dragged her to kneel like some suppliant at his feet. His fingers were like iron talons in her soft flesh, but she was too stunned to protest.

"How much do you think I will take from you?" His voice was deep and rough. His breathing was ragged.

"Stay away from Leathe, or by God, you'll have a lover, but that lover will be me, whether you want me or not."

She slapped him before she knew she was going to, before she had time to think through the wisdom of such an act. His eyes leapt with answering fire, then his head lowered to hers and she could feel the brush of his breath against her skin. Fear rose in her throat and she began to tremble.

"Deborah," he said softly, "when will you learn it's not wise to provoke me?" And he brought his message home with the kiss he forced on her.

Frustrated passion and naked jealousy poured out of him as his lips took hers. His mouth was hot and hard, and his arms wrapped around her in savage possession. He was glad that she had given him this excuse to release the rage that boiled inside him, glad that he could prove to her he was not the gelding she seemed to think him. For weeks past she had ignored him as though he were nothing, reserving her soft words and flirtatious smiles for a set of fribbles who fluttered attendance on her. It didn't matter that those fribbles had come to his house at his invitation. He was a man, more of a man than she had ever known, and he would be damned if he would let her forget it. In one wrenching movement, he lifted her to lie across his lap.

The kiss was a mistake. He knew it as soon as he felt her lips begin to soften beneath his, felt the arms that restrained him begin to draw him closer. Because he was ravenous for the touch and taste of her, he was caught in his own trap. He didn't want to let her go, not when he knew she was his for the taking. For one moment more, he struggled to hold on to his scruples, but he knew it was hopeless. Already he was giving himself permission, promising himself that afterward he would make everything right.

He unbuttoned the back of her frock and pulled it down, then her chemise, baring her breasts. His thumb rubbed her nipple into a tight peak and he felt her body clench in pleasure. He drank her small whimpers of arousal like a castaway dying for lack of fresh water. It was happening again. He had hardly touched her and he was desperate to get at her, desperate to pin her beneath him and bury himself inside her. It had never been like this with another woman. He shifted her in his arms, giving him freer access to her body. As his mouth closed over one hard nipple, one hand slipped beneath her skirts, and began a slow sweep from her ankle to her thigh.

Deborah's thoughts were not unlike Gray's. It was happening again. He had only to touch her and she became like potter's clay in his hands. He could do with her whatever he wanted, make her whatever he wished. He was powerful, virile and demanding, and reckless with it. She should be terrified. She reveled in it.

She wanted, desperately wanted to hold on to him. It could never be. He hated the name Montague, her name. But it was more than that. One day soon, she would have to leave his house and sink into obscurity. She had thought of little else since arriving in London. Everything was changing. There was no place for her with Quentin or with Gray. She didn't know what the future might hold, except grief and pain and a longing for what she had lost. She should live for the moment, take what she could before there was nothing left to take. Memories, that's all that would be left to her. She tugged on his hair, bringing his head up for her kiss.

He tasted her tears on his tongue, and he pulled back to look down at her. He read reproach in the eyes that stared back at him.

"Gray?" She didn't know why he had stopped.

"Don't say a word." His eyes stayed on hers for a long time. He knew that he could have her, but he didn't want a reluctant lover. Swearing, he rose and pushed her into the chair.

He waited until he had control of his breathing, then said, "I mean what I say. Stay away from Leathe. If you encourage him, then I shall know you are any man's for the taking. Then nothing will save you from me, Deborah. Nothing."

And with that infuriating insult, he turned and left

her. Hurt and shock held her speechless as he shut the door on his way out. Fearing she would weep, she fell back on pride, and she bared her teeth at the empty room and thought of a dozen insults she could have flung at him, each one more cutting than the last.

CHAPTER 15

Deborah's attempts to arrange a meeting with her brother were frustrated at every turn. In the three days before they left for Channings, she was guarded zealously, and not only by grooms and footmen. If she went riding, Gray was sure to go with her. The same applied when she went shopping, or to the circulating library to change her books. Occasionally, she caught a glimpse of Leathe on his huge black stallion, but if he saw her, he gave no sign of it, and she was thankful for his prudence. It seemed that he was as aware as she of Gray's watchful eye. When, however, she heard that Gray was to accompany them to Channings and stay with them for the duration, she broke the rule she had imposed on herself since the night he had almost made love to her. She spoke to him first.

"I thought," she said, "there was a war going on."

They were in Hatchard's book shop, perusing the latest titles. Anyone seeing them would have taken them for strangers. It was only when they were in company that they unbent a little and made a pretense of being civil to each other. But since they were alone on this occasion, they had reverted to long, speaking silences and chilling stares.

"Meaning?" said Gray.

"Shouldn't you be at the Foreign Office, doing whatever you people do?"

Not once did they look at each other. The books on the shelves absorbed all their attention.

"Contrary to what you may have read in the newspapers, Deborah, we are not yet ready to meet the French, nor are they ready to meet us. When that day approaches, you will be the first to know."

"That's not what Lord Denning says."

"What does Denning say?"

"He says that the reason the war has been shelved is because it's the hunting season. Parliament is in recess. The War Office, the Admiralty, the Foreign Office—they've all ground to a halt because English gentlemen would rather ride to hounds than anything."

There was something in what she said, as Gray would have been the first to admit if he had not been sulking. This had nothing to do with Leathe. When he had calmed down and thought about it, he saw that Deborah had been doing her best to protect Meg. Deborah was so straitlaced she would never take up with someone like Leathe. It was the viscount's motives he distrusted. He had been hovering around, like a hound on the scent, and Gray was determined to keep him at bay. No. What got his goat was that Deborah was punishing him for daring to lay his hands on her. She had liked what he had done to her, but she would never admit it.

"Lord Denning," he declared, "is a blockhead, as anyone with an iota of intelligence would know within two minutes of meeting the man."

Eyes flashed, locked together, and glared.

"Are you saying I lack intelligence?" demanded Deborah. It never occurred to her to defend Lord Denning.

Gray brought his nose so close to hers that she could see flecks of gold scattered on the rings of his irises. "If the cap fits, wear it," he said.

With that, Deborah snapped the covers of her book together, turned on her heel, and stalked out of the shop. With a face like granite, Gray went after her and sailed straight into the path of a boy selling toffee apples from his barrow. The barrow tipped, the apples went flying, and the irate boy was not appeased until Gray had tossed him a golden guinea for his losses. Deborah said nothing on the way home. Clutched in her hand was a note the boy's companion had pressed on her during the confusion.

In the privacy of her bedchamber, she smoothed out the one-page epistle. It was from her brother, informing her that he knew of the projected trip to Channings, and that if she could slip away she would find him at the White Swan in Dartford, where he had reserved rooms for the following week. His rooms were right above the front portico and she could not miss them.

Channings was within walking distance of the village of Dartford.

❧

Their welcome at Channings was exactly as Deborah expected. Before they had alighted from the carriage, Hart came out the front doors and pounced on them, kissing and hugging for the ladies, and back-slapping for Gray, and just when she was getting over it, Quentin and Jason came tearing around the corner of the house and launched themselves at the new arrivals.

Quentin was almost unrecognizable, and the same could have been said of Jason. Their breeches were out at the knees, and their jackets were spotted and stained. Their faces and hands matched their garments. Deborah stared at them hard, then something inside her seemed to dissolve, and she joined in the general laughter.

"We've been cleaning out the stables," said Quentin. "Mr. Perch said we might."

Hart elaborated. "Mr. Perch is my head groom. There is nothing he doesn't know about horses and he has promised to teach the boys, as long as they are willing to pull their weight."

"And we all know what that means," said Gray, and there was more laughter.

She was righting her bonnet, talking and laughing on the same breath, when her eye was caught by Gray's.

The coldness was gone, and the smile in his eyes was warm and intimate. She felt herself responding to that look, then her attention was diverted by a young man whom she had overlooked in the confusion of their welcome.

Gray made the introductions. Mr. Jervis was Quentin's "tutor." He seemed a pleasant enough young man who reminded Deborah of Gray's secretary, Philip Standish. But Mr. Jervis possessed one proficiency that Mr. Standish did not. As Gray had put it, he was a good man to have in a fight.

"No," said Gray, in answer to something Hart had asked him. "Nick will not be joining us. He is visiting friends in Hampshire."

"Skirt-chasing, I don't doubt," said the dowager to Gussie in a stage whisper.

Quentin was hopping from foot to foot. There was something he was bursting to share with Deborah. "Deb, Charlie's had pups. Would you like to see them? They're in the stables, tiny little things with black spots on them. Or is it white spots? I can never remember. She is ever so good about letting strangers pet them."

"Charlie?" said Deborah dubiously.

"Charlotte, our dalmatian," said Jason.

"I can't resist puppies," said Deborah. "Give me half an hour and I'll meet you there."

The boys ran off, dragging Mr. Jervis with them. Deborah was thoughtful as she watched them go. She could see with her own eyes that Quentin was in the best of hands. The Graysons were good for him and good to him. Gray had been right about a lot of things. Then why did she feel like weeping?

Her gaze strayed involuntarily to Meg. Though the others wouldn't notice it, Meg had withdrawn from her. The girl was confused and hurt, and Deborah did not know how to put things right. She could not tell her the truth. Besides, Gray would never allow Meg to marry Stephen. The sooner the girl got over him the better.

"Why so pensive?"

She jumped at Gray's softly intoned question. The others were entering the house and she started after them. "I like your family," she said. "I like them a lot. It's a pity that—"

When she stopped in mid-sentence to pick up her skirts before mounting the steps, he finished for her. "That I'm not more like them?"

She did not return his bantering tone, but gave him a look that he could not decipher, and which made his own smile die away. "That there are so *few* like them, is what I was going to say."

For the rest of the afternoon, she devoted herself to Quentin. She'd expected that Jason and Gray or one of the others would be there too, but everyone made excuses, and she guessed that Gray had arranged for her to have this time alone with Quentin.

Her first impressions of Quentin were confirmed. His horizons had expanded and he was in his element. She wasn't sorry, but it made her feel terribly alone. Everything seemed to taste of a bittersweet flavor. She didn't want to think about the future. She refused to think about the future. The present was all she had, and she was going to make the most of it.

Dinner was a lighthearted affair. It always was with the Graysons. Later, when they had repaired to the drawing room, Gussie began to describe the pleasures of country life. The country, Gussie told her, had everything the town had to offer and more besides. Though the assemblies might not be as brilliant, many a match had been made right there on the dance floor between a country lass and an illustrious nobleman who had come into the area for the hunting season. When the gentlemen's hoots of laughter had died away, she went on to praise the shopping in Dartford and the riding on the downs. There were interesting walks as well as many ancient ruins.

"And there is Sommerfield," said Gray when Gussie paused to draw breath. "It's worth a look."

"Sommerfield?" asked Deborah.

Hart answered. "The seat of the earls and barons of Kendal for three centuries. You can see its roof from the upstairs windows. That's Gray's place, didn't you know?"

"Yes, now that you mention it, I believe I did."

"We would be there now," said Gray, "except that workmen are redoing the plasterwork. One of the ceilings collapsed and the others looked as though they were ready to follow suit. Oh, it's safe enough, though rather dusty. If you like, and if you have time, I'll show you over the house and grounds."

He was offering her an olive branch and she was glad to accept it. "Thank you. I should like that."

Hart made a derisory sound. "Best beware, Deborah. Gray sets great store by that heap of old bricks. Say one word against it and you may find yourself at the short end of his temper."

"It's a showplace, then?" She knew all about showplaces.

The countess answered innocently. "Any house is a showplace when there are no children in it. That is easily remedied."

This gibe provoked more gibes, all at Gray's expense, and though Deborah laughed dutifully, her heart wasn't in it. She was beginning to feel too cozy, too much at home with this congenial family.

There flashed into her mind a picture of her father entertaining guests at Belvidere. He smiled in a way that was totally unfamiliar to Deborah. In fact, she scarcely recognized him. He was a gracious, affable host, and very approachable. There was no frost in his eyes as there invariably was when he looked at her or Stephen. He hated them, seeing them as their mother's children, and they could never do anything to please him.

She remembered one occasion in particular, when Stephen had come home for the holidays. This was their first venture into grown-up society and they were on their best behavior. The guests had hardly departed when the earl rounded on his son, and the frost was back in his eyes. Stephen's table manners were atrocious; his conversation did not bear repeating. He was not fit to be the heir to the title and estate of Belvidere. Deborah would have slunk away with her tail between her legs. At fourteen years, Stephen was beginning to flex his muscles. The day he inherited Belvidere, he retorted, he would put a torch to it. He'd known he would pay for that remark, and he had.

Somewhere in the house, a clock chimed the hour. Eight o'clock, thought Deborah. In a few hours, she would be with Stephen. *Patience,* she told herself, even as she automatically responded to something the countess said. She could never escape detection during the daylight hours, but when everyone had retired for the night, she could slip away unseen and make her way to Dartford. She would have to walk the two miles. To borrow one of the horses from the stables was too risky. Besides, a two-mile hike was nothing to her. She hoped to God that Stephen was alone when she got there. He didn't know she was coming. There was no way to let him know.

Her eyes flicked to Meg. The girl was very quiet, very subdued. Poor Meg, and all women who loved unwisely. A thought came to her, not quite formed, and she resolutely pushed it away.

❧

The clock on the mantel struck the hour. Gray looked up from the papers he had been studying and saw that it was an hour past midnight. His muscles were cramped and his neck was stiff. For the last hour or two, he had been poring over all the information he had gathered on various subjects. There was a report from Jervis on Quentin's progress, and a report from the physician on his health and state of mind. There were also notes on two conversations he had had with Sophie Barrington, one shortly after Gil's death and one that had taken place less than a week ago.

One thing was clear. He was no closer to discovering the identity of the person who had murdered Gil Barrington. He did not think he would ever know until Quentin regained his memory, and that likelihood was fading. The thought that he could set a trap for the murderer using Quentin or Deborah as bait continued to tickle his mind, and he was equally persistent in rejecting it. Deborah would never agree to it. She would think it was too risky. There *were* risks involved, but sometimes risks were worth taking. One had to weigh everything in the balance. He thought about it for a long time, toying with the idea, thinking of possible strategies. He always came back to the same thought. Deborah would never agree to it.

Deborah. He was no nearer to solving *that* mystery either. He might have called Lawford in to help him, but he was reluctant to do this. What he wanted was for Deborah to come to him of her own free will and *tell* him what he wished to know. She had told his mother that she had been born and bred in Ireland. She'd lied of course. When he'd looked into it, he'd discovered there was no such place as Beg in the county of Antrim. Who was she and what was she running from?

He rose to his feet and stretched his arms above his head, then took a few paces around his bedchamber. He did not feel like going to bed, but Hart and Gussie kept country hours, and the house was as silent as a tomb.

He was restless and well aware of the reason for it. He wanted her. In fact, she had damn near become an obsession with him. He had even begun to have fantasies about her, and not only the typical masculine ones of taking her to his bed. The talk of Sommerfield had set him off tonight. He could quite easily picture her there, presiding at his table, with a brood of infants hanging on her skirts. The boys would have blond hair and blue eyes, in the image of their father, and the girls, naturally, would have auburn hair and green eyes in the image of their mother.

It was a womanish fancy and not worthy of a real man, and why the hell he was smiling was more than he could understand. He was tired of wanting, tired of thinking. What he needed was some hard physical exercise to take the fidgets out of him. The explicit images this thought evoked had him cursing fluently, and on the spur of the moment, he decided to go for a brisk walk. He had passed the door to Deborah's chamber, when another door behind him creaked open.

"And how is Leathe?"

He whirled and saw his sister Meg. Her eyes were

red rimmed and she was in her nightclothes. She backed away from him. "Oh, it's you, Gray. I beg your pardon."

"Who did you think I was?"

Her face crumpled and she choked out something unintelligible, then turned back into the room. He could not let it rest there, not when she was so distraught. He didn't wait to knock, but followed her into the room and shut the door.

"You didn't answer my question, Meg. Who were you expecting? Who did you think I was?"

"No one. I . . . I made a mistake. Now may I go to bed?" She crawled beneath the bedclothes and indicated the candle. "I was just going to snuff it out."

He regarded her steadily. "Something has upset you, and I want to know what it is. Is it Leathe?"

"Please, Gray, I don't want to talk about it, all right?"

Baffled, he looked around the room, but there was no clue there. "Have you quarreled with him? Or Deborah perhaps?"

She scrubbed at her wet cheeks with her balled fists. "Don't mention that woman's name to me."

He frowned. "You thought I was Deborah, didn't you?" *And how is Leathe?* His eyes flared in sudden comprehension, and he snatched up the candle, turned on his heel, and made for Deborah's chamber. The bed was made up and there was no sign of her. Furious now, he retraced his steps.

"Where is she?" he asked.

"Truly, Gray, I don't know." Her eyes were wide with fear. She had never seen him so livid.

"But you know that she went to meet Leathe? What did she tell you? Answer me, Meg, or I shall shake the truth out of you."

She shrank from him and shook her head.

"For God's sake, if you know something, tell me! She can't go traipsing all over the countryside in the dead of night. Anything could happen to her. She could be lying dead in a ditch."

"I don't know where she went!"

He gentled his voice. "But you saw her leave the house?"

She nodded, and looked away.

"And you think she went to meet Leathe?"

"Who else would she go to meet?"

"And where can I find Leathe?"

"I don't know. He didn't tell me where he would be staying. He is friendly with Matthew Derwent and his parents. He could be staying with them, but I don't know."

"But you do know he has come into the district?"

"Yes," she whispered.

He breathed deeply. "How do you know?"

"Because I sent him a note, telling him that we would be here, yes, and received a reply. He said he would find a way to meet me." Her shoulders shook and fresh tears welled in her eyes. "I thought it was me he loved, but all the time it was Deborah. I told you they knew each other from before. Oh Gray, what am I going to do?"

❧

Viscount Leathe poured out a glass of wine and handed it to his sister. He was glad to give his hands something to do to smooth over the awkward moment. They had never been particularly demonstrative, but somehow the quick kiss she had pressed to his cheek when she had entered his rooms did not seem adequate to the occasion. It was almost nine years since he had last seen her. He wanted to hug her, but feared it might seem too effusive to be sincere.

A fire burned brightly in the grate, and Deborah was sitting so close to it that every few minutes she switched her skirts to prevent them scorching. It helped pass the awkwardness, for what she really wanted to do was fling herself into his arms and cry her eyes out.

"You are blue with cold," he said, handing the glass to her. "What the devil possessed you to come here at this ungodly hour? You might have been attacked by footpads or worse. You should have waited till morning.

God knows what the landlord thinks of a woman in my rooms at this time of night."

Her tone was on the dry side. "From all I hear of you, Stephen, he won't think anything. Your reputation is not exactly spotless, as I'm sure you know."

He grinned, seated himself, and stretched his booted feet toward the grate. "It wasn't my reputation I was thinking of, but yours."

She studied the wine in her glass. "An accused murderess doesn't have much of a reputation to protect. Anyway, he didn't see me. I crept up the stairs when his back was turned."

He gave her a moment or two to collect herself, then said, "I don't believe you are a murderess, Deb. I never did. When we were children, you used to collect injured birds and animals and nurse them in that makeshift infirmary of yours in the disused barn behind the stable block, don't you remember? You couldn't bear to see anything get hurt. And if I took a tumble or a scrape, God save me, you would almost kill me by pouring Father's best brandy on the wounds, then dose me with a foul-tasting potion you had either bought or purloined from the gypsies."

She laughed. "That's one of the advantages of being the elder, even if it's only by a year. The younger thinks you are so much wiser, he will let you get away with anything."

"I didn't always let you get away with things. Do you remember the time you gave me that blancmange you had made yourself?"

She nodded. "It was my first attempt, and I was so proud of it. And you! You went into convulsions, or so I thought, and I went screaming for Cook. I thought you were dying."

"That's what I wanted you to think."

"Boys are so hateful!"

"I know."

There was no awkwardness now, but a sense of intimacy, as though the years between had made little difference. Gradually, their smiles dimmed, but the residue of warmth remained.

His voice was husky. "I didn't know or think how much you must have suffered when I went away to school. I made friends there, but there was no one at Belvidere for you."

"It was inevitable. And it wasn't so bad."

His brows rose and she replied, "It could have been worse. I had a governess, don't you remember her? Miss Hare. She made a great impression on me. If it were not for her, I would not have managed to escape Father's clutches."

"I don't think I recall her. Well, I wouldn't, would I? I was hardly ever home once I went away to school. And in the holidays, I'd go home with friends before I'd go to that pile of marble Father worships. I'm sorry, Deb. I wasn't thinking of you. And she was there, our step-mother, insinuating that we would come to a bad end, just like our mother. I wanted to choke the life out of her, and was afraid that one day I would not be able to restrain myself."

"She disliked us both," said Deborah, "but you especially because you were the son and heir. What do you hear of them?"

"As little as I can possibly manage. Surely that does not surprise you?" He allowed a moment to pass, then said gently, "I swear I did not betray you, Deb. I went to that inn in Windsor, as you asked in your note. I would have done anything to help you. God knows how Father found out. I went crazy when I saw the militia drag you away."

"It wasn't me."

"What?"

"I was dressed as a boy. I don't know who the girl was, but it wasn't me. And I wasn't going to ask for your help. I only wanted to say goodbye."

An interval passed as he absorbed her words. "I see. I was told you had escaped, but no one explained how it had come about. And you went away thinking I had set a trap for you?"

Deborah swallowed, but met his eyes. "I should have known better, I suppose. But what could I think? You were only a boy of fifteen. I thought Father must have put you up to it."

His lips twisted in the sneer that had been so evident at Richmond. "Father has no influence over me. He never did, and as soon as I could manage it, I followed your example. When I turned sixteen, I ran away from school and enlisted. For the past eight years, I have been a soldier, Deb."

"So I heard."

"What have you heard?"

She searched his eyes. "That you know how to fight and command men, but you are a thorn in the flesh of your superiors. They say you left India under a cloud."

"Who says?"

"The gentlemen who tried to provoke you into a duel at Richmond, you know, when I ran away from you."

He swirled the ruby-red wine in his glass, looked up at her and grinned. "That's about the sum of it. I disobeyed orders, and if I had to do it over, I'd do it again. My commanding officer was a dolt, one of those self-important bores who think they know everything. He'd never seen active service. Oh yes, that happens all too frequently. Men buy their commissions and think they are experts on warfare. When he ordered me to take my company of light horse against enemy guns, I affected deafness. Unfortunately, the man had influence in high places. He should have been court-martialed. I was made the scapegoat and given a posting to Dublin. Damn boring place, Ireland. No fighting worth mentioning."

She surveyed him silently as she sipped her wine. There was so much anger in him, so much bitterness that she no longer doubted the stories she had heard about him. She could well believe that he was wild and ungovernable. He was suddenly without a target to fight, so he fought the world. And though he would never admit to it, he was still fighting their father.

"What?" he asked, watching her expression.

"Did you really think I was dead?"

"What else could I think? It was easy for you to find

me, if you wanted to. I wasn't in hiding. But you never wrote, never left any messages with my friends. Where have you been hiding yourself all this time?"

She moved back a little from the fire before answering him. "For the most part, I've been with Miss Hare, the governess I told you about. When she left Father's employ, she opened a school in Bath. She's been wonderful to me, Stephen. She never doubted my innocence. Later, that is, for the last four years, I've been Quentin's governess. And here I am."

"And it never occurred to you to send word to me, if only to let me know that you were alive?" He answered his own question. "You thought I would tell Father. Shame on you, Deb!"

She managed a smile. "You have yet to tell me what you hear of Father and his wife. Our sister must be nearly sixteen by now. What is she like?"

"I know very little except that Elizabeth takes after our father in looks. The word is they are hoping for a brilliant season leading to a brilliant match for her."

"At least," said Deborah, "Elizabeth is safe from Father's schemes."

"Why do you say that?"

Her eyes searched his face. "She's not an heiress, is she?"

"No, of course not. It was our mother who had all the money, not Father. Father merely lined his pockets at our expense. As far as I can judge, he squandered those moneys on his picture gallery and collections. When he dies, I suppose those will pass to Elizabeth."

She shivered, and held out her hands to the blaze. "I'm glad Elizabeth has no money of her own. Then she will never have to go through what I went through."

His eyes narrowed on her. "What did you go through?"

She shook her head.

He took her hand and gripped it tightly. "I want to hear what happened, Deb. I know what Father said happened, and I know what everyone else says, but I've never believed any of it. You could never commit murder. Tell me what happened."

For a long time the only sound in the room was the hiss of the burning coals. When he touched her arm, she shivered and raised her eyes to his. "Do you know the man I killed?"

He nodded. "Albert Hollander, our stepmother's cousin. Father said you were engaged to be married. You changed your mind. There was a quarrel, and you attacked him, and deliberately pushed him to his death from the top of the circular staircase."

"That's partly true. What Father didn't tell you was that he was forcing me into this marriage. When I refused to go through with it, he beat me and locked me in my room, then he sent Albert to me. Albert was supposed to ravish me, you see, on the assumption that I would docilely accept my fate. He tried to, but I fought back. I ran from him, and he trapped me at the top of the circular staircase. Yes, I went for him. Yes, I pushed him. He fell against the rail. It gave way and he fell to his death, so I suppose that makes me guilty of murder."

Rage darkened his face. "That is not murder! And what kind of man would attack an innocent sixteen-year-old girl? I know Father hated us both, but what could he possibly hope to gain by forcing you into a marriage you did not want?"

"If you had known Albert you would understand. He was tall, dark, and handsome. He was also a simpleton, and I mean that quite literally. He couldn't count beyond ten. He could neither read nor write. I believe it happens sometimes to a child when a woman has a difficult birth. I didn't find this out till it was almost too late." As she spoke, her voice began to thicken. "Father did not want me to find out until after Albert and I were married."

He was frowning. "I still don't understand what he hoped to gain by marrying you to a simpleton. That makes no sense at all."

She smiled bitterly. "Stephen, what happens to a woman's property when she marries?"

"Her husband controls it."

"And if she marries a simpleton, who do you think controls her property then?"

"I presume the simpleton, or whoever takes care of his affairs." He made a grimace of disgust. "That would be Father, of course."

She made no answer, none was necessary, and he went on. "Then he'd finally be able to get his hands on your fortune which you inherited when Mother died." After a moment of horrified comprehension, he said quickly, "There must be some way around this. If I could find a way to force Father to retract—"

"Now you are being stupid. Of course Father will retract, just so long as I marry the man of his choice— another Albert. He doesn't want to see me hang. He wants my fortune. He as much as told me so."

"Then marry someone of your own choice. That should spike Father's guns."

"In that event, I think Father would set the law on me. He's vicious. You know he is. Besides, why should I exchange one tyrant for another? I don't wish to marry."

"What? Never, Deb?" He was smiling.

"You can ask that when you know the kind of life our mother led?"

"Not all men are like Father."

"It's a gamble I'm not willing to take. And anyway, who would be willing to take a gamble on me, an accused murderess?"

"There's a way out of this maze, and I intend to find it."

"No! Leave it alone! I'm in enough trouble as it is. You must have heard about Lord Barrington's murder. If all this comes out, who do you think will become the prime suspect? Please, Stephen, let sleeping dogs lie."

"But—I thought Lord Barrington was murdered by a thief who broke into his house. Meg told me so."

She wasn't up to telling him the whole story behind Lord Barrington's murder. She was tired and out of sorts, and longing for her bed. "That's only a theory," she said. "Stephen, promise me you will do nothing without my consent?"

He gave in reluctantly. "You have my word on it. But we'll find a way out of this, I promise you."

The conversation drifted then, as each recounted what had happened to them in the intervening years. When the clock chimed the hour, Deborah rose reluctantly. There was still so much to say, so much to learn, but it would have to wait until another time.

She made the return journey to Channings riding pillion on her brother's stallion. When he let her down in the lane that led to the gatehouse, she drooped with weariness.

"Do you know," he said, "we hardly spoke of Mother."

She blinked up at him and reached for his hand. "You look so much like her."

"Do I?" His voice was hoarse. "When I try to recall her face, I can't seem to do it. There is no portrait of her. Nothing. It's as though she never existed."

"No," she whispered. "Not as long as you and I have breath in our bodies. We shall always remember her. Besides, I do have something that once belonged to her. Her locket. Don't you remember it? She gave it to me on that last Christmas before . . . before she went away. Her portrait is inside it."

"May I see it?"

"I don't have it here. I gave it to a friend, Miss Hare, to keep for me. When I reclaim it, I'll bring it to you."

"When will that be?"

She shook her head. When Quentin was safe; when she was safe; when, when, when.

"It's all right, Deb. It's all right. I understand."

She went on tiptoe and caught his lapel, drawing his head down. His arm went around her shoulders, bringing her closer, and they clung to each other as they had never done, not even when they were children.

She broke away with a laugh. "Now go!" she said, pointing in the direction of the village. "I'll come to you when I can."

She watched his progress, cloak billowing around her, and her hands stuffed in the pockets of her white rabbit-skin muff. When horse and rider had disappeared into the gloom, she slipped through a gap in the hedge and tiptoed around the gatehouse so as not to disturb the sleeping porters. The main house was in darkness, except for the lanterns burning at the front doors. She stepped off the grass verge on to the gravel drive and breathed a sigh of relief that turned into a squeal when a voice, as smooth and venomous as distilled hemlock, hailed her.

"Very affecting," said Gray. "So Meg was right. You and Leathe are lovers."

CHAPTER 16

He loomed above her, astride his great roan, and the play of light and shadow on his features gave him the appearance of some ghostly warrior knight. She wasn't given a chance to respond to his taunts. His hand shot out, and she was plucked off her feet and hauled across his saddle. The rabbit-skin muff went tumbling to the ground. She tried to wrest herself from his grasp, but one arm crushed her to him, and she soon gave up the attempt.

"You have no right—"

"I have every right," he said harshly. "When you became my mother's guest, you came under my protection. I warned you what would happen if you tried to defy me."

She cried out when the horse leapt forward. Though she was deathly afraid, beneath the fear, her own anger began to simmer. He was doing it again, using his superior strength to force her to his will.

He did not make for the house, as she anticipated. They vaulted a hedge, and rode at breakneck speed. The moon, the stars, hedgerows, and formless shadows flashed by her in terrifying confusion, making her head swim. She closed her eyes, pressed herself into the curve of his body, and clutched at the arm he had wrapped around her to steady her. When she felt the horse slow, she opened her eyes. There was only a moment to register the outline of the house before he jumped down and reached for her. A slap on the roan's flank sent it trotting toward the stable block.

"This must be Sommerfield," she said. "Why have you brought me here?"

His fingers bit into the flesh of one arm, and he hauled her unceremoniously up the front steps. When she stumbled, he lifted her by the arm and dragged her into the house. "My mother is tenderhearted," he said. "I'll not have her upset by your screams when I give you the thrashing you have brought upon yourself."

She tossed her head. "Dare to lay a hand on me and you will answer to Leathe for it."

His eyes flashed with an emotion so powerful that Deborah instantly regretted her rash threat. "Fine," he said. "It's more than time someone taught that young whelp a lesson."

In the hall, a porter came forward to hold the doors. Deborah pulled the edge of her hood forward to hide her face and shrank into the folds of her cloak.

"Thank you," said Gray. "No need to rouse the housekeeper, Ames." He gave no explanation for bringing a woman to his house so late at night, but brushed by the porter, lifted a candelabra from the hall table, and made for the stairs. Deborah's face was flaming in mortification as he dragged her behind him, forcing her to match his pace.

He opened a door at the top of the landing and thrust her inside. She caught herself as she fell, then recoiled as she realized she was in a bedchamber, a very masculine bedchamber with dark pieces of mahogany furniture, and blue and maroon bedhangings. His chamber.

Whirling to face him, she cried out, "How dare you bring me here!"

His face was a mask of scorn. "I have no designs on your person, if that's what you are thinking. Even I, degenerate that I am, have my limits. I've never yet taken a woman who came from the arms of another man. This room suits my purposes because it is private. No one will interfere." He set down the candelabra, stripped off his gauntlets, and threw off his cloak. Slowly, pitilessly, he began to stalk her. "What? Nothing to say for yourself, Deborah?"

Her brain was numb. No reasonable explanation for being with her brother came to her, and she retreated, step by step, carefully skirting the bed. Her throat was so dry that her voice came out in a raspy whisper. "What are you going to do with me?"

"What I would do with my own sister. I'm going to put you over my knee and beat the defiance out of you. Then I shall track down Leathe and demand satisfaction."

When he lunged, she screamed and dived for the other side of the bed. "Gray, you've got it all wrong. Leathe is not my lover." Mercifully, her brain began to function. "I went to see him about Meg, to try to reason with him."

"Liar," he hurled at her. "I saw you kiss him!"

"It was an innocent kiss. Hart kisses me, doesn't he? And Nick? It was innocent, I tell you. Why won't you believe me?"

"Because I know you to be an accomplished liar, but I never took you for a slut until tonight."

The vicious word had the effect of making Deborah's temper blaze so hotly that she could not speak for it. When she found her voice, it was low and venomous. "You dare to say that to me, you . . . you hypocrite! Who is it that keeps a house in Hans Town for his string of women? Who is it pays his mistresses off with the price of a gold bracelet?"

He made a savage motion with one hand. "That is neither here nor there. Those women are professional courtesans. They are not pretending to be something they are not."

"Now who is the liar?" Her voice had risen to a screech. "You gave Helena Perrin a gold bracelet with a ruby in it. I saw it with my own eyes, yes, and Meg winked at me as though it were a huge joke. And Helena is a respectable, married woman."

Before she could take evasive action, he had vaulted the bed and had taken her shoulders in a punitive grip. He shook her so hard that her hood fell back. "Helena has many lovers. That I was one of them is of no consequence. It happened before I met you."

"What are you saying? That there have been no women in your life since you met me? Again you lie! You visited that bawdy house in Wells, and had the temerity to bring those . . . those jewels to the cottage for your pleasure. I was there! I know what I saw."

The furious light in his eyes gradually dimmed. For long, endless moments, he stared at her as if he had been struck by a blinding revelation. Finally, dropping his hands, he took a step back. When he spoke, there was no anger in his voice, only a kind of weariness.

"Is that why you went to Leathe? To pay me back in my own coin? It was quite unnecessary, you know. I can only repeat, I have not been with another woman in that way since I first met you."

He turned aside and went to stand by one of the windows. He spoke with his back to her. "I won't let you go to him, Deborah, no matter what. The boy is too reckless, too wild." He emitted a low laugh. "I held off because I thought you were too good for me, that I was unworthy of you. Hell, you made it plain enough that that's what you thought too. Then someone like Leathe captures you. I don't think I shall ever understand the mind of a woman."

"I never thought I was too good for you, leastways, not the way you mean. You abducted me! You frightened me! You still frighten me. Half the time, I don't know what to make of you."

"I have explained all that, but it makes no difference what I say. If you don't know that I would never hurt you, you are right—you don't know me at all."

As her anger ebbed, the confusion in her mind gradually took shape and became comprehensible. She could hardly believe what her brain was telling her. Her own jealousy came as no surprise, but she had never dared to believe, hope, that he really cared for her. She had to know.

Her voice was scarcely as loud as a whisper. "Gray, are you jealous of Leathe?"

He didn't answer her, didn't look at her, but stood there motionless, staring out at the dark night. She felt the prickle of tears, and a bittersweet ache tightened her throat and slowly spread through her. She took a step toward him, then another, and with each step, everything became clearer, simpler. When her skirts brushed his legs, she halted. "Leathe is not my lover," she said. "It's not what you think."

He turned to look at her. "Isn't he? Then explain it to me so that I can understand."

She had already made her decision. Going on tiptoe, she reached out and traced his lips with her fingers. It was something she had wanted to do for a long, long time. At the first brush of her fingers, his whole body went rigid. "Gray," she said, "Leathe and I have known each other since we were children. He is more like a brother to me. I've never had a lover. There is only one man I've ever wanted, but he rejects me at every turn."

"Who is he?" he asked hoarsely.

Her dimples flashed. "Who is he?" she mimicked. "You, you blithering idiot. Gray, please don't reject me this time around. I don't think I could bear it."

"*Reject* you?"

She nodded. "I'm warning you now, I'm going to have you, and there's nothing you can do about it."

He looked like a man turned to stone and her confidence began to waver. Had she misread him? Misheard him? Then she saw the helpless need burning in his eyes, and she breathed out a soft sigh. She didn't know how it had come about, but she sensed that the power he had always wielded in their relationship had slipped from his hands into hers. It fueled her confidence. It made her tender. It made her generous in victory.

She cupped his neck with one hand and drew his head down for her kiss. His eyes remained open on hers, open and disbelieving. "Don't look so frightened," she murmured. "This time, I promise not to bite you."

Her lips brushed lightly over his, and when he didn't respond, she moved in closer, adjusting her body to the fit of his. She skimmed her hands over his chest and shoulders and felt hard masculine muscles clench beneath the tips of her fingers. He was lean, hard, and powerful, but there was nothing to fear here. His brute strength was not a weapon he would use against her. His threats, as always, were empty, and now that she had finally taken his measure, she knew that she would never fear him again.

She deepened the kiss, using the tip of her tongue to separate his lips. When he stopped breathing, she laughed softly into his mouth, then her lips moved on his, demanding his surrender.

Gray's hands fisted at his sides. She didn't know what she was doing, didn't know what effect she was having on him. Somehow, his words had convinced her that he was as harmless as a tabby cat. She no longer feared him. But she would fear him if he yielded to his baser instincts. He'd suffered through hell in these last hours, imagining her in Leathe's arms. His emotions were still in a turmoil. The murderous rage that had possessed him had turned into a lethal resolve to be master of his own woman. He wasn't harmless. He was dangerous. He wanted to tear off her clothes and tumble her on the bed. He wanted to crush her beneath him, and make her surrender everything to him, and that was only the beginning of what he wanted from her. He wanted to be intimate with her as he had never been intimate with any woman. If she only knew how desperate he was to have her, she wouldn't look at him with such big, trusting eyes. She would run screaming from the room, and if he didn't get a hold of himself, that's exactly what she would do. With every ounce of his considerable will, he forced himself to remain passive beneath her innocent, questing touch.

"Put your arms around me," she whispered. "Now, kiss me back."

He obeyed, but already his mind was working on logistics. The bed was made up and the room was far enough away from the servants' quarters to ensure their privacy. He could get her back to Channings before dawn, and no one would be the wiser. The rest would follow naturally; the engagement, the round of parties and balls in her honor; the wedding. One thing he must impress upon her. He didn't believe in long engagements.

She brought the kiss to an end and smiled up at him. She sensed that he was unsure, and that pleased her. It made her bolder. "I think," she said, "we would be more comfortable on the bed."

A wave of lust roared through him, making his head spin. He rode it, bridled it, and forced it to recede. This time, he wasn't going to frighten her off. This time, he was going to have her, and if that meant he had to play the part of a gelding, he would do it, up to a point. Moreover, she had told him this was her first time, and he believed her. A man would have to be a brute if he did not curb his passions and treat his woman with the utmost restraint. Even then, he was going to hurt her. Did she know it?

He spread one hand under her chin, bringing her face up, and he pressed whisper-soft kisses to her eyes, her nose, her cheeks. "I shall be very, very careful with you," he said softly. "You need not fear that I shall deliberately hurt you."

Her eyes smiled into his. "I trust you Gray, implicitly. And I shall be very, very careful with you."

He opened his mouth and quickly shut it. He had warned her. A man couldn't be expected do more than that, could he? His conscience was clear. Besides, he couldn't describe in lurid detail what she might expect, for he hadn't the faintest notion. He had never initiated a virgin before.

"What is so amusing?" Her eyes searched his face.

He pressed a kiss to her open palm. "I've been told that sometimes a woman's first time can be a bit of a disappointment."

"Then we shall have to try again, won't we?"

His eyelids drooped. They would, nothing was surer, and next time around, they would do it his way. "Might I suggest we get a fire going? There's a distinct chill in the air."

"A fire?" Her gaze followed his to the grate where

kindling and logs were already set, needing only a spark to get a blaze going. She loved the way he thought of her comfort, loved the way he deferred to her. Smiling, she plucked a candle from the candelabra and touched the flame to the rolled papers beneath the kindling. When the fire crackled to life, she turned to replace the candle, and saw that he was already on the bed. He had removed his jacket and was working on his neckcloth.

"Take off your cloak," he said. "You'll be more comfortable."

She had a flash of recall, an impression of her ruthless captor ordering her to take off all her clothes, then he smiled at her, in that way of his, and the image faded, and she saw Gray, only Gray.

She replaced the candle. With eyes wide on his, she unbuttoned her cloak and threw it over the back of a chair. The fire was behind her, and the flames cast a flickering, reddish glow from floor to ceiling. The room seemed smaller, warmer, and her skin began to heat. She could smell the faint fragrance of the potpourri in the glass bowl beside the grate, and the rosewater which she'd splashed on her skin after her toilette, earlier that evening. As her senses heightened, she became aware of other things. Gray's chest was rising and falling and his breathing was audible. Her own breath caught and became shallow, erratic.

He held out both hands, palm up. "Come to me," he said.

There was no hesitation in her steps when she crossed to the bed and grasped his outstretched hands. It took only a tug and a twist and she was up on the bed, half sprawled over him. She smelled the starch on his lawn shirt and the clean male scent of him, then she raised herself slightly to join her lips to his as his head descended.

It was so easy, so warm and sweet, that she wondered why she had ever been frightened of this. She had never suspected that he was capable of such tenderness. But she should have known. She'd lived with him now long enough to know that when he cared deeply, he could be as fierce as a lion or as gentle as a lamb. *My lion, my lamb,* she thought dreamily, and emitted a soft sigh of repletion.

He drew her closer with a moan, and rolled with her on the bed, bringing them to their sides to lie face-to-face. He didn't want her to feel the bulge in his groin or the full force of his weight, pressing her into the mattress, didn't want to remind her that his strength far outstripped hers. He was rigidly tempering the savage in him so that she would feel secure in accepting him as her mate. It was devious, it was unworthy, and at the same time, it was knowledge that came from the deepest reaches of his masculine psyche. As his hands roamed up her back, slipping buttons from buttonholes, he distracted her by deepening the kiss.

No one had told her that kisses could be like this. His tongue had penetrated her lips and was tentatively exploring the inside of her mouth, surging and retreating, inviting her to reciprocate. When she tentatively complied, touching her tongue to the roof of his mouth, he pulled back as though she had struck at him with a dagger.

"I'm sorry," she cried out, scanning his face anxiously, "I'm not very good at this."

He breathed deeply. "You are better than you know," he said, and drew her close again.

His kisses grew hotter and wetter. The hands roaming over her became less comforting, more erotic. Her skin was so hot, she was grateful when he slipped her dress over her breasts, then whisked it over her hips to drift somewhere on the floor. She was less grateful when he tried to do the same with her chemise. She felt suddenly shy, and her fingers closed around it, holding it to her breasts.

He didn't argue the point, didn't try to pry her fingers from the edge of her chemise. He simply fastened his lips through silk to first one erect nipple then the other, working at them with teeth and tongue, and while she moaned and panted, he relieved her of her drawers.

She watched mutely as he rose from the bed and began to peel out of his clothes. Not a word was said, but the air between them was charged with a dark energy. He didn't disrobe completely, but left on his shirt. It fell to his knees in folds and the sight of the hairy, masculine legs that stuck out of it made her lips twitch.

He was smiling too, as though he could read her mind. For a moment he toyed with the shirt buttons at his throat, then seemed to come to a decision. "No, not yet," he said, mystifying her, and without removing his shirt, he stretched out beside her on the bed.

Her disappointment surprised her. She was curious, of course. She had never seen a naked man before, except in white marble statues that were to be found at Belvidere. She supposed he was deferring to her modesty, and she felt quite touched by the gesture.

His tone of voice was very serious, very matter-of-fact, and that got her attention. "I told you that the first time is sometimes, no, is almost invariably disappointing for a woman. I want this to be perfect for you, Deb. I've never wanted anything so much in my life." He tunneled his fingers into her hair, and stopped for a moment to kiss her ardently, plundering her mouth with his tongue in some vague attempt to give her a hint of what was to follow. "Trust me, give in to me, and I promise you, it will go easier with you."

Go easier with her? Somewhere, in a corner of her mind, she puzzled over his words, but she couldn't hold on to them. His hands had edged up her chemise and they were stroking along the inside of her thighs with tantalizing languor. She stopped breathing, then gasped when his fingers found her and probed gently. Time had no meaning. She was aware of nothing but the pleasure he was so skillfully building inside her. His slow, relentless caresses, there, between her thighs, gave her no respite, and her whole body tightened in anticipation.

She reached for him and tried to draw him over her. He resisted, and kept them both on their sides. His hand cupped the back of her knee and drew her leg over his flank. His chest rose and fell rapidly as he continued to stroke into her, stretching her tightness for his fuller possession.

"This way is easier for a first time," he soothed.

She was too steeped in passion to recognize the

warning in his words. He braced one arm around her back like a vise. The hand on her leg fettered her in position. Then it came, the burning, stretching sensation as he imposed his body on hers. He silenced her cry with his mouth. She couldn't move, couldn't throw him off, and her struggles only seemed to drive him deeper into her body. She felt a tearing sensation, a flash of pain, and the torment was over.

Gray held himself rigidly in check. When he felt her body relax, he raised his head. Tears stood on her lashes, and he kissed them away. He didn't give her time to speak, didn't give her time to think. Locking their bodies together, he turned her on her back and rose above her, then he began to move, slowly at first, carefully, coaxing a response from her.

His patience was rewarded. Her breath caught on a wave of pleasure and she strained against him. She moaned. He smiled. Exultant now, he increased her torment, drawing her by slow degrees toward the edge of oblivion. When it came, she jolted beneath him and cried out in helpless abandon. He held back so that he could watch her face. Her eyes glazed over and her head thrashed on the pillow. The hands on his shoulders clenched and unclenched as the spasms shook her. She said his name, and her desperate plea was more than he could endure. As the rapture overwhelmed him and hurled him over the crest, he muffled his hoarse cry of triumph against her throat.

CHAPTER 17

"I had hoped that I wouldn't hurt you."

"Mmm?" Deborah slowly opened her eyes and looked around her. The fire in the grate blazed brightly, evidently with fresh logs, and Gray, now in a dressing robe, was at the washstand, pouring water from a china pitcher into a basin. She was under the covers and had a vague recollection of Gray putting her there as she was drifting off to sleep.

"I had hoped that I wouldn't hurt you," he repeated, and looked over at her as she struggled to sit up.

The smile in his eyes made her feel warm all over. She stretched languidly and smiled back at him. "You made up for it," she said.

"I wanted to make it perfect for you."

She glanced at the basin of water he had set down on the table by the bed. "It *was* perfect," she said. "It was the most wonderful experience of my life. Was it . . . was it perfect for you too?"

He chuckled. "Not exactly. I hope I never have to go through that again."

She was disappointed, to say the least. She almost pouted. "What did I do wrong?"

He sat on the edge of the bed and raised one of her hands to his lips. His eyes danced wickedly as he nibbled on first one finger, then another. "You didn't do anything. It was your first time. That's what made it so difficult for me. Next time, it will be better, for both of us."

Now she did pout. He was used to experienced women, women who knew everything there was to know about pleasuring a man in bed. She wished she were one of them so that she could have made it perfect for him too.

He had drawn one of her fingers into his mouth and was sucking strongly. She felt the tug of his lips as though he had fastened them to her nipples. Distracted, she brought an arm to her breasts and rubbed gently in an effort to quell the throb that had started there. The throb intensified and she let out a shivery breath. She didn't want to appear gauche and inept. She wanted to please him. Should she suck on his fingers too?

She couldn't hold on to that thought. He was fingering her ear, now brushing inside it, now slowly drawing out of it. She must be very wicked for the picture that flashed into her mind had nothing to do with ears at all. A jolt of heat raced from ear to loins, and another throb got started. Deborah squirmed and stifled a whimper. She was so hot, she could feel her bones begin to melt. If this went on much longer, she was sure she would set the bed on fire.

Gathering her scattered wits, she made a stab at introducing an air of normalcy. She indicated the basin of water on the table by the bed. "Is that for me?"

"Yes," he said.

She jumped when he suddenly pulled back the bedcovers. Her chemise was around her waist, and she reached for the sheet to cover herself. He prevented it.

"You were a virgin," he said. "This will make you feel better."

Her eyes followed the path of his gaze, and she flushed when she saw the dried streaks of blood on her thighs. This was as nothing, however, when he wrung out a washcloth and she grasped his intent. She snapped her knees together and shook her head. "Oh no," she said, "oh no."

His voice was very soft and threaded with a shade of amusement. "Intimacy, Deborah. It's natural between lovers. You mustn't be shocked by it." He waited an interval, then said even more softly, "There's more to loving than joining our bodies. I want to know your body as intimately as I know my own, and I want you to know mine intimately too."

His words did something peculiar to her insides. A melting sensation spread from her womb to the extremities of her toes and fingers. Her limbs felt weightless, and each breath became shallower, less regular. When he parted her legs and draped one of them over his thighs, opening her body to him, she threw back her head.

The cloth was warm, almost hot, and it registered dimly that he must have fetched the hot water himself from below stairs. None of the servants would be up at this time of night.

"Deborah," he said, "uncover yourself for me. I want to see you naked."

The words came automatically. "No one has ever seen me naked before."

"I have, once. When I abducted you. You were asleep, and I wanted to examine your injuries. That picture has been branded on my mind. You'll never know the torments I've suffered since then, watching you, knowing what was concealed beneath your garments."

Deborah was suffering her own torments. The washcloth was between her thighs, rubbing, invading gently, parting the folds of her femininity to his questing fingers. Another jolt of heat shot through her. She stifled a moan and reached for the hem of her chemise. She was struggling to get it over her head when his finger flexed inside her. She could hardly draw her next breath.

"You are beautifully formed," he said, "lovely, in fact. Especially here." His fingers parted her.

The chemise came over her head, and she flung it to the end of the bed. She was panting as if she'd run up three flights of stairs. He was smiling his lazy smile, with his eyes half hooded, shielding his expression.

"Warm, Deborah?"

Hot as Hades, but she couldn't tell him that. It was too embarrassing. "Actually," she said, "I find it a tad chilly in here."

"Then we must try to make you warmer."

It wasn't possible. Then she discovered it was possible. He planted a kiss on her abdomen, and trailed his lips downward, ever downward, to the triangle of dark reddish hair between her thighs. She watched in awed fascination as he kissed her there, in the secret place between her legs. This was intimacy with a vengeance. It was wicked. It was wanton. And it made her wild to have him. *Kisses*. She remembered his tongue, thrusting into her mouth, and though, in that moment, he did no more than lightly touch his tongue to her, her imagination did the rest. She cried out and arched off the bed like a tensed crossbow, burying his face between her thighs.

There was a moment when they both froze. He moved first. When he slowly raised his head to look at her, and saw the hot color that ran across her cheekbones, he wasn't exactly laughing, but his amusement was patent.

"Ah," he said, "I see you have already figured it out. God, you tempt me. But no, I think not. Not yet."

She couldn't hide her disappointment. "You mean, that's it? You're not going to . . . well . . . finish what you started?"

"What do you think?" he said.

He smiled at her eagerness, and swiftly rising, shrugged out of his robe. He turned to face her.

Though they'd made love once, this was the first time she had seen him naked. Her eyes moved over him slowly. Her first impression was of sheer masculine beauty, but as her eyes lingered, taking in the breadth of his shoulders, the hard muscular physique and the jutting sex, she became acutely aware of his brute strength. She wasn't afraid; she was fascinated. In the act of love, all that beauty and power had been hers to command.

She ran the tip of her tongue over her lips and looked up at him.

"What?" he asked, frowning at her.

He looked curiously uncertain, as though he feared she might not like what she saw, and that touched her. "If I'd known what *you* were concealing beneath your fine clothes, I would have seduced you long before now."

He laughed and came down beside her. "You didn't seduce me. Seduction implies reluctance, and I have wanted you for a long, long time." She looked skeptical, and he nodded then went on. "Almost from the first, in Miss Hare's parlor, with those atrocious girls. They were running rings round you, and I was sorely tempted to box their ears."

Her fingers twined in his hair. "I think I lost my heart to that nice Mr. Gray."

He kissed her softly. "But I really knew it was all up with me when you ran from me in Wells, in the cathedral. Do you remember?"

"How could I forget?" She stopped playing with his hair. "I was terrified of you!"

"I know." He kissed her lips, softening them. "And I was angry because you didn't trust me. I wasn't thinking only of Quentin. I think I knew even then that I would never let you get away from me."

She frowned, and sensing an argument, he kissed her swiftly. When she relaxed beneath him, he made love to her in earnest. He bent to take a nipple in his mouth, and sucked gently, then strongly as he felt her response. His fingers brushed through the hair between her thighs and slipped into her. He felt the liquid heat that both excited him and reassured him, and he came up on his knees. She was wet and ready for him.

"Oh Gray," she said. "Oh Gray," and she reached for him.

He pulled her to her knees, facing him. "It's your turn. Touch me, Deb. Pleasure me. I've shown you how easily it can be done."

Her eyes were drawn to his swollen sex. She didn't know the first thing about pleasuring a man, but supposed that it wasn't so different from what a man did to a woman. She grasped the length of his shaft in both hands and that's as far as she got.

Gray came off the bed like a rocket. She was flung back, but he caught her before she went flying to the floor.

"What did I do?" she cried out, and grasped his shoulders to steady herself.

"What did you do?" He started to laugh. "You damn near castrated me! Your fingers closed around me like a steel trap. Here." He caught her hand and guided it to the thrusting length of him. "Gently," he said, "softly, like this." He curled her fingers around him, showing her just what he wanted.

She was fascinated by the smooth, satiny feel of him, fascinated by the way his rigid staff pulsed and moved beneath her soft caresses. Wide-eyed, she looked up at him. His nostrils were flared; his lashes flickered against his cheeks; his lips were parted and she could hear the breath rushing in and out of his lungs.

"Kiss me," he said.

"Where?" she asked.

He opened one eye, and when he saw that she was serious, he rolled on his back and flung one hand over his eyes. His shoulders were shaking. "*Where,* the lusty wench wants to know," he gasped out. "Oh God, every man should be so lucky!"

She was done with being the butt of his hilarity. A considerate lover would have known she hadn't a notion of what was expected of her. A considerate lover would have answered her question. With a snort of wounded pride, she made to get off the bed. He pounced on her and rolled her beneath him. She glared up at him and opened her mouth to upbraid him, but she wasn't given the chance. He swooped down and kissed her into silence. She wrapped her arms around him and kissed him back.

He released her mouth and buried his face against her throat. "It's never been like this before. I never dreamed that there could be a woman like you for me. You are everything I've ever wanted."

"Truly?"

He raised his head and their eyes locked, his intensely blue, hers as dark as raw emeralds. "Truly," he whispered.

In one smooth thrust, he entered her. He moved. She responded. He braced himself on his arms, sinking deeper into her body. She shifted her position to accommodate him. They both smiled.

"Perfect?" he asked.

"Perfect," she agreed.

Then their smiles dissolved, and they knew nothing beyond the driving need of their bodies to make them one.

❧

She was curled into him, and her breath tickled his armpit. Disengaging himself carefully, so as not to waken her, Gray rolled from the bed and went to add another log to the fire. When he returned to the bed, he lay on his back with his arms crossed behind his neck. Deborah sighed, nestled closer, and pillowed her head on his chest.

He draped one arm around her inert form, drawing her closer. Something sweet and ineffably tender moved him. Nothing in his varied experience of women had prepared him for this one slip of a girl. He couldn't remember a time, not once, when he had convulsed in laughter during the sexual act. His usual experience was a great deal of skill and finesse, moaning and panting, and a tumultuous climax that had left him replete, but hardly hungering for more. He knew that there would never come a time when he would be sated with Deborah. He would always hunger for more.

Turning his head, he looked down at her. Her hair was different in this dim light, darker, almost chestnut. Her features were love-soft, her skin was love-flushed. When he traced a finger down her patrician nose, she batted his hand away, then began to make sniffing noises which lapsed into intermittent snores. He knew there was a big smile on his face. That *she* should be the one to capture him both surprised and delighted him. She was perfect for him, but if someone had tried to tell him so before he had met her, he would have laughed himself silly.

He smiled down at the top of her head and twisted one short, silky curl between his fingers. Even when she had played the part of a dowd, he had felt the tug of attraction. She had felt it too. It would have been so much simpler if they had met under normal circumstances. She would have been his that much sooner. *His,* he thought, and something dark and primitive moved inside him.

He groaned. He couldn't take her again. She was an innocent. This was all so new to her. Only a brute would give in to his baser instincts. Gritting his teeth, he fought to master his body.

Deborah wasn't helping. One hand was absently stroking along his shoulder and the other was caught between their bodies, pressing against his groin. Just thinking about it made him go hard with wanting.

She stirred, and came to herself slowly. "Perfect," she murmured. "It was perfect."

"How do you feel?"

She raised on one elbow to get a better look at him. "Wonderful," she said, smiling. Her fingers curled around his shaft, squeezing and stroking with exquisite pressure.

Gray writhed; he groaned. "I should never have taught you that trick." His teeth were clenched. "I thought you were sleeping."

"Hardly," she answered demurely. "This is all so new to me. I must be shameless, Gray. I can't get enough of you."

He took her at her word. Surging against her, he carried her to her back, and he crushed her mouth beneath his. There was no gentleness in him now, no restraint. She could have stopped him with a word, a touch. Instead, she incited him to greater passion. His urgency was matched by hers. His desperation fed her desperation. Together, they went hurtling toward the edge of mindless delight. Once, she stilled his movements, and she grasped his hands and showed him what she wanted. He laughed in sheer triumph, then groaned when she touched him intimately, the way he had taught her. Catching her wrists, he held them above her head. Panting, bucking, she strained against him, demanding he take her.

There was a moment when he savored her expression, the passion-dazed eyes, the trembling lips, the flush of desire on her skin. Then she begged him to take her once too often and his control shattered. She gasped when he drove into her.

"Deb?" he said on a breath of apology.

In answer, she wrapped her legs and arms around him, locking him to her. She set the pace. He followed, exulting in her unfettered response. This was more than pleasure, more than passion, more than anything he had ever known. She was his. He was hers.

"Mine," he said fiercely, as he felt the rhythmic spasms begin deep inside her. "You are mine," he said again as she writhed beneath his thrusting body. Then coherent thought disintegrated, and he gave himself up to his own explosive release.

They lay for a long while after, trying to recover their breath. In the aftermath of spent passion, Gray was appalled at himself. He knew he had been rough with her. "Violent" was not too strong a word for it. He was sure there would be bruises on her white shoulders where he had held her down at the last. And what on earth had possessed him to suck on her delicate skin as though he were a vampire straight out of hell? No woman should be subjected to such treatment from her lover.

He pulled from her body and rolled to his back, bracing himself for the reproaches that were sure to follow. "No woman has ever had this effect on me," he muttered, thinking aloud.

"I'm sorry," she said. "I'm really a very gentle girl. I don't know what comes over me in the throes of passion."

He opened his eyes and looked up at her. "What?"

She bit down on her lip. "Are they very painful?"

When she brushed her fingers over his shoulders, he looked down and saw the scratches and red scores from her fingernails. The knot of tension inside him uncurled. "I like your marks on me," he said.

"You're not . . . disgusted?"

"Ask me that in a few hours when you see the marks I've left on you."

Her eyebrows rose.

They both smiled.

Quite unconcerned for her nakedness, she slipped from the bed and began to gather her discarded garments. Gray pulled to a sitting position, one knee drawn up with his arm resting across it. A smile tugged at his lips. The light from the fire dappled her skin, enhancing her soft curves and contours. It pleased him that she could be so natural with him. This was real intimacy, and he'd had enough of the other kind to last him a lifetime.

She was examining a torn stocking. When he made a sound, she looked over at him. "This is nothing to laugh at," she said. "These are silk stockings. They are incredibly expensive." She poked her finger through a hole in the toe and waggled it at him. "Fortunately, it's easily mended."

"Don't worry, love. When we are wed, you will never have to worry about the price of silk stockings again."

When she stiffened, he hastened to explain. "I shall be a generous husband, Deborah. You'll have more pin money than you will know what to do with."

"Husband?"

He realized that he had shocked her, and he sat up a little straighter. More cautious now, he went on. "I thought we could manage it within the fortnight if I procure a special license. That should give you time to arrange for bride clothes and whatever trifles are necessary to satisfy a woman on such an occasion."

She moistened her lips and glanced nervously at the clock on the mantel. "Speaking of time," she said, "shouldn't we be on our way? The sky is beginning to lighten."

He studied her for a long time then said softly,

"Marriage, Deb. It's not a dirty word. There's nothing to fear. People get married every day."

She made a small sound of derision, moved to a leather armchair beside the grate, and began to pull on her stockings. "It never entered my head that you were thinking of marriage," she said. "Why should it? You do this kind of thing all the time."

That did it. He let out a roar and sprang from the bed. When he bent over her, with his hands supporting his weight on the armrests of the chair, she shrank back, then lowered her lashes to shield herself from the effect of those powerful bunched muscles in his chest and arms. Her pulse leapt wildly in her throat, but not entirely in fear. She knew the feel of him now, knew his touch and taste.

"I have never trifled with innocent young women," he said in a voice that made her wince. "I am no reprobate. I know the score. And I knew what the consequences would be when I claimed your innocence for myself."

"Must we talk of this now?" she murmured and glanced desperately at the door.

"Damn right, we must. I'm warning you, Deb, until we thrash this out, you are not leaving this room."

"Then would you mind if we got dressed first?"

"Why?" he snarled, ignoring the appeal in her huge, pleading eyes. "So you can pretend that nothing happened between us? I know every inch of you intimately now, and I promise you, I'm going to know you intimately again and again. When I want to take you, I shall, and you won't stop me. Do you know why, Deb? Because you'll want it too."

Her lips parted and a blush spread from her throat to hairline. "I know," she said in a constricted tone. "In fact, it's what I hoped you would suggest."

"What?" he asked, nonplussed.

Her eyes dropped away. "You know. I'm not sure how these things are managed, but you do have that empty house in Hans Town. I really haven't given it much thought, but . . . couldn't we meet there from time to time?"

Suddenly straightening, he combed his fingers through his hair. "Deb, you can't mean what I think you mean."

"Why can't I?"

"Because . . . because you're not cut out to be a man's mistress."

Her mouth tightened and her eyes ignited. "I wasn't suggesting that I become your mistress. I have no wish to be a kept woman. I'll not have a gold bracelet pressed upon me when you grow tired of me." She leaned forward to make her point. "I want us to be lovers, Gray, *lovers.*"

"Lovers?" The word exploded from his lips. "Lovers? And what the hell do you mean 'when I grow tired of you'? I love you, dammit. I want to be with you for the rest of my life."

Though his words moved her, they did not weaken her resolve. "Gray," she whispered, "I shall never marry. You had better make up your mind to that right now."

"You don't love me?"

She swallowed the lump in her throat. "I don't know what love is, but from what I've seen of it, I wouldn't wish it on my worst enemy. No, listen to me. Even if I did love you, it wouldn't make any difference. I still wouldn't marry you."

But she did know what love was. He could see it in her eyes. All was not yet lost. Slightly mollified, he grabbed a sheet from the bed, wrapped it around himself, and sprawled in the chair opposite hers.

"It really is time for us to be on our way," she said, pleading with him.

"Oh no, Deb. You'll not escape me that easily. I asked you to marry me, and I'm entitled to an explanation for your refusal."

She darted him a small smile. "Actually, you didn't ask. In your usual high-handed fashion, you told me that we were to be married." There was no answering smile on his lips, and after a moment, she lifted her shoulders and said, "I'm not averse to the institution of marriage. My quarrel is with the laws of England. Gray, do you know what happens to a woman's property when she marries?"

"Since you don't have two pennies to rub together," he said nastily, "I don't think that's relevant."

She stiffened. "Just for the sake of argument, let's say I was a great heiress. If we wed, you would have control of all my moneys."

"Control, perhaps, but that does not mean I could do whatever I wished. You don't think I shall allow Meg to marry without tying up her fortune so that she and her children are well provided for?"

"Oh yes, I know what happens in theory, but in practice, things are very different, and the laws of the land allow it. Do you know, if Meg found her marriage intolerable, and left her husband, she would lose her children? They would be his, and he could prevent her from seeing them ever again. And if she found work to support herself, her earnings would belong to him too. She would be destitute, and in the end, she would be glad to go back to him, if only to survive."

"I'd kill him first."

Very quietly, very seriously, she said, "Meg is fortunate to have brothers to look out for her interests. Not all women are in that happy position."

"I see." He took a moment or two to review her words in his mind. Finally, he said, "Is that what happened to your mother? Did she leave your father?"

She nodded. Her voice came out a cracked whisper. "She tried to take us with her, but he prevented it. I never saw her again. And when she died, neither my brother nor I were allowed to go to her funeral. As for my father"—she emitted a choked laugh—"he married again before the mourning period was half over."

He should feel sympathetic, and to a certain degree he did. But the emotion that swamped all these softer feelings was akin to outrage. That she could lump him with such a man! That she would believe him capable of such unscrupulous behavior! He got up and began to prowl the room.

Suddenly rounding on her, he said emphatically, "I sympathize. I really do. But what in the name of God has any of that to do with us? I'm not your father. I don't make victims of the women who are entrusted to my care. Ask my mother. Ask my sisters. Don't you understand? I don't want to take things away from you. I want to give you everything you've ever dreamed of. I want to take care of you."

"You say that now, but can you promise me that you'll say that in another year or two? When love fades, good intentions fly out the window. I know what I'm talking about."

He held on to his temper with the greatest difficulty. "Your opinion of me is not very high, is it, Deborah?"

She shifted uncomfortably, but she kept her eyes steady on his. "It's not you, Gray. It's not even men in general. It's the laws of the land, as I told you."

There were other compelling reasons why she could not marry him. She could well imagine his horror if she were to tell him the truth about herself. But that wasn't why she was refusing him. She would never put herself in a man's power. She would never be as helpless as her mother.

"And nothing I can say will make you change your mind?"

"Change the laws of the land and I'll marry you tomorrow."

"There are no laws that I know to regulate love, Deb."

"I'm sorry," she whispered.

When he began to dress, she followed suit. "About the house in Hans Town," she began, hesitated, then plunged on. "Will you give me a key to it?"

"Now why should I do that?"

For a moment she was stymied. "You know, so that we can be together."

When he was dressed, he crossed to her, turned her around and began to do up the buttons at the back of her gown. "You want my body, but I'm not good enough for you, is that it?" It was a line of conversation that had been flung at him by many a disappointed damsel who had hoped to lead him to the altar, and he relished the words as they tripped from his tongue. He wasn't really angry. He knew he could stir Deborah's passions, and if that was the way to lead her to the altar, he was not going to allow a few scruples to stand in his way.

She spun to face him, her eyes wide with contrition. "Oh no, Gray. It's not just your body I want. How could you even think it? I admire your mind, your intelligence. I like you a lot."

And that was a line of conversation he had used on more occasions than he cared to remember. He couldn't help grinning. "We've got our roles reversed," he said.

"What?"

"You can't have my body until you put your ring on my finger. That's the next line in this play."

She peered up at him. "Are you all right?"

"I mean it, Deb. Until I have my ring on your finger, you can't have my body."

"You are not being fair."

"All's fair in love and war. That's a line from a different play." He was enjoying himself enormously, and that annoyed her.

"Will you stop talking nonsense and start making sense?"

"Perhaps this will explain what I'm trying to say."

He lowered his head and kissed the sensitive spot he had discovered just below her earlobe. When she moved closer, he settled his hands on her waist. Her head came up and he accepted the invitation. His lips sank into hers, lavishing her with wet, openmouthed kisses. His thumbs brushed the undersides of her breasts. She whimpered and wilted against him. When he felt her fingers clench and unclench on his shoulders, he dropped his hands to her bottom, and he lifted her against him, grinding her mound against the bulge in his groin.

"Please?" she said, panting. "Oh Gray, please?"

He released her slowly, steadying her with one hand splayed on the small of her back. That he managed to control his own breathing, he counted as a major victory. He gave her a moment to come to herself before he spoke. "Here's another line I remember. Set a date for our nuptials, and I shall be all yours."

"I can't and I won't." She was beginning to get angry.

"Then I suggest you enjoy your chaste bed."

She poked him in the chest with her index finger. "And if I don't? If I won't?"

He misread her meaning and the smile left his eyes. "If you so much as let another man lay a finger on you, he'll answer to me for it, and you also. I mean it, Deb."

"Idiot!" she snapped. "I'm not like you. One man is more than I can manage, thank you very much."

He had the last word, as she knew he would. "One man is all you are going to get. But on my terms. Think about it, Deb."

It was only when he had her safely back at Channings and he was stretched out on his own bed that he began to pick up clues she had let slip, in all innocence, during their various conversations. It was time, he decided, to pay that overdue call on Viscount Leathe.

❧ ❧ ❧ ❧ ❧ ❧ ❧ ❧

CHAPTER 18

Gray stood just inside the entrance to the White Swan, his eyes trained on the young man who was at the counter settling his bill with the landlord. A shaft of light touched the viscount's crop of dark locks, gilding them with touches of reddish-gold. His chin was square. There was no sneer on his face now. He was smiling at something the landlord had said, and his cheeks creased in much the same way that Deborah's dimples flashed when she was amused. He did not know the color of Leathe's eyes, but he could make a calculated guess. When Leathe turned and his eyes flared at the sight of him, Gray had his answer. Green eyes. Deborah's eyes. Why hadn't he seen the resemblance before?

"I want a word with you," said Gray quietly.

Leathe bristled with hostility. "Much as I hate to disoblige you, Kendal, I fear I must decline. There is a matter in town that requires my immediate attention. You know my direction. Seek me out in a day or two, and I shall be happy to exchange insults with you."

He made to brush past him, but Gray reached out and grasped his arm. "It's about Deborah," he said.

"What about Miss Weyman?"

"I know she's your sister."

All the color washed out of Leathe's face. He stammered, then said harshly, "Whoever told you that is a damn liar."

Gray said nothing, and after a moment, Leathe scowled and said, none too civilly, "Oh, very well. Come this way."

He led the way to the parlor where he and Deborah had conversed the night before. The fire was reduced to glowing embers, and a leather portmanteau sat on one of the chairs. Leathe removed it, and indicated that Gray should seat himself. He took the chair opposite.

"How did you find me?"

"I paid an early-morning call on the Derwents. Matthew Derwent told me you were putting up here."

There was a silence, then Leathe said, "Now, would you mind explaining that remark about Miss Weyman?"

Gray got right to the point. "I mean to marry her, you see, and before I do, I have to know what kind of trouble she is in so that I can fix it for her."

Leathe stared, and went on staring. Pulling himself together, he said scornfully, "You mean to marry her, believing she is my sister? You must take me for a fool. I know what you think of my family. Shall I remind you, on the odd chance that you have forgotten? My mother died in an insane asylum. My sister, whom you believe to be Miss Weyman, murdered her betrothed, and is wanted by the law. My own career is well documented. I'm a wastrel, a drunkard, a ne'er-do-well. Your sympathies are all with my poor, long-suffering father and his countess. Is that not so, Kendal? And you want me to believe you are eager to ally yourself with my disreputable family? I hardly think so."

Gray looked down at his clasped hands, then looked back at Leathe. "You had all that from Meg, I suppose? Yes, I did make those comments to her. They were said in the heat of anger. You are not a suitable young man for her to know. Nothing has made me change my mind on that point. However, I apologize for speaking out of turn. I allowed rumor to color my thinking. Having met Deb, and knowing the kind of girl she is, I see now that I was prejudiced. I'm sorry."

Leathe was assessing Gray in much the same manner

as Gray had assessed him when he had entered the inn. At length he said, "I accept your apology, but I cannot help you with Miss Weyman."

Gray let out a sigh of exasperation. "Let's not waste time bandying words. I presume Deb has sworn you to secrecy or some such foolish thing. We have to help her, in spite of her wishes. Don't you see that? If you won't tell me what I wish to know, I can easily find out from other sources."

"What sources?" asked Leathe quickly.

"Your father. I'm on my way to see him now."

"Damnation!"

A long look was exchanged, then Leathe breathed deeply. "As it happens, I was just on my way to pay a call on my father too." He paused, hesitated, then seemed to come to a decision. "Before I admit to anything, I want your word that you mean Deb no harm."

"You have it."

Leathe shook his head. "I don't know why I should trust you. I don't even like you. But if you are going to stir things up with my father, I have no choice but to take you into my confidence."

"Good," said Gray, "then you can begin by telling me what Deborah is running from. She is accused of murdering her betrothed, that much I remember from rumors that were circulating at the time, but if I'm to help her, I need to know everything about her in minute detail."

"Everything?"

"Everything."

"It's a long story, and goes back to before Deborah and I were born."

Gray settled back in his chair. "Take your time," he invited. "The more I know and understand, the better equipped I shall be to help her."

With many pauses to marshal his thoughts, Leathe began to relate the events that had led to Albert's death and Deborah's subsequent disappearance. Though he told the tale without passion, Gray was electrified, for it seemed to him that he was there, as a bystander, with no power to intervene, and more than anything, he wished he could pluck Deborah and her mother and brother from the clutches of the mercenary monster who had them in his power.

"The odd thing," said Leathe at one point, "is that I believe my mother once loved him. What she ever saw in him, I shall never know. Deb doesn't know this, but our stepmother, the former Lady Hepburn, was his mistress long before he married our mother." To Gray's questioning look, he answered, "A boy gets to hear things at school. There were taunts, innuendoes, that sort of thing. And some of the servants were loose-tongued. My father was not exactly the most revered of masters.

"At any rate, he and his blue-blooded mistress chose an ideal victim in my mother. The Rossiters were wealthy, and my mother was heir to everything. Naturally, her father wanted the best for her, and he chose *my* father. In short, my grandfather was taken in by her suitor's charming façade. So they married. When Grandfather died, my mother found herself alone in the world, with no kin to turn to. After this, my father became intolerable. My mother tried to stand up to him, but it was hopeless. She died in the insane asylum where my father had committed her."

There was a challenging look in Leathe's eyes, but Gray merely remarked, "You were very young at the time, I believe."

"Deb was seven. I was a year younger. We inherited my mother's fortune, not that we were aware of it. It was only later that we realized how cursed we were. In our father's eyes, we weren't children. We were the source of his income. Money. That's all we ever meant to him. Deb bore the greater burden because she was a female. There was no escape for her. I was sent off to school, thank God."

"And Deb, thank God, had Miss Hare," said Gray with feeling. "I'm sorry. You were saying?"

"I never realized until Deb told me last night, how it must have galled my father to think that he would lose our income when Deb married and I reached my majority. In his twisted mind, he believed the money was his in all but name—his by virtue of having stooped to marry a merchant's daughter. You have heard of my father's reputation as a fabulous collector, the showplace he has made out of Belvidere. None of it would have been possible without our income, and it absolutely maddened him to think it could all slip through his fingers. So he devised a scheme to keep Deb's share.

"At the time, I was away at school, and Deb wrote that she was going to London for her first season. My father has a house there, too, Strand House. Do you know it?"

"That old cathedral of a place that's been lying empty for years?"

"That's the one. My father has been trying to sell it. With Deb and me gone, you see, he doesn't have the money to keep up two houses. Well, that's where it happened."

In mounting revulsion and rage, Gray listened intently as Leathe revealed the last episode as Deborah had told it to him only hours before.

There was a long silence, then Leathe said, "Deborah had no one to turn to. I was only a boy of fifteen. How could she have prevailed against my father? How could I? So she disappeared, and because she never wrote to me, I came to believe she was dead. You can imagine my shock when I came face-to-face with her in Richmond Park."

An hour passed while they talked at length, Leathe clarifying points as they arose in Gray's mind. Gray was beginning to have an idea of how to deal with Leathe's father.

He sat back in his chair. " 'Where your treasure is, there is your heart also,' " he quoted, musing to himself.

"Beg pardon?" said Leathe.

Gray looked at him sternly. "Don't you know your Bible, man?"

"Not particularly."

"What the devil do they teach boys in school these days? Oh, never mind! What it comes down to is this. The driving force in your father's life appears to be the collections he has amassed over the years."

Leathe's sneer was pronounced. "My father sees

himself as a man of culture, and a great connoisseur. That he is a thief and stole the money to finance his collections, from first my mother then from Deb and me, does not trouble his conscience."

"If anything happened to Deborah, what would become of her fortune?"

"The bulk of it would come to me, unless she marries. That's why my father has never bothered to take legal action to have her declared dead."

"How much money are we talking about?"

"My income is in excess of a hundred thousand a year, as is Deborah's. Coal and cotton are quite lucrative."

Gray's jaw went slack. "Good Lord! I think I begin to understand." He thought for a moment, then said, "When I arrived, you were on your way to see your father. Why?"

"I thought I might pick a quarrel with him, and possibly kill him, just to avenge Deb's sufferings."

"*That* would not help Deborah."

"No. But it would help me. Do you have a better idea?"

Gray smiled an unholy smile. "I'm a diplomat, Leathe. My methods were learned at the courts of Europe."

"Diplomacy," said Leathe, flicking Gray a dry look, "has never been known to work with my father."

That remark earned a smirk from Gray. "That's because you've never tried it, not as it's practiced by His Majesty's ministers. You're a hothead, Leathe. Diplomacy requires patience, cool nerves, and a straight face."

Gray had risen and Leathe did likewise. "I presume," said Gray, "your father is in residence at Belvidere?"

"Yes. They never come up to town until the hunting season is over. How did you know?"

"Because Deborah would never have come to London if she thought her father was likely to be there. We can be at Belvidere by evening, spend the night at Windsor, and be back here by tomorrow afternoon."

Leathe was still reflecting on what Gray had said.

"What kind of diplomacy is practiced by His Majesty's ministers?" he asked.

"I'll fill you in on the way to Belvidere. You are to take your cue from me. Understood?"

They were in the inn's lobby when they caught sight of Meg. She was tethering her horse to the hitching post in the courtyard.

"What the devil is she doing here?" demanded Gray.

"I sent her a note," said Leathe, flinging the words at him.

Gray gritted his teeth. "Oh, you did, did you?"

They were both bristling, like dogs about to go on the attack.

"Well, get rid of her," said Gray. "We don't want Deborah to know that we are leaving together. She would guess that we are up to something."

Gray took cover in the deserted taproom and watched with mounting irritation at the spectacle that took place in the inn's courtyard. The young whelp actually had the effrontery to take Meg in his arms and kiss her. Only one thing mitigated Gray's annoyance. Meg was chaperoned by a groom. Soon after, Meg and the groom rode off, and Leathe returned to the inn.

"I have a hired chaise waiting," said Leathe, stiff as starch, indicating the vehicle in question. "We can stable our mounts here until we return."

Nothing more was said until they were inside the chaise. "I meant what I said," said Gray. "You are not a suitable young man for my sister to know."

Leathe's response was equally blunt. "Those are my sentiments exactly with respect to yourself. You are too much in the petticoat line for my taste, Kendal, and I'm warning you now, I shall do everything in my power to protect Deb from you."

"You had better not take that tack in the presence of your father," Gray said between his teeth. "My strategy depends on convincing him that Deb will soon be my wife and thus under my protection."

"I can playact as well as you," was the stiff rejoinder.

They glared, they hunched their shoulders, and each affected an interest in the passing scenery.

❧

They reached Belvidere a little after eight o'clock. Though they had unbent enough to discuss their strategy, their manner toward each other was polite rather than friendly.

"I've heard a lot about Belvidere," said Gray, looking around him with interest. "It's reputed that your father rebuilt it into the most magnificent private palace in the whole of England."

"You heard correctly," said Leathe, "and it was money from coal and cotton that is responsible for all this grandeur." He made a gesture with one hand, encompassing the neoclassical façade of white marble steps and Greek columns. "My father lived like a king while my mother languished in an insane asylum. I shall never forgive him for that."

Gray had prepared himself for a finely appointed house, but even he was taken aback by its splendor when Leathe ushered him into the vast entrance hall. A set of twelve Greek columns with gilt Greek statues upon them seemed to hold up the intricate plaster ceiling with its mural of some scene from Roman history. Beneath his feet was a marble mosaic in white and blue to match the columns.

"The columns," said Leathe, "were discovered in the river Tiber in Rome. My father had them brought to Belvidere on the occasion of his marriage to my mother. You might say they were a wedding present to himself."

The footman who took their coats and hats gave no sign of recognizing Leathe. Leathe had warned Gray to expect this. He had not set foot in Belvidere since he had run away from school.

"You may tell his lordship," Gray told the footman, "that Lord Kendal presents his compliments and requests a few moments of his time."

Within minutes, the footman had returned and was politely ushering them into a gold and green anteroom.

Paintings which Gray recognized at once as executed by Raphael and Titian adorned the walls, and gilt pedestals were set around the room with objets d'art displayed to effect on each one.

Leathe was amused by Gray's expression. "Look at the mural on the ceiling," he said. "Can you believe it? It's of my father. Yes, it's a Greek myth and he is portrayed as the Greek hero Theseus."

He broke off as the door opened. Gray had never met the Earl of Belvidere, and nothing had prepared him for the gentleman who entered. After listening to Leathe's account of all that he and Deborah had suffered, he had expected an evil-looking monster. What he saw was a remarkably handsome man, dark hair, and a thin face dominated by deep-set dark eyes. His garments were of the finest materials and exquisitely tailored, but he wore them easily. His whole bearing was majestic, but it was also gracious. A prince presiding at his court. It came to Gray then that the house and its contents were no more than a stage setting to gratify this man's ego. He should have been amused. He found the spectacle chilling.

One slim hand gestured, hinting a welcome, and rings flashed, reflecting the light. "Kendal," said the earl affably. "This is an honor! Pray be seated." He indicated a gold upholstered chair against the wall.

"I believe you know my companion," said Gray.

Leathe took a step forward, and the smile on Belvidere's face dimmed, but only momentarily. The voice was rich and smooth. The tone was ironic. "Does this mean that the prodigal son has returned?"

Leathe's voice was not so level as the earl's. "You know better than that. Only something extraordinary could have brought me back to this house."

Again that thin hand made a brief gesture. "I see that your manners have not improved, Leathe. Gentlemen, why don't we sit down and make ourselves comfortable? Something extraordinary, you say? I'm all ears."

As they seated themselves, Belvidere spoke to Gray. His voice was amused, tolerant. "I presume Leathe has made me out to be some kind of ogre? It seems to be his life's object, to blacken my character. As you see, I'm only a country gentleman." He ignored Leathe's soft imprecation. "The boy is prejudiced. His mind has been poisoned against me. If we are to have a reasonable conversation, Kendal, it's best that you understand that."

Gray said pleasantly, "All families have quarrels. I'm not so green as to take everything Leathe says at face value."

Belvidere smiled and settled back in his chair. "Well then, how may I help you?"

"I'll come right to the point," said Gray. "You have a daughter whom you have not seen in nine years. We have found her, Belvidere. Deborah. Your daughter, Deborah. That's why we are here."

For a moment Belvidere's mask slipped, but then he mastered himself.

"Deborah!" The earl pressed a hand to his eyes. "I have always wondered . . . what I have suffered, not knowing . . . Deborah!" He looked up, and his features were set in an expression of regret. Only the eyes betrayed him. They were blank.

He said, "I was sure she must be dead, but I refused to give up hope. Where is she?"

Leathe's patience came to an end. "Where you'll never find her! Do you think we are taken in by your playacting? You never cared for Deborah, any more than you cared for me or our mother." He had half started to his feet.

Gray said quietly, "Leathe, get a hold of yourself."

When Leathe subsided, Belvidere gave Gray a deprecating smile. "Thank you. Whatever Leathe may think, I have always had my children's best interests at heart."

"Then explain Albert," said Leathe vehemently, "and how you accused Deb of murder, yes, and set the magistrates on her."

Those long hands moved in an elegant gesture, and rubies and diamonds flashed. Belvidere said gently, "Leathe, I don't have to explain myself to you. Whatever I said, you would dispute. And as for Lord Kendal, I hardly know him." His eyes moved to Gray, questioning. "What is it you wish to tell me about Deborah?"

Any normal father would have been showing some emotion, firing off questions, demanding to know what had happened to his daughter in their long years of separation. But there was nothing but that cold, bland mask.

"I'm going to marry Deborah," Gray said.

"Ah, I think I understand," Belvidere said. "She's quite an heiress."

Gray said cheerfully, "Yes, isn't she?"

Belvidere chuckled and spread his hands. "I wish you happy, I really do."

"Thank you," said Gray, "but there is one small problem."

"Yes." There was an infinitesimal pause, then that rich, smooth voice went on. "You could call murder a small problem. It's a tragic business. I tried to use my influence to have the charges against her dropped, to no avail."

Leathe made an inarticulate sound.

Gray said, "Now that relieves my mind."

The earl looked at him curiously. "Unhappily, there were witnesses, servants, whose evidence was irrefutable. They saw Deborah push poor Albert over the balustrade."

"I thought there might be witnesses," said Gray, "but you know and I know that if it went to trial, no jury in the land would convict Deborah for defending herself. But think of the unpleasantness, the speculation, the gossip. I'm afraid I cannot allow it."

"Indeed?" replied Belvidere. "And how do you propose to stop it?"

Gray made a steeple of his fingers. "What I propose," he said, "is that you try again. To put it bluntly, if those charges against Deborah are not dropped, I shall take punitive action."

Belvidere gave a disbelieving laugh. "You're *threatening* me?" There was real amusement in his eyes when he looked at Gray.

"I don't wish to threaten you," said Gray. "I'd prefer to make a bargain with you."

"What bargain?"

"Leathe, please enlighten your father."

Leathe adopted the same tone as Gray. "The paintings and collections belong to me and Deborah. I've consulted a barrister as well as my solicitor, and I'm told that any court in the land would find in our favor. You had control of our income. It was yours to invest for us, not spend on yourself. My solicitor tells me that Deborah and I owe you a debt of gratitude. Over the years, these collections have appreciated in value. Of course, I never cared for money, and neither did Deborah. But you do, and unless you want to lose everything, you'll do as we say."

Belvidere's face was livid with scorn. "I'd see you dead before I'd part with a single porcelain button. The collections are mine, and when I die, they will pass to my daughter, Elizabeth. Take me to court and try to prove your case! Do you think I'm a fool? There are no records. As for your moneys, I shall plead bad investments or incompetence in handling your affairs, and that's not a crime."

Until this moment, the earl had confined most of his remarks to Gray, but now that Leathe had entered the debate, it was as if Gray had ceased to exist. Both father and son had risen to their feet, facing each other. The hatred in the air was palpable, and Gray felt the fine hairs on the back of his neck begin to rise. It was clear to him that the earl's façade had developed a crack. The threat to his precious collections had done this, a threat that had come from an unexpected quarter, his son and heir.

"There isn't a decent bone in your body." Leathe stopped to even his breathing, failed, and went on hoarsely. "It shouldn't be necessary to bribe you. You're Deborah's father, for God's sake. But you've never loved anyone in your life. You're incapable of love. All you cared about was things."

"Love?" Contempt blazed from the earl's eyes and his lips were drawn back in a sneer. "What a sniveling cur you are! Pride in our heritage is what matters. Loyalty to our family name. This house and its contents are reputed to be the most enviable private palace in the whole of Europe, on a par with Windsor and Versailles.

And it is my doing! But that means nothing to a wastrel such as you."

"You married my mother for her fortune and spent it on this house. You didn't care what happened to her."

"Your mother!" He spat the words as though they were tainted with poison. "It was a marriage I soon came to regret. I married beneath me. Your mother had no conception of her duty to the great family she had married into!"

Leathe's voice cracked. "The great family she married into destroyed her. She was your victim, as Deb and I have been your victims. God have we not! We were young and helpless, and you took from us the one person who made life tolerable in this . . . this petrified mausoleum. At least I was able to escape you when I went away to school, but Deborah . . . Deborah— when I think of Albert, I could kill you." He drew in a great shuddering breath. "But that's too easy a revenge. No. I'm not going to kill you."

"Kill me?" Belvidere laughed. "I'm trembling in my boots." The silk in his voice became velvet. "Leathe, have a care. You can't fight me and win. You never have; you never will. And do you know why, Leathe? Because you are your mother's son. You're a weakling and a wastrel, and that's all you'll ever be."

Something shattered on the floor behind them, and both men spun round. Gray was on one knee, picking up the pieces of what had been an urn. At that moment, two armed footmen burst into the room and came to a sudden halt.

"Good Lord!" exclaimed Gray. "How careless of me." He held out two jagged fragments to the earl. "This was Mycenaen, was it not? What a pity! I shall pay for it, of course." He smiled sheepishly as he rose and joined father and son. "Or, if you like, you may regard it as a wedding present, you know, for Deborah and me."

The footmen looked at their master, and receiving no direction, quietly withdrew.

Belvidere was as rigid as one of his own marble statues. He didn't blink. He didn't breathe. The eyes weren't dead. They were burning with a violent intensity, and Gray was satisfied that his message had been received and understood. A son might not have the stomach to take on his father, but there was nothing to stop the Earl of Kendal. And Gray knew where to hurt him. His precious collections. A less cautious man would have ordered his footmen to throw them out. Belvidere would want to know just how far they were prepared to go. Good. At last the earl was taking him seriously.

"If I were you, Belvidere," said Gray, "I would pack my treasures away where thieves cannot break in. This place is a robbers' paradise."

That formidable control came into play. Belvidere unfroze, but he couldn't quite steady his voice. "You think I'm foolish enough to leave my treasures unguarded? You saw what happened just now. Ask around, Kendal, and you will discover that every thief who has ever broken into my house has ended his life on the gallows."

"Point taken," murmured Gray. "Leathe, what do you suggest?"

"Fire," answered Leathe at once. He had recovered his poise, and belatedly remembered the plan they had agreed on. "I always wanted to torch this place, and nothing has made me change my mind."

"But Leathe," protested Gray, "this is your ancestral home. The house is entailed on you. Fire would destroy everything, not only the collections."

"Then I would rebuild it to my own taste."

"What a pity I won't be here to see it," snapped the earl. Then to Gray, "What exactly do you want from me?"

There was no pretense at civility now. Gray was as grim-faced as the earl. "If you had managed to get Deborah in your clutches again, you soon would have taken steps to clear her of the charges against her. You had a plan of some sort. Use it. At the end of a week, two weeks at the most, I shall expect to hear that the matter has been settled."

"And my collections?"

"Leathe?"

"Shall we say that the collections remain intact until Lord Belvidere dies, and on his death, a half share shall go to Elizabeth and a quarter share to Deborah and me? Our solicitors can draw up the agreement."

"That's very generous," said Belvidere. He sounded bored. "But I fear I must decline. Your threats don't frighten me." His eyes fastened on Gray, and a murderous rage blazed in their depths. "You made a mistake coming here, tonight, threatening me in my own home. It's a mistake you will live to regret."

"Two weeks," said Gray. "That's all the time I will allow you. Fail me in this, and I'll take everything away from you, piece by piece, down to the last porcelain button.

"A word of advice. Even now, you are under surveillance. Make one move toward Deborah or Leathe, and I shall hear of it."

As they turned to leave, the earl addressed his son. "You take after your mother."

Leathe said nothing.

"She was mad, Leathe. And her blood runs in your veins."

The vicious words froze Leathe to the spot. Not so Gray. He stepped between father and son and calmly rammed his fist into Belvidere's face, sending him hurtling to the floor. Legs splayed, hands fisted, Gray stood over him. The blood spurted from the earl's nose and dripped onto his snowy-white cravat.

"That's for Deborah," said Gray. "Oh, not the past. Nothing short of a long, lingering death would suffice for how you abused your role as father and guardian of two innocent children. No, that was because you failed to ask after Deb's welfare, expressed not one word of regret, nor an interest in how she has managed to survive in the last several years. My inclination is to call you out. You're lucky that for Deborah's sake, I want no more scandal."

When the door closed on Gray and Leathe, Belvidere wiped the blood from his face with the back of his sleeve. He was so incensed, he was unaware of what he was doing. He didn't cry out for servants to come and assist him. The humiliation of being found like this was not to be borne.

He pulled himself to his knees, then to his feet, and supported himself on the back of a chair as he struggled to even his breathing. This was not over yet, he promised himself. He would see them both dead for the humiliation they had heaped on him, but he would make them suffer first. It might not happen tomorrow or the next day, but it *would* happen. He was a patient man. Then he would find Deborah and deal with her too.

❧

Not a word was spoken between Gray and Leathe until they were in the carriage and making for the village of Windsor where they were to lodge for the night.

"Well," said Leathe, breaking the silence, "if that was an example of how British diplomats conduct themselves at the negotiating table, it's no wonder that we're always at war. Striking a defenseless man!" He chuckled. "I was never more shocked in my life."

"Are you still convinced your plan will work?" asked Leathe.

"I'm more convinced than ever. Those collections really are an obsession with your father."

"You're not really going to burn the house to the ground, are you?"

"Your father will never let it go that far. Trust me, Leathe. I know what I'm doing. Oh, would you mind if we spent tomorrow in town? There are some things I have to arrange."

"Things to do with my father?"

Gray folded his arms across his chest. "I'm going to enjoy this," he said.

"What are you going to do?"

"Mmm? Oh, negotiate, of course, in a way that your father will understand. That's what diplomacy is all about, my boy."

"Well, if that was an example of how British diplomats conduct themselves at the negotiating table, it's no wonder that we're always at war. Striking a defenseless man!" He chuckled. "I was never more shocked in my life." After a moment's reflection, he went on in a more serious vein. "What did you think of him?"

Gray did not mince words. "Cruel. Vindictive. Contemptible. He really hates you and Deborah. I don't think I fully understood that till now. And that part at the end about your mother, that insanity runs in your veins—he really knows how to twist the knife in you."

"You . . . you don't think there's something in it?"

Gray turned his shrewd blue eyes on Leathe. "I can't vouch for you, of course, but I know my Deb. I'm staking my future and my children's future on my instincts. She's saner than I am."

Leath laughed and stretched out his long legs.

From this point, the conversation dwindled, and finally passed into a companionable silence that was not broken until they were almost at Windsor.

At that point, Gray said suddenly, "You have my permission to accompany Meg when she goes out riding, but on the clear understanding that she is chaperoned at all times."

"What!"

"And when we return to town, you may drive her out in your curricle, but only in public places, Hyde Park, and so on."

Leathe sat up straighter and Gray went on. "Should you happen to encounter her at balls and other such functions, you have my permission to invite her to dance, but mind, no more than the conventions allow. I suppose it's all right if you take her into supper on the odd occasion. I shall confer with my mother on that point." He paused. "This is not to say that I am giving you permission to pay your addresses to my sister. Is that understood?"

"Yes, sir," said Leathe.

"You have a reputation to live down, a character to establish. When I am satisfied that you have made progress, we shall speak again. Do you take my meaning, Leathe?"

"Perfectly. And might I say, sir, that I extend to you the same privileges with respect to Deb?"

It was meant as a joke and they both laughed, but Gray's laugh was forced. He was beginning to understand Deborah's antipathy to the institution of marriage, and the more he thought of it, the more his mood soured.

CHAPTER 19

Gray returned to Channings to find everyone in a great state of agitation. Hart met him at the door and whisked him into a small waiting room.

"Has something happened to Gussie?" Gray asked.

"No, no, nothing like that. But I thought it best if I spoke to you first, before you meet with the ladies. They are rather upset by the incident."

Gray stood with his feet apart, jerking his gloves through the fingers of one hand. "Go on. I'm listening."

Hart spoke quickly. "There was a shooting accident. Well, not an accident exactly. More like a mishap. No one was hurt, that is, no one was wounded. However, Quentin had a bad shock. It's brought on that chest complaint of his. Dr. Tait has already been to see him, and he says there's no real harm done. No, really, Gray, I mean it. The boy is fine."

"Then what did Tait mean when he said that no *real* harm was done."

"We thought at first Quentin's mind might be affected. He fainted, you see, and when he came to himself, he was babbling about France and someone pursuing him. However, whatever it was that disturbed him seems to have passed."

"I see." Gray turned this over in his mind, then said, "Tell me about the accident."

"It *was* an accident. You can be sure of that, Gray," said Hart, knowing what was going through Gray's mind. "It happened early this morning. The boys and their tutor were out walking. Unfortunately, at the same time, our neighbor's son, Matthew Derwent, and a party of friends were out grouse shooting. They had lost track of their surroundings and had strayed onto my land."

"Just tell me what happened, Hart."

"All the guns went off at once. Jason says it was quite an explosion. Even he was shocked. Quentin's reaction, however, was extraordinary. He screamed at the top of his lungs. When Jervis, the tutor, took a step toward him, Quentin backed away, then took off like a hare. Jervis gave chase. When he caught up to him, Quentin fainted. As for young Derwent, I've never seen anyone in such a state. He blames himself. He was here for hours, waiting until Dr. Tait had examined Quentin and assured him that the boy had suffered no real harm."

"I presume Deborah and Quentin are in his chamber now?" Gray was already striding for the door.

Hart hastened to catch up with him. "Yes. Deborah can't be induced to leave him, and—" Gray was taking the stairs two at a time. Shaking his head, Hart went after him.

At the top of the stairs, Gray was met by his mother and sisters. "We thought we heard your voice," said the dowager, and she reached up to press a kiss to his cheek.

As the ladies began to fire off questions at him, he raised both hands, palm up, silencing them. "I should have warned you that something like this might happen. There's nothing to be afraid of. Look, Gussie, I haven't eaten since breakfast. Would you mind arranging something for me? I should like to speak with all of you after I have spoken with Deborah. Why don't you go down to the breakfast room and wait for me there?"

He entered Quentin's chamber to find Deborah sitting on a chair on one side of the bed, and the tutor nervously pacing in front of the window. Gray then looked at Quentin. He appeared to be sleeping, but when Deborah tried to disengage her hand from his clasp, his small hand tightened, holding her fast. The air was thick with vapor and the scent of herbs which came from a small copper pot that was steaming over the fire. In spite of the measures that had been taken to ease the tightness in Quentin's chest, his breathing was rough and labored.

"Sir?" intoned Mr. Jervis.

Gray put a finger to his lips, silencing the tutor. "You look done in, man." He spoke quietly, so as not to disturb Quentin. "Go down to the library and pour yourself a stiff measure of brandy, several if you like. I shall be down directly." When the tutor hesitated, Gray pointed to the door. "Go!"

The door closed softly at Jervis's exit. Gray crossed to Deborah, offering her his hand. She carried it to her face and turned her cheek into it.

"Oh Gray," she said in a shaken voice, "I was never more glad to see anyone in my life."

The expression on Gray's face as he looked down at Deborah would have shocked family and friends alike if they had been there to see it. It was warm and sweet, devastatingly sweet, the same look that Lady Helena had surprised on his face at his mother's soirée.

"Tell me about Quentin," he said.

"I wasn't there when it happened. I heard the commotion and ran out of my room. Mr. Jervis was carrying Quentin up the stairs." She couldn't voice the next thought, that at sight of Quentin's still, white face, she had feared he was dead. "Quentin had fainted. When he came to himself, he thought at first that he and I were still in Paris, running from his father's murderer. He's had a bad shock, and that brought on an attack of asthma. I thought he was growing out of it. And now this!"

Gray kept his voice neutral. "I thought you said that Quentin had no memory of anything connected with his father's death?"

"That's true. But later, I told him what had happened. He must have been thinking of that."

Gray did not respond to this, except to squeeze her shoulder. This was not the time or place to say more.

A movement from the bed put an end to their conversation. Quentin stirred, wheezed, and turned on his side toward them. "I'm thirsty," he murmured drowsily. "And I don't want that barley water of yours, Deb. I want a real drink. Tea or ale."

Gray laughed, but Quentin's words produced a different effect on Deborah. She sniffed, felt in her pocket for a handkerchief, and blew her nose.

"Go on down, Deb," said Gray, "and find him something to drink. Tell Hart to join me here in ten minutes. I'll take over for now. You'll find my mother and sisters in the breakfast room. Wait for me there."

She would have argued with him but his attention was not on her. He was helping prop Quentin up against the pillows, and they were both joking about sherry and how Uncle Gray would know where to look if any of his decanters were ever to go missing again. There was a smile on her face when she left the room.

For the first few minutes, Gray spoke gently about the shooting and how fortunate it was that it was grouse the hunters were after and not deer, for their guns were pointing up. By degrees, he gently led Quentin to describe what had happened.

Gray listened in silence, and though Quentin wheezed and coughed from time to time, he let him go on until all the facts were known to him. Quentin's account was approximately the same as Hart's.

"I suppose," said Quentin, "Jason and everyone is laughing at me? I suppose they think I'm a baby?"

"Why should they think that? Jason was shocked, too, when all those guns went off at once. He was frozen to the spot. You bolted. Only a stupid person would carry on as if nothing had happened. Why, even at this moment, your tutor, Mr. Jervis, is helping himself to your Uncle Hart's best brandy just to steady his nerves. And Uncle Hart doesn't begrudge him one drop."

"Truly, Uncle Gray?"

"Truly." Gray kept his voice light and easy. "Besides, we both know that you had far more reason to be frightened than either Jason or Mr. Jervis. They have never been chased by a murderer before."

If Quentin had betrayed horror or agitation, Gray told himself he would go no further. But Quentin seemed relieved to have the chance to explain himself.

"When I heard the guns go off, I was sure my father's murderer was trying to kill me. I was running to find Deb, and when Mr. Jervis caught me, I thought he was someone else, you know, the murderer."

"Deb seems to think that you thought you were back in France?"

"In France?" Quentin squinted up at Gray. "Why would she think that?"

"I don't know. Perhaps it was something you said. She must have made a mistake."

Quentin's fingers began to work at the coverlet. "You are never going to find out who murdered my father, are you, Uncle Gray?"

"If your memory comes back to you, we shall know who he is."

"But why can't I remember? I've tried and tried, and I still can't remember what happened. I *want* to remember, but—" He broke off, looked down at his hands and smoothed out the lumps he had made of the coverlet.

"I promise you," said Gray, "I'm going to find the man who shot your father, whether your memory returns or not. Ah, here is the maid with—good Lord—it's a tankard of ale! Now that should prove to you no one considers you a baby. Here let me help you with it."

"Watered-down ale," complained Quentin after the first sip.

"Well, what did you expect from Deborah?" said Gray, and they exchanged a man-to-man look, then laughed.

Gray hid his disappointment. He had hoped for so much more. It seemed to him that Quentin *was* beginning to remember, but only at the periphery of things, and only when he was frightened. It would take something extraordinary to get him to remember everything, and Gray did not wish that upon the boy.

Not for the first time, Gray was thinking that until

the murderer was caught, Quentin's life would always be in danger. This could not go on. For Quentin's sake, he had to do something about it.

When Hart came to relieve him, his half-formed resolve began to harden into a solid determination. This was no life for the boy. There would not always be people around to guard him. In another month, he was due to start the new term at Eton. Deb could not go with him, nor could his tutor. Moreover, boys could be cruel if they detected a weakness in another boy. He could well imagine some of the tricks they would play on Quentin if it became known that he panicked when surprised by a loud noise and that he was afraid of the dark. They would make his life miserable.

He had known all this months ago, had known that if he failed to unmask the traitor, there was only one way to lay Quentin's fears to rest. Against his better judgment, he had allowed Deborah to persuade him to let sleeping dogs lie. But Deborah was wrong. If he could not make her see it, he would act without taking her into his confidence.

He spent the next few hours questioning anyone who was anywhere near the scene of the shooting, going so far as to interview Matthew Derwent and his friends. As he expected, there was nothing sinister in what had happened. It was exactly as Hart had described. In a last desperate effort to avoid a course of action he knew would set Deborah against him, he borrowed Hart's library and sent for her.

She saw the gravity in his face, sensed the seriousness of his purpose, and this made her sit up straighter. He remained standing, and she waited for him to begin.

He smiled and said, "Poor Quentin. You know, this would not have happened if we had caught his father's murderer. Quentin would know that he had nothing to fear."

"I've been thinking the same thing," she said, surprising him.

"Have you? And what do you suggest we do?"

"What I've said all along." She looked earnestly into his eyes. "Since you haven't caught your traitor, I think

Quentin should go to his uncle in the West Indies, oh, not forever, you understand, but to give him time to get over what happened in Paris. He'll feel safe with his uncle, knowing that he has put miles of ocean between himself and the man who wishes to harm him. In another year or two, when he is over it, he could return here and take up his life again. By that time, he might even have recovered his memory."

"Or we could try some other way to find out who the murderer is," said Gray. She stiffened, quite visibly, and Gray knew he could never persuade her to agree to the plan that was forming in his mind.

He moved on to something else. "You know," he said, "I'm not convinced that you have told me all that you remember of that night. Perhaps you saw more than you think you saw. What I propose, if you are up to it, is that we go through the events of that night step by step."

The breath that she was holding was exhaled on a rush. She'd been afraid he would suggest using Quentin as bait to trap the murderer, and his words relieved her worst fears.

"I'll do anything if it will help Quentin," she said simply.

It soon became clear that he meant to do more than put a few questions to her. It was to be a reenactment. He made her stand by the door, and on her advice, positioned the desk exactly as she remembered it in Lord Barrington's library.

"How many candles were lit?" he asked.

She had to think about that. "Two. There was one on the desk and one on the mantelpiece."

"Where was the mantelpiece?"

"Over there, facing the door. Weren't you ever in the house?"

"No. I preferred meeting Gil on neutral territory."

"What does that mean?"

"Sophie," he replied succinctly. "She is a born coquette. It made things awkward between Gil and me. However, on the night of our appointment, I was sure

Sophie had already left Paris. I'd no idea you and Quentin were still there."

As he spoke he positioned a small table to represent the fireplace in Lord Barrington's library. Having done that, he set a candle on it.

"Lord Barrington thought you were late for your appointment that night. He was waiting up for you."

He turned to look at her. "Poor Gil."

She swallowed and nodded.

He moved around the room extinguishing candles till there were only two left. "And the windows? Where were they?"

Goose bumps were coming out on her skin. She moistened her lips. "They were just where the windows are now, behind the desk."

"Were the curtains open or drawn?"

"Drawn." She frowned. "They were drawn. I never remembered that till now. And that was unusual, because Lord Barrington never bothered to draw the curtains. But Quentin did. It was one of his favorite tricks, hiding behind curtains, then springing out at me. I'll bet he hid in the library, knowing I would come after him."

"How could he know that?"

"There was a storm that night. I never sleep through storms, and Quentin knows it. If he did not come to my room, I would go to his." She made a helpless gesture with her hands. "I don't like to be alone during a lightning storm, that's all. Quentin would also know that if I found his bed empty, I would search the house till I found him. Why are you frowning?"

"It seems odd to me that a boy would play tricks on his governess in the middle of the night."

"Oh, Quentin is full of tricks. Did you think he was all sweetness and light? Oh no! There was more to it than that, though. He was afraid of storms, too, but he didn't want anyone to know it. I thought he was showing off, you know, as boys do, proving that he wasn't afraid of anything."

"I see. Let's begin then, when you found Quentin's bed empty. What were you thinking?"

"I remember that very well. I was annoyed. Quentin

was just getting over a fever. If he was hiding from me, I was going to give him the sharp edge of my tongue. Apart from anything else, I thought he might be running around in his bare feet. At the same time, I was annoyed because I had no candle. I had to feel my way down the stairs in the dark."

"How did you know to go to the library?"

"There was light shining under the door."

"Yes, go on. You were feeling your way down the stairs. You saw the light shining under the library door. What then?"

She inhaled a long, slow breath. "I called out Quentin's name, not enough to waken the house, but enough to show him that I was not well pleased. There was no answer, and I went on down." Her eyes were wide with shock. "Do you know, I had forgotten that too? On the landing, I called Quentin's name. Do you think they heard me in the library, Gray?"

He answered her carefully. "What do you think?"

"I . . . I can't say. I'm not sure."

"Let's not think of that now. You approached the library door, ready to pounce on Quentin. What happened then?"

She frowned in concentration. "I heard voices. I told you that before."

"Gil's voice?"

"Yes."

"Who else was there?"

"I don't know."

"Could it have been one of the servants?"

She shook her head. "No. The servants spoke French. They were speaking in English."

"A woman's voice, then?" He gave her no time to pause, no time to think. "Yes or no, Deborah?"

"No."

"A stranger's voice?"

"Yes. No. That is, oh Gray, I don't know."

"Don't worry about it. Let's go on to something else. Tell me Gil's exact words."

"I can't remember them exactly. As near as I can remember, he said something like, 'Let the boy go! You, of all people! Have pity. Kendal, Lord Kendal, don't harm him!' Then he shouted, 'Quentin, run for it!' "

They were both white, both shaken as they stared at each other. Deb swallowed and whispered, "I heard a thud, then the gun went off, and I threw the door wide."

Gray said hoarsely, "You are, beyond doubt, the bravest, most resourceful female of my acquaintance. Even a grown man would have quailed before opening that door."

She smiled weakly. "I wasn't brave. I wasn't thinking. I acted out of sheer instinct."

He was trembling, just thinking of Gil's last desperate moments, and of how close both Deborah and Quentin had come to being killed as well. Suppressing these harrowing thoughts, he straightened and took a step toward Deborah. "Don't think of Gil," he said. "Let's concentrate on his attacker. Now close your eyes. You've just heard the shot and you throw the door wide. I am the attacker. I've just shot Gil. Open your eyes, Deborah. Am I in the right position?"

"No. You're too close to the desk. Take a step back and turn to face me."

When he did as she asked, she said, "That's better."

"Deb," he said softly, "look at me. Can you see my face?"

The light from the candle on the desk cast eerie shadows on his face. But she could see his features clearly.

"Gray, I didn't see the murderer's face."

"Why not?"

"I don't know. The candle on the mantelpiece was right behind him. It flared, I think, and my eyes moved to it. I honestly don't know. Too many things were happening at once. I saw Lord Barrington sprawled on the floor . . ."

"Show me where and how."

"There," she said, "right at your feet, and . . . and Quentin came at me suddenly . . ."

"From where?"

She pointed to a corner of the room, between the window and the door. "And I was terrified the murderer might have another pistol."

"Did he?"

"No, just the one."

"How do you know?"

"Because I was looking straight at it," she cried out.

Her bosom was heaving, and her breath came in short sobs. In her imagination, she could hear the sound of the gun going off, feel the vibrations of the spent pistol, smell the acrid stench of burned powder.

"I think that's enough for now," he said quietly.

"No, Gray. If this is of any help to Quentin, I want to go on with it." She gave a short laugh. "The worst is over. What more can you ask me?"

"Only one thing more. Are you sure you are up to it?"

"Quite sure."

He studied her for a long moment, nodded, then said, "Close your eyes."

She closed her eyes and heard the sound of the desk drawer being opened. There was a rustling, then the drawer clicked shut.

"Remember, I'm the attacker," said Gray. "I've just shot Gil, and I'm coming after you and Quentin. Remember also what you told me. You are not going to look at my face, Deb. Now, open your eyes."

He had taken a step closer to her and the pistol in his right hand was clearly illumined by the light from the candle on the desk. Her eyes darted to his left hand. It was empty. She let out a shaken breath.

"Gray," she said, astonished, "the murderer had something in his right hand, a handkerchief, I think, but his left hand was holding the pistol. The murderer was left-handed, Gray."

❦

She had been of immeasurable help to him, but not in the way she thought. There was not nearly enough to go on to unmask the murderer. What they had were lures to bait a trap.

Gray inhaled deeply from the cheroot in his hand, then threw the stub into the smoldering coals in the grate. Gil and he had often spent a quiet hour or two enjoying a smoke and a glass of fine French cognac before a roaring blaze. But that was before Sophie. After Gil had married, it seemed that his time was never his own. And then there was no time left.

He rose and crossed to the turned-down bed. After discarding his robe, he slipped between the verbena-scented sheets. He wasn't ready for sleep. His mind was still sifting through everything Deborah had told him.

In his mind's eye, he had a fairly clear picture of how things had progressed. Gil had answered the door, thinking that he, Gray, had come to keep his appointment. Quentin had slipped into the library and was hiding behind the drapes when his father and the murderer had walked in. He had been discovered. Gil had ordered Quentin to go to his room. But this the murderer could not allow, for Quentin would be able to identify him. He would have killed Gil first, of course. Then it would be easy to deal with the boy.

Deborah's cry from the landing must have given him a rude shock. Now there would be three of them to deal with. All this must have been going through Gil's mind too. Had he started to argue with the killer in order to distract him? And at the last, had he lunged for the gun? Was that the thud Deborah had heard? He was almost sure of it. It's what he would have done. As Deborah said, in such a crisis, one didn't think. One acted from instinct.

There was something else at the back of his mind, something that teased but remained elusive. What was it?

His head turned when the door to the servants' staircase creaked open. Deborah stood on the threshold, a candle in one hand, the other holding the edges of her warm woolen robe together.

"I thought you would come to me," she said.

He forced back a smile. "Now why should I do that?"

"Because this has been a miserable day. Because you must know I need comforting. Because I need *you*."

He tossed the sheets aside and patted the mattress

beside him. "It seems I have no willpower where you are concerned. You really are unscrupulous, Deb, to take advantage of me like this."

As she deposited her candle on the dresser, she made a sound—a husky murmur of assent or approval—and she sped across the carpeted floor, shedding her robe as she went. His arms caught her, and he hauled her into bed.

Supporting herself on his chest, she stared down at his face. "You're not wearing a nightshirt," she said.

"I always sleep naked. You'll get used to it."

She dipped her head and told the tiny mole on his left shoulder, "I never knew it could be like this."

"Like what?" His hands moved over her in light, leisurely strokes, not arousing, but calmly possessing every curve and hollow, every bone and sinew that belonged to him. He kissed the little frown on her brow, then her eyebrows, and finally the dimples that suddenly flashed to life in her cheeks.

"I told you. It's not just this." She pressed a kiss to his lips. "It's you. It's . . . I don't know. Missing you when you're not there. Wanting to be held by you. Wanting to hold you."

"I never knew it could be like this either. I think it's called 'love.' "

Her gaze faltered before the intensity of his. "Gray, why can't you just accept what we have and let it go at that?"

"You," he said slowly, "are a coward. You do love me, you just won't admit it. But all that aside, there is something I want to tell you, something I would have told you when I returned this afternoon if I had not been catapulted into another crisis. I wasn't at the Foreign Office, Deb. I was in Windsor—Belvidere to be precise."

She looked into his eyes and saw a knowledge that made her tremble. "What do you mean?" she whispered.

"I mean," he said, "that I know you are Lady Deborah Montague. You are the daughter of the Earl of Belvidere. Leathe is your brother. I know everything,

Deborah. I know about Albert and that you were accused of his murder. Need I say more?"

She stared at him in blind, speechless horror. When
she remembered to breathe, she sucked air into her lungs
in an audible gush. "Leathe told you?"

"No. I figured it out for myself, from things you let
slip."

Her voice was hoarse. "What are you going to do?"

"Protect you, of course. Did you doubt it?"

She pulled out of his arms and sat back on her heels.
"You went to see my father without consulting me?"

"Leathe went with me."

"Leathe!" She felt as if someone had punched her in
the stomach. "My God, he, at least, should have known
better."

He grabbed her when she made to slide off the bed.
"You can't keep running from your father for the rest of
your life!"

"Oh, can't I? Just watch me!"

He had to shake her to get her attention. "What
about Quentin? Are you going to abandon him? He's
not going with you, Deborah. He stays with me."

At mention of Quentin, all the color drained out of
her face. Her eyes were swimming. "Oh Gray, what
have you done? It's not just me now. Don't you understand? If you've made an enemy of my father, he'll find a
way to punish you too."

"There is no need for so much anguish. Your father
is only one man. Everything is going to be fine."

His reasonableness in the face of her terror infuriated
her. "Tell me what you have done!"

He went on in the same reasonable tone. "What I am
going to do is persuade your father to have the charges
against you dropped. In a week, two at the most, things
should be settled. There will be no case against you, and
you will no longer need to conceal your identity. You'll
be free, Deborah, free."

He was smiling the way he sometimes smiled at
Quentin. But she wasn't Quentin. She knew Gray wasn't
a demigod. He was human, and mortal, and could be
hurt. And her father was a monster.

Torn between fear and fury, she cried out, "I never wanted to bring you into this. Leathe promised he would do nothing without my consent. You don't know my father. You don't know how vicious he can be, how tenacious, how vindictive. Don't you understand anything? By meddling in this, you've put your own life in danger."

He kissed her gently on the lips. "I am more careful than that. Your father will do exactly as I tell him because he knows, or he soon will, that if he fails me, he will lose what he loves best in the world."

"My father doesn't love anything."

"Now there, my pet, you are wrong. He is a man possessed. He loves his collections, Deb, and will do anything to preserve them."

"Meaning . . . ?"

His fingers moved gently, tracing her profile. "Every day that he delays, he is going to lose part of his treasure. I've already taken steps to set things in motion. Don't worry, Deb. I know what I am doing."

"You've set things in motion? What does that mean?"

"I am not without friends. Powerful friends. They are acting on my behalf. Your father will soon know that if he doesn't take steps to clear your name, he will lose his precious collections."

She wished she could believe him, but she knew her father better than that. "And if your plan doesn't work? What then?"

He shrugged indifferently. "Then let them press charges against you. We can weather the scandal, but it will never come to trial. No one could blame you for what you did. It was a mistake to run, Deb. There was no real case against you."

She closed her eyes in despair. She didn't know how to convince him that it wasn't that simple. Her father was devious. It was a mistake to underestimate him. He never forgave or forgot.

She shivered and pillowed her head on his chest. Her whole world was in chaos. Her shoulders were not strong enough to carry her burdens. She thought of

Quentin, the murderer, and now her father, and Gray. There was no end to it. She was trapped in a maze of fear and there was no way out.

Once again, he read her mind. "Trust me, Deb. I know what I'm doing. Let go and let me take care of things."

The soothing words did not act on her as he thought they would. One moment she was nestled trustingly against him, and the next she was on her knees, her eyes spitting fire.

"Listen to yourself!" she stormed at him. "You sound just like my father! He wanted me to let him take care of things too! If I had listened to him, I would have married Albert. This was my business. You had no right to interfere."

"Damn you!" He caught her wrists and yanked her so that she was sprawled over him. His face was only inches from hers. "How can you compare me to that miserable snake? I want only what's best for you."

"What's best for me? I'm the one who knows what's best for me! I knew it would be like this. I was a fool to trust you, a fool to come here. From now on, I just want to be left alone."

Gray's eyes were dark with answering fire. "In some things, Deb, you are nothing but a pitiful, sniveling coward."

Before she could strike him, he rolled with her on the bed, and his mouth came down violently on hers. He dispensed with her nightdress, uncaring of her sharp intake of breath or the tiny pearl buttons that spilled over the bedclothes and onto the floor. She didn't try to resist him. She wasn't afraid. She couldn't think when he touched her like this, kissed her like this. She could only feel. She was alive, gloriously alive, and if only for a short while there would be a respite from all her cares and troubles. She clung to him, inciting him to do more.

He knew he was driven, but he couldn't seem to stop himself. There would be other nights when he would take her with all the tenderness and finesse of which he was capable. But not tonight. Tonight he would be satisfied with nothing less than her total surrender. He had been too patient with her, too intent on overcoming her initial distrust of him. He was done with gentling her. After tonight, she would never deny him again.

She went hurtling into an explosive, mindless climax with a velocity that stunned her. She reached for him, trying to draw him over her. He held her at bay till she was shuddering in the aftermath of spent passion.

"Does that feel as if you want to be alone?" he demanded, his voice almost savage. "You love me as much as I love you. Tell me, damn you!"

The lie trembled on her tongue, then died into silence. There was something in his expression she couldn't bear to see. "Gray—"

"Tell me, dammit!"

She choked back a teary sob. "I love you," she cried out, and wondered if she was wise to put so much power into a man's hands.

"Don't look so appalled," he whispered, and his eyes were smiling. "It isn't the end of the world. I love you too. That makes us equal."

"I wish I could believe that."

"Believe it."

When he entered her, there was a change in him. He lavished her with feather-light kisses and soft words of praise. He told her in husky, erotic whispers that he loved the way she responded to him, loved the way she abandoned herself to him in this ultimate act of trust between a man and a woman.

His words became more erotic, and she felt herself yield to that dark and sensual part of him that was so blatantly male. As she yielded, raining wild kisses over his face and shoulders, she could feel his control slipping away.

With a soft cry, she arched, hovering on a crest of unbearable pleasure. He gave her what she needed. Locking her to him in an inseparable embrace, he rode her to a furious, shattering climax that made them both cry out. Beneath him, Deborah shuddered for a long time after, then her whole body gradually went lax.

Later, when he pulled from her and rolled to his side, she gave a small, replete sigh and promptly fell asleep.

He smiled, seeing in this a pattern that had already become established between them. He lowered his mouth to her bruised lips, kissing them softly. Her eyes opened slowly and she gazed up at him.

"I expect you to do the honorable thing," he said.

"What?"

"Marriage, Deb. It's the only possible way for us."

"Kendal, do you never give up?"

"Never."

She managed a smile, but already she was slipping into sleep. "I'll think about it," she murmured, and edged closer till she was half sprawled over him.

One of them had to stay awake if only to make sure that she got back to her own room before the maid arrived with her morning chocolate. Smiling tolerantly, he propped himself against the pillows and decided he was feeling very pleased with himself. He was sure now, very sure, that he had finally overcome the mistrust and suspicion that had dogged them since he had abducted her. She had finally admitted she loved him. That was a decisive victory. She might not know it yet, but he had already won the war.

He thought about her father for a long time, wondering if it wouldn't be wiser simply to call him out. It would give him a great deal of satisfaction to put a bullet in his brain. Whether Belvidere set things straight with the magistrates wasn't crucial. He had meant what he'd told Deborah. It would never come to trial. But there would be a scandal and the suspicion of murder would always dog her heels. For Deborah's sake, he would let the snake live.

Dismissing Belvidere from his mind, he turned his attention to the night Gil was murdered, and he retraced all that he had learned from Deborah when they had reenacted the murder in the library. He dwelled on that scene for a long time, carefully sifting through everything. And then he had it! The elusive thought that had teased him came sharply into focus, and with it, a face.

CHAPTER 20

During the night, Quentin took a turn for the worse. Though his breathing was easier, he suffered from severe headaches, and the usual remedies had no effect. Deborah slept late and knew nothing of this till she came downstairs as the family was rising from the breakfast table.

The countess looked harried. "Dr. Tait is with him now," she said. "Gray would not let us awake you. He said you were completely worn out. Don't be alarmed, my dear. Gray has things well in hand."

Deborah did not wait for breakfast, but hurried up the stairs to Quentin's room. She had passed it on the way down, when the door was closed and she had assumed Quentin was asleep. Gray and the doctor were just coming out of the room when she stepped into the corridor, but beyond a few pleasantries, Dr. Tait had nothing to say to her. He and Gray turned aside and conferred in hushed tones.

She found Quentin sitting up in bed and drinking from a glass the tutor held to his lips. "A headache powder," Mr. Jervis explained, "to ease the pain."

"My head hurts, Deb," said Quentin.

He moaned when he lay down, but he was asleep before Deborah had finished fussing with the pillows and covers. His breathing was quite normal and that surprised her.

When Gray returned, he took her by the elbow and led her into the corridor. The look on his face alarmed her.

"What is it, Gray? What did Dr. Tait tell you?"

"He does not know how to diagnose Quentin's illness."

"Illness?" she said nervously.

"Headaches. I should have said headaches. Tait thinks they may be the result of the shock he got yesterday."

"Oh God! What are we going to do?"

"Nothing, for the moment. They may pass. And if they don't, Tait gave me the name of a man in town who may be able to help us."

"What man?"

"He's not a doctor exactly, though he goes by that title. He has a place, a hospice in Pall Mall, quite close to Bell's Coffee Shop. Dr. Marchand. Have you heard of him?"

"No. His name sounds French."

"He's a Swiss, and a disciple of Dr. Mesmer." To her blank look he added, "The famous Dr. Mesmer, you know, the miracle worker who has cured innumerable patients of disturbances of the psyche."

She touched a hand to his sleeve. "Oh Gray, I don't like the sound of this."

"Deb, there's nothing to worry about, I promise you. Marchand is a good man. Quentin will be in the best of hands. Don't look so anxious. It might be nothing at all."

His words reassured her, and she nodded.

With a quick look around to make sure they were unobserved, he took her in his arms and kissed her.

"What was that for?" she said when he released her lips.

"What was that for?" he chided, shaking his head. "Honestly, I don't think there is an ounce of romance in a woman's soul. That was because I love you. That was because you love me. That was because in two weeks' time we can blazen to the world that Lord Kendal has captured the hand, if not the considerable fortune, of Lady Deborah Montague. I shall be the envy of every fortune hunter in the land."

"What? I don't remember saying I would marry you."

"No, but you said you'd think about it, and if you have a grain of intelligence in that pretty head of yours, you'll see it's the right thing to do."

"Since when did you become so straitlaced?"

"Since I fell in love with you. My mother told me how it would be. Alas, I was too young to understand."

She wasn't going to win this argument, so she changed direction. "What about your family?" she asked. "What are they going to think when they learn I have deceived them?"

"Don't be such a worrier." He smiled down at her. "Deb, that will be the least of what they think. They are going to start counting the months off on their fingers before our first child is born, knowing that we should have been married months ago."

Her cheeks bloomed and he nodded. "Maybe we should be counting them too. Now, would you mind? I intend to catch up on the sleep I lost last night. There will be plenty of time later to discuss Dr. Marchand and whether or not we should consult him about Quentin."

She spent what was left of the morning in Quentin's room and was heartened that he slept peacefully. When Gray wakened, he joined her, and they shared a light repast together, but there was not the opportunity to talk further of Dr. Marchand. Leathe arrived at the house, asking for Deborah, and she went down to see him.

As soon as they were alone, he said, "I told you there would a way out of this maze, Deborah, and by Jove we found it."

There was no answering smile on Deborah's face. "What is it?" he asked.

"*What is it?* You can ask me that when you know what Father is like? I was hoping you would talk some sense into Gray. He seems to think that he has dealt with Father."

"And so he has, or so he will. Father has finally met his match, Deborah. I'm convinced of it."

"And if he hasn't?"

"I will kill Father before I'd let him harm a hair of your head. I know Gray feels the same."

She wanted to stamp her foot in sheer frustration. She wasn't afraid for herself. She was afraid for Leathe and Gray. Her father would find a way to punish them, or at the very least, he would try. There was no persuading Leathe, and finally she gave up trying.

It turned out that she was not the only reason Leathe had come calling. He and Meg had arranged to go for a walk, but only if they could find someone to chaperon them.

"Oh no, Leathe," said Deborah. "You and Meg? Gray would never permit it."

Leathe laughed. "Not only does he permit it, but he is the one who suggested it. No. We are not exactly the best of friends, but we are no longer at each other's throats. Ask him if you don't believe me."

She was still trying to digest this when Gray and Meg entered the room together. Far from opposing the outing, Gray insisted that the change of air would do Meg and Deb a world of good.

"And while you are out," he said, "why don't you have a look around Sommerfield? I don't believe you have seen the house yet, have you, Deb?"

A faint blush crept into her cheeks. The only part of Sommerfield she knew well was Gray's bedchamber, and the laughter in his eyes told her that he knew what she was thinking. "No," she said, and to cover her confusion, she added as an afterthought, "Perhaps Gussie would like to come with us?"

They chatted amicably while a footman went in search of her ladyship. Gray's manner toward Leathe was natural; Leathe's verged on the respectful; and Meg's reserve had completely melted. Deb was humming under her breath when she went to fetch her coat.

"You're leaving *today?*" Meg's voice was low, but there was no mistaking her petulance. "But why so soon?"

Leathe directed a look at Deborah and Gussie, but they were so far ahead on the bridle path that there was no chance they could overhear his conversation with Meg. "I have some urgent matters to discuss with my solicitor. It's only for a week or two. You'll be back in town before I go north to look over my business enterprises, won't you?"

"A week or two?" She spoke as though it were a hundred years. "Why don't I persuade Mama to return to town now, then we could be together for longer?"

"No," said Leathe. "We couldn't see each other anyway. I'll be too busy. And so will you. You told me you had fittings with your dressmaker, and shopping, and whatever females do to get ready for Christmas."

"For the new season," corrected Meg. "We shall be back here for Christmas, at Sommerfield. Will you come too?"

"No. Not unless your brother invites me."

"I meant with the Derwents. You could stay with Matthew."

"No. He's coming to town with me."

There was a pent-up silence, then Meg burst out, "You've changed your mind about me, haven't you, Stephen?"

His look of astonishment calmed her fears. "Don't be a goose," he said. "The only thing that has changed is that your brother has given me permission to court you. That's what it amounts to, Meg. I thought you'd be pleased. There's no need for us to meet in secret, or to elope."

"But Stephen, from what you told me, it could be months, even longer, before Gray gives his permission for us to marry."

"That will give me time to set my affairs in order, look around for a suitable house for us and so on. I have coal mines and cotton mills I've never set foot in, workers who have never set eyes on me, or I on them. It's time I took control of my business enterprises. You were the one who wanted me to become respectable. You were the one who didn't want to elope. So why all the objections?"

She laid a hand on his sleeve, halting him, and he turned to face her. "Not too respectable," she said, "or I won't know you."

He grinned down at her. "Say that to me when we look in on Sommerfield on the way home."

Her face brightened. "There's a conservatory we could slip away to—"

"No!"

"It's Deborah, isn't it? She's the one you love?"

He grabbed her when she would have turned away from him, and he made no attempt to shade what smoldered in his eyes. When he saw that she had read him correctly, he dropped his lashes and his expression became less intense.

"Meg, I may steal the odd kiss, but that is as much as I dare. Once I start touching you, I can't stop myself, and you are no help at all."

"But I like it when you touch me. I don't want you to stop."

"Try to understand. Your brother has put me on my honor—not in so many words, but by virtue of the fact that he has given me his trust. Six months. That's all I am prepared to give him. That's not too much to ask of us, is it? He's giving me a chance to prove myself and I don't intend to disappoint him."

She looked up at him with an expression of arrested surprise. "Gray's respect means that much to you?"

He shrugged. "Not as much as your respect. You loved me when I was at my worst, but you loved what was best in me. How did we get onto this? Can we talk of something else?"

She felt a tightness in her throat, remembering what he had told her of his early years, but she managed to speak without betraying the pity she knew he would scorn. "And if Gray still doesn't give us permission to marry?"

"Then he's not the diplomat I thought he was. He knows I won't hold off for longer than that." He flicked a glance at Deborah and Gussie, then swiftly kissed her. "Simpleton," he said. "Are you blind? Can't you see it's your own brother who loves Deborah, and she him?"

"That's what everybody tells me, but you can't deny that she is special to you, Stephen."

They started walking again, and Leathe kicked a stone with the toe of his boot, sending it rolling toward the river. "She is special to me, but not in the way you think. In two weeks, I shall explain everything. And in six months, I swear I shall marry you, with or without your brother's consent. Will you wait for me for six months, Meg?"

Her fears had totally evaporated, and she smiled up at him. "If I had to, I would wait for you till the end of the world."

It was he who felt the tightness in his throat now. "Let's catch up on the others," he said gruffly, "or I won't be responsible for my actions."

❧

Deborah returned to Channings with a glow on her cheeks and a spring in her step. They had been gone for some time, but that was because they had lingered so long at Gray's house. It was a remarkably preserved mansion of Tudor origin, with not a Greek column in sight, no marble, and no gilt worth mentioning. Warm oak paneling was everywhere, and small mullioned windows and a splendid three-story oriel window in the Great Hall. Her father would have scorned to live in such an old-fashioned house with its small rooms and closets. The Graysons were proud of it. Every room seemed to have a story attached to it, going back to the days of the Wars of the Roses. There were collections there too, but these were of weapons and suits of armor and parchments or prayer books—historical relics of former generations of Graysons. And there was Old

Warwick, the stuffed war horse that held pride of place in the Great Hall. She didn't know why, but that shabby, battle-scarred destrier had caught her fancy.

She was eager to tell Gray how much she had loved his house, but just as she was taking off her coat, the countess entered her chamber. After a long disjointed preamble about Gray's numerous failings, the countess explained that Gray had suddenly decided to take Quentin to London to consult with Dr. Marchand. Jervis, the tutor, had gone with them.

"And what mystifies me," said the countess, "is that Quentin seemed quite recovered from his ordeal. He was laughing and joking as though it were a great adventure."

There was a letter from Gray, and Deborah read it in stunned silence. Quentin, Gray informed her, had awakened to think he was back in France. He had managed to calm him, but had decided it was no longer possible to accede to Deborah's wishes. It was in Quentin's best interests to recover his memory, and he hoped that Dr. Marchand would accomplish this.

There was more, about how she was not to worry, and how he would keep her informed. And it was only for a short time. He would see her in a week or so in Berkeley Square, with his mother and the others, when they returned to town. In the meantime, on no account was she to take chances with her own safety. This last was underlined. There was still a murderer at large, and they must never forget it.

"Why wouldn't he wait and take me with him?" Deborah asked faintly.

"But how could he, my dear?" said the countess. "Without me to chaperon you, you and Gray could not reside in the same house. Don't look so crestfallen. It's only for a week. Then we shall all return to Berkeley Square together."

It was a reasonable answer, but somehow, it did not satisfy Deborah.

Gray adjusted the wrap around Quentin's knees, then settled back against the banquette. "Warm enough?" he asked.

"Yes, thank you, Uncle Gray."

"You should try to get some sleep."

"I slept all morning," protested Quentin.

"Oh? I thought that was just a sham, you know, to throw Deborah off the scent."

"That's how it started out, but I did fall asleep, without meaning to." He didn't sound too pleased about it.

"Headache all better?"

"It was only a little headache. Do you think Deborah knows that I was pretending? She's very clever, you know."

"In this case, I think she believed you. You played your part so well, you had *me* believing you." Observing the uncertain look on Quentin's face, he said in a more serious vein, "You mustn't feel bad about deceiving Deborah. We are only exaggerating the truth a little."

"Deborah says that it's all right to tell lies, but only as a last . . ." He floundered.

"Resort?" offered Gray.

"Yes. That's the word."

"Now that surprises me. When did she say this?"

"You know, when we were coming home to England, Deborah told lies all the time, and not just little ones. Some of them were great whoppers, Uncle Gray."

Gray was grinning hugely. "That makes me feel much better about this whole escapade," he said.

"Is that a last resort?"

Gray's expression sobered. "That's exactly what it is, Quentin. Listen to what I say very carefully. I hate lies and deceit, and you must grow up hating them too. There is only one reason ever to use them, and that is in a matter of life and death. I wish I could have told Deborah everything, but if I had, she would only spoil all our plans, and we don't want that, do we?"

Quentin thought about this for a minute. "Is it a good plan, Uncle Gray?"

"That remains to be seen. Now, would you mind if I

caught forty winks? Unlike you, I have been up half the night setting things up."

❧

Gray's plan got under way as the first rumors began to circulate in London. Matthew Derwent, who had returned to town with Leathe, created some minor interest when he related details of the shooting mishap to members of his club. They were in the card room at White's, enjoying a quiet game of whist.

"Quentin Barrington?" murmured Lord Denning, dragging his thoughts from the perpetual problem of finding a mother for his two motherless daughters. He kept his face impassive as Leathe took the last trick with his trump. He was thinking that either Leathe's manners had improved since he had last met him, or he had misjudged the fellow. He wasn't such a bad-tempered young whelp. In the right company, he could be positively likable.

It was his turn to deal. Picking up the cards, he continued. "Miss Weyman told me that he was just getting over the tragedy of his father's death. Poor boy. Is he quite deranged, then?"

"God, I hope not," cried out young Derwent, raising a few brows. "If he is, I shall blame myself."

Leathe had rehearsed in his mind what Gray had told him to say, and while he scanned the cards in his hand, he threw out casually, "Don't be absurd, Matthew. The boy had suffered a memory lapse and the sound of the guns going off gave him such a shock that he began to remember things. That's all it was."

"A memory lapse?" asked one of the gentlemen interestedly.

"Yes," said Leathe. "His father's murder had a strange effect on him. He could remember nothing before or immediately after the event. It's true that his mind is disturbed, but Lord Kendal is confident that there is some doctor in London who can help the boy. They are here now."

"But how can you know all this?" asked Lord Denning.

"Because Jervis, the boy's tutor, told me when I invited Lady Margaret to go walking with me." He frowned. "I don't think Kendal wants it known, however."

It was the remark about Lady Margaret that was taken up with relish.

"You and Kendal's sister?" demanded Lucas Spry incredulously. "Kendal would never allow it."

Leathe laughed. "Lord Kendal is not the ogre you think he is," he said.

The outcry that these words produced completely eclipsed the story about Quentin, but only temporarily.

Lord Denning mentioned it the following afternoon to Sophie Barrington when they were taking a turn in the park in his carriage. She was the boy's stepmother and he assumed she knew all about it, so he began by asking how the boy fared, and stirred up a hornet's nest.

The day before, a note had arrived from Gray canceling her visit to Channings, and her mind was rife with suspicion. She'd heard from Helena Perrin about Gray and Deborah Weyman, and it did not sit well with her. In fact, it infuriated her.

"Gray said nothing in his note to me about Quentin being unwell," she said.

"Oh dear," said Lord Denning, belatedly remembering that Leathe had said something about Kendal not wanting it generally known. "Perhaps I should not have mentioned it. Perhaps there's nothing in it."

She banged her reticule on the cushions, and the maid who was chaperoning her jumped. Lord Denning was taken aback. Having failed to make progress with Miss Weyman, he had cast his eye around, and it had finally settled on Lady Barrington. The girl was young, sweet-tempered, and malleable, or so he'd thought.

"And Gray did not even have the decency to come and tell me in person!"

She was practically foaming at the mouth, and Denning, thinking of his two darling, motherless girls in the nursery, on whom he doted, began to tick off in his mind all the advantages of the single life.

She was so angry, she hardly knew what she was saying. "Do you know what I think? I think she put Quentin up to it. This is a ploy to keep us apart. She doesn't want me there because she knows he is partial to me. Oh, he's tried to hide it, but a woman knows these things."

Truly bewildered, Lord Denning asked cautiously, "Who doesn't want you there?"

"Miss Weyman, of course."

"But why should she try to keep you and Quentin apart?"

"Not Quentin, you fool! Lord Kendal."

As soon as the words were out of her mouth, she realized she had committed an indiscretion. Lord Denning stiffened up like a poker, and though Sophie quickly reverted to her usual flirtatious self, he barely spoke two words to her before he set her down at her house in Manchester Square.

When she ventured out that same afternoon with the same maid in tow, Sophie had herself well in hand. On arriving at Gray's house in Berkeley Square, she presented her card to the footman and asked sweetly if Lord Kendal might spare her a moment of his time. When she entered the library, however, leaving her maid to sit outside the door, it was Philip Standish who came forward to meet her.

She had met Philip in Paris, at various diplomatic functions, and though she found him a bit of a dry stick, on this occasion, she used all her powers to charm him. Her charm slipped a little when he told her that, as far as he knew, Gray was still at Channings.

"But how can that be?" she asked. "The note I received from him only yesterday was marked 'London.' And Lord Denning told me, not an hour ago, that he and Quentin had come up to town."

"How odd." He removed his wire-rimmed spectacles and began to polish them with his handkerchief. "He hasn't been here, or I would have known it."

"Could he be putting up at one of his clubs?"

"With the boy? I hardly think so. Is this urgent, Lady Barrington? Do you wish me to find him for you?"

Sophie concealed her disappointment behind a bland smile. "No, not urgent," she said. "It's just that it threw me into confusion when Lord Denning told me about Quentin. I am the boy's stepmother, after all, and it seems to me that I should be kept informed about what has happened to him."

Her look was so appealing that for a moment, Mr. Standish lost the thread of what she was saying. Coming to himself, he stammered, then said, "What has happened to Quentin?"

She related as much as Lord Denning had told her, and ended by saying, "I would not have known if Lord Denning had not told me. That does not seem right to me. And now, not even to know where Lord Kendal has taken him! Perhaps Miss Weyman can tell me. Do you know where I can find her?"

"I had supposed that she was at Channings also."

She threw him another of her particularly appealing looks. "If only I weren't alone in the world, if only I had someone to act for me, I would soon satisfy myself that Quentin has suffered no grievous harm."

It was her second appealing look that put Mr. Standish wise to her little ways. He remembered how in Paris she had made a spectacle of herself by pursuing Lord Kendal and embarrassing her husband into the bargain. He did not think she was concerned so much with Quentin's welfare as with Deborah Weyman as competition for his lordship's affections.

Nevertheless, he was puzzled. It was not like Lord Kendal to keep his whereabouts a secret from his secretary. Something very strange was going on.

He pushed back his chair, indicating that their tête-à-tête was at an end, a useful trick he had picked up by watching his employer. Lady Barrington rose with him.

"Why don't you leave this with me?" he said. "I'm sure there is a simple explanation and the mystery will be resolved in a matter of days."

❧

Mr. Standish was wrong. The mystery was not resolved in a matter of days. No one knew how it happened, but the rumors spread like wildfire, and each rumor became more fantastic than the last.

"As I heard it," said Eric Perrin to his wife, "our people are no longer satisfied that Barrington was murdered by a thief who broke into his house."

They were standing at the rail of the gallery of Carleton House, the Prince of Wales's private palace in Pall Mall. Below them, in the great octagonal entrance hall, a throng of London's eminent citizens were moving slowly in line toward the double staircase. Helena was enjoying the spectacle. It was not often that ladies were invited to functions at Carleton House. The prince was estranged from his wife and it made things awkward for him when he wished to entertain.

She raised her glass of champagne to her lips and took a small swallow. "How strange," she said.

Any other woman would have been dying to hear what he had to say. Eric Perrin looked at his wife and wondered what it would take to crack that controlled, unshakable composure of hers. In bed, she was a passionate woman, but even then, she veiled her feelings. He never knew what she was thinking.

He took a healthy swallow from his glass and said carelessly, "It seems that the boy was there when his father was murdered. It's only now that he is beginning to remember things, and then only in snatches."

He had the satisfaction of seeing that he had cracked her composure. "He was there? Oh, how *horrible* for that poor boy! And he is beginning to remember things?"

"So it would seem, but it's coming back to him only in snatches."

"What does that mean?"

"It means he remembers that the murderer was English and he was left-handed."

Her hand jerked, and several droplets of wine spilled

to the floor. He smiled and nodded. "Yes, I know," he said. "I'm English and I'm left-handed."

There was a huskiness in her voice when she spoke. "Eric, where were you the night Lord Barrington was murdered?"

He did not mince words. "With a woman," he said. He was watching her closely, but there was nothing in her expression to gauge her reaction to his bald statement. Tipping his glass, he drank it to the dregs. "I met her in the precincts of the Palais Royale. She was French, of course. I don't even know her name. So you see, I have no alibi."

A moment passed as she tried to interpret the venom she had detected in his words. Unsure of what to make of it, she said, "Do you think you will need an alibi?"

"You know there is no love lost between Kendal and me. What do you think?"

"But what possible motive could you have for murdering Lord Barrington?"

"Men like Kendal invent motives to suit their ends."

She felt her hand begin to tremble and turned away so that he would not see it. "Has Gray said anything to you?"

"No. Kendal has not said anything to me. No one has seen anything of him for more than a week."

"What do you make of it?"

"I suppose he fears, now that Quentin's memory is returning, that the murderer will try to get to the boy, and he's taking no chances. No one knows where he can be found, not even our own people at the Foreign Office. The rumor is Kendal is waiting for the arrival of some eminent doctor from the Continent who is an expert on disturbances of the mind. This doctor may be able to help the boy regain his memory."

"There's one person who will know where to find Gray," she said."

"Who?"

"Deborah Weyman." She nodded in answer to the question in his eyes. "She would never let Quentin go into hiding without knowing where he was. Besides, I'm more than half convinced Gray means to marry the girl. If he has confided in anyone, it will be in Miss Weyman." When the silence lengthened, she said, "What is it, Eric?"

"Nothing." He turned away, and saluted someone in the hall below. "There's David Banks and his sister," he said.

She looked over the railing. "I remember him from Paris. He works with you at the Foreign Office, doesn't he?"

"He does, and no, I do not know whether Banks is right- or left-handed."

In the Great Hall, David Banks and his sister were also discussing the rumors that were rampant. Beside them was Lord Lawford, dressed to the hilt in white satin breeches, fancy claret coat, and shoes with silver buckles on them. He kept adjusting his neck cloth, as though it were choking him.

Banks was hiding a smile. He knew how much Lawford detested these formal affairs, but when the Prince of Wales did the inviting, there was no refusing without incurring His Royal Highness's undying enmity.

"Dr. Mesmer?" said Rosamund Banks. "I've never heard of him."

Her brother had. "But surely, sir, he is a charlatan. He's been thrown out of half the countries in Europe for his heretical practices."

"So was Galileo," replied Lawford, bending the truth to make his point, "and his theories have been proven correct."

"What practices?" asked Rosamund.

Banks answered her. "He puts people into a trance, don't ask me how it's done, and tries to cure them of their demons."

"He has a theory about animal magnetism," added Lawford.

Rosamund wrinkled her nose. "I don't see how that can help Quentin regain his memory. In fact, I think it sounds rather frightening."

Lawford said, "It is drastic, but I suppose Kendal

sees no other way. Marchand, the first quack he consulted, could only take the boy so far, and advised Kendal to invite this Dr. Mesmer to London to treat the boy."

"You're very well informed," observed Banks, quizzing his lordship.

Lawford smiled and said with a touch of condescension, "At the War Office, my dear boy, we make it our business to chase down rumors. It's a habit that has carried over into my private life. You mustn't take what I say too seriously, though. I'm only repeating the rumor as it was related to me. Whether it's true, I cannot say."

Hours later, in the comfort of his own house, Lawford reflected on the evening just past. He sat before a blazing fire, in his nightshirt and dressing robe, his feet immersed in a basin of hot water, and his dogs reclining comfortably in the crook of each arm.

"It's surprising how many left-handed people there are in this world," he told his dogs.

Jezebel licked his face. Salome growled encouragingly.

"I counted fifty at Carleton House before I gave up. Do you know what I think, girls?" He chuckled. "I think there are a lot of people at the Foreign Office who are going to become ambidextrous overnight. Well, I would too. Wouldn't you?"

Both dogs barked.

"Remind me when this is over," he said, "that Kendal owes me a big favor. Starting rumors is one thing. Having them circulate with no one knowing who is fanning the flames is not as easy as one would think. And as for the plagues that have descended on poor Lord Belvidere—the slimy bastard—I could go to prison for a hundred years. Oh yes. At the very least, Kendal will be buying me dinner for a long time to come."

Two long tails thumped ferociously on the arms of the chair.

"I think I shall wait a day or two before disclosing the date of Dr. Mesmer's supposed arrival. I'd best check that out with Kendal to make sure everything else is going as planned. What's that you say? Oh, you may well ask who the murderer is. Frankly, I don't know. However . . ." The fingers that were scratching behind the dogs' ears stilled. "I think Kendal knows, or he has a very good idea."

CHAPTER 21

The first Deborah heard of the rumors that had taken London by storm was when she returned to Berkeley Square with Meg and the countess. They came back early, in response to a letter from Gray's secretary, asking if they could give Mr. Standish his lordship's direction. It was a great mystery, he said, but no one seemed to know what had become of Lord Kendal and his ward.

Though Hart had escorted the ladies, he was not planning to stay. Gussie and Jason were still in the country and he was eager to get back to them. He was sure the mystery of Gray's whereabouts would soon be solved. His plans changed, moments after entering the house, when it became clear to him that Mr. Standish was referring to more than Gray's prolonged absence.

"Are you saying that Lord Kendal never arrived in London?" asked Hart incredulously. "You must be mistaken. He wrote to us about Quentin, leastways, he wrote to Miss Weyman."

"That's true," said Deborah. "I have the letter somewhere. I'm sure it came from London."

"That may be so," said Mr. Standish. "All I am saying is that his lordship did not come here, to Kendal House. And no one knows where he can be found. I'm thinking of calling in the magistrates. This is not like Lord Kendal at all."

They were milling around in the hall as footmen maneuvered boxes and portmanteaux through the doors. At Hart's suggestion, they moved to the library.

When they were seated, Hart asked Mr. Standish to tell them everything he knew. He did this very concisely, though he was thrown off stride a time or two by their many questions.

At the end of his account, the countess exclaimed, "I knew that Quentin's mind was affected by his father's death, but I never knew he was *there* when Lord Barrington was murdered. Deborah, did you know anything of this?"

The question took Deborah off guard, and she answered while her mind was still reeling from the shock of what Mr. Standish had told them. "Yes, yes. I knew. That was why Gray came up to town. He was going to consult with Dr. Marchand, in hopes that—" Suddenly realizing that she might be saying too much, she changed direction. "That he might be able to do something for Quentin's headaches."

"That's true," said Mr. Standish. "Lord Kendal did consult with Dr. Marchand. He has a hospice in Pall Mall, and I went to see him. All he could or *would* tell me was that he had advised his lordship to consult with a certain Dr. Mesmer."

This disclosure led to more questions about Mesmer and his work. Hart was shaking his head in wonder when he asked Mr. Standish if he knew where they could find Dr. Mesmer.

"No. I tried to find him, but there is no doctor of that name practicing in London. Rumor has it that he is a foreigner, and that Lord Kendal has sent for him to treat the boy."

The countess smiled at Mr. Standish. "I am in your debt, Mr. Standish. My son is very fortunate to have you as his secretary. I am only sorry that you had to face all this unpleasant speculation alone."

Meg leaned forward in her chair. "It must have been

very difficult for you, Philip. You should have summoned us sooner."

Mr. Standish colored up. "It has not been easy," he allowed. "I am only sorry that Lord Kendal did not see fit to take me into his confidence."

Hart said brusquely, "And I am sorry that Gray did not see fit to take *any* of us into his confidence. Unless . . . " He looked at Deborah with raised brows.

She, too, colored up. "No," she said, "I know nothing."

They soon discovered that Mr. Standish had been very conservative in his description of the rumors making the rounds. Over the next day or two, there was a steady stream of visitors to the house, and every morsel of gossip was related at length. Because none of the Graysons or Deborah knew what Gray was up to, they answered all questions vaguely. When some seconded Mr. Standish's impulse to call in the magistrates, Hart made light of it. Because of Gray's work at the Foreign Office, his absence might well be connected to matters of state. More than that he would not say.

In private, they were not so assured. They were as puzzled as everyone else, more so when Hart and Mr. Standish combed London, discreetly, and came up empty-handed. No one had any idea where Gray was.

"I am beginning to suspect," said Hart, "that the rumors are true, and that Gray has hidden Quentin away to keep him safe from the man who murdered his father."

Deborah absorbed everything and began to sift things through in her mind. She was beginning to wonder if Gray was setting Quentin up as bait to catch the murderer. The thought was chilling. In her mind's eye, she stacked each rumor like a building block. It was now known that Quentin had witnessed his father's murder and that the horror of it had affected his memory. It was also known that the shock of the shooting mishap at Channings had worked in the opposite direction. That Dr. Marchand and Dr. Mesmer were celebrated students of the science of the psyche was no secret either. Add to that the description of the murderer as English and left-handed, and it seemed self-evident that Quentin was recovering his memory. Only she knew that she was the one who had told Gray all these things when they had reenacted the murder in the library at Channings.

There was one thing, however, that exonerated Gray from the terrible suspicion that hovered in her mind. If he were setting Quentin up as bait, he would want the murderer to know where he could be found, or there was no point to it. His extreme caution in keeping his whereabouts a secret must mean that he was taking no chances with Quentin's safety.

The rumors, however, continued to disturb her. How could they have started if Gray were not behind them? How could they be so accurate? Hart was able to reassure her on this point. As near as he could make out, he said, Matthew Derwent had stirred things up inadvertently when he had told his cronies about Quentin's reaction to the guns going off. It seemed, also, that Dr. Marchand was not as discreet as he might have been. When Sophie Barrington had called on him, demanding to know what had become of her stepson, the doctor had let slip more than he had meant to. After this, the rumors had spread like wildfire.

No, she refused to believe Gray would use Quentin as bait. She trusted him now, trusted that he would never take such chances with Quentin's life. Deborah thought, hoped, that Gray would get a message to her, if only to relieve her worst fears about Quentin. She saw that Quentin would never be safe now unless the memory of that night came back to him, and he could identify his father's murderer. Gray must be pinning his hopes on Dr. Mesmer. The murderer must know this and must be waiting his chance to get to Quentin before Dr. Mesmer treated him. The more Deborah thought of it, the more convinced she became that Gray had done the right thing, and she told Hart to stop searching for him. If and when Gray thought it was safe, he would get a message to them.

Though she knew it was farfetched, she began to study each person who came to the house as if he might be the murderer. Was he left-handed? Was he in Paris at the crucial time? What motive could he have for murdering Lord Barrington? She knew that Gray thought the murderer and the informer at the Foreign Office were one and the same person, but she was not convinced of it. Lord Barrington could have made enemies that Gray knew nothing about.

Her speculations took a bizarre turn the day Leathe came to the house to invite Meg to go driving in his curricle. Meg and the countess were keeping an appointment at the dressmaker, but Deborah was at home and needed little encouragement to accept her brother's invitation.

"What do you make of the rumors?" he asked at one point.

"You won't believe this," she said, forcing a laugh, "but it's got so that I cannot look at someone without trying to discover whether they favor their right or left hand."

"You will observe," he responded with mock solemnity, "that I am left-handed."

She watched for a moment as he expertly directed his team with a delicate touch of the whip. "I had forgotten that," she said. "Now I remember! Father used to tie your left hand behind your back so that you would favor the right. Evidently, it didn't work."

"If it were not for that, I think I might have been right-handed. I'm almost ambidextrous. But you know me. I would do the opposite of whatever Father wanted." He saw her frown and he laughed. "Oh ho! Does this mean you suspect me, Deb?"

"Hardly. You were not in Paris when Lord Barrington was murdered."

He threw her an odd look. "But I was. I thought you knew. That's where I met Meg. All the Graysons were there."

"All the Graysons? Nick and Hart too?"

"Deborah, half of London was there. Paris had been closed to us for—what was it?—ten years. When peace was declared, Paris came into fashion. Even Father was there with our stepmother and half sister. Oh, not that we ever acknowledged each other. We were very civilized. When we caught sight of each other, we simply looked away, affecting an interest in something else."

For the rest of the drive, they spoke of other things, and Deborah managed to conceal how shaken she was by what Leathe had told her. She tried, to no avail, to suppress the horrible thoughts that crowded into her mind. What if she and Gray were on the wrong track? What if *she* had been the target and not Lord Barrington? She did not know how her fortune was to be disposed if anything happened to her. She had never consulted a solicitor, never made a will, never discovered if there were conditions on the moneys that came to her through her mother. For all she knew, on her death, it would all pass to her father. Or to Leathe.

On entering the house, she made straight for her bedchamber. She removed her bonnet and gloves, but did not take the time to remove her coat. In the escritoire, she found notepaper and pen and ink. The last will and testament that she drew up was quite simple. Everything was to go to Gray, and it was left to his discretion to decide how much of her fortune should go to Quentin, as well as others whose names she added as they occurred to her. When the ink was dry, she went in search of the housekeeper and butler and, after swearing them to secrecy, had them witness the deed.

❧

On their fifth day in town, Nick came bursting in upon them during dinner, demanding to know if the rumors were true and how the devil they had got started in the first place.

Deborah looked at him carefully, weighing every word and gesture, every expression, and though she realized that suspicion was poisoning her mind, she no longer trusted anyone.

Hart's answer was testy. "I suppose you're annoyed because you had to leave your friends in Hampshire. Well, you are not the only one whose plans have been ruined."

Nick delayed responding to this when footmen entered with the first course. He didn't wait for them to set a place for him, but fetched his own plate and cutlery from the sideboard and seated himself at the head of the table, where Gray usually sat. When the footmen had withdrawn, he said cheerfully, "I beg your pardon, Hart. I see from your long faces that this has all been a terrible strain on you. I can't think why. If anyone knows how to take care of himself, it's Gray."

"Have the rumors reached as far afield as Hampshire, then?" asked the countess anxiously.

"Oh, yes. I also met Helena Perrin in Piccadilly, and she had a score of questions for me, questions I could not answer. Meg, what's this I hear about you and Viscount Leathe? You are to keep away from him, do you understand?"

Meg bristled, but before she could go on the attack, Hart took charge of the conversation. "Gray knows about Leathe," he said. "No, no, we can argue about it later. What I want to know is what else Lady Helena told you."

Nick told them. For the most part, it was no more than they already knew, except for one item. Lady Helena had given Nick the date of Dr. Mesmer's arrival in London.

"The day after tomorrow?" said Hart. "And where, pray tell, did Lady Helena get her information?" He sounded angry.

Nick did not seem to realize that he had confounded everyone by this careless remark. He was carving the saddle of lamb that had been set at his place. "What? Oh, Helena said that it's common knowledge at the Foreign Office. She had it from her husband, and he should know. She tried to pump me, to see if I knew where Gray was, but, of course, I didn't." He looked up at that moment and caught Deborah's eye. "If anyone knows where Gray is, it will be Deb. Where is he, Deb?"

His question took her by surprise. She stared at him in stupefied silence, then stammered something to the effect that Gray had not confided in her. No one said anything, but when she chanced to glance around the table, she saw the same speculative look on each face.

❧

The countess was hosting one of her informal soirées that evening. Deborah was in her chamber, trying to decide what to wear, unable to concentrate on anything, when she heard a soft tap on her door. Before she could answer it, Nick entered. He put a finger to his lips, as though to silence any outburst she might make. There was no outburst. She was gripped with a curious tension, then relief shivered through her. Everything was going to be all right. Even before he spoke, she knew what he was going to say.

"I'm taking you to Gray," he said. When she said nothing, he cocked his head to one side, studying her intently. "Did you hear me, Deborah? I'm taking you to Gray."

"When?"

"Right now. There's a hackney waiting for us on the corner. No one will miss us for an hour or two. Put on your coat and come with me now."

There were a thousand questions she might have asked him. Not one of them mattered. Soon, she would be with Gray, and he could answer them all.

Her coat was in the wardrobe. Nick helped her into it. "You don't seem surprised," he said.

"But I *am* surprised. From what you said at the dinner table, I was sure you arrived in town today. And when you asked *me* where Gray was staying, what could I think but that you knew nothing?"

"That's what's known as laying a false trail."

They left by the servants' staircase. Nick went first, and when he was satisfied that the coast was clear, he motioned Deborah to follow him. Out on the square, lanterns above doors gave off a feeble light. There were few people coming and going, for it was not yet eight o'clock. In another hour or two, the square would be choked with carriages as well-dressed members of high society set out or arrived on their first party of the evening.

The address Nick gave the cab driver was on a quiet

cul-de-sac just off the Strand. Deborah knew the area well. Her father's house was just around the corner.

There was a short delay as their driver waited for a crested carriage to negotiate the turn into Charles Street, then they were off. It seemed to Deborah that Nick was as nervous as she. He did not say a word till the hackney had turned into Piccadilly.

"One can't be too careful," he said, suddenly aware of her scrutiny. He felt in his coat pocket and brought out a pistol. "Have no fear, Deborah. You'll be safe with me."

Pistols and Deborah did not mix well together. That's all it was, she chided herself. She was not unlike Quentin in this, and for the same reason. Guns could kill. She stared at the pistol in Nick's right hand, watching the play of light from the coach lamp glint off the muzzle, and she began to remember.

Not liking her thoughts, she turned them on Nick. There was nothing to fear here, she told herself. She had watched him carve the joint of mutton at the dinner table, and he really was right-handed. Beyond that, she had always liked and trusted him. When Gray had abducted her, it was Nick who had befriended her. No, Nick had deceived her. He had pretended to be her friend, but all the time, he had been playing a part, deliberately misleading her.

She shivered involuntarily. Once again, suspicion was poisoning her mind. If she went on like this, she would end up by suspecting Gray . . . again.

"How is Quentin?" she asked, trying to distract her thoughts.

"Fine. He's fine."

Even now, Nick's attention was not on her, but on the way they had just come. He was only being careful, of course.

"And Gray? When did you last see him?"

"Just before I came for you."

She could not tell whether he was telling the truth or lying. His answers were so vague.

"Is there someone following us?" *Someone who is left-handed?*

"Don't worry about it. I know what I'm doing."

"Why didn't we take Hart with us?"

"Hart has nothing to do with this."

She knew that his smile was meant to reassure her, but it had the opposite effect. She moistened her lips. "What about Leathe?"

She had his full attention now. "Why do you ask about Leathe?"

Not even a vague answer this time. She, too, could be vague. "No particular reason."

They were just coming to Charing Cross, on the corner of the Strand. On the right was her father's house, and Deborah's eyes were inexorably drawn to it. It was an enormous mansion even by London standards, and could have housed a garrison of soldiers. The front porch was lit up, as prescribed by law, and she could make out the two great marble lions that guarded the entrance. Beyond the house, unseen from the street, the gardens sloped down to the river Thames. It was a magnificent house, but she would always think of it with loathing. Shivering, she turned away.

She gave a start when Nick suddenly rapped on the roof of the cab and ordered the driver to halt. On the pavement, she looked around her, taking her bearings. Across the Strand were the grounds of the old Savoy Palace with the Savoy Chapel. Somerset House was to its left. She looked at Nick. He was glancing back over his shoulder. Making a casual half-turn, she, too, glanced back to see what had caught his interest. A cab had drawn up a good way down the street, and a man was descending from it. He was too far away for Deborah to recognize, but when she looked at Nick and saw the expression on his face, she was sure that he knew who was following them, and he was *pleased*.

Her whole body contracted and her pulse raced as instinct took over. What was she doing here with a man who had once betrayed her, allowing him to lead her to a dark and lonely stretch of road with easy access to the river? No one knew where she was. If she drowned, it would look like an accident. Everyone would think that she had stolen away to be with Gray and Quentin. It's what Nick had made people think at the dinner table. It *was* a false trail, a trail that led away from *him*. No one would suspect him, least of all Gray. No one would know that Nick had an accomplice. No one would guess that *she* and not Lord Barrington had been the murderer's target that night in Paris.

❧

From an upstairs window in a house on the corner of a quiet cul-de-sac, Quentin looked out over the Strand, and he watched avidly as Nick turned to pay off the driver of the hackney. Quentin stood well back, careful that no one from the outside would catch a glimpse of him. He wasn't supposed to be at the window. Uncle Gray had told him that everything in the house must appear normal when they sprang their trap. His door was locked from the inside, and he wasn't to leave his room until Uncle Gray himself told him it was safe. He couldn't leave, even if he wanted to. Mr. Jervis was next door in the dressing room with orders to make sure that he obeyed Uncle Gray's orders. The door to the dressing room was open, but the tutor could not see him looking out the window because he was looking out the window too. Quentin knew this because he had checked. There was another room in the house with a candle lit where he was supposed to be sleeping. He wasn't quite sure how Uncle Gray meant to trap the murderer, but he knew it had something to do with that room.

He emitted a soft gasp as he saw Deborah suddenly pick up her skirts and dart across the road, away from the house, dodging riders and carriages. Uncle Nick didn't see her. He was still paying off the driver. What was she doing? She would spoil everything!

Mr. Jervis suddenly appeared in the adjoining doorway. "Wait here," he barked out, "and lock the door behind me," and he took off at a run.

Quentin hardly noticed. His eyes were glued to what was happening in the street below. For a moment, it looked as though Deb would hail a hackney, but the cab passed her without stopping. She hesitated for a moment, then turning aside, she slipped into the grounds of the Savoy Chapel. Nick had seen her by this time and he was giving chase. Then Quentin saw the other figure. He, too, darted across the road and slipped into the grounds of the Savoy Chapel. Did Deb know someone was following her? Did Uncle Nick?

He didn't think of what he was doing. He flew out the door, along the corridor, and thundered down the stairs to the front of the house. "Uncle Gray! Uncle Gray!"

Mr. Jervis stopped him on the landing. "Get back to your room. Your uncle can't see you right now. This minute, Quentin. I mean it."

"But . . . but it's Deb. She's run off, and—"

"Yes, we know. Go back to your room, Quentin. At once!"

Jervis watched as Quentin turned with obvious reluctance to go up the stairs. Satisfied that the boy had obeyed him, he went to the front doors and locked them, as Lord Kendal had instructed before dashing from the house. By the time he did the same to the back doors, Quentin was already gone.

≈

The voice that came to her from out of the shadows was the one she least expected to hear. *Quentin*. Fearing her mind must be playing tricks on her, she did not respond, except to flatten herself against the nearest wall. She had come out on the walled gardens of Adelphi Terrace, on the south side of the Strand, hoping to take refuge in one of the houses, only to find that every gate was locked and barred.

It was sheer agony to hold her breath, and she covered her mouth with her hand to stifle the harsh sobs that tore from her throat.

"Deb?"

Her mind wasn't playing tricks on her. "Quentin. Over here."

He came out of the dark with such speed that she went stumbling back when he flung himself into her arms. His breath was spent, but he managed to make himself understood. "They think you are hiding in the chapel. I saw you from the window. I knew you were not there."

"They are looking for me in the chapel?"

"Yes, Uncle Nick and another man. I came to warn you."

"Where were you?"

"In Uncle Gray's house."

So Nick had not been lying about the house. That did not mean she could trust him. What should she do? Oh God, what should she do?

From the direction of the chapel, there was a sound that might have been a firecracker going off, or a pistol shot. Her eyes desperately searched the darkness, but there was no clue to how close her pursuers were. "We'll talk later," she said. "We must be very quiet. Do you understand, Quentin? We don't want them to find us."

"Not even Uncle Nick?"

"Especially not Uncle Nick."

Her mind worked like lightning as she weighed her options. She had Quentin to think of now. Already, his breathing was labored. He couldn't go on much longer like this. They had to find refuge, and soon. With the next thought, her mind calmed. Her father's house was empty and close by. She could hide Quentin there and go for help.

She pointed, indicating the river, and Quentin nodded. The turf was hard with frost and Deborah clutched Quentin close to her to prevent him slipping. Every few minutes, she looked back over her shoulder, and though there was enough light from houses along the Strand to give her her bearings, she could see nothing, hear nothing but the desperate sound of their own breathing.

She chanced one more question. "Does Uncle Gray know about Nick and the other man?"

His voice was as whisper-soft as hers. "I think so, but I don't know."

It wasn't far to the house, but they had taken the long way round, coming at it from the river. Deborah was sure their pursuers would expect them to come out on the Strand, where there were hackneys and people to whom she might appeal for help. Once she had Quentin hidden away, that's exactly what she would do.

The walled grounds ended at the river's edge in a stone boathouse that could have housed several families quite comfortably. In its heyday, Strand House had been one of the wonders of London. By present standards, it was too big and monstrously expensive to keep up. As a consequence, it had fallen into a sorry state of neglect. This worked in their favor. They found a gap in one of the crumbling walls and squeezed through into the gardens. The back of the house rose up against the skyline like an armed fortress. It was a forbidding, gloomy sight, and one that Deborah had hoped never to look upon again. She frowned, observing the lights that shone from several of the ground-floor reception rooms. She hoped they had been placed there by caretakers. Either way, it didn't matter. They had to go on.

"Almost there," she said, and froze as she heard someone stumble against the wall.

Her head whipped round to the gap they had just squeezed through. Nick was there, or his accomplice. She could hear him as he clambered over fallen bricks. His breathing was thick and harsh, reminding her of that other time.

"Hurry!" she whispered in Quentin's ear, and with their eyes fixed on the lights shining from the downstairs windows, they made their way quickly toward the house.

CHAPTER 22

The Earl of Belvidere stood in the center of the former picture gallery of Strand House, admiring its noble proportions. It was one hundred and sixty feet long, twenty-six feet wide, and two stories high. Its former owner had once entertained six hundred guests in this very chamber, to celebrate the coronation of George III. Those days were long gone.

The earl was incensed that Strand House was passing into the hands of strangers, but he lacked the funds to keep up two splendid houses to the standard his aesthetic taste demanded. The picture gallery, in particular, was a great loss. Though he had moved everything of value to Belvidere, one could not remove the magnificent gilt stucco ceiling or the murals that were painted on the walls. The four large crystal chandeliers were another matter. When he met with Lord Holford in the morning, he would try to persuade him that the chandeliers were not included in the sale of the house. These little extras must be negotiated as separate items.

He had come to Strand House for two purposes. The first was to make an inventory, before showing the house to Lord Holford, of all the fine pieces of furniture, carpets, and bric-a-brac that, when put together, should fetch a tidy sum. The other reason was to refresh his

memory on the many outstanding features of the house
which should impress a prospective buyer. Strand House
did not lack these, and he was more angry than ever that
he had to let the house go.

It galled him to think he had been reduced to these
straits. If it had not been for that bitch, who was no
daughter of his, it would never have come to this. He
would have had funds in plenty. On his death, his children would have come into their inheritance, if they had
only been the sort of children he had wanted. Instead,
they had turned against him, all except Elizabeth, and
had provoked his undying hatred. As though coal and
cotton could be compared to the things of beauty he had
amassed in his lifetime. The one was dross, the other
was pure gold and should have been treasured by future
generations of Montagues. He should have known that
the spawn of a tradesman's daughter would never appreciate the finer things in life.

He wasn't done with them yet. Lady Deborah and
Lord Leathe had much to learn if they thought they were
a match for him. For the moment, it suited his purposes
to allow them to think they had won. They had found a
powerful protector in Lord Kendal. That would not save
them. He would find a way to bring them all down. He
would not be satisfied till he had repaid with interest all
the indignities he had been made to suffer these last two
weeks.

His thin face went from white to purple as he recalled how it had all started. He'd wakened that first
morning to find his dressing room in a shambles and
every porcelain button on his garments smashed or
cracked. He'd understood the message. *I'd see you dead
before I would part with a single porcelain button* is
what he had told Leathe. He'd been truly amused over
those cracked buttons. If this was the best Kendal could
do, he might as well concede the game. All the same,
he'd doubled his guards and put all his footmen on the
alert.

On the second morning, he'd come downstairs to
find an Egyptian urn lying in tiny fragments on the marble floor. He'd raged, he'd wept, he'd called in the mag-

istrates. And the magistrates had told him that charges were pending against him for receiving stolen property. They'd removed several "questionable" paintings until they had time to investigate reports of similar paintings that had gone missing from Lord Lawford's house.

He'd been fit to be tied, but he hadn't let his anger master his good sense. Kendal wanted Deborah. He could have her, for a while. He'd taken care of the sworn statements and witnesses, but a large sum of money had changed hands before his good "friend," Justice Porter, could be persuaded to destroy the evidence and keep his mouth shut. Two days later, his paintings were back on his walls, and the magistrates were fawning all over him, offering him their abject apologies. The day after that, Leathe's solicitor had arrived with a document disposing of his collections at his death. He'd signed it, but this wasn't the end of it.

In his mind's eye, he envisioned an "accident" with boats or possibly with footpads and highwaymen. And once Kendal and Leathe were out of the way, he would be free to deal with Deborah. She'd be glad to marry someone like Albert by the time he was finished with her.

He was still lost in reverie when he heard the sound of breaking glass. He wasn't alarmed; he was infuriated. He'd set his caretakers to clean the place to create a good impression when he showed the house to Lord Holford in the morning. If they had broken something valuable, he was going to take it out of their wages.

Snatching the candelabra from one of the many mantelpieces, he stormed into the hallway. He was almost sure that the sound had come from across the hall. It took him only a moment or two to go around the circular staircase, traverse the hall, and enter the library. The words to flay them died in his throat when he saw the young woman and boy who turned from the window to face him. His mind immediately jumped to the conclusion that they were thieves. A glance at the French doors confirmed his suspicion. They were open, and broken glass lay scattered on the parquet flooring. He moved quickly to cut off their escape, placing himself between them and the French doors. They, in turn, retreated to the other side of his huge, flat-topped desk that sat in the center of the room. He had them now.

"So," he said, "you thought the house was empty and you could rob it at your leisure. Unfortunately for you, you have been caught in the act."

The girl's mouth worked and her eyes stared.

"Oh yes, my good woman, I see you know what this means. It's transportation for you and the boy, and good riddance is what I say."

"Deborah?" said the boy.

Belvidere's head jerked, and his eyes slowly traveled over her. "Deborah? No, I don't believe it. It can't be! By God, it is you!"

For a moment, he thought it was a trap, and Lord Kendal or Leathe would suddenly materialize, but when he saw the stark terror in her eyes, he knew that the fates had answered his prayers.

Suddenly, he laughed, and the sound of it jumped from wall to wall. "It was foolish to come here, Deborah. Foolish to put yourself in my power. Of course, you would not expect to find me at Strand House. You would think I was at Belvidere. This is fate, Deborah. I have you now, and Kendal will never get you back."

The shock that had rooted Deborah to the spot was beginning to wear off, leaving her sick and trembling, but at least her mind was beginning to work. She tightened her grip on Quentin's hand and took a swift step toward the door. The earl moved like lightning, and caught Quentin by the shoulders, dragging him from Deborah's grasp.

"Father," she cried out. "I'll do anything you say, *anything*, if only you will help us. Someone is after us, a murderer. He'll be here at any moment. You *must* help us, you must."

"Help you?" He didn't believe her, but the words he spoke came straight from his heart. "I'd as soon shake the hand of the man who made away with you."

Her glance jerked over the earl's shoulder. She saw the figure of a man in the shadows, just outside the French doors, and she cried out. When the earl turned to see what had provoked her reaction, she reached for Quentin and gathered him in her arms. Every nerve in her body was poised for flight, but as the figure advanced into the room and became recognizable, she went limp with relief.

Gray's secretary looked so ordinary, so solid and unthreatening, that she would have given in to hysteria, except she knew they were not out of danger yet.

"Philip," said Deborah, and she sobbed, "I can't tell you how glad I am to see you."

The earl took a step forward. "I don't know what game Kendal is playing, but—"

"Don't move," said Standish. "Don't anyone move." From the folds of his coat, he brought up a pistol.

Deborah looked at the pistol in his hand, his right hand, and it emboldened her to say, "Please. You don't understand. Nick is after us, and he has an accomplice."

He seemed to be staring at them as if he were in a trance, and Deborah said urgently, "We must get away from here, all of us, before it's too late."

"I never meant to hurt anyone," said Standish. "I never meant it to go this far."

Quentin's hand was clasped in Deborah's. It trembled, then tightened convulsively. "It's him," he whispered. "He's the man who shot my father."

The gun came up so suddenly that everyone stood stock-still.

"I thought I was safe," said Standish. His eyes were on Deborah. "I knew I had nothing to fear from you. We met at the boy's picnic but you did not raise the alarm after I killed Lord Barrington. Why?"

"I didn't see you clearly," she whispered, not knowing that she had spoken aloud.

"That's what I thought. What a pity, though, that the boy's memory came back to him. They told me it never would."

The earl's mind was beginning to thaw, and he was shaking his head, backing away from Standish. The candelabra was held high in his right hand. Through the fog in his brain, it was beginning to dawn that Deborah had told the truth and that he stood in mortal peril of his life. "You want her and the boy?" His voice shook. "I give them to you. They mean nothing to me. I don't know you. I never saw you before in my life. And when I leave this room, I will forget we ever met. Don't you understand? I hate her too."

Deborah did not flinch from the hate-filled words. It was no more than she expected from her father. Her eyes were fixed on Standish, watching and weighing, every sense alive to each small change in his expression.

"I never hated anyone in my life." He was so sincere it was terrifying. "I was taught to love my fellow man."

Horror welled up in Deborah. He was the son of a vicar. He was practically a member of Gray's family. They had *trusted* him. "You were the traitor," she said. "Philip, *you,* of all people!" Those were the very words Lord Barrington had used before he was shot. Standish was the last person anyone would have suspected.

"If only he had not seen me with Talleyrand. But he did see me, and I had to do something about it. Surely you see that? I was supposed to be in Rouen. What could I say to Lord Kendal if he questioned me? He would know I was the informer, and I would be disgraced."

She couldn't help herself. The words came automatically. "Philip, have pity. Let the boy go. Lord Kendal knows we are here. He will come for us at any moment."

It was all so familiar, and she saw from his expression that he was remembering too. She knew what would happen next. Gray had explained it to her. There were three of them. First, he would kill the one who was the greatest threat to him, then he would turn on the others.

Her mind was numb with fear. There was something of great moment she wanted to say to her father, something that would wash out the past and put everything right between them. "Father, I wish—"

"Don't speak to me! I don't know you!" her father screamed. And to Standish, "This is so unjust. I have nothing to do with this. I don't even know what's going on."

"I'm sorry," said Standish. "I'm so sorry." And leveling the pistol, he shot the earl in the chest.

Belvidere's eyes registered his shock a moment before he went stumbling back. Deborah screamed, then cried out, "Quentin, run! Hide yourself."

"Stay where you are!" Standish had withdrawn another pistol from his pocket and it was aimed at Quentin. "You see," he said, "I learned my lesson from the last time. This time I have come prepared."

Quentin made a sound, and Deborah drew him to her. Her eyes were fastened on her father. His body lay in a boneless heap, and a dark stain was spreading across the front of his jacket. The candelabra he had been holding was entangled in the silk drapes.

Her head swam and she sagged against the desk. Her hand brushed against something smooth and hard, and when she straightened, her fingers were curled around an onyx paperweight.

There was a whoosh, and tongues of fire swept the curtains from floor to ceiling. Deborah and Quentin clung together. Standish barely looked at them. Nothing seemed to excite him. He had just murdered a man. The room was going up in flames. Sparks were flying, fanned by the breeze from the open French doors. And he looked at them without blinking an eyelash.

"I have to kill you," he said. "And the boy too. You must see that."

To her surprise, her voice was quite calm. "It won't do you any good. Gray knows that you are the murderer." It was a lie, but she told it convincingly. If she could only make him believe that it was too late to escape Gray's wrath, he might let them go. His next words shattered that illusion.

"It doesn't matter if Lord Kendal knows. Without you and the boy, he will never prove it. Without proof, my father will never believe him. That's as much as I can hope for now."

"Don't you understand?" she cried out. "If anything happens to us, Gray will kill you, with or without proof."

He smiled gently. "It's you who doesn't understand, Miss Weyman. I don't care what happens to me."

He had made up his mind to die, but not before he had silenced the witnesses who could identify him. In a convoluted, bizarre way that made perfect sense to her, she saw that he was doing it for his father.

"Your father would never sanction this," she cried.

He looked shamed. "No."

"Why?" She really wanted to know. "What was worth all this?" One hand gestured, taking in the prone figure of the earl, and the blazing drapes.

"I did it for money," he said. "A secretary's income is not adequate for the expenses involved in keeping up with Lord Kendal's friends. And this time, I was determined to become one of them."

"This time?"

Her mind was working on two levels at once. She wanted to keep him talking. Unseen by Mr. Standish, the wall paneling behind him was blistering. Soon, it would go up like the drapes. When it did, she would be ready to act.

He shrugged. "Most of us were at university together. I was always the odd one out. I had no money, you see, and couldn't keep up with the others."

"I know how you feel." She was hardly aware of what she was saying. She was talking to delay him. Why wasn't the paneling bursting into flames? "Governesses are often made to feel like the poor relation."

Her eyes strayed to her father. She didn't know why she felt like weeping. She couldn't remember a time when he had said a kind word to her. He wasn't like Quentin's father. He wasn't even like Mr. Standish's father. Then why so much regret?

He went on. "I was almost sure that Lord Kendal was setting a trap for me. It didn't matter, just as long as I got to the boy. I knew you would lead me to him eventually. You must see that my one aim now is to spare my father pain. He would die of shame if any of this got out. I didn't mean it to go so far." A pleading note had crept into his voice, as if he were begging for her understanding. "It started from such small beginnings. No one really cared about the information I passed on. It wasn't a matter of life and death."

"But it became a matter of life and death when Lord Barrington threatened to expose you."

He frowned at her ugly tone. "As you say," he said. "Forgive me," and he took a step toward her, then another.

She could almost feel the vibrations of the pistol shot, taste the acrid smell of burned powder, just like that other time. She had to do something, say something before it was too late. "But you were left-handed," she cried out.

"No. I had burned my right hand with sealing wax. It was bandaged. Quentin must have missed that."

"But that's just it, Philip, you see Quentin—"

She heard a roar and the whole of one wall burst into flames. In the moment that his attention was distracted, Deborah pushed Quentin toward the door. "Run, Quentin," she shouted, and drawing back her arm, she launched the paperweight at Standish, catching him on the shoulder. He dropped the pistol but he retrieved it before she could get to it. Deborah scrambled away and bolted for the door. In the hall, she could hear someone shouting. Somewhere close by, a window shattered. Help was at hand. She had to find Quentin.

"Quentin!" she screamed.

His voice drifted down the well of the circular staircase in a ghostly whisper. "Up here, Deb."

She sobbed in horror. This was something out of her worst nightmares. This was time playing tricks on her. This was how she had run from Albert. "Oh God," she sobbed.

The library door opened, and she went haring across the hall and up the stairs, expecting at any moment to be felled by a bullet. On the first floor up, she came to a gallery with long corridors leading off in every direction. "Quentin!" she called out.

"Up here!"

Her heart sank. *Not there, Quentin. Oh, not there.* The gallery at the top of the stairs was purely decorative, and there was no exit except the stairs down.

"Come down to me!"

There was no answer, but she could hear him wheezing. Then she heard the tread of footsteps behind her, and she took the last flight of stairs. Above her, there was a great glass dome through which she could see the moon and the stars. On every side there were alcoves with marble statues, flanking windows with views over London and the Thames. There was no candle, but there was enough light from the windows to pick out shapes and objects. Events were moving so fast that she dared not take time to comfort Quentin. Ignoring him for the moment, she tried one window after another. None of them would open, and even if they had, there was only a ledge, and no way down. She had done this once before.

She went down on her knees and put her arms around Quentin. He wasn't panicked; he wasn't crying. His dark eyes were great pools of trust. That look moved inside her like the sharp edge of a blade.

"Deb, I remember everything, *everything*," he wheezed out.

"I know, I know, darling." She grabbed him by the shoulders to get his attention. "Listen carefully. You must keep your wits about you, and when you see your chance, you must get out of the house as fast as you can. You mustn't look back. You mustn't stop for anything. Do you understand?"

His bottom lip trembled. "Where will you be?"

"I shall be right behind you, but you mustn't wait for me."

"No, Deb. I want you to come with me."

"Think of your father. He would want you to do as I say. It's just like that other time, and we are going to escape—"

She had run out of time. A sound on the stairs warned her of Standish's approach. She led Quentin to one of the alcoves and pushed him down behind the statue. Then she moved along the gallery, where she hoped to lure Mr. Standish away from Quentin.

She heard wheezing, and her heart stopped, fearing Quentin would be discovered. Then Standish stepped onto the gallery and she realized he was the one who was wheezing. She should have *known*, remembering that night in Paris when the murderer came after them. He was fighting for breath just like Quentin.

"You can't escape me," said Standish, not threateningly, not viciously, but as though they were talking about the weather. "Can't you smell the smoke? Don't you know what's happening? The fire is spreading rapidly. There is no escape for any of us."

As if in answer to his words, there was a roar, then an explosion. Smoke billowed up the well of the staircase and great tongues of fire were reflected in the glass dome, then bounced grotesquely from window to window. The fires of hell could not have been more terrifying.

She spoke desperately. "You've lost, Mr. Standish. I led you on a false trail. As you can see, Quentin isn't here. He will tell the world all that he remembers, and everyone will know that you murdered Lord Barrington."

He was blocking the one exit. All she wanted him to do was take a few steps toward her. Then she would launch herself at him, and the way would be cleared for Quentin to escape. Why didn't the man move?

"Quentin," he said, "if you don't come out of your hiding place at once, I shall put a bullet through Miss Weyman's brain."

It was the smoke that betrayed him. Quentin began to cough, and Standish smiled. "Come out, Quentin," he said. "I promise I won't hurt you."

When Quentin stumbled from his hiding place, Standish grabbed him. "I mean to keep my word," he told Deborah. "I won't hurt either of you. We shall just wait here quietly, and allow the fire to do its work."

She was helpless. Even if she launched herself at Standish now, Quentin would never escape. He didn't know the house, and with the ground floor burning, he would not know which way to turn.

Smoke blinded her, and she reached for the balustrade to steady herself. At the same moment, something smashed into the great glass dome above, shattering it. Her head jerked up and when she turned to see what had caused it, she saw Gray slowly ascending the stairs with a smoking pistol in his hand.

"Stand back, Kendal, or I shall blow the boy's brains out." As he spoke, Standish edged away from the stairs, hauling Quentin with one arm locked around his throat.

Gray stepped onto the gallery. "You will be happy to know, Mr. Standish," he said, "that Nick survived the bullet you put in him. It was a clean wound, straight through the shoulder and out the other side. You should also know I heard the other shot. Deborah, what happened?"

"He shot my father."

"Ah," said Gray. "Two shots. That's what I was hoping you would say."

Deborah didn't understand what was happening, but she sensed something new in Standish's desperation. Suddenly he moved. He flung his pistol aside and lunged for the balustrade, dragging Quentin with him. She wasn't aware that she screamed. She knew what was in his mind. He was going to jump to his death and take Quentin with him. As Gray went to intercept him, she went for the pistol. Her hand was shaking when she pulled back the hammer and leveled it.

Gray's fist smashed into Standish's face, and he went sprawling, taking Quentin with him. Quentin's teeth sank into his captor's arm and Standish slapped him hard, then he quickly scrambled to his feet, holding Quentin in front of him. In the struggle, he had lost his spectacles. Deborah moved in close till she had a clear shot of the back of his head.

"Let the boy go," she said, "or I shall pull the trigger."

Standish laughed. It sounded carefree, and all the more demented, to Deborah's ears, because of it.

"Deborah," said Gray, "stand aside."

Gray didn't understand, and there wasn't time to explain it to him. Her finger tightened on the trigger, and she hesitated. It was a terrible thing to take a man's life. Then Quentin sobbed, trying to get breath, and her resolve hardened. She pulled the trigger. The gun clicked but there was no explosion, no bullet in the chamber.

Before her horrified eyes, Standish began to hoist Quentin onto the balustrade. Gray's hand lashed out, and there was a sickening crack as Standish's arm snapped. Deborah grabbed for Quentin and wrenched him clear by the coattails.

"Get out of here," yelled Gray, "before the whole place goes up."

In the moment when Gray's attention was on Deborah, Standish dragged himself to his feet and collapsed against the rail. Half leaning over it, he fought to drag air into his lungs. The rail swayed, and with an ominous crack gave way beneath his weight. Before their horrified eyes, he teetered on the edge, then went toppling into the abyss. There was no scream, no sound until he hit the marble floor, three floors below. Deborah's arms were around Quentin, keeping his face averted, though there was nothing to see now.

White-faced and grim, Gray reached for the two of them. "Now let's get the hell out of here," he said.

❧

Outside in the Strand, the street was blocked with carriages. Red-coated militia were ordering the crowds back. Flames were already creeping along the roof. The back of the house was an inferno and the fire was quickly spreading to the front of the house.

Lady Helena Perrin was in her carriage, watching the spectacle with detached interest. Her detachment fled when she saw and recognized Nick Grayson as he flung out the front doors. His face was blackened from smoke, and his arm was in a sling. Frowning, Helena opened the door of her coach and, ignoring her coachman's protest, gingerly stepped onto the street. She was immediately swallowed up by the jostling crowds.

"Move along! Move along!" bellowed the captain of the militia. "Or I shall read the riot act!" He was mounted, and the spectators pressed back to avoid being crushed beneath the horse's hooves.

Helena elbowed her way toward the front of the

crowd. "Captain," she called out. "What's going on here?"

The cultured accent stayed the rude retort that came to the captain's lips. The dazzling beauty of the lady who had put the question to him softened him even more. "A damnable business," he said. "There are people trapped inside the house."

"Who?" asked Helena. Her heart was beating frantically.

The captain pointed to Nick. "That gentleman's brother, for one. He went to the rescue of a lady with a boy. A brave man. A very brave man." The crowd surged forward and he turned away, bellowing to his men to hold their positions.

There were faces in the crowd that Helena recognized, people of her own set. The crowd was so dense, however, she could not get to them. She had to know what was happening. She had to know.

"Lord Lawford," she cried out.

Lawford heard her cry, and turned his head. He smiled, nodded, and tried to make his way toward her. The crowd was too dense.

"What's going on?" Helena shouted above the noise of the crowd.

"I believe Kendal has caught his murderer," he shouted back.

There was a cry and the crowd went wild as three people came out the front doors. Gray, Deborah Weyman, and Quentin. Nick went forward and flung his good arm around Gray's shoulders. Gray smiled and said something to the captain, and two militiamen came forward and led them away. No one else came out of the house.

A terrible feeling of doom possessed Helena. She acted without reason, a thing of the wild in a panic. Pushing, shoving, she forced her way out of the crush, then, blind to everything and everyone around her, she started to run. Her coach driver saw everything but could do nothing since he was hemmed in by other carriages. He motioned to the other coachman, who then descended from the box and went after her.

She had only one thought in her head. She must get home. Eric had agreed to escort her to Lady Kendal's informal soirée that evening. She prayed as she had never prayed before that he would be at home waiting for her.

As soon as she entered her house, she called his name. There was no answer. Picking up her skirts, she went tearing up the stairs and burst into his dressing room.

He looked up from the newspaper he was reading and in a lightning glance took in her disheveled appearance, the panicked breathing and fear-bright eyes. "Helena, what is it?" he asked urgently. He had never seen her look like this.

She sagged against the door and tears welled in her eyes. "Kendal has caught his murderer," she said. Her voice broke. "Oh Eric, I thought it was you. I thought it was *you*."

"Who is it?"

"I don't know. I think he perished in the fire."

He came to her then and clasped her by the shoulders. His eyes devoured every expression. "And would it have mattered to you if it had been me?"

"How can you ask me that when you know that I love you?"

He closed his eyes, then opened them wide. "I thought you didn't care for me."

She shook her head. "Perhaps at first, because I knew you married me for my connections, but later—"

He shook her hard. "I have loved you from the moment I set eyes on you." She looked at him uncertainly, and he shook her again. "It's always been you. I thought you married me for my money."

"I did, but I was a fool."

He kissed her as he had never dared kiss her before, betraying all that he felt for her, and the Kendals and their informal soirée were consigned to oblivion.

CHAPTER 23

Lady Kendal's informal soirée was not precisely a raging success. Some of those invited were among the spectators at the demise of Strand House, and when the red glow over Charing Cross lit up the sky, the remaining guests took off to investigate, taking their hostess and her daughter with them. Nick was glad to have no mother fussing over him when the physician arrived to doctor the "scratch" on his shoulder.

Having seen the physician off the premises, the survivors of the fire assembled in Gray's library, and were soon fortifying themselves with their favorite tipple. Hart was there, but only because he had returned home to find the house empty. The atmosphere was subdued but far from grim. Gil's murderer was finally caught. They had escaped with their lives. Quentin was safe, and though he had been through another harrowing experience, he had come through it well.

At one point, Gray said quietly, "Tell us, Quentin, exactly what happened that night in Paris."

Quentin swallowed and nodded. "I was playing a trick on Deborah, but when I heard Papa's voice, I came out from behind the curtains at once. Mr. Standish was with him, and he had a pistol. He said 'Don't move. Don't anyone move.' Then we heard Deborah calling my name. Papa told me to leave, but Mr. Standish wouldn't allow it."

When he stopped speaking, Deborah put her arm around him. "Don't think about it if you don't want to," she said.

"But I *do* want to think about it." There were tears in his eyes. "When Papa told me to run, I thought he would run too. But he sprang at Mr. Standish. Then, then, I don't know. The gun went off, and Deborah was there, and we were running, and . . . and I forgot everything."

"Well," said Gray, "tonight your papa must be very happy."

"Do you think so, Uncle Gray?"

"I know so. If it were not for you, we would never have caught Mr. Standish. Your papa knows that too. I'll bet he is . . . um . . . looking down from Heaven with a big smile on his face."

Quentin said eagerly, "When I remembered who Mr. Standish was, I was frightened, but I didn't cry, did I, Deb?"

"No. You were very brave."

"And I bit him on the arm, didn't I, Uncle Gray?"

"You were a real Trojan. Ferocious, in fact."

"He slapped me hard, Uncle Nick, but I didn't cry out. Uncle Hart, do you think I shall have a bruise on my face when I wake up tomorrow?"

"I don't think . . ."—observing Quentin's hopeful look, Hart changed in mid-sentence—"there's any doubt of that. Why, it would not surprise me if we scarcely recognized you."

"That's what I thought you would say. I can hardly wait to show Jason. Deb, may I have more ale?"

"You may not! In fact, young man, you should not be here. It's long past your bedtime."

"Then I'll have some of your barley water, and you may put as much honey and lemon in it as you like."

"Fine. I'll bring it up to you in a few minutes, once you are settled. All right?"

"I'll ring for a footman," said Hart.

"Oh, not one of the footmen. Can't I have Samuel?"

"And who," asked Deborah, "might Samuel be?"

"My valet," said Gray. "And he is Mr. Farley to you, scamp."

Hart pulled on the bell rope to summon a footman who, in turn, went to fetch Mr. Farley.

Quentin jumped up and ran to the door to greet him. "Farley," he said, "you'll never guess what's happened. We caught the man who shot my father. I lost my memory, did you know? And when everything came back to me . . ." He left without a backward glance.

Those remaining smiled and chuckled.

"I'm glad to see," said Nick, "that Quentin is recovering from it all. I know I shall have nightmares for a long time to come."

"I know how he feels," said Gray. "It *was* a harrowing experience, but he is elated that his father's murderer has been caught. Not only that, but he helped catch him. He's proud of himself, and so he should be."

Deborah sipped at her tea and kept her opinions to herself. She was not so sure that Quentin was untouched by the events of that night, and took comfort from the thought that Dr. Mesmer would be arriving in a day or two to examine him.

Nick had moved to the window and was staring out at the fiery sky. Suddenly shivering, he pulled on the ropes to close the curtains. When he came back to his place, he offered the others a crooked smile. "I don't think," he said, "I shall ever forget finding Strand House going up in flames when I arrived with the militia. I didn't know where to begin to look for you. We tried every room on that ground floor before the heat and smoke drove us back. When you came down the stone staircase and out the front door—" He swallowed hard as the memory came back to him.

"And," said Gray, "I shall never forget the dash along that long upstairs corridor. It seemed to go on for miles. Hell, it did go on for miles. We could hardly see for smoke, and the floor beneath our feet was so hot it was burning holes in my boots."

Deborah said, addressing Nick, "How did you know I would make for Strand House?"

"Gray told me. But what I can't understand is why. You took me completely by surprise when you ran away, Deb. Why did you do it?"

She couldn't bring herself to tell him the bare truth, that she had suspected *he* was the murderer. "I knew someone was following us and I panicked." Then, to distract him, "What happened when you followed me?"

"What happened was I was too clever for my own good. I knew Standish would be armed, of course, and I tried to draw his fire as a safeguard. I succeeded as you can see." He patted the arm in the sling. "When Gray arrived upon the scene, I was in no condition to go chasing after you, but at least I could tell him which direction you had taken and how far Standish was behind you. Then I hailed a hackney to take me to Whitehall, where they insisted on putting this cursed sling on me, and had them call out the militia. And that takes care of my part in the affair."

Deborah was not quite satisfied with this. "You knew Mr. Standish was following us?"

"I did."

"But how could you know?"

"I made sure he was in the house before I came for you."

Deborah frowned at this, then said to Nick, "Then you knew Philip was the murderer?"

"No. But Gray did."

"The devil he did!" exclaimed Hart. "And did it not occur to you, Gray, to warn the rest of us? Standish has been at leave to come and go in this house like a member of the family. No one questioned him. He could have murdered us all in our beds."

"You don't believe that," said Gray. "And how could I warn you? You know yourself, Hart, that you are not exactly an accomplished actor. If Standish was the murderer—and I had no proof—it was essential for my purposes that he suspect nothing."

"All the same," said Hart, not the least mollified, "you should have warned Deborah. He might have tried something with her."

"Oh no," said Gray. "I was very sure he would not.

Deb did not recognize him when she came here, and she had not lost her memory. His target was Quentin, and he was counting on Deb to lead him to the boy."

There was a question hovering in Deborah's mind, but Gray's words shifted her focus. "He knew I had not seen him clearly that night in the library. Well, everything happened so fast, and the light was not good."

"How did he know?" said Nick.

"We had been introduced at Quentin's picnic. If I had seen his face clearly, he knew I would have remembered it, and would have told Gray. He told me all this."

"What else did he tell you?" asked Gray.

"He never expected Quentin to regain his memory. His exact words were, 'They said it would never happen.' "

" 'They' presumably being the French?" asked Hart.

Gray replied, "Oh, I don't think there is any doubt of that."

There was a long period of silence, then Deborah asked quietly, "What made you suspect Philip, Gray? Was it what happened in the library at Channings when we went through the murder step by step?"

"It was, though it did not come to me in the library, but only when I had time to reflect on things."

There was a moment of silence, then Hart said in the same aggrieved tone, "Well, don't stop there. You have us all agog. Do tell how you managed to solve the mystery when the rest of us were rubbing shoulders with a murderer morning, noon, and night, only we did not know it."

Gray handed round the decanter of brandy before commencing, but Hart was the only one who availed himself of it. "As Deb said," began Gray, "she and I reenacted Gil's murder in the library at Channings and some interesting things came to light, things Deb had forgotten until she went through them step by step. She told me that in his right hand the murderer was holding what she thought was a handkerchief, and that the pistol was in his left hand. That did not make sense to me. Why would a murderer be holding a handkerchief?"

"It wasn't a handkerchief," said Deborah. "Philip

had burned himself with sealing wax. His right hand was bandaged."

"It was a great inconvenience in a secretary," said Gray. "During the peace talks in Paris, I had to share one of the other delegate's secretaries."

"And you deduced it was Standish from that?" demanded Hart incredulously.

"Hardly," said Gray. "There were other things, small things that got me wondering."

"What things?"

"Something Gil said. 'You of all people' were his words. I knew then that the man I had suspected all along was innocent. And before you ask, Hart, the man I suspected was Eric Perrin. Oh, I know he would not betray secrets for money, but I thought he might do it to embarrass me, you know, at the Foreign Office. After all, I was responsible. It reflected badly on me. I've known for a long time that Perrin doesn't like me. With Gil's words, however, it seemed to me that the murderer must be, ostensibly, a man of high moral character, which Perrin is not, or someone close to me or close to Gil."

"Very close to you?" asked Nick.

Gray couldn't resist saying, "Naturally, I thought of you and Hart first."

Nick came up from the back of his chair and the wound in his arm made him gasp.

"That's not funny," said Hart, glowering at Gray.

"No, it's not," agreed Gray. "And you will be happy to know I discarded that thought almost as soon as it occurred to me."

"Oh?" said Hart, smiling through his teeth. "And why was that?"

"Because there had been many opportunities for both you and Nick to make away with Quentin, and you had not availed yourself of any of them."

Nick was laughing. Hart looked as though he might explode, and Gray said wickedly, "However, thinking that it might be someone of high moral character certainly narrowed the field."

"Oh ho," said Nick, "so that's what disqualified us

as suspects. I think, Hart, he is telling us that we were not good enough."

Gray ignored the banter. "And Deborah had assured me that the murderer was not a woman. And so, my eye alighted on Mr. Standish. Well, who else could it have been? Think of it. Standish was English. He worked with me at the Foreign Office. Though it's true that he did not have access to my personal correspondence, he could have intercepted letters and messages without too much difficulty." He shook his head. "I don't know how Gil found out that Standish was the informer—"

"I can answer that," said Deborah. "He admitted it to me there, in Strand House. He said that Lord Barrington had seen him with Talleyrand when he was supposed to be in Rouen."

"And that's all?" asked Gray. When Deborah nodded, he said, "It sounds to me as though Standish panicked. Poor Gil. He should not have entrusted anything to paper. That was unwise. But I suppose he did not think that Standish would stoop to murder." A moment went by, then he went on in a lighter vein. "Add to that, on the night in question, Standish's right hand was immobilized. He had the opportunity. You must remember, everything was in chaos those last few days when everyone was trying to get out of Paris. No one seems to have had an alibi except for Sophie Barrington."

"I had an alibi," Hart burst out. "I was with your mother and sisters! We weren't even near Paris. You insisted we leave as soon as we heard that the borders were to be closed."

"Hart, I know. I was only joking when I said I suspected you."

"I didn't have an alibi," said Nick.

"Yes, I know that too. There was one other thing," said Gray, and both Nick and Hart groaned.

"What?" asked Deborah, sending the mockers a quelling look.

Gray went on. "Deb mentioned the murderer's breathing. It had made a great impression on her, yes, and on Quentin too. That was something else I could not understand. Why should he be breathing so hard?

Shooting a man with a pistol does not involve hard physical exercise."

"I think," said Deborah, "Mr. Standish suffered from the same complaint as Quentin."

"I know he did," said Gray. "When we were at Oxford, he was frequently indisposed because of his weak chest. I remember I felt sorry for him."

"That's as may be," said Hart, "but this is all circumstantial. If you want my opinion, I think it was just a lucky guess on your part, Gray, or you would have confronted Standish with what you knew."

"That's true. I had to be sure."

Hart seemed pleased with this concession. He sat back in his chair and slapped his knees. "Now," he said, "will someone please tell me what happened tonight? I have only the vaguest idea. I understand everything up to the point where Deborah ran from Nick. But how did Quentin come to be with her? And how did you know, Gray, that she would make for Strand House?"

"Deb?" said Gray quietly.

She sat still, looking down at her hands, and whatever it was in the last hour or two that had buoyed her up seemed to have slipped away. She couldn't be sorry that they'd escaped with their lives. She only wished that things had worked out differently.

She said, "Quentin was watching from the window of the house Gary had rented. He saw Nick and Philip following me and he slipped away to warn me."

"And where were you, Gray?" asked Hart pointedly.

"Oh, I had seen everything too. I left the house before Quentin. In fact, I did not know he was with Deborah until I came upon them in Strand House."

"Why Strand House?" asked Hart, looking at Deborah.

There didn't seem any point in going on with the charade now. She wasn't sure if her name had been cleared, but it no longer mattered to her. "I was familiar with the house," she said. "I should be. It's my father's house. Lord Belvidere is my father. Leathe is my brother. I don't want to go into all that now. Gray knew. He also knew that the house was empty and that my father was trying to sell it. Where else would I hide Quentin when a murderer was pursuing us?"

The silence was so absolute that Deborah felt that if a snowflake had fallen on the carpet, she would have heard it. Only Gray was looking at her. The others were looking at their hands.

Nick spoke first. "I could bite my tongue out! To think that we were joking just now! What you must be suffering! Forgive me, Deb, I'm not usually so uncouth."

"No, really, there's nothing to forgive. I hardly knew my father. The grief I feel is what I would feel for any stranger who was murdered in cold blood." It was the truth, and it was a distortion of the truth. She was grieving but she didn't know why.

Hart said, "Oh Deb, I'm so sorry." He shook his head. "Gray should have told us."

Deborah forced herself to speak naturally. "I didn't want anyone to know. After everything that's happened, it doesn't seem to matter."

"Did you know your father would be there?" asked Hart.

"Oh no. To be frank, things were so bad between us that if I'd known he was there, I would have gone somewhere else." She swallowed hard. "I don't know where."

Gray regarded her closely, trying to read behind the calm words. He wondered exactly what had taken place between Deborah and her father before Standish had caught up to her. Nothing good, if he knew Belvidere.

Looking only at her, he said, "It was just his bad luck to be there when Standish came upon him." This was mere rhetoric on Gray's part. He was more than glad that Belvidere had been present. Had he not been there, Standish would have used his last shot on Deborah, and it would have been easy for him then to deal with Quentin.

"It was horrible," said Deborah. "It was so reminiscent of that other time with Lord Barrington. There was one major difference, though. This time, Mr. Standish had two pistols. I didn't know that the second one had no bullet in it. But you knew, Gray."

"I was sure of it. One bullet had passed through Nick's shoulder. There had been no time to reload. I was approaching the house from the back when I heard the other shot go off. I found Belvidere's body on the floor of the library and—"

"You entered the library?" asked Deborah.

"When I saw the blaze, I thought you must be there. As you may imagine, I did not linger." Only long enough to make sure that neither Deborah nor Quentin was lying there too. A memory of that terrible fear shuddered through him, and he went on abruptly. "It was impossible to cross to the door, so I ran along the terrace and broke into the room next to it. I heard you call for Quentin, and followed the sound of your voice to the circular staircase."

"Then what happened?" asked Hart.

Gray lifted his shoulders fractionally. "Standish was there, and I was sure he meant to throw Deb and Quentin over the rail of the staircase. There was a fight. He fell rather heavily against the banister, and the thing gave way. He plunged to his death. The rest you know."

Everyone was very still. Even the room seemed to have stopped breathing. A dying ember cracked and everyone looked at the fire.

Hart cleared his throat. "Why did he do it? He was the son of a vicar. What on earth could have induced him to sell information to the enemy?"

"I asked him that," said Deborah. "It was for money. He wanted to fit in with Gray's set, and he needed money for that. At Oxford, he had always felt like the odd man out. But at the end, the only thing that mattered to him was that his father be spared the pain of knowing that his son was a traitor and a murderer." She caught Gray's eye, and looked away.

"And so he was driven to murder again." Nick shook his head. "It's his father I feel sorry for. I suppose there is no way of keeping this quiet?" He was looking at Gray.

"No," said Gray. "Too many people saw us leaving Strand House tonight. They are not stupid. Even if we wanted to conceal it, they would soon put two and two together. Besides, apart from the fact that he murdered my friend, what he did and tried to do tonight was iniquitous. I feel cheated. What I wanted was to see him in the dock, publicly charged with his crimes, and made to face the consequences. Now, all there will be is an inquest. Yes, I'm sorry for his father. Who wouldn't be? But I refuse to perjure myself to save Standish's reputation. That is asking too much."

His gaze was locked with Deborah's, and she shivered involuntarily. She sensed in him the same unbending force that had frightened her when she was his captive. As she was turning this over in her mind, he spoke quietly to Hart and Nick.

"Would you mind giving me a few minutes alone with Deborah? There are some things she and I have yet to discuss."

There was a moment of awkwardness, then Hart and Nick rose, and after making a few noncommittal remarks, they left the room.

Suddenly, unbidden, her mind was filled with snatches of this and that, threads of conversation that she had been too keyed up to grasp at the time. Her eyes searched that hard, uncompromising face, and she knew she had missed something important, something that she ought to have known. And she had known it, but she had refused to believe it.

Her brain began to make lightning connections, and her voice shook as outrage rose in her. "You led me to believe that Quentin could only be free if his memory came back to him. And all the time you were setting him up as bait to entrap the murderer."

He didn't try to deny it, nor did she expect him to. She could see from his face that he had decided there was no point in trying to conceal it from her. Sooner or later, she was bound to work it out.

"I could not be sure that Quentin's memory would ever come back to him. This was the only way to remove the threat that Standish posed."

"The rumors—you were behind them! Quentin's memory wasn't coming back to him. You used what you learned from me at Channings to bait your trap."

He reached for the decanter and refilled his glass. "It was the only way, and when you have time to think about it, you will see it too."

His calm assurance that he knew best had her spitting like a wildcat. "Do you know what threw me off? You were so careful not to be discovered. No one knew where you and Quentin were."

"Yes," said Gray. "I knew if it were too easy, Standish would suspect a trap. I had to make it difficult for him, but not too difficult."

"So, you used me to lead him to Quentin!"

"Deb—"

Her voice was rising. "There is no such person as Dr. Mesmer."

"Oh, Dr. Mesmer exists, and he is exactly as I described him to you. He lives in Switzerland, now, I believe, though he did live in London at one time. As for treating Quentin, no, it was never in my mind to put my ward into the hands of quacks and charlatans."

"*Your* ward? *Your* ward?" Her whole body was quivering. "I am his guardian too. You should have consulted me before you embarked on this wild escapade. Do you realize how closely Quentin and I came to losing our lives tonight?"

He watched her for a moment without expression. Finally, he said, "I know very well. I made a mistake there. I thought you trusted Nick and would do exactly as he said. If you had entered the house where we were lying in wait as you were meant to, things would have turned out very differently."

She had risen to her feet, and as she paced, he watched her in silence, occasionally drinking from the glass in his hand.

Suddenly rounding on him, she said, "Do you know you sound just like my father? If I had only done what *he* wanted me to do, today I would be married to a simpleton, or I would be locked away in an insane asylum."

Anger flashed in his eyes and was swiftly subdued. "How could I consult you? You allow your emotions to rule your logic. You have never stayed to face a fight.

Oh, I'm not saying you are not brave. That is not in doubt. But only when you are cornered. You run away from things, Deb, you know you do. And some things have to be faced."

"That is so unjust!" She was hugging herself with her arms. "What should I have done when Lord Barrington was murdered? Should I have stayed to fight Philip Standish with my bare hands?"

"What you should have done was go to the authorities. I know those were exceptional circumstances, but when you reached London, you should have gone straight to the magistrates, yes, and told them that you suspected *me* of the murder. Instead of which, you took Quentin and ran. I don't think I shall ever forget that night on the roof when he slipped toward the edge."

She shrilled at him, "If you had not been so single-minded in pursuing us, we would never have been on that roof."

"You are missing the point. What about your life these last eight or nine years? You've hidden yourself away, playing the part of a dowd, becoming old before your time. For what? You ran from your father and a trumped-up charge. If you had stayed, there is no jury on earth that would have convicted you. Instead, you became a fugitive, always looking over your shoulder. Is that the kind of life you wanted for Quentin?"

"Of course not! He could have gone to his uncle in Nevis—"

He cut her off with a violent motion of one hand. "Listen to yourself, Deb! Running away is no way to solve one's problems."

"Oh, it's easy for you to speak. You are a man. You have power and influence. You cannot know the terror of being weak and helpless, with no say over your own fate. Women and children are chattels, did you know that?"

"You will never hear my mother or sisters speak like that. Doesn't that tell you something, Deb?"

She laughed, a hollow sound, even to her own ears. "Oh yes. It tells me they are not married to you. Gray, you frighten me. You really frighten me. With you, the end justifies the means. You don't care how you do things, just as long as you get your own way."

His features tightened and seemed to harden into a wooden mask. He rose to face her. "That's not true."

"How can you deny it?" she cried passionately. "From the very first, you abducted me and panicked me into leading you to Quentin."

"Oh, so we're back to that again, are we?"

She shook her head bleakly, incapable of putting her thoughts into words. But he was reading her, and he said the words for her.

"You think I'm like your father. Is that it? My God, how can you compare me to that worm?"

"I don't say you are wicked. You're not, of course. But you are ruthless. You manipulate people, events. You trick people. You lied to me—"

"I did not lie to you!"

"Then you deliberately misled me."

"I did what was necessary to bring matters to a right and proper conclusion. Are you sorry that Standish is no longer a threat to Quentin? I assure you, Quentin is not sorry."

She raked her fingers through her hair in a gesture of frustration. "No, I'm not sorry about that, but I'm sorry for the way it was done. You should have discussed it with me first."

"What was the point when I knew it would do no good? You don't trust me, you never have. Everything I do becomes a battleground for us. In some perverted way I cannot understand, you see your father in me. That's the sum of it, isn't it, Deborah? *Isn't it?*"

"Yes!" she cried out.

He took a step back, as though her passionate affirmation had struck him like a blow. They stood there staring at each other, the girl hugging herself to stop her trembling, the man as though he were hewn out of a block of stone. When she spoke, there was a catch in her voice.

"When I left my father's house, I made a vow that I would never again put myself into the power of any man."

His eyes were careful, wary. "I thought you had got over that?"

"I thought you were different!" she cried out. "I thought your love for me had changed you! But you are just the same."

"I see." He shrugged, as though it were of no moment to him. "You're running away again, following your usual pattern. I shouldn't be surprised. I won't try to dissuade you. I won't—how did you put it?—manipulate events to suit my own purposes. It seems we both made a mistake. I hope you find what you are looking for, but I see now you won't find it with me. I could never be happy with a woman who was forever questioning my integrity. And you have questioned it once too often. If you don't commit yourself to me now, this is the end for us. Be very sure I mean that, Deb."

She felt as though her heart were being torn from her breast. Unable to bear that cold look, she turned away and took a step toward the door, just as it opened to admit Nick.

"Deb," he said, "Lord Leathe is here and wishes to speak with you."

Leathe was in the vestibule and his face was stark and white. "Deb, there has been a terrible accident. It's Father."

"Yes, I know. He's dead."

He clasped both her hands and subjected her to a searching look. "If those tears are for him," he said, "you've come to the wrong person for comfort."

"They're not only for him. They're for us too."

"What does that mean?"

But she couldn't explain it, not even to herself.

CHAPTER 24

The Earl of Belvidere was young and handsome, and immaculately turned out in his blacks, but the mourners at his father's funeral found little else to recommend him. His expression was austere. His responses to their condolences were cold and unrevealing. His manner was distant. When the service was over and the old earl's coffin was duly lowered into the ground, they remained standing about only as long as good manners required, then they made their excuses and filed out of the churchyard.

Belvidere, as Leathe was now known, watched for a moment or two as the grave diggers began to heap the dark, bloodred earth into the gaping grave. He felt nothing, not a single regret for his father's demise. If he regretted anything, it was that Deborah had persuaded him to accompany her on this senseless pilgrimage. He felt like a hypocrite, decked out in mourning. It wasn't a mark of respect for their father, he assured himself, but in deference to their sister, Elizabeth. He wasn't mourning. He was completely indifferent to the old sod's fate, and when he and Deborah left this place, the mourning clothes would be packed away.

For no reason, his eyes began to sting, and he turned away with a soft imprecation. He was a man now, not a boy, and he refused to let the past mold him to its whim. That was the argument Deborah had used to persuade him to accompany her. They were, she'd said, going on a pilgrimage to face their ghosts and finally lay them to rest. He feared it would be easier said than done. He thought of Meg, and it was like inhaling a breath of fresh air. He would allow nothing to come between them, not even Kendal. Suddenly realizing that the others had outdistanced him, he hastened to catch up.

The dowager was leaning heavily on the arm of an elderly gentleman, some relative whom Deborah understood was now Elizabeth's guardian. Her half sister, Elizabeth, walked silently at Deborah's side and flashed her a furtive glance from time to time. Deborah was hardly aware of it. She was steeling herself for what was to come. Belvidere was only a short drive away and the house, in her mind, represented something that was beyond her comprehension. She only knew that if she could come to terms with Belvidere, she would understand all mysteries. The thought made her smile.

Raising her eyes at that moment, she caught and held Elizabeth's stare. The girl was the image of their father, thin faced, and with dark, long-lashed eyes. There was a question in those eyes, then suddenly the girl smiled, and her face was transformed as dimples flashed at Deborah.

Deborah smiled and nodded. It wasn't much. It wasn't nearly enough, but it was a communication of sorts. As she smiled at her sister now, Deborah regretted that she had hardly spared the girl a passing thought since the day she had left Belvidere. She had never really known Elizabeth. Her stepmother had kept them apart. She hoped they could do better in future.

"You must come and have tea with me one day soon," she said to Elizabeth.

Again the girl's face was transformed by her smile. "I should like that of all things. And . . . Leathe too?"

"Of course. He is your brother. Naturally, he will wish to see you."

"Elizabeth!" The dowager countess's hand was on the coach door. Her eyes were as sharp and piercing as a hawk's. "Come along, child. You will ride with us."

"Yes, Mama." Elizabeth's head dipped, and she moved quickly to obey her mother.

Deborah let out a small sigh and allowed the coachman to help her into her brother's carriage. She wished there was something they could do for Elizabeth, but she didn't know what. The girl had a guardian now, and it was out of their hands.

On the drive to the house, she and Stephen said very little. Occasionally, they pointed out landmarks they remembered, but when the house came into view, not a word was exchanged.

It was just as she remembered, a neoclassical palace modeled on the temples of Greece. Her eyes were drawn to the roof of the house, and traveled that long stone pediment with niches where statues of pagan gods looked down on all who passed by. As they drew closer, her eyes picked out the stately Ionic columns, the intricately chiseled borders of vines that decorated each window, and the ornate ironwork. There was a set of massive white marble steps leading down to the fountains, and another set that led up to the great portico and the front doors. When Stephen helped her down from the carriage, her breathing was not quite regular.

"It's rather intimidating, isn't it?" she whispered, as though she feared to betray her presence to whatever gods resided there.

Her brother's eyes flicked over the house indifferently. "It's a shrine to one man's ego," he said.

"It's yours now, Stephen. Will you live here with Meg?" There was no question in Deborah's mind now that her brother and Meg would make a match of it. Young as they were, they were both strong-willed and very much in love.

"If Meg wishes it." He grinned. "She says that it's only a house and when we fill it with babies I won't recognize it. I'm going to make other changes, of course. For a start, I'm going to obliterate all the murals where Father is portrayed. There's one other thing I'd like to do. With your permission, I'd like to have our mother's portrait done. There is an artist I know who is gaining quite a reputation for himself as a portrait painter. He tells me that he can do it from the miniature you have in our mother's locket. He's done this sort of thing before."

"I think that's a splendid idea."

"There's nothing to stop you from sending for it now, is there? Your name has been cleared. You're a free woman."

Free. She was not so sure that she would ever be truly free. "I'll write to Miss Hare at once."

In the great marble hall, her steps slowed to a halt. More Greek columns towered threateningly on either side of her. Scenes from Roman history were depicted on the ceiling. Her breath caught painfully when she saw her father's face staring down at her. In this awesome chamber, he was depicted as Julius Caesar. Until her brother mentioned it, she'd forgotten that in almost every room, her father was portrayed as some mythical hero or character from history. As a child, she had been terrified. It had seemed that his eyes were always following her.

"The solicitor is going to read the will," said Stephen. "There's nothing in it for us, of course, but I intend to be present if only to annoy the old harridan, and see that they do right by Elizabeth."

Deborah nodded, but her gaze remained fixed on her father's face.

"Aren't you coming in?"

"What?" Her head jerked round.

He said gently, "The solicitor and the others are waiting for us in the library."

"No. I shall wander around, if you don't mind. This is what I came for."

He touched a hand to her cheek. "Are you all right? You look rather pale."

Her smile was meant to reassure. "I'm fine, Stephen, really. This won't take long. When I'm finished, I shall wait for you in the carriage."

He gave her a long look, nodded, and entered the library. Like a sleepwalker, Deborah remained where she was, trying to fight off the potent atmosphere that seemed to be saturating every particle of her being. She gave herself a mental dressing-down. It was only a house after all. There was nothing to fear here. Breathing deeply, she began on her pilgrimage, beginning with the rooms of state on the ground floor.

Perfection, cold perfection—those were the only words to describe the house. Her father's personality seemed to be stamped on every room. Not a thing was out of place. There was no dust, not a scratch on any piece of furniture, not a chip or a crack on any of the porcelain. It looked as though the rooms had never been used. She tried to imagine Quentin and Jason running through these rooms, and failed. But when she thought of herself and Stephen, she could remember how it was very well. They had been afraid to put a foot out of place, quite literally. She remembered sitting for what seemed like hours, without speaking, without moving a muscle. Their place had been in the nursery and school-room on the top floor, or better yet, in the cellars where their father never ventured.

As she moved through each successive room, a feeling of panic began to grow in her. She had the strangest sensation that she was that young girl again, and she was locked in time with no hope of escape. She had awakened from a dream, and it was gradually receding. There was no Gray, no Quentin, no Channings or Sommerfield. The Graysons were only a figment of her imagination. She had never loved or been loved. In another moment, even the memory of the dream would fade.

"No!" she cried out. "No!" And picking up her skirts, she ran for the stairs that led to the nursery. She flung herself into that room as if the furies were after her and came to a sudden halt. The room was choked with furniture and odds and ends that she recognized had come from Strand House. She didn't know what she'd hoped to find in that room, but whatever it was, it was there no longer.

She knew she was imagining things, but she couldn't help what she was feeling. It seemed to her that something malevolent stalked her in that house, some shade from the past that had bound her with invisible threads that were as hard to resist as iron manacles. She wanted to pick up her skirts and make a dash for freedom, then she would be off and running, running, running . . .

You run from things, you know you do. Some things have to be faced. Gray's words filtered into her mind and the panic receded a little. She could fight the house's spell. She was stronger now. Gray had done this for her. As if in answer to that thought, pictures of another house drifted before her eyes. *Sommerfield.* It, too, was stamped with the personality of its owner. It was an old house, solid, battle scarred, but it radiated warmth and benevolence. Without the least difficulty, she could picture hordes of noisy children marching through its hallowed halls, leaving their footprints on the parquet floors, or their grubby fingerprints on the highly polished surfaces of the oak furniture. Her mind wandered over that house and finally focused on the huge, stuffed war horse in the Great Hall, and she found herself smiling. If anything in that house personified Gray, it was that stuffed war horse. It, too, was battle scarred, but it stood there proudly, a lonely sentinel guarding the house. Warwick was its name, Old Warwick, and Gussie had told her that they would never part with it. If it were not for Old Warwick, the course of the Graysons' fortunes would have been far different.

She stood there for some time with a smile on her face, looking at everything, looking at nothing, thinking of Sommerfield and what it represented. Gradually, the image faded, and with it her smile.

If it were not for Gray, the course of Quentin's life might have been far different. "Mine too," she said, her voice anguished, "mine too." Her name had been cleared and there was no need for subterfuge now. It was public knowledge that she was Lady Deborah Montague, and she could come and go as she pleased. She should be ecstatic. She was free, but she didn't feel free. The past was still taking its toll on her. If she were truly free she would not be so afraid.

As if her thoughts were not torment enough, she heard Gray's voice as he had last spoken to her: *It seems we both made a mistake. I hope you find what you are looking for. But I see now you won't find it with me. I could never be happy with a woman who was forever questioning my integrity. And you have questioned it once too often. If you don't commit yourself to me now, this is the end for us. Be very sure I mean that, Deb.*

He didn't understand. It wasn't *him.* It was the ghosts of Belvidere. It was her father and the power that was invested in him. How could a woman fight a man and win? Her mother had tried and lost.

You will never hear my mother or sisters speak like that. Doesn't that tell you something, Deb?

For a long, long time, she remained motionless, veering between black despair and tremulous hope. She was no longer that frightened girl who had been so easily intimidated. She was stronger, but was she strong enough? And what was the point of so much anguished debate anyway? Gray would never take her back now. He had made it impossible for her to work her way back into his good graces. In the last three days, while he had stayed on at Kendal House, spending every spare minute at the Foreign Office, she had gone down to Sommerfield with Quentin and the rest of the Graysons. She could not remain there much longer. She had a brother now, and it was expected that she would go to him. She wouldn't, of course. She would set up her own establishment and be perfectly happy doing whatever took her fancy.

On that happy note, she marched out of the nursery and descended the stairs. The house's spell was strong, but hers was stronger. "Old Warwick," she told the Greek columns and marched on by. "Old Warwick," she told her father's eyes as they followed her down the stairs. She was crossing the hall to the front doors when Stephen came out of the library.

"How was it?" he asked.

Her smile was brilliant. "It's smaller than I remember."

"No ghosts?"

"No. That's over and done with now." Suddenly conscious that he seemed preoccupied, she said in a different tone, "What's wrong, Stephen? What happened in there?"

"Nothing much. It was just as I anticipated."

"Then why the long face?"

"It's our sister, Elizabeth. She's a little mouse, afraid of her own shadow. I fear that her life with her mother and that guardian of hers is going to be no better than ours was with our father."

"But that is intolerable. What's to be done?"

"With your permission, I intend to buy them off, or threaten them into letting Elizabeth come to us. It could cost us a packet, you know."

She went up on her toes and pressed a kiss to his cheek. "We must do whatever is necessary to bring matters to a right and proper conclusion," she said.

He grinned. "I was hoping you would say that. It's best if you wait out here. This could become very unpleasant."

"Oh no you don't. I'm coming with you."

He bowed. She curtsied. Arm in arm, they swept into the library.

※

Gray spent his days at the Foreign Office and his nights at his clubs. As far as possible, he tried not to think of Deborah. His first instinct had been the right one, and now he regretted that he had not held to it. She would never overcome her fear and distrust of men. Her father had seen to that. If the old bastard were not already dead, he would be tempted to put a bullet in his brain. And besides all that, he and Deborah had got off to a bad start. It would always poison her mind against him. He had faced the truth and finally come to terms with it, and that was that. It was time to get on with his own life.

A fortnight after Deborah and his family had removed to Sommerfield, he went to the King's Theater and afterward mixed with the performers in the green room, imbibing the obligatory glass of champagne. This ritual was the time-honored way for gentlemen of rank and fashion to acquire a mistress. The scantily clad opera dancers flirted and paraded themselves, showing off their lithesome bodies in hopes of attracting a rich protector. Gray had a flash of recall—Deborah, hanging on to her shift as if her life depended on it. That's when he had removed her drawers.

His absent smile was noted by one of the opera dancers, and she left the young lordling who, she knew, was on the point of offering her carte blanche, and sauntered over. She knew of Lord Kendal, knew of the house in Hans Town that had stood empty for more than four months, and she did not see why she should not be its next occupant. She wasn't thinking only of Lord Kendal's wealth and title. She was thinking that she would be the envy of her peers. Kendal exuded power and something that his finely tailored clothes and natural charm could not hide. He made her think of a sleepy, tawny lion that would turn savage when roused. The thought excited her.

Five minutes' conversation with Miss Clarke put Gray in a foul mood. He realized that he had been premature in thinking he was ready to take a mistress. It wasn't that the girl didn't appeal to him. He would have had to have one foot in the grave not to be affected by that lithe body and the sultry look in those violet-blue eyes. It was the crushing weight of guilt that put a damper on things. He felt as though he were betraying Deborah, which was utter nonsense. That episode of his life was over and done with. He would never take up with Deborah again, not even if she were willing. A man had to know that his woman was committed to him come what may. She wanted a man who would be her lapdog, and he was not that man.

Thoroughly incensed that he could not bring himself to make the offer which he knew Miss Clarke would jump at, he made his excuses and stomped out of the theater. His empty, lonely house held no appeal for him, and he walked the short distance to his club in St. James's. In the reading room, he came upon Lord Lawford. Had the old codger not seen him, Gray would have removed himself to another corner of White's where he could get drunk in private, but Lawford had seen him and had waved him over, and Gray was obliged to answer the summons.

Lawford was drinking port, and after requesting one of the waiters to bring another glass, Gray found himself drinking port too, when what he really wanted was strong spirits, something to dull the edge of his black humor.

"I have been hoping to run into you," said Lawford.

"Oh?" said Gray. He grimaced as he drank the port.

There was a shrewd look in Lawford's eye. "That business of Philip Standish—he *was* your murderer, was he not? That story you told at the Foreign Office, that Standish lost his life while trying to save Lady Deborah, it *was* pure fiction from beginning to end. Am I right?"

Gray hunched down in his chair. "Confidentially?" he said.

"Need you ask?" There was a faint reproach in Lawford's tone.

"No. I beg your pardon. Your help in unmasking him was crucial. It was Standish, as you say."

"Why the secrecy? I would have thought you would want the whole world to know."

"I met his father," answered Gray. "He has enough grief to bear without me adding to it."

"Ah. The vicar?"

Gray shrugged. "He made a great impression on me."

Lawford smiled. "Do you know, Kendal, I always liked you and now I'm beginning to see why."

At least someone liked him, thought Gray peevishly. His own family had abandoned him and carried Deborah off to Sommerfield. He wasn't sorry that Deborah had friends to support her at this time. It just seemed callous that no one spared a thought for him.

Appalled, he looked at the glass of port in his hand. He was beginning to think that port and champagne were a lethal combination. In another minute or two, he would be wallowing in self-pity, telling anyone who would listen to him the sad story of his life with Deborah.

There was a commotion in the vestibule as some

young gentleman cried out that he had won the bet that was wagered in White's famous betting book.

"What's that all about?" asked Gray indifferently.

"That," said Lawford, "was a bet on Eric Perrin's new flirt."

Gray's lip curled. "Who is the lucky lady?"

Lawford smiled. "His wife, Lady Helena." Lawford nodded, answering Gray's blank look. "I see from your expression that you did not know Perrin has been hopelessly in love with his wife these many years?"

"*Perrin?*" said Gray. "If he was, he never showed it. He made a spectacle of himself, parading his mistresses before Helena. I felt sorry for her."

"And I was sorry for Perrin. Lady Helena was hardly aware of his existence. What was the poor man to do?" When Gray did not answer, Lawford laughed. "Don't look so morose," he said. "I have a premonition that you will be as lucky as Perrin."

"I am not Perrin," said Gray. "I don't have his patience."

"I know," said Lawford and laughed again.

An hour later, Gray was in Kendal House, wandering from room to room with a glass of brandy in his hand. The house looked as empty as he felt. There was nothing of Deborah here now. Nick had kept him abreast of things. It seemed that she and her brother now had charge of their younger sister, and the girls would go to Stephen once he had found a suitable house. In the interval, Deborah and Elizabeth were his mother's guests at Sommerfield. No doubt they were all having a wonderful time without him. He knew what would happen if he dared show his face. Deborah would take her sister and flee as if he had brought the plague down with him. And really, there was no need for it. He was as resolved as she to sever their connection.

He thought he had entered his own bedchamber, but when he looked around, he recognized it as Deborah's. It hardly mattered since she would not be returning. Now he *was* wallowing in self-pity. Laughing mirthlessly, he took a long swallow from his glass.

When he set his glass down on the table by the bed,

he noticed a scrap of lace, one of Deborah's dainty handkerchiefs. He picked it up, put it to his nose and inhaled the flowery scent. Another memory rushed into his head—Deborah fishing in her pocket for a handkerchief, and blowing her nose into it whenever she was overtaken by a crisis. That's where all his troubles had started. She'd been so damn brave yet so vulnerable, he just couldn't resist her.

By this time, he was feeling very mellow, and he stretched out on top of Deborah's bed. His most endearing memories of Deborah, he decided, were when she had turned to him with that special look in her eyes, the one that betrayed how glad she was that he was there to shoulder all her burdens. It was too bad it couldn't last. It wasn't just him. It was all men. She feared their power, and he did not think she would ever get over it.

He must have dozed, because he wakened with a start, knowing that there was someone moving about in his library on the floor below. It might have been one of the servants, but he couldn't help hoping. He didn't run, but he moved quickly. When he entered the library, however, it wasn't Deborah who turned to face him, but his new secretary, Mr. Riddley. Lord Lawford had recommended him. He was in his late thirties, married, and with a young family to support. There would be no question of him practically living at Kendal House. As soon as Mr. Riddley found accommodation, his family would be joining him from Oxford.

"How is the house-hunting going?" asked Gray.

Mr. Riddley made a face. "I didn't know that lodgings in London were so expensive. Mary says we shall just have to economize in other areas."

"Mary?"

"My wife."

"Of course. You know, Mr. Riddley, I don't expect you to work so late into the night." Gray smiled to show that there was no censure in his words. "You have your own life to lead. I understand that."

"Thank you, sir, but without Mary and the children, I'm at a loss. I don't mind, really. I say, now that you are here, perhaps you wouldn't mind taking a look at this.

The housekeeper gave it to me, and I think it might be important."

Gray took the sheet of vellum from his secretary's fingers and quickly scanned it. It was Deborah's last will and testament. He read it several times, read between the lines, and all his agonized soul-searching, all his uncertainties drained out of him.

"I see it *is* important, sir."

"What?" Gray looked up and gazed unseeingly at his secretary for a long time. Finally, he said, "No, not really. It's a spur, if you like, but I would have come round to it myself sooner or later."

"Sir?" said Mr. Riddley, mystified.

A slow smile spread across Gray's face. "Do you know, Mr. Riddley, I think I may be in a position to help you?"

"Sir?"

"It just so happens that I have a little house in Hans Town that has been lying empty for quite some time. It's begging for new tenants, no really, and I should be grateful if you would take it off my hands, for a nominal sum, of course."

❧

The report that Gray's notorious house in Hans Town was soon to be occupied spread throughout society circles like a raging forest fire. At White's, the betting book did a brisk trade as members wagered which opera dancer or high flyer had caught the earl's fancy. Lord Lawford's bet was the last to be entered before the book was closed. "No, to all of the above," was his wager, and though it was slightly irregular, the members who had charge of the book decided to let it stand. Irregular bets at White's were so common they were almost regular.

At Sommerfield, the report reached Deborah when her brother came down to advise her that suitable houses in London were hard to come by, and he was still looking for a place. He mentioned the house in Hans

Town for only one reason, so he said, and that was to convince her, supposing she needed to be convinced, that she was well rid of Kendal.

Deborah agreed with him wholeheartedly, fished in her pocket for her handkerchief, and blew her nose.

❧❧ ❧❧ ❧❧ ❧❧ ❧❧ ❧❧ ❧❧ ❧❧ ❧❧

CHAPTER 25

Gray's carriage was on the approach to Sommerfield when he was held up by highwaymen. He heard their strident demands just as the lamp outside the coach popped, throwing everything into darkness, and he reached automatically for the pistol that was kept primed and ready in the holster by the banquette. As the door was thrown open, he cocked the pistol and fired. There was only a click as the hammer came down on an empty chamber.

He launched himself at his assailant even as it went through his mind that someone's head would roll for that empty pistol. His momentum carried him and his opponent through the door and onto the hard-packed road. His arm went back to deliver a stunning punch, but before he could act on it, rough hands were laid on him and he was hauled to his feet. He wasn't finished yet, but he heard a voice he thought he recognized, *her* voice, and before he had recovered his senses, they had trussed him like a chicken.

"I demand to know—" he began, and someone laughed before shoving a gag in his mouth.

Gray was seething. This didn't have the feel of a real robbery, but of a prank that young bucks might get up to just for the hell of it. If that were the case, when they finally released him, he would not be satisfied until he had tracked them down and horsewhipped the lot of them.

His dignity suffered another blow when he was thrown over a horse and tied down like a sack of potatoes. They broke into a trot and then a canter. He heard their voices, but they were muffled. All the same, he sensed their jubilation. It was a long, long time before they stopped. By this time, his head was throbbing and his arms and legs were numb. They cut the bonds on his hands and ankles, and thrust a pistol in his ribs to dissuade him from trying anything foolhardy. He was in no condition to try anything.

The house was small, more like a cottage, and looked vaguely familiar, but he wasn't given time to examine anything. He was hustled upstairs into one of the bedrooms, and his hands were tied behind his back to one of the bedposts. His three attackers were masked, and there was not enough light from the lone candle to make out any distinguishing features. One said something in an undertone to the others and they all left the room laughing.

Outside the door, he heard voices conferring, but it was a long time before the door opened and someone slipped into the room. At sight of her, Gray began to struggle in earnest, straining at his bonds, moving his head and working his jaw till he had dislodged the gag. "What the hell is going on here?" he yelled.

Deborah cowered, then quickly recovered herself. It was essential that she show him it was not a little mouse he had to deal with but a woman confident of her own power. She was a match for him and he must be made to see it. She stood as straight as an arrow. "I have abducted you," she said.

"Abducted me? You? Don't be ridiculous, Deb. Abductions are not your style. You haven't the stomach for it."

She took this to be an insult, and lost her temper in earnest. "Oh, I'm learning. Two can play at your game. Look around you, Lord Kendal. You are completely at my mercy."

He laughed. He actually laughed. *"Ruthless!"* he said, and shook his head. "What is this place?"

"I believe," she said coldly, "it belongs to one of your former tenants."

"I thought I recognized it. This is Tom Baldwin's place?"

"I wouldn't know."

He looked at her intently, then said, "You wrote that letter purporting to come from my mother?"

"I did."

"There is no emergency. The ceiling in the Great Hall did not collapse? There was not the least necessity for me to post down to Sommerfield?"

"No. No. And no," she said.

"Was my mother party to this?"

"Certainly not! As though the countess would lend her aid to something disreputable! As though I would ask her! I forged that letter to bring you down here."

He suddenly bellowed, "Don't you realize that someone might have been hurt tonight?"

When the ringing in her ears had subsided, she said calmly, "I am not such a fool. I told them to be gentle with you."

"You were there?"

She answered him proudly. "Of course I was there. I was directing things."

His teeth ground together. "Let me see if I can guess who your accomplices are. Hart? Nick? And the third one would have to be your brother."

"You're very quick," she said admiringly.

He bit out, "As they will discover when I get out of here. Now, would you mind telling me what this is all about?"

Now that it was time to explain her purpose, she saw that she had allowed things to get out of hand. He was supposed to be gagged and immobilized, and she was supposed to be contrite. All this glaring on both their parts was putting her off her stride.

It wasn't going to work. He was too angry. She was too craven. She had been a fool to think she could force him to listen to her. He could be as stubborn as a mule when he liked. The door beckoned and her resolve wavered, but only for a moment. She had come too far to draw back now.

"Gray," she said, as humbly as she could manage, "I went to Belvidere. Two weeks ago, my brother and I went to Belvidere."

"I'm aware of that."

"Yes, but what you can't possibly be aware of is the effect it had on me. That house and my father are inextricably woven together in my mind. Oh, it's so much more than that. I was looking for answers, Gray, and I found them."

"How fascinating," he said in a bored drawl.

She said desperately, "I realized then that you are nothing like my father, not even superficially. Deep down, I always knew it." Her look pleaded for understanding.

His expression was inscrutable. He said nothing.

She elaborated. "Belvidere and Sommerfield? There's no comparison."

"I see. Is that all you wish to say to me?"

She heard the indifference in his voice and winced. Pretending she *hadn't* heard the indifference in his voice, she went on quickly. "When we were at Belvidere, we met our sister, Elizabeth. We liked her, we liked her very much, but we didn't like her mother or her guardian, so we decided to do something about it."

"Is this relevant?"

There was only so much a girl could tolerate. "Will you hold your tongue and let me get on with my story? This isn't easy for me, you know."

She couldn't be sure, but she thought he was biting down on a smile, and she was incensed. "Pray continue," he said, not mocking her, not taunting her, and her annoyance abated.

Composing herself into the proper frame of mind, she started over. "As I said, we liked Elizabeth, but we were afraid that her life was going to be no easier than ours. So we persuaded her mother and guardian to let her come to us."

"And was Elizabeth agreeable?"

"Oh Gray!" She blinked rapidly to dispel the burning sensation in her eyes. "If you had only seen the look on her face when she realized that we weren't going to take no for an answer, and that we would give anything, do anything, to bring her to us. It would break your heart."

He spoke very quietly. "Go on, Deb. Tell me how you managed it."

She sniffed and breathed deeply. "First we offered them our share of Father's collections, and when that didn't work, we threw in fifty thousand pounds in hard cash."

His brows shot up. "You surrendered your father's collections, then topped your offer with fifty thousand pounds? And Leathe permitted it?"

"Actually, no. I persuaded Leathe to try it my way first. But it didn't work. They refused every offer."

"Then what happened?"

"Leathe said we must take a leaf out of your book." Her eyes were dancing. "It was horrible. Threats. Intimidation. You know the sort of thing I mean. They wavered, and I threw in my trump card."

"I don't know if I can bear to hear this. What was your trump?"

She sounded proud of herself. "I told them if they didn't settle at once, I would call *you* into the affair. Gray, it worked like a charm."

"You did well. Now, would you mind telling me what point you are trying to make?"

There was a point to what she was telling him, but the expression in his eyes was not very encouraging. Her shoulders slumped.

"The point, Deborah," he prompted.

She answered persuasively. "I don't care who you have found for your house in Hans Town, Gray, but she will never love you half as much as I do."

"My house in—? Ah, you had that from your brother, I suppose?"

There was a glint in his eye that gave her encouragement. "I mean it, Gray. I'm the woman for you. I'm not as fearful as you seem to think. I stood up to Elizabeth's

mother and guardian, and I won. I faced the ghosts in
Belvidere. I abducted you, and have made you my prisoner. You must see, I *can* be the girl you want me to be."

His voice snapped out at her, making her jump.
"You *are* the girl I want you to be. You always were."

He looked so grim, she wasn't sure if he was being
sarcastic, and she did not know how to answer him.

He took a deep breath. "Deborah," he said, "where
the hell do you think I was going tonight when you
waylaid me?"

"You were coming to Sommerfield to look over the
damage."

"I don't give a damn about the damage to Sommerfield. I was coming for *you*."

Her heart slammed against her ribs, and she swallowed the lump in her throat. "Why? What made you
change your mind?"

He answered simply, "I found your last will and testament. It wasn't sealed. I didn't know what I was reading until it was too late. When I read it, I realized there
was hope for us. I thought you would never get over
your fear of men, you see."

"I'm not afraid of men!"

"What I should have said was the *power* of men. Yet,
you trusted a man to dispose of your fortune. I would
have expected to see Miss Hare's name, or even my
mother's. I knew then, all was not lost."

He paused, shook his head and laughed. "No, that's
not it. Even if I had not read your will, I would have
come for you eventually. I'm sorry about the laws of the
land, but that's not my doing. I know this, you will
never find a man to love you half as much as I do. We
may not be a perfect match, but in this imperfect world,
we'll do."

Joy shivered through her. "You were coming to Sommerfield to beg my forgiveness and promise that you
would try to change too?"

His eyes were very blue. "I was going to abduct you
and keep you my prisoner till you damn well came to
your senses."

This display of his habitual arrogance raised her

hackles. Recollecting, however, that she had bested him by abducting him *first* made her smile in sheer feminine triumph. Then she remembered the house in Hans Town.

"What is it?" he said.

"Hans Town. I should warn you, Gray, I am not so liberal as Lady Helena."

He grinned. "And I am no Eric Perrin. The house is let to a respectable gentleman and his family. My new secretary, to be precise."

"But Stephen said—" She frowned, trying to remember what her brother had told her.

"Deborah," he said, "Hart, Nick, and your brother were supposed to be helping *me* to abduct *you*. Doesn't that tell you something?"

She was at a complete loss, and stared at him dumbly. He was wrestling with his bonds. There was a snap and his hands came free.

Laughing, he captured her in his arms. "You don't see it yet, do you?"

"No," she said.

"My darling Deb! They've abducted you too. If you don't believe me, try the door and see if it will open." She made to obey him, but he said, "Later, try it later. Take my word for it. We've both been abducted."

He crushed her in his arms so fiercely that every sensible thought went out of her head. His lips on hers were hard and demanding. With a little cry of surrender, she threw her arms around his neck and kissed him back. So caught up were they in that kiss, they didn't hear the key grating in the lock, or the tread of feet that stole up on them. It was the sound of the pistol cocking that brought them out of the kiss.

Gray didn't look up; he didn't release Deborah. "Go away," he said, and kissed her again.

Nick laughed, then made an exaggerated show of clicking his tongue. "Gray, old man, have you no shame? You're corrupting the morals of your baby brother."

"Yes, indeed!" said Hart, trying not to sound sanctimonious. "Of all of us, in fact." When there was no response to this, he said to his companions, "I told you it was a mistake to lock them in a bedchamber."

"Kendal," drawled the Earl of Belvidere, "I warn you, I have honed my skills in diplomacy since last we met." He aimed the pistol straight at Gray's head. "I give you two choices. You either marry my sister or you marry my sister."

Gray ended the kiss with obvious reluctance. He smiled down into her eyes. "Which is it to be, Deb?"

She smiled up at him. "You choose," then as an afterthought, "Doesn't that show how much I trust you?"

Gray threw back his head and laughed.

※

The wedding took place that very night in the Great Hall at Sommerfield. There was no evidence that it was a hastily contrived affair. The hall was garlanded with flowers. The special license, which was necessary with no banns read in church, was in perfect order. The bride's dress was laid out on her bed, as were her flowers, and those for her maid of honor, her sister, Lady Elizabeth. The cleric who was to perform the ceremony said that he was honored despite the lateness of the hour. The guests, who were confined to members of both families including the children, gave no indication that the marriage came as a surprise to them. In short, there wasn't a shadow of doubt in Gray's mind or Deborah's that they had been well and truly duped. And it did not dim their joy one whit.

The last thing Deborah did before leaving her chamber to join Gray in the Great Hall was to go to her jewel box for her mother's locket. It had arrived from Miss Hare the week before, along with a jubilant letter, congratulating Deborah on her vindication of all the charges against her. Her brother and sister were with her, and Elizabeth, sensing a private moment, turned away and began to arrange the bric-a-brac on top of the dresser.

Deborah opened the locket, and she and Leathe looked down at their mother's likeness. This wasn't the first time Leathe had seen it, but the effect on him had not lessened.

"I wish—" he began, then stopped.

"What?" asked Deborah.

"Oh, that she were here, that she could see us now."

Deborah smiled through tears. "I think she *is* here. I think she knows. I can feel it here." She touched a hand to her heart. "Put it on for me, Stephen."

He took the locket from her and fastened it to her throat. For a long, long time, they stared at their reflection in the looking glass, Deborah with her mother's locket, her brother behind her, with his hands cupping her shoulders. Then Nick's voice called to them, and the moment passed into memory.

On her brother's arm, with her sister in attendance, Deborah descended the stairs. Gray's eyes never strayed from hers, nor hers from his. At the last, when she placed her hand in his, he smiled.

When it came time to exchange their vows, Deborah handed her posy of freesias to her sister, Elizabeth. She faltered only once. It was a solemn occasion, of course, and Gray's face reflected that he was aware of it. Deborah, throwing him a veiled look as he repeated his vows, was struck with the sheer power and strength that seemed to radiate from him, and her hand trembled in his. He turned to look at her, and that look sent a piercing sweetness flooding through her. Her voice was not quite steady when she made her own vows.

When they knelt before the priest to have their marriage blessed, Gray had never felt more humble in his life. It seemed incredible to him that Deborah had prevailed when the odds were so heavily stacked against her, and he fervently thanked God for His unceasing vigilance on his beloved's behalf. He thought of her mother, and Miss Hare, and her brother, Stephen. He thought of Gil. Finally, he thought of her father and Philip Standish. He prayed for them all, not knowing how to pray, hoping it was enough.

Deborah's prayer was very simple. She was thinking of Gray and only Gray.

When the priest raised them, and Gray looked into

Deborah's eyes, he thought his heart would burst. He kissed her softly, reverently, and in that kiss there was a promise for their future life together.

Nick said something rude and everyone laughed, then they were seized and amid laughter and cajolery led off to the dining room for the toasts and wedding feast. Deborah looked around at the faces she loved best in the world, and her gaze finally came to rest on Quentin. He caught that look and smiled, and she knew that the memory of that smile would be forever locked in her heart.

❧

She was petting Old Warwick when the last of the guests trooped off to bed. Gray came to stand behind her and he enfolded her in his arms.

"I know what you're thinking," he said.

Her dimples quivered, and she patted Old Warwick affectionately. "I doubt it."

"You're thinking this house is hopelessly old-fashioned. You're thinking that it's about time it was refurbished. And you're right. Well, look at this shabby old war horse." He whacked Old Warwick on the rear end, and a cloud of dust floated up. Gray was taken aback. Deborah giggled. "Yes, well," said Gray, grinning, "it's more than time Old Warwick was put out to pasture. I mean it, Deb. You have my permission to start afresh. Do what you like with the house. Decorate it to your own taste. I don't care what it costs."

It was pathetic. Poor Gray. She could see from his expression that he had steeled himself to make this generous offer. "You're an idiot," she said. "You don't understand anything. I don't know why I bothered to explain things to you. Oh, for heaven's sake, kiss me. At least you do *that* well."

It looked as though he might argue with her, then, shrugging, he turned her in his arms and kissed her nose.

"Not there," she said.

He kissed her ear. She shivered, but shook her head. "Not there."

He kissed her lips, and when he pulled back, she shook her head.

"Where?" he demanded to know.

She went on tiptoe and whispered something in his ear. He let out a whoop of laughter and reached for her.

"No, Gray! No!" She laughed as she backed away from him. "It was only a joke."

"You wanton hussy!" he cried out, and pounced.

Shrieking, laughing, she went darting away from him. He gave chase. She knocked over a chair to slow his progress. When he vaulted it, she screamed and dashed for the stairs, bumping into a suit of armor in her blind haste to get away from him. It rocked on its heels, then toppled to the floor with enough din to wake the dead. Gray caught her at the foot of the stairs. She was swept up in his arms and held high against his chest. He kissed her fiercely, and the shrieks of laughter dwindled to giggles, then to little whimpers and moans. She twined her arms about his neck, and they murmured softly to each other as he carried her up the stairs.

ABOUT THE AUTHOR

Elizabeth Thornton holds a diploma in education and a degree in Classics. Before writing women's fiction she was a school teacher and a lay minister in the Presbyterian Church. *Dangerous to Kiss* is her seventh historical novel. Ms. Thornton has been nominated for and received numerous awards, among them the Romantic Times Trophy Award for Best New Historical Regency Author, and Best Historical Regency. She has been a finalist in the Romance Writers of America Rita Contest for Best Historical Romance of the year. Though she was born and educated in Scotland, she now lives in Canada with her husband. They have three sons and two granddaughters.

If you loved *DANGEROUS TO KISS*,
don't miss

DANGEROUS TO HOLD

by award-winning author
Elizabeth Thornton

On sale in spring 1996

Read on for a preview of this spectacular
new historical romance . . .

Spain, December 1812

She made an arresting picture, seated at the small table in front of the fire, completely absorbed in her task. Marcus lay unmoving on his pallet and feigned sleep while he watched her dip pen into ink and begin to write. If he blocked out the drip of rainwater that fell through gaps in the roof and ignored the scorched walls, he could almost imagine that he was in England. It was a reverie Marcus had evoked many times when the pain from his wounds made sleep impossible.

The small priest's cell would be a lady's parlor, and the woman at the table would be at her escritoire, catching up on her correspondence or answering invitations to various functions. They would be at Wrotham at this time of year, to celebrate Christmas. There would be dinner parties and balls and beautiful women in pale, transparent gauzes, with fragrant hair and soft skin. But as lovely as these fair English girls undoubtedly were, none could compare to the woman at the table.

The steady stream of rain on the tiled roof became a torrent, and the pleasant reverie faded. This was not home. This was not England. This was a burned-out, God-forsaken monastery in the hills overlooking the border between Portugal and Spain. He was behind enemy lines and fortunate to be alive, rescued from a French patrol by *El Grande* and his band of guerrillas. And the lady who was so assiduously writing at the table was, in all probability, keeping a tally of the ammunition her group of partisans had expended in their pitiless war against the French.

She was a guerrilla, and was as dangerous as she was beautiful. The pistol lying on the table by her right hand was no empty threat, nor was the sharp dagger that was thrust into the leather belt at her waist. These women fought side by side with their men, and their savagery to their enemies knew no equal. Fortunately for him, the British were her allies.

Catalina. He liked the sound of her name. He liked the sound of her voice. He didn't know how long he had been cooped up in this place, slipping in and out of consciousness, but he knew that he had her to thank for nursing him back to health. *Catalina.* When her hands touched his body, he couldn't think of her as a soldier. She was soft and womanly, and he wanted to get closer to her warmth.

Still feigning sleep, he moaned, not because the wounds in his shoulder and thigh were giving him more pain than usual, but because he wanted her to come to him. She wouldn't approach him when he was fully awake. If he called for her by name, she would leave the room, and a few moments later her place would be taken by Juan.

He felt her cool hand on his brow and he allowed his lashes to lift a little so that he could get a better look at her. This woman was worth looking at. She had long dark hair and strong, regular features in an oval face. Her eyes were deep-set and shadowed by long black lashes. She wore a man's shirt and divided skirts, something Marcus had seen only on partisan women. Her masculine attire did not detract from her femininity, but only emphasized it. He had known many beautiful women in his time, but none with this woman's allure. When he looked at her, something moved in him, something entirely masculine and primitive that made him want to reach out and take.

The thought amused him. If he as much as laid a finger on her, she would make short shrift of him in his present weakened condition. She would think nothing of slipping that sharp dagger between his ribs. And even if he could prevent it, one cry from her would bring Juan storming through the door, and he would finish the job for her. In Spain, a man risked life and limb if he dared take liberties with a virtuous girl.

Hell! When had that ever stopped him?

She was examining the wound on his shoulder, checking the bandages for blood and pus. He groaned softly. "Isabella?" He knew perfectly well that the woman's name was Catalina.

She stilled for a moment, then sensing he posed no threat to her, she made soothing sounds and drew back the sheet, draping it to preserve her modesty before she checked the dressing on his thigh. Marcus almost smiled.

He moved his hands as casually as he could manage and rested them on her waist. His eyes remained closed. "Isabella, *querida*. Kiss me."

Evidently assuming that he was half delirious, she reached for the tin cup of water that lay on the floor beside his pallet. With one arm supporting his head, she brought the cup to his lips. Marcus sipped slowly, very slowly. The soft contours of her breasts brushed against his chest, and beneath his hands her waist felt slim and supple. When he had finished the water in the cup and she made to leave him, he tightened his hold and raised his head. Surprise held her immobile, and he quickly kissed her. It wasn't the way he wanted to kiss her. It was no more than a chaste peck. Even so, he braced for the slap that was sure to follow. When she didn't slap him, he drew back and gauged her expression. Her eyes were heavy lidded and uncertain. Blue eyes, and that surprised him.

"Catalina?" he said hoarsely, forgetting the part he was playing.

Then she slapped him. When he groaned, this time in earnest, she pushed out of his loosened hold and quickly put the distance of the room between them.

He grinned and raised carefully on one elbow. "My apologies, *señorita*. I mistook you for someone else. *Comprende?* I thought you were Isabella."

Hands on hips, she let fly at him with a spate of Spanish. When he shrugged, showing his confusion, she took several long breaths and started over in broken English. "*Madre de Dios!* This is *España*. Spain, *señor*. If my brother . . . if *El Grande* . . . you must never touch me, never kiss me. *Jamás!* If you do, you will be punished. *Comprende?*"

Marcus was well aware that *El Grande* was a man to fear, but it was the French who had reason to fear him. In Marcus's opinion, however, the stories that circulated about *El Grande* became exaggerated in the telling. No man could be that barbaric. What he knew for a certainty was that *El Grande* was tireless in his war against the French, and sometimes extreme. One French commander had tried to clip his wings by ordering Spanish hostages shot whenever *El Grande* attacked his soldiers. The guerrilla leader retaliated by executing four Frenchmen for every Spaniard shot. It was the French commander who eventually backed down.

He eased himself to a sitting position and gave her

his infectious grin, but it did not soften her. "*El Grande* will kill me. Is that it?"

He wasn't taking her seriously, and that made her temper boil over. "He will do a lot worse that that."

"Torture? I hardly think so. It was an honest mistake."

She was silent for a moment, then said, "Worse than torture."

He detected the mockery in her tone and decided to take the bait. "What could be worse than torture?"

"Marriage, *señor*. Does that not frighten you?"

"One needs a priest for that, *señorita*."

She smiled a slow smile. "*Sí*. A priest. Our *padre* is playing cards with Juan. Shall I fetch him for you?"

Marcus did not return her smile. "Point taken, *señorita*."

Her eyes searched his face, and after a moment she began to gather her writing materials together.

"No, don't leave me," Marcus protested. "*Por favor*. Stay. Talk to me." He searched his mind for the few Spanish words he knew, but most of those he'd picked up from the whores who followed the army and those words were of no use to him with a virtuous girl. What was the Spanish for "talk"? "*Parler*," he said. It was a French word, but he hoped it would do.

She hesitated, then slowly seated herself. "What do you wish to talk about?"

"Well, your brother for a start."

"*Sí?*"

"I wish to thank him for rescuing me."

"*El Grande* is not here. He is . . . how do you say? . . . making war on our enemies."

"When will he return?"

"Soon, very soon, when the rains stop. The rivers . . ." She shrugged helplessly. "It's too dangerous to cross."

"Then who is in charge here?"

She frowned at him. "Who . . . ?"

"Who is your captain?"

"Ah. Juan."

He said incredulously, "Juan? My nursemaid? Is he the only man here?" Juan was seventy if he was a day.

Her eyes were downcast and he had the strangest impression that she was laughing at him, but when she lifted her head, she was unsmiling and her eyes were clear. "There are the women soldiers, *señor,* and the *padre,* and the other English."

"What English?"

"Soldiers, like you. *El Grande* rescued them too."

"How many?"

She held up six fingers.

"So many? Who are they? Where are they?"

"I cannot say. I do not talk with the English. My brother forbids it. I shall send Juan to you. He will answer your questions."

She rose gracefully and thrust the pistol into her belt, gathered her writing materials, and locked them in a carved commode that flanked the hearth.

She was almost at the door when Marcus called out, "Wait!"

"*Señor?*"

She had stiffened at his peremptory tone, and Marcus immediately moderated it. "You visit me, don't you, and I'm English?"

"I come to be alone, *señor,* and for the candle and the fire. And yes, to nurse you when Juan cannot come. But now that you are well, you see how it is. My brother would be very angry if he knew I was here."

Marcus was staring at the carved commode. "This is your room, isn't it?" Another thought struck him. "You come here to write?"

She inclined her head gravely.

"What is it you write?"

"How do you say . . . my journal, *diario.*"

"You keep a journal?"

"*Sí.*"

"And what do you write in it?"

"Things that are dear to a woman's heart."

"And what is dear to your heart, Catalina? Do you dream of love?"

Her smile was hard to read. "Doesn't every woman?"

"No. Some women dream of fine clothes and precious jewels and a soft life." His lips parted slightly and he inhaled a slow breath. "Could a woman like you dream about a man like me, a poor soldier with nothing to offer but a hard life?"

"She might. You are very handsome, I suppose, in your English way." She studied his dark hair and deeply tanned face.

"Some people," said Marcus, "say I could pass myself off as a Spaniard."

"*Jamás!* You are too big. Juan cannot find clothes to fit you."

"I presume my uniform was ruined by those French lancers?"

"And the blood you lost. *El Grande* said you were very brave."

"And you are very beautiful."

For a long, silent interval, she gazed at him, but when she spoke, all she said was, "Remember, *señor,* no more Isabella. *Jamás! Comprende?*" She was unsmiling.

"*Jamás*," promised Marcus. "Will you come to me tomorrow? I'm quite harmless. No, really, I mean it."

"We shall see." She closed the door softly as she exited.

Over the next three weeks Marcus gradually regained his strength, and the more his strength returned, the more he strained at the bit to be up and doing. These were critical times. Wellington and his armies were falling back toward Lisbon while the French regained lost ground. When they finally made a stand, the British would be vastly outnumbered. And here he was, an experienced cavalry officer, stranded in the middle of nowhere, going nowhere. He might as well be marooned on a desert island.

The other English soldiers who were forced to endure *El Grande*'s hospitality were not so impatient as he. Their injuries were superficial, and the senior officer, Major Shepherd, kept them busy, deploying them to augment the women guerrillas who had been left to guard the monastery. Marcus could sometimes catch glimpses of them from the small turret window that overlooked the courtyard. There were six Englishmen in all, three cavalry officers whom Marcus knew slightly, a young ensign, and two enlisted men, Riflemen of the 95th. Had Marcus not been gravely wounded when the guerrillas brought him to their hideout, he would have been billeted with his countrymen in the monastery's crypt. He was not yet well enough to be moved and his comrades, taking pity on him, would take turns visiting him to relieve his boredom and keep him abreast of what was going on.

Catalina was never present during these visits. With

the exception of Marcus, she gave the English a wide berth. She came to him every evening and stayed until the candle burned low. Sometimes she wrote in her journal, but more often than not they talked. She was curious about him, as he was about her. She told him about the Spanish peasants and their terrible sufferings at the hands of the French soldiers, and he told her about England and the life he would return to if he survived the war.

There was one thing, however, that he kept to himself. He was not the ordinary soldier he pretended to be. She knew him as Captain Marcus Lytton of the 3rd Dragoons. In fact, he was a wealthy English lord, the earl of Wrotham, and the possessor of vast holdings in England. Though his title was no secret in army circles, he never permitted anyone to address him by it. He despised the toadying that his title invariably incurred, or conversely, how it distanced him in the minds of men he liked and respected.

With women it was a different matter. Sometimes Marcus used his wealth and title quite unscrupulously to lure them to his bed. He had discovered that a woman's head was easily turned by the attentions of a man of property, however worthless that man might be in himself. As a consequence, his opinion of women in general was not very high. He saw them as grasping opportunists who would sell their bodies for a few worthless trinkets.

This was not how he thought of Catalina. He admired her courage and dignity. Her life was hard, but it was the life she had chosen. With her face and form, she could easily have found a rich protector in Lisbon, or become a rich man's wife. Instead, she had thrown in her lot with the partisans. Marcus wasn't sure how she would feel if she knew who he really was. He didn't want to change anything between them. She saw him as a man, and what she saw she liked. Marcus was very sure about that. When they were together, the air between them was charged with a sexual energy. Sometimes, when he forgot to guard his expression, she would stop in midsentence and, ignoring his protests, quietly leave the room. But she always came back, and he knew that she wanted him almost as much as he wanted her.

Three days after the torrential rains had stopped, *El Grande* and his band of guerrillas returned to the monastery. Marcus watched their arrival from the turret window. They were a motley lot, some dressed in peasant homespun and others in the jackets of various French regiments, booty they'd stripped from soldiers they'd killed. Their black horses were in better condition than the men who rode them, and Marcus's respect for the partisans rose.

He turned slightly when the door opened. Catalina came to stand beside him at the window. She was wearing a long white dress and her dark hair streamed over her shoulders. Her eyes were misted with unshed tears. Marcus forgot about the men in the courtyard.

"The fords are passable," she said. "You will leave tonight. All the English are going."

He didn't want to frighten her, so he did no more than clasp her hands and bring them to his chest. "Listen to me, Catalina." He spoke earnestly, trying to convince her of his sincerity, though she might not understand all his words. "This isn't the end for us. I'll find a way to come to you. Do you understand? Even if we have to wait until the war is over, I'll find you. I give you my word."

Her voice trembled. "Once, just once, I want to feel your lips on mine."

He kissed her chastely, no more than a gentle pressure of mouth on mouth. He was drawing away when her teeth bit savagely into his lower lip. His head jerked, and in the next moment she struck him across the face with her open palm.

He wasn't angry, he was frozen in shock. Then he remembered that she was an innocent, and he blamed himself for frightening her. "Catalina," he said, "don't be afraid. I would never hurt you."

She backed away from him, and he saw the blood, his blood, smeared on her lips. He heard the tread of boots on the stairs, and laughter, and a man's voice above the din, calling her by name. And even when she tore her dress from hem to waist, exposing bare thigh, Marcus still stood there stupidly, not understanding what was going on.

She called out in rapid-fire Spanish, and there was a sudden silence on the other side of the door. Then she whipped out her dagger as if to threaten him, and she said in a deadly tone, "*El Grande* will kill you when he sees how you have tried to rape me."

Comprehension ripped through him like a bolt of lightning. It wasn't the first time a woman had tried to compromise him, but it was the first time a woman had succeeded. His bloodied lip, her torn dress, and the mark of her blow that still stung his cheek—the evidence against him must seem incontrovertible.

He went for her just as the door crashed back on its hinges. She discarded the dagger and flung herself into the arms of the man who crossed the threshold. Marcus had an impression of a young man, younger than Catalina, with dark ascetic looks, then several armed partisans pushed into the room and hauled Marcus back, shoving him against the wall. He was so incensed, felt so betrayed, that he fought them like a mad man. His injuries were forgotten. He felt no pain. Every muscle bunched and strained as he tried to throw off his attackers so that he could get to the girl. It took three of them to subdue him, but it was not until the knife at his throat drew blood that he finally quieted.

He could not follow her outburst, but one word jumped out at him—*Wrotham*. Now he understood everything. Somehow she had discovered who he was and she had made her plans in meticulous detail, down to the moment her brother would return to the monastery. He could not contain his bile. She had duped him as though he were a green boy. Everything was a sham. She wasn't attracted to Marcus Lytton the man. She wanted what every woman wanted, position and money.

When she had run out of words, *El Grande* set her aside and crossed to Marcus. Not a flicker of emotion showed in his dark eyes. His accent was flawless. "Is this how the English repay a friend's hospitality?"

Marcus did not answer. His eyes blazed with hatred as they fastened on Catalina. "You lying bitch! I should have taken what you were offering while I had the chance. *Puta!*"

El Grande's blow sent him to his knees. Marcus swallowed a mouthful of blood and gritted through clenched teeth, "I will never marry her. *Jamás!*"

Another blow followed, and Catalina cried out. When *El Grande* lifted his fist again, she threw herself in front of him. Her voice was low and pleading, and she